LINDA NEEDHAM

Marry the Man Today

An Avon Romantic Treasure

AVON BOOKS
An Imprint of HarperCollinsPublishers

This is a work of fiction. Names, characters, places, and incidents are products of the author's imagination or are used fictitiously and are not to be construed as real. Any resemblance to actual events, locales, organizations, or persons, living or dead, is entirely coincidental.

AVON BOOKS
An Imprint of HarperCollins*Publishers*
10 East 53rd Street
New York, New York 10022-5299

Copyright © 2005 by Linda Needham
ISBN: 0-06-051414-0
www.avonromance.com

First Avon Books paperback printing: June 2005

Avon Trademark Reg. U.S. Pat. Off. and in Other Countries, Marca Registrada, Hecho en U.S.A.
HarperCollins® is a registered trademark of HarperCollins Publishers Inc.

Printed in the U.S.A.

10 9 8 7 6 5 4 3 2 1

To Brad,
*still my favorite hero
after all these years.*

Chapter 1

Tend to his every part in the bath, dear reader, fondle his manly shapes, linger where he seems to most enjoy your touch.

Elizabeth Dunaway, *Unbridled Embraces;* or
Fifty Proven Techniques for an Intimate Marriage, 1852

The Admiralty
Whitehall, London, England
July 1853

"From now on, Blakestone, you'll just have to watch her like a bloody hawk."

"Of course, Lord Aberdeen." Ross Carrington, the first Earl of Blakestone, was finding it difficult to conceal a snort at the prime minister's unnecessary warning. "However, if I watch her any more closely, I'm liable to cause an international incident. We can't risk that."

And Ross had deflected too many of those lately for his luck to hold much longer.

"Fine, Blakestone, but just don't let her get the upper hand in the situation."

1

"I won't, Aberdeen," Ross said, "no matter how outrageous her royal demands." He turned pointedly from the tall windows that overlooked the wide expanse of Whitehall and its bustling midday traffic to look at Drew Wexford, a lifelong friend who surely understood the royal mind like none other.

The man had married one two years ago.

Drew leaned back in his chair and laughed in that maddeningly contented, happily married way that had overtaken him. "She's not the least bit shy about asking for the impossible—"

"Exactly what I'm afraid of, Wexford," Lord Clarendon said, dropping into a chair. He picked up a troop report and fanned his wilted face. "We can't bend to her."

"Nor is she at all shy about putting us in one untenable position after another." The First Lord of the Admiralty launched himself out of his chair.

Aberdeen threw up his hands. "Never stopping to consider the cost of her conceit to anyone around her."

"Completely irresponsible," sputtered Lord Weldon.

"Mollycoddled at every turn!" Clarendon shook his fist toward the ceiling.

"Gentlemen, please!" Ross said through his clenching jaw. "Anyone would believe that we were gossiping about a beautiful woman instead of thrashing over the wiles of Mother Russia and her scheming tsar, Nicholas."

"Now, there's a pity we're not, Blakestone." Lord Aberdeen grunted, scratching at his steely gray temple. "At least with a beautiful woman we could dazzle her speechless with a bauble or two. That bastard

Nicholas wants the whole of the Ottoman Empire all to himself."

"Careful, Aberdeen," Jared Hawkesly said with a slow grin from the sprawling comfort of his chair. "If you value your life and your fortune, you'll never let my Kate hear you be so flip about a woman."

"Or my Caro," Drew added. "I learned the hard way that an angry ex-princess can be just as deadly as one with a glittering crown and an empire of her own."

"You'd best take heed, Aberdeen," Ross said, feeling singularly distracted by a curious noise drifting through the window. A clattering rumble from the direction of Trafalgar Square, though he couldn't quite place the exact nature of the sound.

"No need for your kind warnings, gentlemen," Aberdeen said, "I've partnered both ladies in whist and now refuse to play against them."

Deadlier than the male, Ross was going to say. But he now found himself intrigued by the rising sounds in the street. He pulled aside the sheering drapes and, feeling like a lunatic, leaned partially out the window.

What the devil?

A cluster of people had formed up into a parade of some sort at the upper end of Whitehall. Now they were beginning to walk south toward the Admiralty.

Four abreast, six lines, a limp banner lagging between two of the marchers. And a half-dozen signs being jabbed into the air. None of the words readable yet.

Utterly amazing!

Because the mob consisted entirely of women.

"I just don't know what's wrong with these young ladies of today," Lord Weldon said in a voice as rattling as the tremors in his hands. "Seem to have grown minds of their own. No respect for an old man's opinion."

"All the fault of permissive fathers, I say." The Lord Admiral clacked the bowl of his pipe against the fireplace grate. "Give a young woman an inch and she takes the whole of the street and half the curb."

Indeed, all of Whitehall. Ross nearly laughed out loud as the carefully lettered signage came into sharp focus from the street below.

WOMEN'S RIGHTS!
LIBERTY! EQUALITY! SORORITY!

And in the vanguard, one sign was being thrust repeatedly into the air like a galvanizing call to arms, the most preposterous sentiment of the lot:

VOTES FOR WOMEN!

Not only preposterous, but carried by the most enchanting woman Ross had ever seen.

Damnation, she was a lush bite of brazen womanhood. He could see the shape of her clearly, though not the fullness of her face.

Unabashedly golden hair, slashed with pale copper, uncovered and piled in an unruly knot at the back of her head. Bits of curls floated outward at her temples with the impetuous force of her spirited forward stride. All that glittering pride held high, her chin perfectly shaped, tipped toward the world she so obviously resented.

Her splendid bosom was a perfect prow for leading her flamboyant female armada through the shoals of carriages, wagons, and horses that now had to steam their way around them.

"Out of the road, you bloody lunatics!" bellowed a ruddy-faced driver from atop the bench of a wagonload of baled wool.

Though the furious man shook his fist at the leader as his wagon wobbled past, the extraordinary woman offered no reaction. Unless one happened to notice the subtle smile of triumph that perched upon her dazzlingly moist lips.

Or the sunlight that grazed the tips of her hair as she spun gracefully on her heel to face the stalwart troops behind her.

"Women of Britain unite!" she shouted, thrusting her sign skyward, rousing her followers to a melodious roar.

"Women unite! Women unite!" The chant became raucous as the women stabbed at the air with their signs and their fists. "Unite! Unite! Unite!"

"What the devil's going on out there, Blakestone?" Aberdeen asked from across the room.

"Sounds like the beginning of a bloody riot." Drew was chuckling even before he joined Ross at the window. "Ah, the fair sex at war."

"Terrifying, isn't it?" Ross said, glad that he'd been born a male in these modern times, because deep in his heart he felt a niggling guilt at the plight of women.

The quashed spirit wanting to be free.

The hidden pride of righteousness.

A heart oppressed and yearning for justice.

"Bloody hell, Jared, isn't that old Tosser Maxton's wife?" Drew gestured out the window at a youngish woman just passing beneath them. "There. In that huge green hat."

Jared joined them at the next bank of windows. "Can't tell, Drew. All I can see is the hat. And one hat looks pretty much like the next to me."

But Ross had definitely recognized the woman as Tosser's wife. "And if I'm not mistaken, gentlemen, the woman beside her is Colonel Broadhurst's mother."

"Good Lord," Clarendon said with a snort as he gingerly peered over the sill. "Have they all gone mad?"

By now every man in the room was leaning out the bank of wide-open windowpanes, first grumbling at the interruption, then blustering at the outrageous sight of two dozen women marching down Whitehall in a show of all-out rebellion against men.

"What's all this?" Aberdeen bellowed as though from the floor of the Commons.

"A protest of some sort, it seems, my lord prime minster." Ross still couldn't take his eyes off the woman who was leading them all. Her shapely stride so vibrant, her shoulders thrown back in pride.

And so damn sure of herself, he could only stare and wonder who she was.

And wish for her to turn and look up at him, to share the fierceness of her gaze. Just a fleeting glance would serve his curiosity, would bank the flame that was licking at his loins.

He had a mad wish to know the color of her eyes, the depth of her spirit.

"Do you suppose these women have anything to do with that new ladies' club on King Street?"

"Ladies' club?" Ross laughed at Drew's outrageous sense of humor and then stopped as he realized that the man was serious. "What ladies' club?"

Drew turned toward Jared for confirmation. "It's called the . . . What is it, Jared?"

"The Abigail Adams," Jared said with a bewildered frown and a shake of his head. "Named, I suppose, for the wife of John Adams, who was the second pres—"

"—the second president of the United States. Yes, yes, I know who the woman was, Jared. What I want to know is, why?"

"Why Abigail Adams?" Drew shrugged and sighed. "Don't ask me."

"I mean why a ladies' club particularly?" Flaunting their revolutionary notions right under the noses of every man in London. Spoiling for an unwinnable fight.

Impatient for no earthly reason, Ross leaned out the window to take another look at the ragtag parade and its wily leader. But they were disappearing around the gentle bend in Whitehall. And his heart dipped, slowed from an acceleration he'd not noticed until now.

"Modern women." The very elderly Lord Weldon tsked and shook his head as he toddled back toward his chair and sat down. "What's the world coming to, I wonder?"

"And what do you suppose the betting book at this club looks like, Jared?" Drew leaned back against the windowsill. "Has it a needlework cover, I wonder, dripping with pale roses and leaping fawns?"

"More's the point, Drew," Jared said, obviously toying with the older men in the room, unconcerned himself, for his own wife was as independent minded as the summer wind, "what do you suppose the women find to bet on? When Mrs. Hume will deliver Mr. Hume of a son and heir?"

"Or how long it will take for their eccles cakes to properly rise."

"That's just the kind of trouble I need, gentlemen," Aberdeen said, gesturing toward the street as he returned to the table.

"Meaning what, Aberdeen?" Ross asked, one eye still on the traffic in Whitehall, reluctant to turn from the window completely for what he might miss below. "Upper class women forming a ladies' club and marching on Westminster in broad daylight, demanding we free them from the prison of their husbands, who just happen to be members of the Lords."

"And members of the Huntsman," Drew added.

Jared joined in the fray. "And Boodles and the Carlton and Travelers."

"You see what I mean, lads. Add women marching in the street to rumors of a war with Russia splattered across every newspaper and discussed in every parlor across the kingdom and that gives me a headache." Aberdeen gripped the ladder back of his chair with spidery hands as shaky as his hold on the coalition of his government. "Trouble on every front, domestic and foreign."

A man in conflict with himself, and a world on the brink of a far-reaching war.

"If it's any consolation, Aberdeen"—Ross handed the man a fleet position chart— "we can lay the blame almost entirely on that bloody, usurping Emperor Napoleon. He stirs up a hornets' nest in the Bosporus, taunts Nicholas into a frenzy by moving his fleet ever closer to the Black Sea. Then coddles the Sultan of Turkey when she screams bloody murder every time Russia herself threatens to overrun her territories."

Ross could see it all coming, an international avalanche roaring downhill, day by day. One he could only hope wouldn't overtake them all.

"Though Nicholas is far from innocent in this." Drew leaned back against the windowsill. "He continues to believe that we agree with him, that the Ottoman Empire is doomed and ought to be partitioned off and gifted to each of the Great Powers. With Russia keeping the lion's share for herself and year-round access to a warm-water port."

Because the tsar had a long memory, of a casual discussion he'd had with Aberdeen himself on the subject. An unofficial, offhanded agreement that Ross had no intention of bringing up to the prime minister.

"Yes, well—" Aberdeen snorted and waved his hand at nothing. "Nicholas is in for a rude awakening. He's always taken Franz Josef's support as unshakable. But with the Russians now sitting on the Danube and hinting of trouble in the Balkans, the Austrians have every right to be suspicious."

"Gentlemen, according to what I saw of the Russian fleet and the French, and the mood on the streets of Constantinople, if nothing changes we are but months from a war that might well spread across the entire world."

Ross heard a noise across the street and lost his train of thought. He glanced out the window in time to see a detachment of Metropolitan Police streaming out of Scotland Yard. A dozen officers, followed by three paddy wagons.

And they were heading south on Whitehall.

Surely they weren't going to intercept the harmless parade of women and attempt to disperse them.

A sickly feeling knocked around in his gut, tumbling with the realization that their beautiful leader wasn't the type to disperse without a fight to the finish.

Not that it was any of his business what happened to the woman or her compatriots.

"Ross's recent charts of the various fleets show belligerent movements on the part of all parties, an increased concentration since only three months ago."

Ross reeled his thoughts back into the meeting. Aberdeen was bent over the maps that he had just yesterday brought from his most recent scouting mission into Europe. Six months of spying and diplomacy.

And not a whiff of peace to be found anywhere, certainly not here in London. Only trouble and more trouble. With the *Times* crying for war against Russia.

"So in the meantime," Clarendon said, with a stubborn cross of his arms against his chest, "England is forced to sit in place, with Russia perched on the

Danube, threatening Austria, ready to overrun Turkey, and all of us waiting for Emperor Franz Josef to instruct his foreign minister to make the next move."

Ross prodded himself away from the window and moved back to the table.

"Count Buol has been talking about bringing the parties together in Vienna to work out a truce."

"Another one?"

"I know it's a very long chance, Clarendon," Ross said, wondering how the devil he'd suddenly been dropped into the middle of a diplomatic mission, when his expertise lay firmly, and by his own design, in the military. Where he didn't have to look on the morass of politics up close. "But it's my assignment to see that the conference in Vienna happens, and that war is averted. At all costs."

Ross reached for the map in the center of the table, having to favor the familiar ache in his left shoulder. A painful encounter that reminded him daily of his near fatal miscalculation a year ago.

"Good, then you're off to St. Petersburg again, Blakestone?"

"God, I hope not, Aberdeen," Ross said, willing to do most anything to postpone another visit to that nest of insanity. "I'm going to start off with a dinner party tonight at the Austrian Embassy."

And hopefully empty his brain of the exotic, thoroughly rousing images of the rebellious woman in the street.

And a dangerous wave of unsuitable questions that he shouldn't be asking.

Completely nonsensical questions like: what does a woman of such obvious free will choose to wear under her sensible fashions?

Surely not whalebone and canvas to straighten her posture, but lace and fine linen, because she's proud enough for a half-dozen women.

And does she dash the sleekness of her nape with pale English rosewater?

Or would he find a tantalizing hint of cinnabar lingering there and across her shoulders, trailing downward, between her breasts?

Not that he planned to find out. He would be far too busy in the next few months trying to avert a war to chase after a stunning woman, no matter the beauty of the prize.

No matter the force of the temptation.

But the mere speculation had heated the room, steaming at his collar, deepening his breathing.

And making him thankful when the meeting finally ended and he could step out into the cooling evening air with his two compatriots.

"I don't know about Drew, Ross, but I doubt that I'll have time to see either of you at the Huntsman tonight. Kate and I leave early tomorrow morning for a week at Hawkesly Hall."

As always, Jared was tugging at the bit to return to his London town house and his equally impatient wife. Hardly the usual kind of husband who had been married four years and had a passel of children waiting for him in the west country.

"Caro and I are attending the theatre tonight with a pack of Swedish royalty." Drew rolled his eyes and shrugged fondly. "My favorite kind of outing, as you well know."

Ross couldn't help but chuckle at Drew's ironic situation. A man who had detested the aristocracy, willingly married himself into a royal pantomime.

Caro was that kind of a woman. The sort that a man would give his life for.

And the entirety of his heart.

If he ever found the proper time.

Or the proper woman.

"Gad, Drew!" Ross said, purposely scattering the images with a clap of his hand against his friend's shoulder. "For an ex-princess, your wife is still in tremendous demand by the crowned heads of Europe."

"Like bees to honey." Drew shook his head and hoisted his satchel over his shoulder. "Bees to honey. Shall we say breakfast in the morning at the Huntsman?"

"Thanks," Ross said, leading them out of the courtyard of the Admiralty, beneath an arch in the white arcade. "With any luck, I'll have something positive to report from my dinner tonight."

Or just another useless tidbit about the growing Crimean conflict to add to the files in the Factory.

Jared and Drew climbed into the cab that the footman had been holding for them, and the vehicle sped north on Whitehall, away from the backed-up traffic that was moving slowly in the other direction.

Ross had stabled his horse at the Admiralty livery and had just turned to head in that direction when he noticed the traffic breaking up and Scotland Yard's three paddy wagons emerging from the jumble.

Curiosity kept him watching from the curb as the wagons, followed by the swarm of policemen, made a flourishing right turn into the alleyway across the street.

He might have turned away from the fracas but for a face peering out of a small, barred window in the rear of the last enclosed wagon.

Damnation! It was her.

His rebel.

And though he could feel the winds of change rise up and surge against him, deeply aware of the shift in the turning of the earth, he tossed aside his good sense and strode across the street toward an unknown fate.

He had regretted few decisions in his life.

Crossing Whitehall might just turn out to be one of them.

Chapter 2

O! when she's angry she is keen and shrewd.
She was a vixen when she went to school:
And though she be but little, she is fierce.

William Shakespeare, *A Midsummer Night's Dream*

"**H**ey! That's my new hat, you brute!"
"Oh, blast it all, I've broken a fingernail!"
"Votes for women! Women's rights!"

Though the sounds of battle weren't quite as brutal as he was used to, Ross was sure he'd been thrust into the middle of a full-fledged war. The courtyard at Scotland Yard was utter chaos, swarming with two dozen finely dressed women squealing at the top of their voices, ignoring the flustered policemen who were trying to calm them.

"Ouch, lady! That's my flesh you're pinchin'!"

"Now, madam, if you'll just tell me your name, Mrs. . . . *yeoull!*"

"You need to sit quietly, my lady."

"Not if you're going to speak rudely to me, young man!"

Whack!

Ross winced for the poor officer as the woman's huge reticule came down with full force on the man's head, already bared of its protective hat.

Ross reached out to catch the next blow, but the older woman turned a large smile on him.

"Why, if it isn't the Earl of Blakestone. When did you get back into town, dear?"

Discovered! Ross flinched at Lady Archer's words. He'd been spotted. And now every woman in the compound was looking hungrily at him, as though they were at a ball and he was the only male who'd had the courage to attend.

"Ross, my dear," the very matronly Lady Charlotte said with a straightening tug at his lapels, "you really do need to insist to these policemen that they not be quite so rough with our gowns."

"Excuse me, Lady Charlotte, but what are you doing here?" Ross asked instead, pleased that the chaos had diminished enough for him to be heard over the noise.

"Votes for women, Blakestone!" another woman said as she stabbed her fist into the air.

"We're protesting."

"Miss Elizabeth said we've done extremely well today."

Miss Elizabeth? Was that her name? And why was his heart suddenly slamming around in his chest?

"Who is Miss Elizabeth?" he asked evenly, looking over the top of their heads for that dazzling red hair.

"She's our leader. They took her inside. She was hoping they would lock her up in a cell."

"I hope they lock *me* up in a cell too!" a starry-eyed young woman said, beaming a smile at him.

Lady Maxton slanted Ross a sly glance from beneath the brim of her hat. "I hope they tie my hands firmly behind my back!"

Wouldn't old Tosser be shocked if he knew!

"See where one of those brutal policemen trampled the hem of my skirt! It's absolutely torn!"

"I scuffed my new satin shoes!"

They were lunatics. The lot of them.

And their unrepentant leader had been taken inside the Scotland Yard police station, doubtless eager to do battle with every man she encountered along the way.

For some reason that he didn't wish to examine at the moment, Ross felt sorely compelled to inquire after the woman's fate before straightening out the scandal brewing in the courtyard.

After all, what harm could a little inquiry do?

"Excuse me, ladies," he said, tipping his hat to the chattering crowd gathered around him. "I think I'll just go speak with the captain about a few things."

Ross quickly escaped up the stairs into the coolness of the lobby. A bit less chaotic than outside, but still more frenetic than he'd ever seen the usually stoic Metropolitan Police station.

"Great heavens, Lord Blakestone! What the devil has brought you here?" Captain Robins grinned broadly, dodging around the busy counter to meet Ross with a sturdy handshake in the middle of the room. "Come to beg a little assistance from your favorite old seadog?"

"You know you're always at the top of my list, Captain. Actually, I was across the street at the Admiralty and saw the commotion. Thought I'd come investigate for myself."

"Damn fool women ought to know better than provoke the police in the middle of the afternoon." Robins twitched his thick gray moustache from side to side and shot an arch-browed glare toward the courtyard. "But they'll be laughing out the other side of their pretty faces when they all find themselves behind bars like the other one."

No doubt he was referring to the inimitable Miss Elizabeth.

"Ah, then, you've decided to let the ladies win the battle, have you, Robins?"

"What do you mean win, my lord?" Robins snorted. "A few days in jail ought to frighten them out of their high-handed ways and keep them off my streets for good. How's that letting them win?"

"That's just what they want you to do, Robins: cause a scandal of gargantuan proportion that scuttles the reputation of the Metropolitan Police."

"*Our* reputation? What about theirs?"

"I can see the headlines in every newspaper now, Captain." Ross gave it all the melodrama he could muster. " 'Ladies of the Ton Manhandled by Brutal Members of the Metropolitan Police in Arrest Raid.' "

"Manhandled?" The captain blew out a burst of indignation, reeling out the ends of his moustache. "We did nothing of the sort. Hells bells, they near jumped into the wagons by themselves the moment my officers opened the doors. Eager as a bunch of silly schoolgirls, with all their giggling and jouncing for a seat."

"That's not what they told me out there. Scuffed shoes and ruffled feathers, bonnets askew. They want your blood, Captain."

"They're not going to get it! My men never touched a one of those women."

"I'm sure your men are as innocent as babes in the woods, Robins. But just who is the press going to believe when the story comes pouring out? You, or the wives and mothers and sisters of two dozen of the most powerful men in London?"

"By God, the press will believe me!" Robins's brows drew together in a sudden, sharp wing, his eyes flaring wide. "Won't they?"

Ross shook his head, slowly, meaningfully. "Everyone knows that a good scandal sells far more newspapers than the unremarkable arrest of a few rebellious women holding a parade down Whitehall. The reporters will tear you to shreds. And then come the gossip sheets."

"Bloody hell!" Robins swabbed his fingers over his gray hair. "So what do you suppose I should do instead?"

"Let them go," Ross whispered.

Robins recoiled in horror. "I can't do that."

"You can and you *must* release them all, Robins. Immediately. No questions asked, and with your deepest apologies. For the good of the Metropolitan Police. For London at large. As well as for the sake of your own job."

The captain's eyes flitted back and forth around the room. He lowered his voice to a conspiratorial whisper. "You make an excellent point there, my lord. Wouldn't want to sully the good name of the police department merely because a few harebrained women got out of hand."

Harebrained. "Exactly."

"Besides, it's their first offense. No real harm done. And they are, after all, merely . . . women."

That was where the poor captain was going to find himself wrong-headed in the long run. If only from a pragmatic standpoint. There was nothing *mere* about the situation he had on his hands, least of all about the women.

One woman in particular.

But anything to settle the matter with as little fuss as possible. Because he felt oddly intimate with the whole affair. Responsible somehow because he had watched from above like a secret arbiter.

"And just to be certain that all goes well, Robins, may I suggest that your men escort each of the women safely home, right to their own front doors."

Robins chewed on the end of his moustache for a moment then nodded slowly. "I see what you mean. Keep the affair as quiet as possible. Good, good."

"Including their leader." Ross tried to sound detached. "Did she give her name?"

A sudden fear flashed across Robins's face, then fell to aggravation. "Hasn't said a word on her own behalf. Though she did demand a reporter."

Not her solicitor.

Not her mother.

Or a husband.

Only a reporter.

Ross nearly laughed at the baldness of the woman's designs. "There's your proof, Robins. This whole bloody incident was a stunt concocted strictly to publicize their bootless cause for women's rights."

"Women's rights, my arse. I'll show them what's what!" Robins snorted and turned back to the large ledger lying open on the desk. He dipped the quill and then scratched through a line of words. "I think I'll leave the ringleader to stew for an hour or two. Get herself a real taste of prison life."

Ross had the distinct feeling that it would take more than an hour or two of prison air to affect the indomitable Miss Elizabeth. "Would you mind if I visited the prisoner for a moment? Perhaps I can reason with her."

"Reason with her?" Robins gave a laugh. He grabbed a ring of keys from behind the desk then started toward the corridor of jail cells. "Be my guest. Though I doubt it'll do you a lick of good."

He wasn't looking for good.

Or satisfaction.

He was looking to assuage this bothersome feeling that now grew in his gut with every step nearer the enigmatic woman's cell.

A sizzling feeling that filled up his chest with the tendriling scent of sandalwood and jasmine, and, yes, by God, cinnabar. Exotic and telling.

Fueled by a crystal clear memory of gilded auburn hair spilling over prideful shoulders.

And the certainty that her gaze would be as un-flinching as her convictions.

"Take care with your hide, my lord," Robins whispered as he shoved the key into the lock. Blocking the doorway with his shoulder, as though the woman might just leap out of the cell and brave a mad escape.

"I'll be fine, Captain. Thank you." Though with the man filling up the corridor in front of the cell door, Ross had yet to set eyes on his target.

"You've a visitor, Miss Whatever Your Name May Be," Robins growled at the woman through the open cell door. When there was no reply, he turned and gave Ross a quick nod before striding off with a muttered, "She's all yours now, my lord."

All mine.

At least for the moment.

There was no sound at all from the cell, no pacing, or shouting, or shoe rattling against the bars.

Feeling suddenly, unreasonably, as though he was about to face down a tigress unarmed, Ross cleared his throat, squared his shoulders, and stepped in front of the cell door.

Bloody hell, he was done for.

The profound memories of her ostentatious pride had sent him trailing after her from the Admiralty, across Whitehall, and into Scotland Yard. Her haunting scent had drawn him along the corridor, tugging at his core.

But he hadn't expected that the sight of her, standing in the center of the cell, the late afternoon sunlight from the window behind her setting little fires against the bright cloud of her hair, could so completely take his breath away.

And her amazing eyes. Sea green and lushly fringed, challenging him to believe in her.

Turning up at the corners with the hint of a smile that seemed to be trying to take purchase on the rosy fullness of her lips.

"How excellent, sir." Her sultry voice lifted across to him like a butterfly, perched itself in the center of his chest. Wings beating a velvety rhythm, brilliant with all the colors of the rainbow. "I see you wasted no time."

Wasted no time? His sodden mind stumbled around the blocky words, wondering what they meant.

Had she been expecting him? How? More's the point, why would she be expecting him?

Damnation, had she actually seen him hanging out the window of the Admiralty? Nearly drooling after her like a besotted chump?

"Shall I go first then, sir?"

"First?" Ross swallowed his confusion and took a long breath to clear out the cobwebs.

She crossed her arms beneath her breasts and tipped her chin at him. "I'm ready to tell you most of my secrets. You can ask me anything you like."

"Anything I . . . ?" Well, now that was an invitation he'd not expected from the woman. The possibilities left him stammering like an idiot.

And yet something was niggling at him. Something the captain had said.

That she was their ringleader.

And unreasonable.

Bloody hell, that she'd sent for a reporter!

"Are you from the *Times*, sir?"

"Am I . . . well—" Hell and damnation! The truth was balanced there on the tip of his tongue, digging in, prompting him to speak it aloud. "That is to say, madam . . . I've—"

Been *to* the *Times*.

Subscribe to the *Times*.

Read the *Times* every morning, like clockwork, with my eggs and toast.

But, no . . . I . . .

"Because, sir, I was hoping that the *Times* reporter would be the first on the scene."

"Oh? Why is that?"

"Circulation, of course." Her fawn-colored brows dipped above her small nose. "I'm sure you know that the *Times* has the largest circulation of any newspaper in London. In the entire kingdom. Fifty thousand copies a day. Imagine that. More than all the other papers combined."

"Indeed."

"And, although every newspaper has its obvious biases"—she reached into the pocketbook hanging from her waist and pulled out a folded sheet of paper—"I have a great deal of respect for the integrity of your editor, Mr. Delane."

"I'll have to tell him so." Bloody hell, the woman couldn't be as naive as that; editors were biased toward the power of the pound.

"Which is why I'm certain that you'll treat me with

equal respect, Mister. . . ." She flashed him a disarming smile. "I'm sorry, I didn't get your name."

"It's Carrington. Ross Carrington."

"Very nice to meet you, Mr. Carrington." She put out her hand to him, as bare and shapely as a swan. "My name is Elizabeth Dunaway."

Given his unreasonable interest in the woman, Ross could only hope that her hand wasn't as silky soft as it looked. He held his breath as he reached for it, and was nearly knocked backward by the bolt of desire that zinged up his arm and into his chest.

He heard himself babble out a guttural, "HowdyadoMissElizabethDunaway," but resisted the seething urge to pull her into his arms and dance his mouth across those lush lips.

Instead, he dropped her hand like a hot stone. He fumbled for the notepad in his jacket pocket and poised the short pencil against the page, ready to write and write, convincing himself that he was only doing what any spy would do in the same situation.

Take advantage.

Complete advantage.

"Tell me everything, Miss Dunaway. Your public eagerly awaits."

Chapter 3

A woman's preaching is like a dog's walking on his hinder legs. It is not done well; but you are surprised to find it done at all.

Samuel Johnson, 1709–1784

Tell him everything?

Elizabeth wasn't sure she wanted to tell this particular man anything at all. Let alone everything that was important to her.

She certainly couldn't tell him the way he made her feel as he filled the doorway of the cell with his broad shoulders, or the delicious way he smelled of bay and lemon and the afternoon sun.

Or the way he was looking at her just now, with his dark, smoke-shadowed eyes. Staring at her, really, charting her. As though he was planning a libertine route that would take him nibbling along her collar-bone, tasting her from nape to toe.

And back again.

As though he would kiss her right here and now.

Or carry her off to some starry-edged kingdom

where he would endlessly pamper and caress her, and lavish her with feathers and chocolate and—

Oh, great heavens above! What an utterly ridiculous daydream to be conjuring! Right here in the middle of her protest.

She couldn't tell a reporter from the *Times* anything like that!

After all, she was the owner of the Abigail Adams and had a reputation to uphold!

Gathering up her scattered senses, Elizabeth threw back her shoulders, struck a firm pose, then directed a scathing glare toward the man who seemed to overwhelm the cell by just being there.

"If you want to know everything about me for your story, Mr. Carrington, then I suggest you begin by understanding that everything I say, everything I do, is in the cause of equal rights for women."

He took a long step toward her, cocked his dark head as though trying to study her from a different angle. "Go on, Miss Dunaway. I'm listening."

"Yes, well . . ." She had expected the man to sneer at her, or snigger. At least to start scribbling down her words on his ruffled notepad. Instead he was still staring at her. Into her.

She blinked away from him for a moment, but the stone floor wasn't nearly as compelling as the sun-bronzed, rough-planed face of this eccentric reporter from the *Times*.

"As you know, sir," she said against the pressing thickness of his silence, her fingers fiddling with the treatise she had been prepared to hand out to members of the press at just the right moment, "today's peaceful protest was intended to illuminate the plight of the female citizens of Britain. As I have shown here in my essay."

She thrust the noisy piece of paper toward him, feeling more clumsy than usual. He had the good grace to glance down at her words. "Interesting, madam."

"Yes, well, sir, we were merely walking down the center of Whitehall, carrying signs and banners, when we were rudely interrupted by the Metropolitan Police."

"And you were also shouting 'Votes for women,' weren't you?" The man leaned back against the bars, arching a brow at her, a smile caught in the corner of his mouth.

"Indeed, we were."

"And liberty, equality, sorority."

"Were you there, Mr. Carrington? Did see our parade?" Not that it made a whit of difference. Except that it meant he'd been witness to her march, her private passions, her shouted protests . . . and well, there was nothing she could do about it now. It just suddenly seemed too intimate an idea for such a small room and with so little space between them.

But he had narrowed his eyes. "The captain reported your activities when I arrived."

"Ah! And was he outraged?" Better outrage than the jeers and laughter she'd heard from the street as the police loaded them into the wagons.

"I wouldn't call Captain Robins outraged, Miss Dunaway, but he was completely scandalized."

Good. Excellent, in fact! Elizabeth hid her smile inside her chest, where the man couldn't see how very pleased she was that she had scandalized the captain.

"Now, I can't help that, can I, Mr. Carrington? Depriving women of the same legal rights that a man has is scandalous. Refusing us an education is scandalous. So is robbing us of all property rights the moment we are married." She reined in the usual bellow of her hustings voice. "But forbidding us the vote is the most scandalous of all."

"I see." The man still hadn't taken down a single note in his notebook.

In fact, he looked thoroughly amused by her speech. He'd moved completely into the room and was leaning against the wall of bars, the heel of his highly polished boot propped against the bench. The rich linen of his suiting still crisp with expensive creases. The finely crested gold buttons matching at his waistcoat and jacket and cuffs.

His deep chestnut hair trimmed just so. His square jaw barbered by a professional.

A man whose hobby must be either chasing the news or tormenting women in jail cells, because the smug Mr. Carrington was just too well dressed to be a penny-poor newsman.

"I don't think you see at all, Mr. Carrington. Though I shouldn't really expect you to. Few men do."

"What about your husband? Does he . . . see what you want him to see?"

"I am unmarried, sir, and have vowed to remain so for the rest of my life."

"Ah, you're a nun, then, Miss Dunaway. Hoping to proselytize to the male masses in Westminster to give women the vote?" He cocked that cocky eyebrow again, surely thinking himself a London wit. "I didn't know the Church went in for that kind of thing."

"I'm not a nun, Mr. Carrington, I'm a pragmatist. And you're not a reporter, are you?"

"No, I'm not," he said without a moment's hesitation. The answer to a question she should have asked the moment she saw him in the doorway looking so . . . feral.

"Then who are you, sir?" She could feel the telltale spots of crimson blooming high on her cheeks, a sure symptom of her smoldering outrage. And not of the trembling embarrassment that the arrogant man would surely surmise.

He straightened and became taller. "I'm Ross Carrington, the Earl of Blakestone."

Blakestone. The name sounded familiar, tinted by exotic images of danger and rife with legends.

"If that's so, your lordship, why did you pretend that you were from the *Times*?"

The lout had the decency to catch his smile behind his teeth before he said, "Curiosity."

"Curiosity? About what? Do you loiter around Scotland Yard just for amusement?"

"Not usually. Then again, Scotland Yard usually isn't brimming over with rebellious women."

"So I'm a curiosity? Like one of the elephants at the London zoo. Or a zebra."

The lout gave a broad, encompassing laugh that echoed against the brick walls and slipped easily between her ribs. "Not like them at all, madam. I merely wanted to see what all the commotion was about."

"Commotion! How dare you! I'll have you know

we're not just a commotion! We're a movement which is growing every day."

"That's just what I'm afraid of." The man's jaw squared suddenly, his amusement gone as he strode toward the door, then turned and reached out for her. "Now come on out of here, please. You're going home."

"I'm what?" Elizabeth glanced down at his huge, open palm and felt her knees loosen at the implication. "What do you mean, going home? I'm not ready to go! I'm waiting here for the press to interview me. The real press!"

"Consider your protest finished, Miss Dunaway. For your own good." He beckoned to her with a lift of his powerful arm, as though he believed she would just walk forward and place herself under his, doubtless considerable, protection. "You've made your statement. Now, you and your friends are going to be taken safely home, where I hope to God you'll stay until this mess blows over."

"Blows over?" She'd never in her life been so angry, so ready to haul off and slap someone. Her heart was thumping with such force, she was certain the man could hear it from the doorway. "Haven't you heard a thing I've said, Blakestone? This so-called mess will blow over only after you find me facedown in the Thames."

Her anger only seemed to add to his calm. "An event that I would dearly regret, Miss Dunaway, but you're not staying here in this cell another moment. Your compatriots have been sprung and taken discreetly back to the bosom of their families. And you're going too."

"I don't have a bosom." That didn't sound right, but it threw the man momentarily off balance. She stalked forward, slowly moving him back out of the cell. "I mean, sir, that I don't have a family. No one is waiting for me at home. So no one will worry if I spend a night behind bars. Or a week. And when someone from the fourth estate finally takes notice of me and the cause of women's rights, I want to be here to tell my story."

With that, Elizabeth took hold of the barred door, pulled it toward her, and slammed it shut between them.

He stood blinking at her for a moment, studying her as she gripped the cool metal bars, planning something that she wasn't going to like.

"So, Miss Dunaway, you're willing to spend a long, cold night in jail, battling the rats for your threadbare blanket, existing on moldy bread and stale water, all for the sake of making a political statement."

"Absolutely." Though she would rather do without the rats. "I have no choice. Because self-serving men like you won't allow me to take my rightful place in Parliament where I could express my opinion and be grateful for the privilege."

He was silent again, a flame-blue light flickering deeply in his gaze. A light that settled softly on her lashes, then glided across her cheeks.

Such a palpably compelling sensation that she hadn't noticed until seconds too late that the black-guard had slipped off his silken stock and wrapped it around one of her wrists.

"Sorry, my dear, but for better or for worse, that's the way of the world." In a single motion he yanked the door open, caught up her other wrist, bound it to the first and then began tugging her down the corridor.

"No! Let me go! Youuu! You're not a policeman!"

"Sorry for the inconvenience, madam."

"I don't want to leave!" Elizabeth planted her heels against the floor to stop him, but he pulled her gently along beside him anyway, her wrists still wrapped within his stock, his broad palm, his hot fingers, spread low across her waist. "The press are coming! You have no right to remove me from my cell, you lout!"

Ross smiled to himself as he wrangled the young woman along the corridor of barred doors, wondering if Captain Robins would appreciate the trouble he was going through just to protect him and the Metropolitan Police from Miss Dunaway's wrath. She would surely have browbeaten Robins until he'd have been forced to allow her to stay the night.

Now that would be a headline London wouldn't soon forget: Beautiful Suffragette Tortured by Scotland Yard.

At least that's the way the story would read if the beautiful lunatic suffragette were allowed to entertain the press in her jail cell.

They reached the lobby with enough racket that Captain Robins had already popped out of his office.

"Ah, there you are, Blakestone!" A smile suddenly lifted the officer's long face, a look of pure relief, as Ross approached him with the nimble Miss Dunaway tucked against his side. "I see you've got your hands full."

"I demand to be put back into my cell, Captain!" The woman stopped struggling and thrust her chin toward Robins, which gave Ross the chance to wrap his free arm around her fully and pull her perfectly rounded backside against his thigh. "Make this lout let go of me!"

"And what about your other guests, Captain?" Ross nodded toward the courtyard, pleased to see it empty of the sea of women. "How are they faring?"

"Safely on their way home, my lord, just as you suggested."

"As *you* suggested?" Miss Dunaway whipped her head around and glared up at Ross, her fine, full lips in a furious pout, a fire blazing deeply in her eyes. "Just who are you, Blakestone, that you can throw your weight around Scotland Yard!"

Ross did his best to glare back into all that indignation, but he found Miss Dunaway deliciously beguiling.

Every part of her. Including that lovely, ripe hip she was mindlessly grinding into his groin as she frowned up at him in her anger, innocently arousing in him a fever she ought to leave be.

Because he was in no position to be dallying with a woman just now. Though, bloody hell, he'd always been drawn toward the Miss Dunaways of the world. Toward this one especially. Her rare, soaring spirit. Her self-possession.

And those deeply glittering eyes that would tempt him to explore.

Dragging in a huge breath to cool his brain, Ross wrenched his illicit thoughts from his prisoner and directed his attention toward Captain Robins. "Now, if you have a paddy wagon and a driver available . . . ?"

"Ah, Blakestone! I thought I heard your voice!" The Lord Mayor of London strode out of the captain's office, his deputy on his heels. "Good to see you, man. I was planning to pay you a visit this evening."

"That still may be best, Lord Mayor," Ross said with a nod, having no hand free to shake the man's hand. "As you see, I'm all tied up at the moment."

"Captain, I asked you to call the press," Miss Dunaway said, turning her glare on the startled Robins and stomping her foot. "Or did you expect me to fall for his lordship's little deception."

"His . . . I'm sorry, what?" Robins crumpled his wiry brow as he cleared his throat. "Actually, miss, I've been a bit busy with . . . you know."

"No, I don't know, Captain Robins. You arrested me for disturbing the queen's peace, and all I want in return is to tell my side of the story. In print."

"Yes, well, I—"

"Blakestone, if I might have a word with you. Just for a moment." Lord Mayor Callis had come to Ross's side, casting a wary glance at his prisoner.

"Go ahead." Ross shifted Miss Dunaway slightly to the side.

"I suppose, I . . ." Callis hemmed a bit, tugged at his ear as he studied Miss Dunaway. "Yes, well, ahem . . . another one has . . . gone missing."

"Either you unhand me, Blakestone," Miss Dunaway said with a hiss and a wriggle, "or I'm going to have Captain Robins arrest you right here and now."

Ross did his best to ignore her, only held on more tightly, wondering what the devil the Lord Mayor was whispering about. "Another what, Callis? I've been out of the country for the last six months."

"Another *woman*." Callis frowned more deeply

and whispered even louder, "Lady Wallace went missing this morning."

"Lady Wallace? Missing from where?" Though he still didn't understand what the man was talking about.

But Miss Dunaway obviously did. She'd gone completely still in his arms, her shoulders drooping precipitously against him. Her pale green eyes wide and worried when she glanced up at him.

"The lady simply disappeared from Regent Street, Blakestone. In broad daylight. That's why I came here to Scotland Yard. I mean to keep it completely quiet for the time being. I had just broken the news to the captain here."

"And I was just about to ask the Lord Mayor why he wanted me to keep the matter quiet," Robins said. "After all, if the woman is missing, shouldn't as many people know about it as possible?"

"As Lord Mayor, I don't want to panic the population. After all, this is the third woman in four months to turn up missing. And we haven't been able to stop a single one."

"A shame, isn't it?" came the unexpected whisper of sympathy from Miss Dunaway.

But Ross hadn't heard a thing about any of it. "I'm sorry, Callis, I'm completely clueless. I've been on the continent. You'll have to fill me in."

"Briefly then, all of the victims have been ladies. Every one of them. From wealthy families. Aristocratic titles. Three identical crimes."

"Identical?"

"Down to the time of day."

"And the motives for these abductions?" Ross

asked, surprised that his prisoner had relaxed so completely.

"Hard to say, my lord." Callis shook his head. "Very few clues left at the scene; though, as I said, each piece of evidence has been identical to the one before. Nothing to alert the passersby that anything is amiss."

"And then what happens? A demand for money?"

"Nothing, my lord. No ransom note. Nor any contact with the family at all afterward."

"No bodies, neither," Robins added, in a whisper meant to exclude Miss Dunaway, though she was listening intently, "we can thank the good Lord."

Three women vanished completely? Three identically orchestrated crimes?

And not a single body?

"Interesting, Lord Mayor." Ross eased his hold on Miss Dunaway's shoulder, trusting that she wouldn't turn and bolt back to her cell. "But how can I help you? I've been away, as I told you."

Callis glanced down again at the becalmed woman. "If I could send over what we've got so far on the Wallace case. It's not much—"

"I'll be at a dinner tonight until well after midnight, but, sure. Have your officer leave it at the club with Pembridge. I'll take it from there."

"Excellent, my lord. Thank you." Callis breathed a huge sigh. "Three women in four months! Bloody hell, it's a crime wave! And it's liable to set the whole city into a fright, right in the middle of the social season, if we don't solve the crimes and put a stop to the criminal."

"The press won't get wind of this from Scotland Yard," the captain said, "I can promise you that."

"And you, Miss Dunaway?" Ross bent down to the sobered young woman, freeing her hands of his stock, but holding fast to her wrists and peering into her eyes. "Not a word from you either."

"I promise, Blakestone," she said, her gaze glittering brightly with something he couldn't read. "Cross my heart. Not a single word, to anyone. May I go home now?"

Home? Now that was a sudden change of direction.

"I thought you didn't have a home." A bosom, she had said. But the woman definitely had a bosom. Shapely and soft-edged, he'd noticed that in particular. "Or have you tired of prison life, madam?"

She shrugged and nodded slightly. "Just putting everything into perspective, sir. Hearing about those poor women. Makes one think, doesn't it?"

"Indeed."

"A paddy wagon, Miss Dunaway?" the captain said, eyeing the woman, his hands on his hips, his earlier hesitance having vanished. "Or can I trust you in a hack?"

"Thank you, I'll walk, Captain. I promise to go straight to my—"

"No. I'll see you home, Miss Dunaway." Ross heard the words escaping his mouth before he could pull them back. Before he had noticed his heart slamming around inside his chest.

Before he realized that he just needed to know where she called home. Because he couldn't quite let go of all that fiery courage. Not yet.

She lifted her eyes to his, searching his face, obviously assessing his motives. "If you promise not to bind my hands and drag me to my door."

Ross glanced at Callis and Robins, who were watching the exchange as though expecting a bout of fisticuffs to break out between them.

"A truce then, madam."

Her smile filled her eyes with a kind of peace. Then she turned and reached out her hand to the captain as though she'd just spent the afternoon in his mother's parlor. "Thank you for your hospitality, Captain Robins. I'll recommend Scotland Yard to all my friends."

Robins's mouth hung open as he shook hands with the woman, before he finally managed to babble out, "You're very welcome, Miss Dunaway."

She turned then to the Lord Mayor. "And the best of luck in your search for the three missing women, my lord. It seems you're going to need it."

Then the remarkable woman flounced out the front door of Scotland Yard as though she had just won the day.

"This way, madam." Ross caught up her hand, tucked it into the crook of his arm and started back toward the Admiralty livery, where he would borrow a carriage and safely return the extraordinary Miss Dunaway to her home.

A full circle completed.

Crossing Whitehall hadn't turned out so badly after all.

Chapter 4

I long to hear that you have declared independency. And, I desire you would remember the ladies and be more generous and favorable to them than your ancestors.

> Abigail Adams, to her husband John
> March 31, 1776

"**Y**ou live at the Abigail Adams, Miss Dunaway?"

Elizabeth delighted in the rumble of surprise lurking in Blakestone's voice. And in the scandal that flared deeply in his dark eyes as he handed her down from the coach.

"So you've heard of the Adams, my lord?"

"Madam, every man in town seems to be talking about the bloody place."

"Because every man in town is terrified of a few women gathering together, unchaperoned by their men folk." There was something wickedly sensual about pausing here with him on the very public circu-

lar drive up in the courtyard of her deliciously controversial club.

Even more so because he held her hand too long,
too possessively, his eyes smoky and unreadable as
his gaze traveled over her brow and across her
cheeks.

"Indeed, Miss Dunaway, you ladies leave us men
folk quaking in our boots."

"Don't mock us, my lord. It only proves my point."

"I'm merely confessing a timeless truth. Whether
you admit it or not, you ladies have us gentlemen completely at your mercy. Always have and doubtless you
always will."

The clever blackguard! So like a man. Wielding his
platitudes with such backhanded grace!

"Very open-minded, Blakestone. But still you object
to the mere presence of the Abigail Adams."

"I have no opinion at all, Miss Dunaway." As
though to prove his disinterest, he gave the practical
sandstone edifice a browsing glance, then swept that
same glance back across her face. "It's just that I
should have realized that you would be a member of
London's first ladies' club."

"I'm not just a member of the Abigail Adams, my
lord. I'm the owner."

One of his brows lifted slightly and then he smiled
like a tiger. "So not only are you a radical suffragette,
but a notorious hosteler as well."

Notorious? Hmmm . . . the notorious Miss Dunaway!

How wonderful! She wanted to giggle at the

thought, but bottled it up inside her belly and struck a dignified pose, tilting her chin at the man.

"I prefer the term suffrag*ist*, if you please."

"What's a suffragist?" His brow dropped skeptically low, as though he believed she would concoct a new word just to confound him.

"A suffragist is any disenfranchised citizen who demands the vote. By adding the French suffix 'ette' to suffrage, one renders an otherwise creditable position feminine."

"And is a feminine position so objectionable?"

"It is when everything feminine is dismissed out of hand."

Another flick of a smile, again setting off her heart at a full gallop. "Meaning that you don't want to be associated with anything feminine?"

"That's right." Though it suddenly didn't sound at all like what she'd wanted to say.

"What a great loss to the world, then." He shook his head slowly, with high drama, clicking his tongue on his teeth. "Attempting to obliterate anything female about yourself."

"That's not at all what I mean." She wasn't sure what she meant at the moment, not with his full attention beaming down on her. Clothed in his crisp linen and glinting gold buttons.

"Then what?" He leaned down from his tremendous height, shading her face from the fading sunlight. "Because, like it or not, Miss Dunaway, I find you quite feminine."

"Me?"

"Quite."

Oh, my!

"Well . . . I, uh . . . I can't help that, can I?" Try as she might to remain unaffected by all that overwhelming maleness, she couldn't keep her heart from thrumming madly against her ears, making it difficult to hear him clearly, causing her to tip her head even closer to catch his every word.

Every single word, because she wanted to feel each of them brushing against her ear.

"I wouldn't want you to, madam."

Wouldn't want her to what? To feel his words against her ear? Steamy as they were. Close as they were—

Dear God, had she babbled her fantasies out loud? "You don't want me to what, Blakestone?"

"To be anything but feminine in everything you do."

Those words were even steamier, closer. And yet their meaning was just now piercing her fogbound brain. The lout had lured her.

No, she had allowed herself be lured, seduced by his voice. His exotic scent. His broad, shadow-casting shoulders. Served her right for succumbing to . . . to . . . whatever he'd done to her.

Said to her.

"Why feminine, Blakestone? To keep me in my place, I suppose?"

"To keep us honest, my dear." His eyes darkened to coal as he lowered his voice.

"To keep who honest?" she asked in a whisper.

"The male of the species."

The male. She didn't know what to think beyond

that single thought. *The male*. Except she was quite sure that nothing in the world would keep this particular male honest if he had a mind not to be.

After all, he'd been playing her like a violin since the moment she'd first set eyes on him.

Though just now his gaze seemed honest in the extreme, able to set her cheeks afire, probing deeply enough to steal her breath away.

Though for all the world, the man had just sounded as though he supported her cause. Not that she could trust anything about him.

The sly, circling wolf.

"Though I'm grateful for your patronage, Blakestone, I was not put on this earth to be the feminine antidote to your manhood."

His eyebrows shot up, one cocked higher than the other. Then a slanting smile filled his eyes with a devilment that made her cast backward for what she had said that would have made him react to—

His manhood! An *antidote*! Oh, heavens, he couldn't possibly have thought she meant—

"Believe me, Miss Dunaway, you are not and never could be the antidote to my manhood."

Dear Lord! A fiery blush had banked itself just beneath her bodice for the last few minutes and now it roared to life, heating her chest and her neck, rising right up to her cheeks and brows.

"Yes, well, thank you for delivering me safely, my lord. Good day." Before her blush could unmask her completely, she clamped her hand against her bosom, turned abruptly toward the sanctuary of the Adams and headed for the front door.

The blackguard had riddled her into a complete dither. Blast it all! She wasn't the dithering type.

No matter. London was a big town. With any luck she'd never see him again.

Except that she could hear the blighter following her like a stalking shadow, his stride long and as possessive as his handshake.

At least she'd had the chance to tame her confusion and regain her tattered dignity as she started up the wide granite steps toward the elegant front door, which, under the keen-edged footman's timing of Mr. Ronald Hawkins, opened wide as she approached.

"Ah, good evening, Miss Dunaway," Hawkins said, with a graceful nod of his blond head. "Welcome back to the Adams."

The young man was learning well. Though his black coat seemed to have shrunk across his shoulders in the last few months.

"Thank you, Hawkins." Feeling her old self again, in charge and at ease, Elizabeth took a quick breath, then turned to face the persistent earl, in all his flagrant manhood, full on. "As for you, my lord. Do give my best to your colleagues at the *Times*."

Blakestone stood there for a long moment, tall and broad-shouldered, looking at her and then past her, past Hawkins, so obviously trying to catch a glimpse of the feminine mysteries lurking inside the shadowy ladies' club.

Let him wonder!

Let him outright suspect!

Let him—oh, dear! He'd taken hold of her hand again, swamping it in his heat.

"The pleasure was all mine, Miss Dunaway." He lifted her hand to his lips. And stunned her with the exquisite heat of his large fingers. "But do take care on your adventures."

"My adventures?"

He frowned deeply at her, then glanced briefly over his shoulder at the street. "There seems to be great danger out there. I wouldn't want to hear that you've become a victim of whatever fiend is prowling the streets of London."

"I assure you, my lord, I'll be entirely safe."

Perhaps she'd said that with a little too much confidence, because the man only frowned more deeply and took her chin firmly between his thumb and finger. "Don't take any foolish chances with your misadventuring, Miss Dunaway. I might not be around to rescue you the next time."

"You didn't rescue me, Blakestone!" She laughed, though she ought to have shinned him. "Not even close."

And still he frowned as he straightened, speaking distinctly between his amazingly white teeth. "Do you understand me, Miss Dunaway? The danger?"

I understand far more than you might ever imagine, Blakestone.

"Of course I understand the danger. I'm not a fool. Three women of good breeding vanish into thin air in the course of a few months, never to be seen again . . . a cautionary tale if ever there was one." But hardly a danger to her. Not like the danger posed by the man whose minty breath was breaking against her mouth. "Now, if you'll excuse me, my lord—"

"Oh, look, there she is!" came a trilling voice from inside the Adams, and then a half-dozen club members poured out onto the porch, surrounding her with their questions, shoving the charmingly irritated Blakestone to the edge of the throbbing circle.

"Gracious! Did you break out of prison with your bare hands, Elizabeth?"

"I'll bet that captain grilled you good and hard, didn't he?"

"Will we be in the morning *Times*?"

"Let's go inside, ladies." Elizabeth found Blakestone's gaze locked hard on hers as she tried to herd the women through the front door into the foyer. "I'll tell you everything. I promise."

Everything but the way the earl's touch had dizzied her, had sent her pulse spinning out of control.

She had only turned away from him for a moment, but when she glanced back to bid him farewell, he was gone.

And the carriage too, leaving her with the oddest feeling that she would be seeing him again soon.

Even more odd, because that would be just fine with her.

"I can assure you, Prince Rupert, the prime minister does see Austria's point," Ross said, tamping down his irritation with the deputy ambassador as he accepted a brandy from one of the embassy's obsequious waiters. Doubtless also Rupert's operative as well.

"Austria's point, Blakestone," Rupert said with a snort, a quick show of that hair-triggered, half-witted

Hapsburg temper, "is that Austria has no choice, not with Russia sitting on her flanks."

"And Lord Aberdeen greatly appreciates Austria's efforts toward fashioning a truce between Russia and the opposition. However—"

"Ah-ha! Just as I suspected!" Rupert glared as he waggled his sticklike finger at Ross. "I told the emperor there would follow a 'however' from the prime minister. What is this 'however,' my lord Blakestone? Sit. Sit, and tell me."

Rupert might only be a deputy diplomat with little authority, but he was a typical spoiled princeling through and through. Commanding the embassy's parlor conversation as surely as he had the dinner conversation.

"As I was about to explain, Prince Rupert, Her Majesty's prime minster seeks only to have all of the parties in the dispute fully represented at any negotiation table."

"Surely that goes without saying, sir?"

Ross had learned the hard way that nothing in international politics should ever go without saying. Without drafting in indelible ink. The devil dwelled in the details.

And Tsar Nicholas was the worst kind of devil when it came to hedging his bets.

"What of the sultan of Turkey?" Ross asked, leaning forward in the wing-backed chair. "Has he been told of this peace conference to be convened in Vienna at the end of the month?"

The prince sputtered for a moment, then nodded. "But of course."

Not as of a week ago, when Ross last spoke to the man. But now was not the time to play that particular card.

"That is, of course, Lord Blakestone, if we convene a peace conference at all, given the tempers involved."

"It's been suggested that you convene something soon, Your Highness. And not to forget the sultan. Because, of course, he would be as resistant to the idea of partitioning his empire as your Emperor Franz Josef would be if the Great Powers divided up the Hapsburg holdings between them."

"Mon dieu!" The prince gasped, launching his monocle off his florid cheek in a perfect arc, before it plopped against his shirtfront, to dangle on the end of its ribbon. "That's not what we . . . ahem . . . That is to say, you can assure Aberdeen that all parties will be represented in Vienna, one way or the other. . . ."

All parties, indeed. Now, there was a plain-faced lie, doubtless told by the Austrian ambassador himself. Though it stunk of the tsar's own infamous manipulations. What the devil were the Austrians up to? And why?

Perhaps a bitter dose of Russian intimidation or a little royal blackmail in exchange for leaving the Danube Territories alone.

It was exactly these kind of relentless pressures that might lead a country or its diplomats down a reckless pathway. Political assassinations, invasions, coups.

"I'm sure Aberdeen will be glad to hear it, Your Highness. Because to exclude the sultan is to anger him. Which will only serve to anger Her Majesty, Queen Victoria. And you of all people must understand her temper when she is made to look the fool."

"Yes, yes, Blakestone, I understand perfectly." Rupert's watery eyes flared to saucers, as though recalling a personal encounter with his regal cousin's sometimes thorny disposition. "But I must ask you, sir, to keep this all quite secret."

"My word of honor, Your Highness."

"Now, how about another brandy, Blakestone?"

"No, thank you. It's getting late." An excuse not to be found in the prince's language.

It took Ross another two hours to escape the man and his sycophants, and no time at all to find his way back to the Huntsman.

On a route that led him directly past the Abigail Adams. A building he'd never paid the least attention to before earlier that evening.

Before his unexpected interlude with the amazing Miss Dunaway. With her challenging emerald eyes and her softly clinging scent, which had teased him through the dinner party and still danced in his imagination.

But he had barely made it through the front door when Pembridge appeared at his elbow, a slight hitch to his aging gait.

"Good evening, my lord." Pembridge handed Ross a folder and a pasteboard box, his neatly trimmed gray brows drawn together. "This came for you. From the Lord Mayor's office."

"Thank you, Pembridge, but you didn't have to stay up and wait for me. You could have left it in my rooms."

"Just as well, sir. I was awake anyway." Day or night for the last fifteen years, the prescient old man had always been ten steps ahead of him. "Anything else, sir?"

"To bed with you, Pembridge. Good night." Ross watched the elderly man, worried to see that he seemed to have grown shorter in the last year, slower. He'd have to bring it up to Jared and Drew.

But not tonight. He wanted to take a moment to study the Lord Mayor's report to see if there was anything he could add to the Wallace case. Although how his own specialty—gathering and analyzing data from naval fleets around the world—could help a local kidnapping investigation, he couldn't imagine. But he'd promised to try.

His shoulder aching and stiff, Ross left the members' area of the club and was just starting downstairs into the elaborate catacombs of the highly secret Factory when he heard footsteps behind him.

"Hold up there, Ross!"

"Drew! What the devil are you doing here? What happened to attending the theatre with your wife and that pack of Swedish royalty?"

"We did. But we came home to a note from the Lord Mayor, pleading with me to help you quietly investigate Lady Wallace's disappearance." Drew went ahead of Ross into the evidence lab and turned up the gaslight at the door sconce.

"Callis is determined to keep this out of the press for as long as he can," Ross said. "Seems to think the London season will be ruined by this spate of crimes against the aristocracy."

"The very reason Caro insisted I join the search. Because of the two women who vanished earlier this year."

"Did she know them? Or Lady Wallace?"

"No. But, you know Caro. A woman who understands the importance of keeping secrets. I came because it was the only way to keep her from joining the investigation herself."

"Then let's get to it." Ross handed Drew the thin Wallace report then dropped the pasteboard box onto the table. "Does it say who first noticed the lady missing?"

Drew leafed quickly through the file then snorted. "Her footman, Whiggens. According to this, he's elderly. Nearly blind, hard of hearing. Apparently he thought it was unusual for his lady to spend nearly an hour in the millinery shop, so he went inside to check on her."

"Didn't find her, then sent for a policeman, right?"

"Exactly. The officer on the corner came running, but the trail had already gone cold. In less than an hour."

"And this is all they found at the scene." Ross reached into the box and pulled out a gaudy blue bonnet, a large kid glove, and a folded, crumpled man's handkerchief.

"Virtually identical to the evidence they found at the first two abductions." Drew lifted the bonnet by one of its ribbons and set it on a table stand. "Though surely not this same style of hat."

"We won't know that until Scotland Yard sends over the rest of the evidence." Ross took a magnifying glass from one of the forensic cabinets and peered through it at the bonnet. "So, they found this in Regent Street."

Drew checked the file. "In the alley behind the shop; lodged between two barrels, but in fairly plain sight."

"And Lady Wallace had been wearing this very hat when she entered the shop?"

"According to the footman and three of the sales clerks." Drew was already busy creating a case file from the few pages of the report, the familiar, metal-cornered box that would contain the particulars of the crime as the Factory investigated the details.

"What color is Lady Wallace's hair?" Ross pulled a glittering strand off the line of stitching that attached the wide blue ribbon to the blue velvet brim of the hat.

Drew gave another quick scan of Callis's report. "Dark brown, almost black."

"Interesting." He held the strand up to the sharper light of the gas flame. "Because this belongs to a redhead."

He plucked two more from the rusching at the nape, and was struck by the softness of the scent.

A wisp of the familiar.

"An imposter?" Drew had asked the very question Ross had been considering.

"Except that all the witnesses identified Lady Wallace in the carriage as well as in the shop." Ross dropped onto a tall stool, sniffed at the handkerchief and grimaced. "Definitely chloroform. Found in the dressing room."

"And this glove found at the end of the alley. Also tinged with the slight smell of chloroform."

"Which could mean that Lady Wallace was chloroformed in the dressing room, taken outside into the alley, then put into a vehicle."

"We need to see for ourselves, Ross. Otherwise I might be forced to believe that Lady Wallace truly did disappear without a trace."

Leaving only the most bone-chilling possibilities.

"That's what disturbs me the most," Ross said. "Because people don't usually disappear completely, for no reason. Without a threat of blackmail or a ransom demand. This makes three, Drew. What the hell's going on?"

"A professional criminal?"

"Clever enough to best Scotland Yard at least twice in the last four months. No wonder the Lord Mayor wasn't going to leave it to the Yard this time. Though I don't mind saying I'm completely stumped."

Not a common feeling here in the Factory. It sprawled for three blocks in all directions beneath the elegant rooms of the Huntsman and other, more ordinary buildings. Its catacombs filled with workshops and laboratories, libraries of information, communication systems, every possible invention and some impossible. Every government agency at their beck and call.

Yet sometimes even they were left completely at sea.

"And the Austrians, Ross? How did that go?"

Ross snorted and lifted the blue bonnet off the stand. "Playing games with the Great Powers, Drew. Dangerous games. With dangerous toys."

And yet suddenly Ross felt he was looking at the most dangerous weapon of all.

Richly scented and marked with strands of strawberry gold hair.

All of which made his brain ache.

And the ache only worsened after he left Drew in

the lobby and reached the small, shared sitting area in front of his suite where he found Lord Tuckerton fast asleep in a high-backed chair, a newspaper draped across his knees.

"Lord Tuckerton?"

Ross touched the old man's bony shoulder and he woke with a snorting start. "Yes, yes, what?"

"Sorry to startle you, Lord Tuckerton, but you seemed to have fallen asleep."

"Ah, good, Blakestone. Just the man I wanted to see." The old man struggled to rise, but Ross bent onto a knee to save him the effort.

"What can I do for you, Tuckerton?"

The old man lifted his watery gray eyes to Ross. "You can help find my lass."

"Your lass?"

"My grandniece, Lady Wallace. She's missing." The whole of his body sagged against the back of the chair.

Bloody hell. "Lady Wallace is your grandniece?"

"My brother's granddaughter."

"I didn't realize." Poor old Tuckerton. Never married. Rarely left the Huntsman for anything more than Sunday services at St. Paul's or the opening of Parliament.

"How did you find this out?"

"That husband of hers, Wallace. He came by here asking if I'd seen her today. But I hadn't, had I? Not since Monday last when she picked me up and we went for a drive in the country."

"When did Wallace come by?"

"Just after lunch." After the abduction. "Can you find her for me, Blakestone?"

"I promise to do my best, Lord Tuckerton. But let's keep this between the two of us."

"Oh, thank you, lad. Thank you."

"But in the meantime, let's get you back to your chamber." Feeling like a heel for having nothing at all to tell him that would buoy the grieving old man's spirits, Ross stood and slipped his hand under the old man's elbow. "Things will look much better in the morning."

Chapter 5

What mighty ills have not been done
by woman!
Who lost Mark Anthony the world?
—A woman!
Who was the cause of a long ten years' war,
And laid at last old Troy in ashes?—Woman!

Thomas Otway, *The Orphan*, 1680

"**Y**ou look every inch the elderly spinster, Lady Ellis!" Elizabeth grinned as she straightened the woman's dowdy black fichu. "Eighty-five, if you're a day."

"I feel a hundred." Lady Ellis sent a skittish glance toward the bustling mid-morning traffic clattering along Threadneedle Street. "And so . . . exposed."

"You've nothing to worry about, my lady." Though Elizabeth remembered being just as frightened the first time. Certain that everyone had guessed at her secret plans. That the police were on their way, ready to clap her in irons.

But now it seemed that the more often she braved

the hazardous undertaking, the easier the job became. And the more she shamelessly craved the challenge.

"Is my wig on straight, then?" The woman grimaced and tugged on the black ribbon tied below her chin. "It feels loose."

"It's fine. Besides, no one will suspect a thing, because no one is paying the least attention to us. A pair of helpless, elderly ladies."

"You do look positively ancient, Miss Elizabeth."

"Then we're both well armed!" Elizabeth pushed her spectacles up her nose, then tapped the tip of her cane on the cobble. "Are you ready?"

"If you think we are . . ."

"I'm quite sure of it." And quite proud. "I've pulled off this stunt dozens of times, without a single hitch."

And she was about to do it again!

They were standing in front of the Bank of England, garbed in their frumpish battle armor, prepared to mount a full frontal assault on the Old Lady of Threadneedle Street.

An indignity that never failed to raise her hackles.

Leave it to men to give an impregnable male institution like the Bank of England a feeble, feminine nickname. While at the same time denying married women the right to open accounts of their own without their husbands' permission.

Their permission! As though women hadn't the sense to manage money on their own!

"Now remember, Lady Ellis," Elizabeth said, tamping back that tic of anger as she hooked the woman's arm and adjusted her aged hunch, "you are Miss Althea Moore."

"Althea Moore. I like the name." The woman started up the wide stairs beside Elizabeth, tottering like an expert toward the bank lobby.

"You've never been married. And you live alone in Pickering Place."

"Never married. Pickering Place. Pickering Place." Lady Ellis sounded perfectly doddering with all that muttering.

"You have inherited the rents on a green grocer and a small boardinghouse, and will be adding to your account regularly."

"Green grocer and a boardinghouse. A regular account." Lady Ellis was gripping Elizabeth's arm in a vise of fear. "I hope I can remember all that."

Elizabeth patted her hand. "Just follow my lead, no matter what, and everything will go swimmingly."

"But what if it doesn't?" Lady Ellis paused as they reached the wide porch and peered at Elizabeth through her wiry spectacles. "What if they catch us?"

"They won't." They can't. She couldn't let them. Because the penalty for conspiracy and defrauding a bank was too many years in a dank, dark prison to endure.

But this time there'd be no meddlesome earl to interfere with her fate.

The footman nodded a bow as he opened the great, glass door for them, and Elizabeth led the trembling woman into the cool air of the vast, vaulted, marble lobby of milling people and bank officials.

The enormously tall windows streamed sunlight across the floor and up the front edge of the rich, oak half-walls of the elevated teller's counter, which spanned the back wall of the room. The faces of the bank clerks peered down on the lobby from between the short wooden struts, putting the customers at a distinct disadvantage.

"So this is the Bank of England!" Lady Ellis had stopped in the center of the marble floor, staring in open-mouthed awe at the pompous, overly masculine atmosphere. "Imagine, Elizabeth, I'm nearly fifty years old, and in all that time I've had no cause to come here!"

"Because your husband has taken care of everything."

"Including the substantial inheritance left to me by my father, which I'm not allowed to touch because I'm a woman." Lady Ellis harrumphed, her eyes now snapping, her mouth set in an irritated frown. "After all, I couldn't possibly be intelligent enough to manage my own personal finances. Though not two months ago my husband insisted that our fifteen-year-old son open his own account. And I wouldn't trust that boy to know a horse from a hairbrush."

"Exactly, my lady." A sobering, hard-fought admission for most women.

Lady Ellis gave a defiant grunt, then tugged Elizabeth toward the wall of teller cages. "Come then, my dear. I'm ready for a little independence."

Brava, Lady Ellis. Elizabeth leaned on the crook of her cane, and then hobbled up to a waiting clerk.

She had to crane her head to see up over the counter and through the short bars to the needle-nosed clerk in a crisp white collar and a staid gray neckcloth.

"May I help you, madam?" the man asked with a

long, doubting drawl that made her want to give him a good whack on his balding head with her cane.

"Let's hope you can, sonny," Elizabeth shot back with a goodly amount of disdain, patting the stoop-shouldered Lady Ellis on the arm as though they were fusty old comrades. "My friend here has come to your bank to open an account."

"Indeed, madam." The man rose up off his perch as though the effort pained him, then peered down at them through his pale brows. "However, according to company policy, opening an account here is a matter for your husband to—"

"Miss Moore is unmarried, young man." Elizabeth rapped the tip of her cane against the foot of the counter.

The man gave a satisfying flinch and then narrowed his eyes at her. "Indeed."

"Indeed, yes. She has come into some money and would like to deposit it and any future gains in the Bank of England. Unless, of course, you do not want her money."

He studied Lady Ellis for another moment, his brows pinching together into a single wriggling, caterpillarlike object. "Indeed, madam."

He hemmed and hawed then spoke in hushed tones to the teller beside him, but when the man finally, grudgingly, poked a card through the bars and growled at his new depositor, Elizabeth knew they were going to win—again.

"Fill this out, Miss Moore. Over there at the counter." He pointed to a slanted writing space at the side of the lobby. "Then bring it back here."

"Thank you, sir." Elizabeth gave the frowning clerk an elderly grin then led her hobbling companion to the desk. "Good work, my lady."

"Dear Lord, Miss Elizabeth! If I'd known it was as simple as that, I'd have opened my own accounts years ago and saved myself from my dear husband's constant carping about every farthing I ask of him. I ought to be able to collect quite a pot over the course of a year. Do whatever I want with it."

Fifteen minutes later the deed had been successfully done; Miss Althea Moore was the proud owner of her very own account at the Bank of England, and Elizabeth was leading her out the door onto the porch of the wide steps.

"This is the tidiest damned back alley I've ever seen." Drew stood frowning at the dry cobbles and the row of barrels against the back of the row of shops.

"No sign of a skirmish anywhere along here." Ross had walked the length of the alley, looking for indications of a scuffle etched into the granite. But there wasn't a single sign of iron wheels scraping against the stone for a quick getaway. No drag marks leading out of the open back door of the millinery shop.

Not a single window looking out onto the alley. The bulk of a carriage would easily mask the commotion of an abduction from the streets at either end.

He'd awakened early to set the Factory's best forensic experts onto the evidence. They would search out the haberdasher who made the bonnet, the chemist who formulated the chloroform, and the glovemaker.

Simple tasks that the Factory's experts did on a daily basis.

Walking through the methods and madness of a criminal required an altogether more refined set of skills.

"Find anything, my lord?" The plump-cheeked clerk watched them from just inside the back door of the shop, her brown eyes a familiar mix of concern, horror, and curiosity.

"The police report says that Lady Wallace was here for nearly an hour. Was that normal for her?"

"Normal for most all of our clients. Miss Verdon encourages her customers to take all the time they need. Attends to them herself, while we girls help out with fetching feathers and trimming and ribbons and such from the boxes."

"Did she seem different? At any point? Fearful, distracted?"

"Not any more than usual."

"Meaning?"

"I shouldn't really say, my lord. Miss Verdon doesn't like us to speak about her customers."

"This is a police matter, Alice. Anything you tell us, no matter how inconsequential it may seem, might just be the information that saves Lady Wallace's life."

"Oh, dear. But it's nothing much, sir. Only that the lady wasn't ever very happy. Seemed afraid all the time."

"Not just yesterday?"

"That's right." Alice leaned out the doorway. "Always jumpy, you know. Fretting about what her husband might think of her hats."

"And that's odd?"

"Most husbands don't care. Wouldn't know a poke from a leghorn."

The one thing Ross knew already about Lord Wallace was that the baron was opinionated, unbending. The sort of man who attempted to control every moment of his existence, and all the people who crossed his path.

"I see. Did she meet up with anyone in the shop? A friend, perhaps? An acquaintance?"

"Sometimes customers meet someone they know. And they chat and gossip while they try on hats."

"But not this visit?"

"We only had three other customers while she was here. I gave their names to the officers yesterday."

"I'll check on those, Blakestone."

"Thanks, Wexford. Now if we could go back inside."

"Yessir."

Ross let Alice precede them through the back door, then he stopped in front of the dressing room. "It says here in the report that Lady Wallace went into the dressing room with her bag and the blue hat she'd come in with, and then she never came out."

"That's right. As though she just turned into a ghost and vanished into thin air."

Drew swung the door open and peered inside. "How long before you noticed her missing?"

"Five minutes, my lord. Maybe a little longer."

Ross stepped inside the windowless, ten-by-ten

room, noticing the barest hint of chloroform that still clung to the chintz. "Did anything strike you as unusual at any point after Lady Wallace stepped inside here?"

"Odd noises?" Drew prompted. "Smells, voices, a demanding customer?"

"The police asked us that yesterday, but I don't remember a thing."

"All right, then, Alice, what happened next?" Ross asked as he knelt to inspect the pristine area around the door latch.

"The footman came in asking about the lady. I knocked on the door here, and there was no answer. So Mrs. Verdon opened the door and there was nothing. No Lady Wallace."

"Nothing but a folded handkerchief on the floor, right here, according to the report. Near the dressing table."

"That's right, Lord Blakestone."

"And her bonnet outside in the alley." Ross ran the flat of his hand along the floor at the edge of the wall. Three small, blue glass beads stuck themselves between his fingers.

"Miss Verdon says it was a good thing it wasn't a hat from our shop."

"Why is that?" Ross asked, pleased to have settled that particular question.

"Because it's a complete fright. Ugly as a blue toad, she said. And I have to agree with her."

Ross stood, palming the beads and sticking them into his trouser pocket. "Did Lady Wallace mention any plans she might have for later in the afternoon?"

"No, not yesterday. But she did once in a while talk about visiting an elderly uncle."

"Lord Tuckerton?" Ross asked, pulling his notepad out of his jacket pocket.

"That's it, my lord." Alice nodded as she thought more deeply. "And a club of some sort."

"The Huntsman?" Drew asked, striding toward them.

"No, sir. It was a lady's name. My mother's name. Abigail."

Ross's hand froze in midair, his pencil poised above his notepad. "The Abigail Adams?"

"That's the one!" Alice beamed.

Bloody hell!

"Now there's a coincidence, Ross. We were mentioning the place ourselves only yesterday."

"Weren't we, though." Hell and damnation, the woman had played him for a fool. "Come along, Drew, I'll drop you at the Huntsman. Then I've got a call to make on my own."

A call that Miss Dunaway wouldn't soon forget.

Elizabeth and the very smug, very, very happy Lady Ellis were celebrating their stunning victory over the Bank of England in the public tea room of the Abigail Adams, still a pair of well-appointed elderly ladies, sharing a very English ritual.

A ritual that always made the new account holder more comfortable with her new role.

"Dear Elizabeth, you are a wonder!"

"And you, Lady Ellis, were the perfect spinster, still look the part to a T." Elizabeth loved her popular public tea room—the cozy chintz, and especially its subversive elements. With a fresh selection of newspapers to read without the husband looking on. With intelligent conversation encouraged. With scones and chocolate and sticky toffee pudding and perfectly brewed cream teas.

Yes, the tea room was proving the perfect tool to recruit new members to the ladies' club.

"I've never had quite so much fun!" Lady Ellis gave a girlish giggle. "I felt just like a spy!"

"You'll have no trouble managing your new account, as long as you come and go from the tea room in an anonymous hack and wear the same wig and bonnet as part of your disguise every time you return to the Bank. You can change into your costume upstairs in the Adams."

"You've thought of everything, Miss Elizabeth."

"I've tried to." Elizabeth poured Lady Ellis another cup of Darjeeling, pleased that she was taking to the disguise so eagerly, even after the fact. "But the important thing is that you never raise suspicions and that your husband never finds out that you have become a woman of independent means."

"One miserly pound at a time. But at least the money will belong to me." Lady Ellis sighed as she idly stirred cream into her tea. "Poor Arthur isn't a bad man, really, he's just . . . well, thick, when it comes to understanding that I might have a life intellectually separate from his. After all, I speak and write seven languages, and he can barely handle the one he was born with."

Such a sadly common complaint among the women

she'd come to know and admire. "Besides which, you manage a household of how many servants every day?"

"Twenty-five."

"And Lord Ellis manages how many employees at his investment firm?"

"Eight." Lady Ellis tsked as though she now pitied the man's insignificant fate. "My mother always said that women ran the world."

"But wouldn't it be better if we had a vote in the casting of the laws that rule the land?"

Lady Ellis shook her head. "You are so wise for one so young."

"Thank you, my lady." It was wisdom hard-won, inspired and encouraged by so many brave women who'd come before her.

"Just think, my dear, if I hadn't joined the Abigail Adams and attended the weekly club meetings, if I hadn't listened to the lectures by the Strickland sisters and Mrs. Green and all the other speakers you've brought to us, if I hadn't met you, then I would never have found the nerve to break out of my prison."

"I merely provided the opportunity, Lady Ellis."

"And the courage. For which I thank you."

"You're welcome." Though she disliked taking credit for the wise decisions made by people who only needed to be shown the way. "Now if I might suggest one last thing regarding your new account."

The woman's eyes sparkled with her smile. "More intrigue, I hope."

"It's just that you should try to carry out each of your transactions with the same clerk, every time. He'll grow so used to you, he'll soon not even notice you."

"Just like my Arthur. He barely notices me at all anymore. Not like when we were first married." Lady Ellis leaned forward, arching a brow into her fusty wig, her words conspiring, barely audible. "You know . . . in the bedroom."

"I see." Though she didn't really, not fully. Elizabeth hadn't meant to still be completely virginal at the ripe old age of twenty-two, but there were such risks for a woman in all things sexual.

And she'd met very few men worth a scandalous pregnancy, let alone an unsuitable marriage.

Which made her think instantly, unreasonably, of that great lout Blakestone.

With his enormous shoulders and broad chest, his rumbling voice that had simply turned her knees to jelly.

And made her heart scamper around like an unhinged hare.

"Which, my dear, is the very reason I'm going back into the Abigail Adams right now, change out of my disguise, and sign myself up for that class on how to seduce your own husband. I've heard so much about it."

"Excellent, Lady Ellis."

Word-of-mouth at work! The class was getting more popular by the day. Taught by an ex-madam who'd married a marquis twenty years ago and had, apparently, kept him the happiest, most faithful man in the kingdom.

Not that she herself ever planned to marry. But at least now, if the worst should happen and she should lose not only her independence to a man, but the control of the substantial inheritance that her aunts had left her, she would know what to do to keep her husband from taking comfort in the arms of a mistress.

At least in theory.

Should the very worst ever happen to her.

"And after that class, Miss Elizabeth, I plan to take your class on how to defend myself from an attack on the streets, or God forbid, an abduction." Lady Ellis was on her feet, still whispering as she adjusted the crumpled black netting on the brim of her dowdy hat. "Then I want to start attending sessions of Parliament like you've been talking about, just to see what those men are up to with my rights."

Oh, this was fine news indeed. Subversion at its best. One mind at a time.

"My plan, Lady Ellis, is that eventually there won't be room enough for all of us in the public gallery." Elizabeth stood, feeling quite smug at the results of her daring to take matters into her own hands. "Then we'll have to start taking our rightful places in the chamber itself."

"Oh, if that could only happen!" The very thought seemed to have put Lady Ellis into a reverie that required a shake of her head to banish. "Well, now you just sit right there, my dear, relax and enjoy your delicious tea, while I change out of my disguise." She squeezed Elizabeth's hand. "And thank you so very much!"

The woman hurried to the rear of the tea room, stopped at the members-only entrance to the Abigail Adams, handed the attendant her membership card, then sped through the open door, giving Elizabeth a little wave on her way through.

If only all her clients could be made as happy with such a small adjustment to their lives.

No matter how delightful it would be to sit at a table, sipping her tea while searching the *Times* for an article about yesterday's protest, there were always more pressing matters to be taken care of.

She hadn't even made it as far as the rear door when it swung open and Cassie dashed through the doorway, her clerk's visor dipped low on her forehead.

"Miss Elizabeth, I was hoping you were here!" The young woman shoved the visor up off her brow, grabbed Elizabeth by the hand and started to tug her through the doorway. "You've got to come quickly! There's trouble."

"What is it?"

Cassie stopped abruptly in the middle of the corridor, thoroughly incensed. "It's . . . a man. In the foyer."

"A man?"

"A very large one. He demanded to see you immediately, then pushed right past Hawkins and planted himself in that chair by the fountain, saying he'd wait. Hawkins tried to put him into the visitor's parlor, but he wouldn't budge."

There was only one man she knew who would be so bloody arrogant. Blakestone.

Furious, Elizabeth reached for the door latch that would have plunged her right into the foyer.

"All right, Cassie, I'll take care of the man this very minute."

How satisfying it would be to throw him out of her club on his fine backside.

But Cassie gasped and grabbed her arm.

"You can't meet a stranger dressed like that." The young woman pointed in horror at Elizabeth's dowdy widow's costume. "What would he think?"

That she was up to something.

And he'd be right.

Damn the man for his power to fluster her so thoroughly!

"Tell his lordship that I'll be down in a few minutes." *And then I'll throw him out!*

Chapter 6

Man is the hunter; woman is his game
Man for the field and woman for the hearth.

Alfred, Lord Tennyson, *Song*

"**M**iss Dunaway said to tell you she'd be down in a few minutes, Lord Blakestone."

Ross glanced up from his folio of reports and into the pert face of a young woman who looked to be every bit as determined and efficient as Miss Dunaway herself.

"And you are?" he asked, getting to his feet. He'd never seen anyone wearing a green clerk's visor with such pride of purpose, or with quite so many pencils sticking out of the lustrous blond knot at the back of her head.

"Miss Cassie MacLauren, Clerk of the Membership of the Abigail Adams Club for Ladies." A very large title for such a petite woman.

"Ah, then, thank you, Miss MacLauren," was all he could think to say.

"Good day, sir." With that, she spun on an efficient heel and disappeared through a doorway beneath one of the two dramatically sweeping staircases.

The Abigail Adams was an impressive sight. Elegant with marble and brass and mahogany. Richly exotic carpets, a small fountain, statuary in niches, a pair of round inlaid tables gracing the center of the foyer, each towering with a massive arrangement of flowers.

And everywhere he looked, doors closed tightly against the possibility of male intrusion.

He'd only just returned to his chair when another woman, older than Miss MacLauren, more sturdy, came through the double doors on the right. He got to his feet again, only to have the woman fix a disdainful eye on him as she crossed the width of the foyer, her arms loaded down with what appeared to be ledgers, her frown daring him to offer to help carry the books, her glare threatening bodily harm if he did.

In the course of the next few minutes a half-dozen different women entered the foyer through various doorways. Each eyed him as though he were a penny curiosity while they strode purposely across the marble floor, then flicked a glare or a scowl at him before heading off on their sundry errands.

He felt wholly plucked and skewered.

Wholly out of place.

Prepared to wait out Miss Dunaway's persnickety temper, Ross sat down again, picked up his newspaper, read only a single word, when he realized that the temperature in the room had cooled to eddies.

The air crackled with a familiar scent.

"Good afternoon, Blakestone."

His breath caught in his gut as her sultry voice drifted down from the landing above.

And caught again when he looked up to find her starting down the stairs, as regal as any queen. He wondered if she knew just how unblushingly her femininity was showing at the moment. Glinting at him through the crystal green of her eyes, from her sly, cat-in-the-cream smile, from the elegantly simple lines and curves of her pale yellow shirtwaist and working skirts.

Her ankles.

Her slippers.

Christ! He staggered to his feet again and moved toward the bottom of the stairs, his mouth dry, his pulse stammering as he tried to recall the purpose of his visit.

Something he wanted to ask her about.

"Yes, good afternoon to you, Miss Dunaway."

"To what do I owe the honor of your visit, my lord?"

Lady Wallace! Yes, that was it!

But before Ross could begin to answer that he had come to dredge the truth from her, the front door opened and a half-dozen women poured in from the glare of the afternoon sun, chattering about yesterday's protest march, laughing at their triumph.

Then stopping abruptly to look at Ross.

"Pay the man no mind, ladies. Lord Blakestone will be leaving in a moment."

The women dismissed him with a single harrumph, then one of them broke out of the pack to meet Miss Dunaway at the bottom of the stairs with the front page of the same newspaper Ross had read earlier that morning.

"Elizabeth! Have you seen the *Times*?"

"We're in it!"

"You're in it!" The first woman held out the paper for Miss Dunaway and jabbed at the middle of it. "See. This is so exciting! 'Elizabeth Dunaway, of the controversial Abigail Adams, was jailed yesterday for causing a disturbance of the peace in Whitehall.' "

"Is that what they called it, Mrs. Niles?" Miss Dunaway's brows dipped as she peered over the woman's arm and quickly scanned the article. "That we were merely disturbing the peace?"

"Let's see, it says, 'Miss Dunaway and her unruly band of women—' See! That's us! Unruly!" Mrs. Niles shared a proud giggle with the others, then pushed her spectacles up her nose and continued. "Um . . . 'band of women . . . were not charged and were released into the care of their guardians.' "

"Guardians!" Miss Dunaway's gaze shot across the room to Ross. As though he had stood over the editor and dictated the copy. "As though we were children!"

"I see what you mean, Miss Elizabeth!" Mrs. Niles was now frowning at the newspaper as darkly as her mentor was frowning at him. "There's not a word here about the fact that we were marching on Westminster for women's rights."

"Nothing about our protest signs!"

"Or our chanting."

"Of course not." Miss Dunaway's full lips drew into a line of disappointed anger. So the unbiased editor of the *Times* had obviously failed her. "We shouldn't really have expected to find a word about the sorry plight of women in this country."

"Oh, but at least your name made the morning paper, Miss Elizabeth!"

"And the Abigail Adams! That's a good thing."

Mrs. Niles carefully folded the newspaper and tucked it into her reticule. "Do join us in the tea room, Miss Elizabeth. To celebrate. Please!"

Miss Dunaway's eyes lifted to his again, her mood deeply serious. As though the stakes in this issue were far beyond the understanding of the women who surrounded her with their eagerness.

"I'd love to, ladies. But I've got so much work to do this afternoon." Which obviously included evicting him from her presence.

The group sighed as one, happily satisfied with their antics.

Mrs. Niles grinned broadly, casting a wry glance at Ross. "Then we'll see you at the meeting tomorrow night, Miss Elizabeth."

"Indeed." Miss Dunaway smiled at the group as they gossiped their frothy way across the foyer then disappeared into what he assumed was the tea room beyond.

She then turned her attention on him again, that deceptively soft gaze, lighting his senses to the marrow, lulling the unwary.

It was a damn good thing he was as wary as hell of the woman.

"You're not supposed to be here in the lobby, Blakestone. The Adams is a club for ladies. We have a visitors' parlor for your type."

"You mean for men? Afraid I'll learn your secrets?"

She waved a dismissive hand at him. "Believe me, my lord, if I had any secrets, you'd never get anywhere near them."

"Indeed." The woman was a bundle of riddles and canards.

"After all, what if I pushed my way past the footman at your club and planted myself in the foyer like a toadstool? Your members would scream bloody murder and have me thrown out on my ear."

Ross had to chuckle at the truth of that. At times the men of the club acted just like a gaggle of old ladies.

"I'm sure you wouldn't have made it past the front door of the Huntsman."

"In that case, you understand the sanctity of one's private refuge and won't mind if I insist that you leave. You've sent my entire staff into a muddle." She started past him toward the entrance, as though she believed she could actually convince him to leave when her falsehoods had brought him right to the front steps of the Abigail Adams.

Miss Dunaway was waiting for him at the front door, her impatient hand resting on the latch. "Please, my lord, don't make me throw you out."

Ross stood his ground and caught back the smile of triumph that was beginning to bunch up inside his chest. "One question first, madam, before you attempt such a feat."

She gave an exasperated little huff. "Make it quick, Blakestone."

"Why didn't you tell me yesterday that you knew Lady Wallace?"

She opened her lovely mouth, whether in shock or to launch into an outright denial, he wasn't sure. But then she closed it again, doing a bad job of hiding her discomfort behind a placid smile.

"What makes you think I know Lady Wallace?"

"Because you own the Abigail Adams, my dear, and she was a member in good standing until yesterday morning when she vanished from the face of the earth."

She shrugged a shoulder lightly. "So?"

"So, you withheld information from me. From Scotland Yard, from the Lord Mayor. I don't like that."

"And I don't like your tone. Are you accusing me of some nefarious crime?"

Of being the most cunning woman he'd ever met. Along with the most beautiful.

But he could hardly accuse her of that.

"My dear Miss Dunaway, since I've been asked by the Lord Mayor to investigate the disappearance of Lady Wallace, it's my duty to follow up on all clues. I've seen the hat shop where she disappeared. I've inspected the evidence found at the scene."

"And now you're here to investigate me?" Her soft brows lifted toward her heart-shaped hairline. "Don't you think you should be investigating Lord Wallace? After all, his wife has been abducted."

"I'll ask the questions. You merely have to answer them to my satisfaction."

"Why? You're not a policeman. You're not from the

press. Why should I have to answer your questions?"

Because he was so deeply buried in the secret affairs of the government that he'd never be free.

"Let's just say that I'm lending my military investigative skills to the City of London."

"What's a soldier doing investigating an abduction on Regent Street?"

"I'm a sailor, madam. A commandant in Her Majesty's Royal Navy, on loan to the Foreign Office. And, as such, I do whatever I'm asked to do by Her Majesty's ministers."

"Stranded here on dry land. How sad for you." She laughed lightly, as though protected from his office by the marble walls of the Abigail Adams. "But I can assure you, my lord commandant, I can't help you. Now if you'll excuse—"

"I can interrogate you here in the foyer, madam, or in a private office. Or if you prefer it, we can take a trip back to Scotland Yard, where, I can assure you, if the press finds you this time, they won't be interested in your thoughts on women's rights."

She glared at him, then gave another irritated huff and stomped past him. "Very well, my lord. I'll give you five minutes."

Or as many as he cared to take.

He followed her lightly flouncing skirts through the foyer and into what must surely be the club room. Much like the club room at the Huntsman, only more delicately fashioned: with tall windows draped in gold-tasseled brocade, sheered lightly with laced curtains. A half-dozen rose-strewn wool carpets covered the polished wooden floor, with pairs of floral upholstered chairs, elegant legged tea tables. Portraits of powerful women, Queen Victoria and Queen Elizabeth, the inimitable Abigail Adams above the marble mantel.

"The club room, I assume," he said as she waited for him at the door on the opposite wall.

"We do all our club business here." She narrowed her eyes at him. "Where we vote on important issues of the day, such as Darjeeling versus China black for the tea room. Red petunias for the urns in the drive up, or pink."

If she wanted a piggish attitude, she could have one. "The gentlemen of the Huntsman talk about similar things. Reform Act, or no? War with Russia, or not?"

"Single malt, or blended. Ah, the important issues of powerful men . . ." She gestured into the smaller room beyond. "In here, my lord, though I know little enough about your investigation. I'm sure you'll be disappointed."

Alone, in a small room, with the beautiful Miss Dunaway and her flashing eyes? Disappointment was impossible.

"I'll wager that you know more than you think you do, madam. Clues often hide themselves in the midst of the faintest memories."

"I have an excellent memory." She snorted lightly as she went directly to a large tidy desk, a daringly intimate sound between them.

"I'm sure you do." He was positive, in fact. "Have you ever met Lord Wallace?"

She frowned and pulled open the knee drawer. "Once. Have you?"

"Not yet." Though he planned to as soon as possible.

"When you do, be sure to ask him where he stashed the body."

"Body?" Ross tried to look nonchalant as he perched on the edge of the desk.

"Husbands kill their wives all the time, my lord." She sat down in the wooden desk chair and leaned back.

"Is that so?" Though he already knew that the sorry statistic was true.

"A wife gets in the husband's way, makes a few too many demands on his time or his money, starts forming thoughts of her own, and off she goes to the country, or to her aunt's, or to their villa in Spain, never to be seen again. Who would ever know if a man killed his wife in a fit of anger and buried the body in the stall of his favorite racehorse?"

"You have a very pessimistic view of marriage."

"A practical view of the facts as I see them."

"Murderous husbands and annoying wives, madam?" Damnation, he liked the outlandish, unafraid byways of her mind. He nearly laughed. "Do you mean to say that you suspect Lord Wallace of kidnapping his own wife and then doing away with the evidence of her murder?"

She raised her shoulders and tented her fingers, judge and jury all rolled into a single efficient package. "Just that I've heard gossip in the tea room."

"What kind of gossip, madam?" At times it was far more reliable than direct evidence. At least as a jumping off point. Smoke and fire and all that.

"That his lordship has the temper of a grizzly." She shrugged. "I can just imagine your interview with him, if you should decide to speak with him."

"Can you, now?"

"He'll be very dramatic. Declare undying love for his dear, devoted wife. Demand that you find her immediately, before scandal erupts and he finds himself embarrassed in the press and in Parliament."

"No comment, madam." Because God only knew what she would do if he confirmed his own suspicions. Take up an investigation on her own, or with her little gang. "Now, the sooner you answer a few of my questions about Lady Wallace herself, the sooner I'll be off your property and out of your life."

A thought that stopped him cold in his tracks. He liked standing here in her presence. She filled him up with something raw and exciting.

Made him want to kiss her soundly. Just to see what she would do or say.

"Go right ahead, my lord."

Bloody hell! Had he spoken aloud?

"Right ahead and . . . ?" He trailed off, hoping the woman would fill in the sudden blank spot in his brain.

"Go ahead and ask your questions, sir."

Ah, that. "Yes, yes. Uhm . . ." He cast about for the subject and recalled that someone's wife had gone missing. "Lady Wallace!"

"What about her? And hurry please. I have a class to prepare for."

"Are you studying for a class?"

"I'm teaching one. Is that your question?"

"Not quite." Completely off track now, Ross yanked his notepad out of his jacket pocket and flipped through to the scribble of notes he'd taken so far. He cleared his throat and turned away. "When exactly did Lady Wallace become a member of the Abigail Adams?"

"Exactly?" She considered the question for a moment, focusing on his mouth and then his eyes, before breathing out a sigh. "I suppose I have that here somewhere."

By the looks of the office, the woman doubtless could put her finger on the least important piece of information in the blink of an eye.

"Of course, she couldn't have been with us very long. The club's only been open since February."

"How often did she come?"

"If I recall correctly, two or three times a week at the beginning." She went to a bank of file boxes lined up neatly on the tall bookshelves against the wall, scanned the labels, pulled down a box and went back to the desk with it.

"And after that?"

She looked up at him from across the desk as she propped open the box lid. "Well, as you can imagine, his lordship didn't approve."

Ross decided to stay put on the edge of the desk instead of standing at her side and blatantly staring at the open file. He could read upside down easily enough. That way she wouldn't suspect he was doing it.

"Wallace didn't approve of what?"

"Of anything his wife did that took her out of his immediate sphere of control." The very thing that the hat clerk had implied. "Ah, yes, here it is, my lord. A copy of Lady Wallace's letter accepting our offer of membership." She held up a single sheet of fine onionskin paper. "She joined us at the end of April. The twenty-seventh to be exact."

"And her last visit?"

A flicker of memory creased her brow as she stumbled around for an answer. "Ah, well . . . it's been two weeks. Perhaps three. Members are encouraged to come and go as they please at the Adams. I make a point of not noticing."

"But you would have noticed had anyone outside Lady Wallace's family come to pick her up?"

"Outside her . . . ?" Her eyes brightened considerably. "Oh! You mean a secret lover?"

Secret lover, indeed. The brazen young woman shouldn't know of such things.

"I didn't mean exactly that, madam. But perhaps someone had been paying her a great deal of attention—"

"Because her husband wasn't?" She put the file box back on the shelf and turned to him with her flashing eyes. "Let's just say that I hope it's true, my lord. I hope Lady Wallace has flown the coop with her handsome, doting lover. That she's left all her cares on her husband's front stoop."

"You hope?" Damnation! Had Wallace's wife been cuckolding him? And had the innocent Miss Dunaway known about it all along?

"Yes, my lord, I hope that her lover swept her off her feet with his raging passion and sailed with her to the clear blue waters of the South Seas where they will live out their lives on torrid passion, coconuts and bananas—"

"Torrid . . . ? Coconuts . . . ?"

"In the warm trade winds."

"What are you saying, madam?"

"Making naked love on the beach whenever they like, in the silvery moonlight and under the blazing bright sun—"

"Excuse me, what?" Ross found himself standing over her at the bookcase, staring into her wildly smiling eyes. Surely not hearing right.

Making naked love on the beach?

Is that what the brazen woman had just said?

Naked love?

Or was he going slightly mad with the scent of her? With the sound of her.

"I'm afraid you've lost me, madam." *Or found me.* He leaned as close to her as he dared. Taking in her scent. A little dizzy, a lot stunned.

"I only meant, my lord, that I haven't the faintest idea where Lady Wallace is at the moment. But that wherever she is, I hope she's found her heart's delight."

He still wasn't sure he'd gotten this right. Should have jotted it down for proof.

"So, Lady Wallace had no paramour who might have spirited her away? You merely plucked these plans for the South Seas out of your dreams."

"Oh, my dreams are nothing like that, sir." Her smile became wry and soft.

"Not"—*naked love*—"escaping to a beach with a handsome lover?"

"Good heavens, no!" She drew her brows together,

her eyes twinkling up at him. "I think the sand would be quite uncomfortable for lovemaking, don't you?"

"The sand?"

"Abrasive, I would imagine"

Bloody hell!

"I'd prefer a waterfall and a sun-warmed pool—"

Bloody hell! He was about to do something very foolish. Kiss that bold invitation right off her glistening, upturned mouth.

Or take his leave through the window.

Or douse himself with the pitcher of water that was sitting on the sideboard.

But he was saved from certain doom by a knock at the door. A rat-a-tat-tat that seemed to shake the brazen lunatic from her enchantment.

The rap again.

"Excuse me, Miss Elizabeth. Are you in there?"

"Oh, yes! I'm coming." The woman blinked up at him, then dashed away, straightening her skirts and her hair before throwing open the door.

"Skye! What is it?"

The young woman's eyes caught his in a worry and caused a deep frown. "Well . . ."

The rest of the exchange was a lightning fast tangle of whispering, tight gesturing, ending with Miss Dunaway turning back to him.

"Ah, you'll have to leave now, my lord. Something's come up."

Damn right it had. Hard and throbbing. And he hoped to hell she hadn't noticed. "I can wait here, madam." Cool down.

"I'm afraid you can't. This will take some time."

She hooked his elbow with hers and drew him out of the room, the young woman trailing after them. "I'll be quite happy to answer any more of your questions later today or tomorrow. Just not right now."

His thoughts had slowed to mush and his head seemed to wobble drunkenly on his neck as she breezed him through the club room, into the foyer, and then right to the front door, where she offered her enthralling smile.

"Until later, my lord," she said.

"Good day, madam." He took his hat from the footman, gave Miss Dunaway and her assistant a generous bow, and left the Abigail Adams while he still had all his faculties.

At least he'd gotten a few answers out of her. The fact that Lady Wallace had been a member since April twenty-seventh, and . . . and that the missing woman didn't have a lover.

Or did.

Or wanted to.

Damnation, he hadn't really learned a single thing for his efforts.

Except that Miss Dunaway was a cunning opponent.

And a beautiful woman.

The most dangerous combination in the history of mankind.

"Where did you put her, Skye?" Elizabeth's heart was still slamming around in her chest. Still juggling the threat of Blakestone's investigation against the new crisis that had arrived on her doorstep.

"She's upstairs in your sitting room," Skye said,

heading toward the back staircase. "With his lordship wandering around here so freely, I didn't think you wanted him finding her and then asking questions."

Indeed, the earl was very good at asking questions.

Very good at answering his own.

But she couldn't let him ask this one.

"Did she give her name?" Elizabeth followed on Skye's heels, terrified of what she would find this time.

"Lydia, I think she said. She was shaking so that I didn't get any more of her name than that."

"You did perfectly, Skye. As ever. Thank you, sweet."

They sped up the backstairs, down the corridor into the easterly wing of the club. Elizabeth's own quarters, her home. And so recently a refuge for the heartbroken.

Skye stayed well out of sight in the corridor as Elizabeth peered through the half-open doorway, expecting the worst and finding plenty of it.

The woman was sitting in an armchair in the pale light coming through the sheer curtains. Her back ramrod straight, her gaze fixed on the floor. She clung to her cloak with white-knuckled fingers, as though she still expected its fine cashmere to be a shield against the world.

Not wanting to violate the woman's silence or to threaten her obviously tattered nerves, Elizabeth took a single step into the room, just to let her know she wasn't alone, then waited to be invited farther in.

Her own heart throbbing against her chest, tears threatening the composure she would need to help the woman through the trauma, Elizabeth finally spoke softly.

"Lydia?"

After a very long time, the woman raised her wary, weary eyes, and Elizabeth knew the rest of her story.

The bruises were already darkening around her left eye. Shadows turning to evidence that would never be allowed to stand in a court of law against the brutal man who had done this to her.

Not when a husband had an inalienable right to his property.

She saw the plea in the once-bright young face, the hopelessness, even before she heard the harrowingly familiar words spill from Lydia's shattered soul.

"They said . . ." Her tremulous pause was long and so courageous. ". . . you could help me. . . ."

Elizabeth cleared the sob from her throat and put on her most hopeful smile.

"Oh, my dear Lydia, you've just taken the first step toward helping yourself to a new life."

And a new chance at happiness.

Just like Lady Wallace had done.

Chapter 7

Women are like tricks by sleight of hand,
Which, to admire, we should not understand.

William Congreve, *Love for Love*, 1695

"'**H**ow to Seduce Your Own Husband Without Giving Him Apoplexy' has been such a popular class, ladies," Elizabeth said from the podium of the crowded club room, "that we've added another session."

The room erupted into applause at her announcement, and Eloise Barnes waggled her hand in the air. "Beginning when?"

"Please, Miss Elizabeth, the sooner the better!" Bonita Deverel said in an unusual burst of eagerness. "From what I've heard from a few of the other ladies who have actually taken the class, well . . . it's rather eye-opening. Even for a woman who's been married a long time."

"*Especially* for a woman who's been married a long time, Mrs. Deverel!" Lady Maxton was quick with her usual wit, always so elegant and poised.

Elizabeth smiled at the woman and pointed to the calendar propped against the easel. "The new session will start two weeks from today, and will run for the following three Mondays, seven to eight in the evening."

"And what of the Abigail Adams Tatting Consortium?" Renata Garrison asked from her familiar perch in the most comfortable chair in the room. "Will we still meet on Mondays at eight as well?"

"Absolutely, Mrs. Garrison." Another program that was becoming increasingly popular.

"That's a relief," Vita Sayers said with an air of keen conspiracy, "because though my dear husband is in full support of me tatting away one night a week, he just wouldn't understand that I've actually been learning the secrets of investing funds from my new bank account on the open exchange."

Eloise laughed broadly. "Imagine my Harold, a banker! He'd surely burst a vein in his neck if he ever found out that I've been putting aside money every week in my own secret account. And that it's not even in his bank."

Using Barnes's bank to house Eloise's account would have been foolhardy in the extreme.

"He'd do worse than that, Mrs. Barnes," Justine Knox said, "if the poor man learned that we'd been making fifteen percent on our money. All thanks to Elizabeth's guidance."

"No, no, ladies!" Elizabeth shook her head fiercely. The point here was independent thought. Taking credit for one's personal successes. "You mean thanks to the research you've all been doing into our target companies."

Who knew that the ladies of the Abigail Adams Tatting Consortium would set out upon London's financial district like a band of highly trained detectives and bring back such pertinent trading information as cotton embargos, coal futures, shipping contracts?

"You taught us the ropes, Miss Elizabeth."

Making her feel suddenly like a Fagin with her wily band of pickpockets.

"Speaking of an abundance of profits," Elizabeth said, purposely changing the subject, "I don't need to remind you of how important it is for all of us to attend Lady Maxton's Charity Ball at the end of the month, and to be conspicuously generous to her dear orphans."

"And if I might add something else about the ball, Miss Elizabeth," Lady Maxton said, rising from her chair to fully face the rest of the meeting, a bright twinkle of mischief in her eyes. "Something I've been hatching in my brain . . ."

"Of course, my lady." Though Elizabeth hadn't a clue what the woman was going to add.

"Well, then, I've been wondering what could be done to increase the charitable giving during the ball. Something besides the fabulous Turkish theme we've chosen. Something exciting that could happen during the dancing, or before, or after. Something possibly even scandalous!"

The rumble that tittered through the group was one of approval and anticipation. The complete opposite of the way the same group would have reacted to the same statement just three months ago.

"What kind of scandal are you thinking of, Lady

Maxton?" Elizabeth asked the question because she was vastly curious and the others were still whispering to each other, speculating on their own.

"Just a hint of scandal, really." Lady Maxton rolled her eyes at Elizabeth. "I was thinking of an auction."

"Auction of what?" Elizabeth asked, wondering how an auction could ever be considered scandalous.

Mrs. Garrison snorted. "Racehorses would grab my Anderson's attention."

"Do you mean like paintings or sculptures, Lady Maxton?"

"Opera tickets?"

"Men," Lady Maxton said finally, letting the word drop onto the carpet.

The room went utterly silent for a very long time.

"Did you say 'men,' Lady Maxton?" Elizabeth finally asked, though she was sure that's what she heard.

"Bachelors, really. Wouldn't that be just the best kind of fun? Bidding on a chance to be escorted to the theatre by one of our eligible swains."

More silence, and then someone said, "For unmarried women only, surely, Lady Maxton."

"Married ladies as well. I don't see why not. It would all be perfectly aboveboard, chaperoned by the husband, of course, and in public. And all for a good cause."

"Isn't it a little bit indecent? I mean, what if the authorities make a raid on your house right in the middle of the ball?"

"Let them try, Mrs. Barnes." A twinkle lit up Lady

Maxton's eyes. "I mean, what better publicity for our charity ball, to have Scotland Yard troop into our ballroom, handcuff us all, and drag us off in a paddy wagon like they did to us two days ago? And who wouldn't bid a thousand pounds to sit beside the Earl of Blakestone in a darkened theatre box?"

Blakestone! Ha! I wouldn't give a fig for a whole week with the lout!

But that didn't seem to be the opinion of the other women.

"Two thousand for the man, Lady Maxton!"

"Three!"

Then they were all laughing with anticipation.

"So there you see, ladies!" Lady Maxton said, obviously pleased with herself and her lunatic idea. "We could make bundles of money for the orphanage."

"Isn't that in poor taste, though?" Elizabeth asked, telling herself that she had no reason at all to be blushing like she was. "I mean, isn't our primary intention to present ourselves as independent of men?"

"What could make a modern lady more independent than openly admiring a handsome man, just for the sake of admiring him? Then bidding for him? Like good horseflesh."

"And there's nothing wrong with just looking, Miss Elizabeth." Renata glanced around at her compatriots for approval and got it in spades.

"The Earl of Blakestone is sure easy on the eyes, Miss Elizabeth." Bonita Deverel's eyes were wide. "You must have seen that for yourself yesterday afternoon. He's to absolutely swoon for."

"And he'll doubtless agree in a flash. That man is a fool for a hard luck story."

Blakestone? Now that seemed hard to believe. "What do you mean?"

"If you need a donation for a ragged school fund or to clothe a family after a house fire, he's your man."

He couldn't be her man. Because they couldn't be talking about the same Earl of Blakestone. The one she knew was hard as steel.

"Well, I suppose the man is civil minded and he's nice enough to look at." If one liked them tall and broad-shouldered, with dark, gleaming eyes and a voice that could turn sinew to warm butter. "But that's beside the p—"

"Your son Benjamin makes quite a fine figure, Mrs. Knox." The elderly Lady Parker jiggled her gray eyebrows.

"Ooo, and have you met that new member of Parliament from Shelton Copse? He's been turning heads at all the best parties this season."

"Too bad Princess Caroline stole away that hunk Wexford."

"And Hawkesly fell hard too. Pity."

Still flushing to the top of her head, Elizabeth clapped her hands together and took back the floor. "As you see, Lady Maxton, your idea is chock full of potential donations for the orphanage. I'm sure it will be a great success! All you need is a few eligible bachelors."

Lady Maxton beamed. "Good, then be prepared, ladies, to bid to the moon."

For the Earl of Blakestone? Not likely!

Elizabeth took a long breath and brushed the man

out of the clutter of her mind. "Next, I'd like to announce a very exciting excursion. To a session of Parliament."

"Parliament?" Eloise looked as perplexed as the others. "Do you mean another protest?"

"Nothing as distracting, Mrs. Barnes. Now, how many of you have ever attended a session of Parliament?"

Everyone shook their heads, bewildered.

"Why would we ever want to do that? Mr. Knox complains constantly about the heat and the arguments and the long-winded speeches."

"But, ladies, what is the price of our freedom?" Elizabeth left the podium to walk among the rapt members. "A little uncomfortable heat and a lot of bombast? How can we hope to ever gain the vote if we haven't the wherewithal to withstand a few hours of discomfort to learn how Parliament operates. Am I not right?"

"Indeed, you are!"

"We also need to know how these men of ours think, and what better way than to listen in as they discuss the laws that govern our lives."

"Why, you're so right, Miss Elizabeth!"

"I never thought of it that way!"

"When is our dangerous expedition, Elizabeth?"

"Tuesday afternoon. We'll meet here in the lobby of the Adams at four o'clock and travel to Westminster as a group and enter the building together. I've hired private carriages for twelve, but I can always hire more."

"Oh, dear, Elizabeth, what does one wear to attend a session of Parliament?"

"The very sort of thing you're wearing right now will do very nicely, Mrs. Osterman. Now if there are no other announcements—"

Coraleigh rocketed to her feet. "I have one! Coraleigh's Confections of Charing Cross Road is officially open for business!"

"You've opened your store already?"

"As of yesterday!" Coraleigh grinned madly to the wild applause of the other members and then began handing out a colorful broadside. "We specialize in creamy chocolates, marzipan and Turkish delight!"

"Ooooo! Yummmm!" And other such mewlings of imagined delight leaped around the room.

"I can't believe that your husband actually let you open a shop."

Coraleigh frowned, a blend of trepidation and triumph. "I haven't told him yet, Miss Elizabeth. He thinks I've been doing charity work at the hospital."

"He's bound to find out, Cora—"

"Let him, I say. After all, what can he do about it: put me in jail? Lock me in an asylum?"

"We won't let him do that, Cora."

"Besides, by my calculations, I'll soon be making far more money than he brings in as the Undersecretary for Streets and Sewers."

Elizabeth gave Cora a huge hug. "Congratulations, Coraleigh. I'm sure we'll all do our sweets shopping at your shop. But speaking of Turkish delight—"

"Oh, dear, have the Russians declared war on that poor little country? It's in all the papers! I hope we send in our ships right away!"

"I don't know the current state of war, Mrs. Colfax." Elizabeth smiled fondly at the woman, a long-time friend of both her aunts. "I just want to remind those of you brave souls who have pledged to wear Turkish trousers to the charity ball to please check with our seamstress for your final fittings."

Vita Sayles popped up. "The London season has never been so exciting, Miss Elizabeth! Turkish trousers and protest marches and sitting in on Parliament itself!" She grabbed Elizabeth by the shoulders and planted a kiss on her forehead. "How can we possibly thank you?"

Raise up your daughters to take charge of their own lives and destinies.

Don't force them to marry men like Lord Wallace.

Don't let them become poor Lydia.

"All I ask is that we make it through the rest of the season without another brush with Scotland Yard."

Because the last thing she needed was the persistent Earl of Blakestone nosing around the Abigail Adams.

No matter that he had a most handsome nose.

"Gad, Ross," Drew said as he dropped into a chair at the Factory's large archive table, "the Lord Mayor promised to send you the files on the missing women, and damned if he hasn't."

"Help yourself, Drew." Ross looked up across the table at his friend who had already snagged one of the *Times* articles from the Hayden-Cole file.

He'd known the man for twenty-five years. Through the worst of times and the very best. Knew that dark, arching eyebrow, and the derisive snort that always ended in half a laugh. That scowl of concentration, fingers laced through and tugging at his hair.

"Damnation, Ross! I've never read anything so utterly bizarre in my life." He shook the article at Ross. "According to this dithering tour guide at the British Museum, Lady Hayden-Cole disappeared in the midst of a crowded mummy exhibit."

"You'll find that the porter at Victoria Station tells the same story about Lady Cladsbury. In both cases leaving a hat, a man's leather glove, and a handkerchief doused with chloroform."

Drew picked up a police report. "I take it there's been no ransom demand in the Wallace case, either?"

"It's been three days. No one's contacted the police, or Wallace, or even poor old Biffy Tuckerton."

Drew sat back in his chair, tenting his fingers in thought. "Any chance that Lord Wallace is involved in his wife's disappearance?"

"All I can say of my interview with him is that the man has a nasty temper." A dead end. "But then so do Lord Hayden-Cole and Cladsbury, according to those files. But I doubt any of the men are involved in any way. Because if these three abductions are connected to each other—"

"As they must be, Ross."

"Then that would mean we have three husbands meeting in secret, conspiring together to have their wives kidnapped and murdered by a third party. Why would they do that?"

"Hell, I don't know. I doubt they even know each

other." Drew blew an exasperated sigh and leaned back against the chair.

Ross started leafing through the pages from the Cladsbury file, disappointed in the scarcity of information.

A police report, notes from an interview with the porter—who had reported the incident to the police at Victoria Station—three witnesses whose stories conflicted completely, the familiar ramblings of the incensed husband.

"Bloody hell, Ross. The connection is here in this mess somewhere." Drew put his heels up on the table-top. "Though right off the stick, not even their ages are similar—"

"Damnation!" His mind a tangle of possibilities, Ross grabbed a sheet of paper and started a list. "The most obvious element the victims have in common is that they are all women."

"That is brilliant, Ross."

Ignoring the man, Ross gave the three files a quick sort, laying out items of interest. "Each from a wealthy family." He stopped and added that to the list. "Each married."

"Each family titled," Drew added. "Two viscounts and a baronet."

"Each of the women taken in broad daylight, and in highly crowded, very public situations."

"Which is damned strange, for a criminal-minded fiend."

A thought flitted past Ross's eyes, escaping him before he could grab it. "As though the abductor knew the victim wouldn't struggle."

"Wouldn't cry out for help." Drew was watching him, following his intent.

"Or couldn't." Ross stared at the list, unseeing, feeling that thought tickling at him again until he was left with a jolt of irritation. "Bloody hell, what does it mean?"

Drew poked at the files. "There's no mention in the reports of fleeing carriages or a noisy scuffle. We only assumed there was a vehicle waiting to carry off Lady Wallace from the rear of the hat shop."

Ross was scrabbling through the pages again, certain that he'd seen something important. "No children. At least none who aren't full-grown and gone from the house." He checked again and started to write that down when he heard something in the dimness beyond the open door, felt something.

Drew froze. "Did you hear that?"

Ross nodded slightly and listened with him out of a shared instinct for survival, a shiver lodged in his shoulders, the hair at his nape standing on end.

It was late, the Factory closed for the night. They should be alone.

"It's probably nothing," Drew finally whispered.

But they both remained still for another long minute, until Ross relaxed his stance and Drew did the same.

"Same thing happened when I was down here a week ago," Ross said, still quietly, yet suddenly remembering the familiar sensation as he stepped into the corridor, "the night I got back from Constantinople."

"A stray cat, do you think? God knows, it's happened before. Or someone working late."

"Possibly, though I looked last time and found no-body."

"Perhaps the fiend has taken up residence here at night while he does his evil deeds in broad daylight."

Ross snorted. "We should be so lucky."

A thought came to him from nowhere. From out of the dimness? A scent? A sound? Something on his sleeve.

"The Abigail Adams," Ross said slowly and under his breath, conjuring a pair of wide, thickly lashed green eyes.

"What's that?" Drew had dropped back into his chair and was scanning the list.

"I was just thinking . . ." About Miss Dunaway. "It's a long shot, but Lady Wallace belonged to that new ladies' club. The Abigail Adams. Perhaps they all attended the same ball this season. Or the opera. Ascot?"

"Good thinking!" Drew started rifling through the Wallace file.

"Perhaps the fiend—as you called him—has chosen his victims from the ranks of women who attend social events, and then stalks them until he catches them."

"The women couldn't have been together at Ascot; Hayden-Cole and Cladsbury had both been taken by then."

"Then I'll have one of the archive clerks comb the social pages for the various soirees and parties and balls from early in the season. We'll then request guest lists from each of the hostesses. We can see where the intersections are and start from . . . well, I'll be damned."

"What? Have you got something?"

"By the bloody tail, if I'm not mistaken."

Ross was looking down at the statement the police had taken from Lady Cladsbury's husband at the time of the abduction.

"Listen to this, Drew," he said. "It's Cladsbury's husband describing her daily routine to the police. Reading to her aunt, fittings, visits to the zoo. All of which the man approved of. And then come the complaints. Apparently Lady Cladsbury had begun to spend entirely too much time at the Abigail Adams."

"The ladies' club."

Certain he was right, Ross grabbed the bulk of the Hayden-Cole file and started flipping through the pages, until his heart ground to a stop.

"Here! Lady Hayden-Cole's footman, a Mr. Rowley, says, 'I was supposed to pick her up outside the museum at two-thirty and drive her to afternoon tea at her ladies' club.' "

Drew shook his head at Ross, obviously not catching on to the biggest clue of all, where it was plain as day to him. "I don't understand."

"Damnation, Drew, the only ladies' club in London is the Abigail Adams."

"And . . . ?"

"Blast it all, that's the connection! It has to be! If I'm not mistaken, all three of these women belonged to the Abigail Adams. She lied to me!"

"Who?"

"Miss Elizabeth Dunaway." Fresh-faced and intensely intelligent. "The owner of the Abigail Adams!

The most stubborn, irritating being on the face of the earth."

Drew was looking at him in bewildered astonishment. "That stubborn, is she?"

"Cunning as a damned fox. She knew I was looking for evidence about the other two abductions."

"How?"

"I met her at Scotland Yard."

"What was she doing at Scotland Yard?"

"It's a very long story. Suffice it to say that she heard about the earlier kidnappings from the Lord Mayor at the same time I did."

"Ah. That is suspicious." Drew raised his eyebrow, obviously amused by the whole thing. "But why would Miss Dunaway keep the information from you? Unless . . . she's the fiend we're looking for?"

"Don't be ridiculous." Though he wouldn't be surprised if the woman had withheld the information just to thwart him. "She's just . . . stubborn, as I said."

"And bloody beautiful, by the sound of your blustering."

"She promised to cooperate with me." Ross's ears began to burn as he started gathering the papers back into the three scattered files.

"Is Miss Dunaway a young woman?" Drew was sitting on the edge of the table, following Ross's every move.

"Old enough to understand the seriousness of this investigation. I'll not have her playing me the fool."

"So I take it that Miss Dunaway is beautiful?"

"She's dangerous. To every woman in London."

"Please, Ross. Caro will have my hide if you don't

give me a few facts about the woman." The man cast him a pitiful look he didn't understand.

"What are you talking about?"

"When I tell Caro about how upset you were about the cunning Miss Dunaway, whom you met at Scotland Yard, she's going to plague me with questions about her."

"Why would you tell Caro?"

"She's my wife. I tell her everything."

"Why?"

"It's safer that way. You'll understand when you're married. Now what will I say to Caro about Miss Dunaway when she asks?"

"I just told you she was stubborn and irritating and—"

"And a beauty. Right?"

Try as he might, Ross couldn't help the smile that filled his chest and overtook his mouth. He started to answer but Drew held up his palm.

"Say no more. I understand perfectly." Drew was grinning broadly at him, as though he'd just confessed his heart in song. "Just remember, my friend, the stubborn ones are the most dangerous of all. Have yourself a good night."

With that, Drew left the archive room.

Ross planned to have a good night, all right.

Miss Dunaway, on the other hand, was going to have a night she wouldn't soon forget.

Chapter 8

Men, some to business, some to pleasure take;
But every woman is at heart a rake.

Alexander Pope, *Moral Essays*, 1775

"You're safe with us here, Lydia," Elizabeth whispered to the shadowed figure curled up beneath the thick down of the counterpane. "Sweet dreams."

But the beleaguered young woman was already fast asleep, her face relaxed now, the livid bruises paler in the soft light of Elizabeth's single candle. Much better than they had been when she arrived two days ago.

Two days that had seemed like twenty. Heralding weeks that overflowed with things to be done.

Yawning with the need for her bed, and finally satisfied that Lydia would have a long, restful night, Elizabeth drew her robe more closely around her nightgown, slipped out of the corner guest room and padded down the corridor to her own spacious suite of three rooms.

The north-facing corner of the Adams was the only

109

home she had at the moment. But she was exactly where she needed to be. Smack-dab in the middle of the bustle of London. Everything so vastly different from the slow-moving life she'd loved in the country with her dear and eccentric aunts.

Great-great-aunts, really. Two of the most remarkable people she'd ever known. The Hasleton sisters had taken her into their hearts when she was orphaned as an infant. They had filled her life with wonders and their country estate with poets and philosophers, adventurers and inventors.

And how dearly she missed them both. Their advice and their humor and their unflagging confidence in her.

"You can do anything with your life, Elizabeth," Aunt Tiberia had been forever telling her, with a shake of her fist toward the sky.

And Aunt Clarice, always trying to best her older sister, "But whatever you choose to do, my sweet, look 'em right in the eye when you do it."

Right in the eye.

"Do you hear that, Blakestone?" Elizabeth said into the long shadows of the corridor. "Right in the eye."

But what if those eyes were dark and fierce and oh, so compelling? What if they had the power to muddle her thoughts? And cause her pulse to flutter wildly?

What if the low rumble of his voice set her heart soaring, made her laugh and sigh? What if she craved the touch of his mouth, yearned for the feel of his hands against her skin, for the intimacies that usually came only with marriage. . . .

Of course, marriage was simply impossible. For a

world of reasons. But most practically, because she could never trust a husband with her financial affairs. After all, her fortune was the sum of her independence. And too many people depended on her independence for her to risk their lives and happiness on a marriage.

Aunt Tiberia had always been quick to advise her to weigh the risk to her future. "To marry, Elizabeth, is to surrender your independence and your considerable fortune to a man. And you'll soon learn that men are only good for one thing, my dear. Though they are very, very good at that one thing."

Aunt Tiberia had always been open with her about the desires of the flesh. Though she'd never gone into much detail about exactly what that one "good thing" was, beyond the act of sexual intercourse itself. Or how she herself had learned this particular fact. Though rumors among those who knew her aunts had always been taken as true. Tales of their brazen lifestyle when they were young—

And foolish, Aunt Clarice would always add with a wistful smile and a throaty giggle.

Yes, marriage was definitely out of the question. Absolutely and forever.

But sex . . . now, that was definitely in her future. When and how brought on another set of questions. However, *with whom* posed a more interesting and immediate question. Because for the first time in her life she had begun to entertain fantasies about a particular man.

Blatant imaginings of the earl himself. Hot. Glistening. Naked. Oh, my yes, she could almost imagine that! Wondering if he would . . . if she could muster the courage to invite him to . . . beg him to—

"Oh, damn and blast!" What foolishness! She didn't even know if he was married or not. And that would make all the difference.

She shook off the intoxicating image, then slipped through her private foyer into her sitting room, with its office alcove in the large bay of the window.

A warm breeze teased its way through the curtains there, riffling the moonlight across the carpeting.

An airy, everyday breeze. Though tonight something about it slowed her progress as she reached the center of the room.

A stirring scent, a familiar heat. A thrilling tumble of sensations.

"Blakestone!"

She felt the man before she saw him. Leaning against the open door to her bedchamber beyond, as though he'd been waiting for her to return to their bed and its rumpled heap of still warm bedclothes they'd been wrapped in.

"Good evening, madam." His voice rumbled across the dimness of the room, caressed her breasts and spread through her limbs like warm honey.

Her heart should have been slamming around inside her at the man's startling materialization in the middle of her rooms. But it was keeping a steady beat, as though it had been expecting him all along.

As though he'd known that she'd been hoping for him to come to her some starry night.

Though he didn't look at all pleased with her just now.

"Good evening, Lord Blakestone." She steadied her breathing and went straight to the side table to light its globe lamp, surprised at the calm of her fingers among the dangling prisms. "Can I get you a cup of tea or a brandy?"

He said nothing, only glared at her from the doorway, taking up the whole of the opening to her bedchamber. Filling her chest with a kind of breathy anticipation that she didn't know what to do with.

"I hope you don't make a habit of calling on ladies in the wee hours by breaking into their homes and frightening them to death."

"You don't look frightened to me."

She wasn't. Not in the least. Though she could feel the caged anger in him, seething in his muscles, directed at her for some unimaginable reason. Making him look larger than ever in the dimness.

"Nevertheless, if you'd be so kind and tell me how you got in here. I'd like to bar the way from the next prowler who might come along."

The next arrogant lout to invade her privacy. Though none could ever be quite so pleasing to the eye.

"You needn't worry on that point, madam. I'll seal my way as I leave."

Seal his way? Of all the bloody, invasive nerve! What did that mean?

And who the devil did the blackguard think he was; coming and going in her home, whenever and wherever he pleased?

Look him right in the eye, Elizabeth.

Right in the eye.

Taking Aunt Clarice's advice into her heart, she

struck a resolute pose, fists on her hips, just to prove that his temper hadn't impressed her, that she wasn't afraid of his unyielding glare.

"See here, Blakestone, I've given you every opportunity to tell me why you've broken into my rooms in the middle of the night. It's late. Now, what is it you want from me?"

She heard him take a long, fierce breath, as though trying to dampen his anger before answering. "What I want from you, Miss Dunaway, is the honesty that you promised me when I started this investigation."

"Honesty?" Oh, that. Oh, dear. Her heart took off like a wild rabbit, thumping madly in her chest, stifling her breathing.

Because she couldn't afford to be at all honest with the man. He'd already gotten too close to a truth that she couldn't possibly reveal to him.

"I'm sure I don't know what you mean, my lord. I've gone out of my way to be honest with—"

"Who is Lady Hayden-Cole?"

Elizabeth caught a breath in her throat, but it closed off into a lump of cold fear, making it even more difficult to breathe. Or to think clearly, with all the questions banging around in her head.

Where was he trying to go with this? What had he learned in his snooping?

She certainly couldn't tell from his stance. The huge man had yet to move a muscle, still stood there like a living mountain, leaning silently against the door frame.

Feigning a nonchalance she didn't feel, Elizabeth idly sat down in her favorite chair, lounging as though he were an afternoon guest at teatime, hoping she could lead him away from the subject and her bedroom door.

But her mouth dried to paste as she asked casually, "Lady Hayden-Cole? I'm sure I—"

"And Lady Gwyneth Cladsbury?" He'd cut her off with a coldly controlled cadence. His teeth gleamed in menace beyond the wall of shadows between them.

And had he just growled at her?

"Cladsbury . . . ?" The rest of her prevaricating stuck in her throat.

"That's right, Miss Dunaway, Lady Cladsbury." He was standing free of the doorjamb now, though planted like a statue in the doorway. "While I was here a few days ago inquiring about Lady Wallace, you neglected to tell me that the two other women who have been abducted from the streets of London in broad daylight were also members of the Abigail Adams."

Dear Lord. He knows!

"Really, my lord?" Trying her best not to tremble, Elizabeth shrugged broadly from the steadiness of her chair, her palms clammy and cold. "The Abigail Adams has been very popular since the very first day we opened our doors. We've nearly two hundred members, and growing every day. I can't possibly keep track of them all."

"Perhaps you'd better start, madam. At the rate your members are disappearing, come next season there won't be enough women left in London for even the smallest meeting. Or don't you care?"

"Of course I care. We've all been quite worried

about our missing members." *Just not worried for the same reason you are.* "I didn't mention their membership because I just don't see how it matters."

"Oh, really? It doesn't matter to you that of all the women in London, the three who have been abducted were all members of the Abigail Adams?"

Oh, damn. What an unfortunate mistake. It just hadn't occurred to her that anyone would make the connection. Well, it wouldn't happen again.

"I'm sure it's just a coincidence that they were members here, my lord."

"Is it?" His voice was still way too calm, his words too smooth.

"What else could it be?"

"Besides suspicious?" Now he was shaking his head. "I don't know, Miss Dunaway. You tell me."

"Tell you what, sir?" Her cheeks began to burn with anger, a flare of outrage that he would have the nerve to suspect her of anything as nefarious as kidnapping. "Confess that I abducted three members of my own ladies' club?"

She didn't abduct anyone.

"I didn't say that."

The women left on their own.

"And what do you think I did with them, sir?" She got to her feet, the untellable truth on the tip of her tongue, raging to be heard. "Killed them, then buried them out in the courtyard beneath our prize-winning azalea beds? Why would I do such a horrific thing?"

Because they asked her to help them escape. And so she did.

Blakestone stood looking at her for the longest time, the angles of his jaw changing and working as he studied her. She'd felt perfectly safe with him planted across the room, glaring at her with his stalking questions.

But now he was striding slowly toward her, his dark eyes fixed on her face.

"Are you a complete lunatic, Miss Dunaway?" He kept coming her way. Slowly, moving into the pale lamplight.

"You, sir, are the lunatic." Though at times like this she could only wonder at how deeply, how irrevocably, she'd become involved. She backed up, stumbled against the upholstered arm of the chair, and then could go no farther, though he came closer and closer still. "What is it you want from me, Blakestone?"

"I'm trying my bloody damnedest to knock some sense into you."

"Oh, so now you're going to strike me? Resorting to violence, are you?" Though she knew without a doubt that he wouldn't. He wasn't the type. He was too sure of himself, of his place in the wide world. Unafraid of his own failings, willing to consider other possibilities. She had seen all that in his eyes from the moment he first stepped into her jail cell.

"Blast it all, Miss Dunaway, if you were a man I'd do more than just strike you for all the bloody danger you've been courting!"

"Danger?"

He was hovering over her now, breathing like a bull in his fury. His anger turned to impatience. "Don't you see what your bloody silence might have cost you personally?"

"My silence?" Now he wasn't making any sense at all. Lady Hayden-Cole had arrived safely in New York nearly two months ago. Lady Cladsbury should arrive there any day now. Lady Wallace would safely board another ship this evening. "How do you mean?"

He clamped his huge, hot hands around her arms, enveloping them completely, and leaned so close she thought he might be planning to kiss her.

"Don't you see the pattern? Three women, from the best families, all belonging to the same controversial ladies' club, all go missing within months of each other."

"I still don't see where you're going." Though she could see the flecks of fire in his eyes. Could feel the soft sparks against her cheeks.

"Blast it all, woman! The Adams is the common piece of evidence between the abductions. And the Adams is you, Miss Dunaway! You're the linchpin of this whole mess."

Of course she was! But she could not possibly admit that to him. Not even to stanch the heat of his frustration. Lives hung in the balance.

"Which, Miss Dunaway, can only mean that someone disapproves of what you do here."

"Someone disapproves?" She nearly laughed out loud. "That, sir, would be every man in London."

But he only gripped her arms more firmly, frowned more deeply. "You've crossed a line somewhere, madam, in someone's evil brain. You've made a malicious enemy who will stop at nothing to close you down permanently. Even if he has to pick off your club members one by one."

"Pick off my . . ." Oh, dear! She'd obviously drawn the wrong kind of attention to the abductions. Certainly the wrong kind of investigator. What the devil was she going to do with him now?

And what a very strange moment to be delighting in the heat of the man's spicy scent that was curling around her, teasing against the gathered linen of her nightrobe, seeping softly into the folds.

To be intoxicated by the fevered strength of his hands on her arms. Hands that even now were tucked absently against the outer edges of her breasts.

Soooo hot and thrilling.

"Don't you see the danger, madam?"

Oh, God, yes! And the danger was as sweet as honey. Calling to her.

"Danger to me, my lord?"

Ross caught himself. Knew better than to confess that particular threat: The surging danger he posed to her virtue.

The danger to his self-control.

He was standing too close to the woman for clarity of thought, too close to her sultry scent, to the whispery rise and fall of her chest against the soft linen of her robe.

He could feel every delicious inch of her through the inference of her curves against his thighs, the softly rounded heat of her breasts.

He should step away from the woman while he still had control of his better nature.

Bloody hell, he shouldn't even have come here tonight. He'd nearly convinced himself to wait until the safety of broad, blazing daylight to confront her with her stubborn, confounding foolishness.

But his uneasiness about the whole mess, about the woman herself, had seethed and bubbled as he pored over the archives in the Factory until it had finally boiled over. He'd made the short trek through the streets of St. James to the Adams on foot, unsure of what he intended, but determined to protect the woman, whether she liked it or not.

And with his every quickening step had come the chilling sensation that he wouldn't arrive in time, that no matter what wicked force was working against the women of the Abigail Adams, its evil was focused on Miss Dunaway herself.

That was the danger he'd set out to protect her from tonight.

Not the danger from himself, the deep hunger she aroused in him.

Not from the temptation to slide his hands down her sleek arms and then around her waist. Over her breasts.

That temptation to taste her mouth, her throat, to carry her into her bedchamber and bury himself inside her.

Not that kind of danger. Not tonight.

Probably never. Because Miss Dunaway was the kind of woman a man married. And he wasn't in the market for a wife.

Even this kind.

So he dutifully released his hands from her arms and stepped back, clearing his throat as he freed her, his gaze still caught up in hers, waltzing there.

"I don't believe I've made myself clear enough, Miss Dunaway."

"Clear enough about . . . ?" She seemed bewitched by something, unfocused, almost amused.

"About the danger to you."

"Me?" She blinked up at him.

Damnation, if he didn't know better, he'd think the woman was simpleminded. Or didn't care about her safety, the safety of the other women. Or wasn't listening to a word he said.

But she was far from simple; the woman was as cunning as a politician.

"Are you listening to me, madam?" He caught her arms again, but this time dropped her backward into the chair behind her. He knelt in front of her bent knees, hoping to see at least a shred of fear, but finding only that calm amusement.

"Of course I'm listening. I just think your imagination is working too hard. I'm sure there's no one hiding out in the alley, plotting to throw a bag over my head and steal me away. Or anyone else."

"Madam, I don't know how much more proof you need that the Abigail Adams has become the target of a madman."

Her lopsided smile held nothing more significant than gentle patience. Even shyness. "I appreciate your interest in the Adams, however—"

He grabbed her wrists and held fast to them, trying

not to speak through his teeth. "I'm sorry, Miss Dunaway, but 'however' just doesn't work any longer."

She frowned, dipping a shapely brow at him. "What do you mean?"

"I mean, that I'm moving into the Adams first thing tomorrow morning."

"You're what?" She yanked her wrists out of his hands.

Bloody hell! The solution had just come to him. Couldn't have startled her any more than it did him. But it was the perfect answer to the situation.

In fact, he would move in tonight.

"You heard me." He stood, his fears finally calmed. "Until these abductions stop, until we find the fiend who has been preying on your club members, the Abigail Adams is going to need twenty-four-hour security."

She looked genuinely horrified, scandalized. "Oh, no, it doesn't. Don't even think it, Blakestone."

"I'll move into the visitors' parlor on the ground floor. And you can just go about your daily business as though nothing has changed—"

"Oh, no, you won't." She threw herself out of the chair and glared up at him.

"I'll put guards at each of the external doors. How many doors have you?" Of course, the woman wouldn't tell him, or couldn't, for the anger in her eyes. Or didn't even know where all the chinks in her armor were.

"Don't be absurd! None of the abductions happened in the Adams."

"Not yet. But a fiend with a grudge against you and

your ladies' club will stop at nothing to do you harm. Surely you can understand that breaking into an unguarded building is the simplest of crimes."

"A fiend? Is that who you think is doing this?"

"A fiend, a madman, a maniac. Call him whatever you will, I'm not going to allow him to take another woman."

Certainly not you.

She just stood there in her simple linen robe looking at him in abject horror, her mouth agape and glistening.

"What if I say no?" she said finally.

"Then, regrettably, I'll have the Lord Mayor shut you down as a threat to the health and safety of your club members."

Or something like that.

"Close the Adams?" She gasped and backed away from him. "You wouldn't dare!"

"I would, indeed, if you don't cooperate with me."

She forced out a sharp sigh and paced across the sitting room to the alcove. She pulled aside the sheer moonlit curtains and looked out the window for a time. The breeze caught her robe around her slim ankles, revealing slender calves and a finely shaped hip.

"What if I hire my own guards?"

"This is a criminal investigation, madam. It requires the intervention of Scotland Yard."

"And a commandant in Her Majesty's Royal Navy, on loan to the Foreign Office and the City of London." Her lithe shoulders sagged. "You've put me in an unwinnable situation."

"It's not a matter of winning or losing, Miss Dunaway." He took a few steps toward her, an offering of sorts, as he tried to gentle his voice. "You and your ladies can come and go as you please—"

She scowled at him. "Under your constantly critical eye. I know your opinions."

"Meaning what?"

"You're a man, Blakestone."

Now there was an indictment if he'd ever heard one. "Guilty as charged."

She had met him halfway to the center of the room, her hands shaped over her perfect hips. "The Abigail Adams is a temporary refuge for women, sir. They come here to relax, to escape the pressures of their households. To be themselves, without the fear of having to perform as the perfect wife, or the perfect mother, or the adoring daughter."

This wasn't going to be as easy as it seemed. "The guards will be posted outside, and when I'm in the house—mostly in the evening and overnight—just tell your ladies to ignore me if they see me."

"Ignore you? You must be joking!"

Oh, this was sticky stuff, uncharted waters. "I'm very serious."

"Excuse me, my lord, but every woman for miles around seems to know exactly who you are and are vastly interested in everything you do."

"Me?" That sounded odd. He was hardly ever in town.

"They were willing to bid thousands of pounds in order to win you for an evening at the opera."

The opera? "What are you talking about, madam? Bidding where?"

"At the bachelor auction at Lady Maxton's Charity Ball. Hasn't she told you?"

"Not a word." A bachelor auction?

"Nevertheless, the club members are sure to want to know the reason that you're loitering in the halls."

"I guarantee that I'll be discreet. Practically invisible."

"Then while you're at it, sir, bring an elephant along from the zoo. We'll put it in the tea room and we can ignore that too. Great heavens, this is ridiculous!"

"But it's the way it must be. I'll do my best to stay out of sight."

"Excellent. Then I'll just tell them we have a ghost."

"Whatever you like."

"I don't like you."

Indeed. But he wouldn't have expected that to hurt as deeply as it did. "I am sorry for that, madam."

"Another thing, Blakestone. If anyone asks, you will not say a thing to any of the club members about the reason you're here."

"They'll want to know—"

"And I'll explain that we've had a few break-ins and I've asked Scotland Yard to look into the matter. That's all. Nothing about the missing women and their so-called connection with the Adams. Do you understand me?"

"Fine."

"Good." She took a deep breath and narrowed her eyes at him. "Now if you'll please leave my—"

"Just a few more questions . . ." He still needed to

think this whole thing through. Square the facts with the crime, and judge them against the threats.

She groaned and leaned against the arm of the chair. "Please, Lord Blackstone, it's nearly two o'clock in the morning."

"I've been looking into the inheritance you received from your aunts—"

"You've been what?" Suspicion flared in her eyes, winging her brows. "You have no right! My financial status is none of your business."

Now was not the time to tell her that he was determined to make everything about her his business.

"You were your spinster aunts' sole heir to a substantial fortune." Nearly ten thousand pounds a year. Most of which she wisely kept in high yield bonds, managed nicely by the Bank of England.

"How could you possibly know that?"

He held back his smile of satisfaction. Because if the woman knew the extent of his resources, she'd throw him out the open window into the alley below. "I have my sources."

She fixed an outraged glare on him that he could feel right through his skull to the back of his brain. "Damn you," she whispered with such naked loathing he drew back from her in confusion.

No longer sure of himself, he toned down his approach. "Was the will ever contested, Miss Dunaway? By a disgruntled relation?" Not that he expected her to answer.

"No. I am a free and independent woman. No one, anywhere, has a claim on my finances. And I plan to keep it that way. Now if you're finished, I've got a busy day tomorrow."

A huge yawn seemed to ambush her. She rubbed her forehead as though she was tired beyond sleeping, making him feel like a complete heel as she shambled toward her bedchamber.

"Busy at what?"

"Club business, if you must know." He didn't like the tone of the frown that she tossed back at him from over her shoulder, or the challenge in her voice as she turned back to him at the door.

"I absolutely must know, madam." And he was just as certain that the woman would absolutely tell him nothing on her own. All right, then; the gloves were off. He plopped down onto the sofa. "Good night, then, Miss Dunaway."

Another scowl. "I thought you were going to use the visitors' parlor."

"Tomorrow. Tonight, I'll be right here. If you should need me."

She cast a wry glance at the spindly piece of furniture, then another at him, with a slow shake of her head. "Does your wife know you're spending the night in my suite?"

He tucked away his smile. "Believe me, Miss Dunaway, if I had a wife, I wouldn't be here."

"Oh." She gathered her robe about her like an armored shield. "Well then, sir, sleep well."

And if *she* was his wife, he sure as hell wouldn't be sleeping out here.

Chapter 9

If particular care and attention is not paid to the ladies, we are determined to foment a rebellion, and will not hold ourselves bound by any laws in which we have no voice or representation.

Abigail Adams, to her husband John
March 31, 1776

"This way to the carriages, ladies!" Elizabeth called into the crowd of milling women in the lobby of the Adams. Their random circling reminded her of rounding up a flock of chickens on her aunts' manor farm.

"Carriages, where, Elizabeth?"

"Outside, Mrs. Deverel, in the drive-up." These were all highly intelligent women, one-on-one, but jam them together into a gossiping mob and they lost all sense. "We've got three carriages. Plenty of room for everyone. Just find a place and sit down or we'll be late."

And the omniscient Earl of Blakestone might appear out of nowhere and discover them leaving on their expedition, then follow them with his blaze of objections right to the steps of Westminster.

Or concoct some obstacle to keep them from leaving the Adams at all. For their safety. For England. For the good of mankind.

She had expected to run his gauntlet of questions that morning on the way out of her bedchamber. Heaven knows, she'd felt him there all night long. Even imagined herself waking to the sight of him standing in her doorway, his bronze chest naked in the moonlight, stalking toward her, his corded muscles shifting . . . Ahem!

But by the time she'd bathed and dressed, he had already disappeared from her sitting room. Her hopes that he'd reconsidered his unnecessary security measures against a nonexistent threat to her and the ladies' club had been dashed when she found three very serious men walking a frowning circuit around the Adams.

Trapped. Observed. For no reason whatsoever.

Except that she'd obviously done her job far too well. But how could she possibly have predicted that secretly arranging steamship passage for one young woman who desperately needed to escape her abusive husband would so quickly escalate into a full-scale clandestine conspiracy to aid and abet two other equally desperate women?

A total of four now, counting Lydia, who was quickly recovering from her ordeal and gaining back that much needed will to triumph over the worst of her fears.

"I thought I'd bring one of our Votes for Women signs, Elizabeth." Justine Knox grinned broadly as she held up the sign between them. "Just to get my husband's attention on the back benches.

"Let's leave that here, Justine," Elizabeth said, gently taking the sign from her. "Remember, ladies—this goes for all of us—we're not attending the session of Parliament to protest this time. Only to listen and learn."

"Awwwww..." They all groaned like a team of cricketers at a rained-out match.

"So we don't want to do anything to call attention to ourselves...."

But, of course, they couldn't really help it. As much as Elizabeth wanted their expedition to be unremarkable, a dozen well-dressed women marching up the public steps of Westminster was bound to cause a furor.

St. Stephen's Hall had been ringing with male voices when the ladies of the Abigail Adams entered the long room, but the sight of the women traveling in a pack seemed to have struck the men dumb.

The stunned silence followed her determined group through the narrow, grandly vaulted hall, right into the central lobby, where the women broke into a chorus of oos and ahs about the impressive architecture, and wandered about among the other denizens of the room.

"Oh, my! Look at that spire!" Mrs. Garrison pointed her gloved finger into the air. "Why, it's grand!"

It was, indeed. The octagonal tower was a full seventy-five feet high, and crowned with tall windows framed by lacy Gothic arches.

"Ooo! And there's the Duke of Argyll!" Mrs. Barnes was heading toward the man and his knot of aides.

Elizabeth hooked the woman's arm and turned her toward the group. "Mustn't interrupt the duke while he's in conference. Now, let's—"

"And if I'm not mistaken that's Sir William Molesworth," Mrs. Deverel said, narrowing her eyes at the man. "The Commissioner of Public Works. Excuse me, dear, I need to see him about a pothole in front of my town house."

"But, Mrs. Deverel, it's time to take our seats in the public gallery. Come along, ladies!"

Elizabeth had visited the halls of Parliament a few times since moving to London, but she'd never made it beyond the central lobby into the gallery of the House of Commons.

Nothing was going to stop her today. Not flood nor famine, nor busybody earls.

Especially not unmarried ones, who had slept the night just outside her bedchamber.

"Have you lost your way, ladies?" An official-looking little man was bearing down on them as they moved toward the Commons, a patronizing tolerance for the weaker sex hovering beneath his neat moustache. "You have found yourself in the halls of Parliament."

"Excellent, sir." Elizabeth met him before he could plow into the center of her party and risk his equanimity. "That's exactly why we had our carriages drop us in front of St. Stephen's Porch."

His smile thinned. "Whyever would you want to do that, madam?"

"Because we plan to . . . to . . ."

Oh, blast it all!

Blakestone!

"Look there, Elizabeth, dear," Mrs. Barnes whispered, nodding slightly toward St. Stephen's Hall. "It's that stunning earl. And he's coming right this way, like a locomotive."

With a full head of steam.

"Let's go, ladies!" Elizabeth left the little official stammering and started herding the women toward the long corridor and the Commons lobby beyond. "Up the stairs to the Public Gallery. Careful now."

Elizabeth could feel Blakestone's eyes burning into her back as she hurried with the last of the group down the narrow corridor.

Knowing she couldn't escape him completely, she waited until the women had reached the Commons lobby, then stopped at the end of the corridor to wait for him.

"Ah, Blakestone," she said as she turned on her heel to meet him. Every massive ounce of him coming toward her as though he would overtake her like a thunderstorm. "Fancy meeting you here in Parliament. Is the Lords in session today? Or are you on loan to the prime minister?"

He took up her elbow and brought his steaming temper against her ear. "Bloody hell, woman, you told my guard at the Adams that you were heading for Kew Gardens."

"You know women. We change our minds as often as we change our hats."

"Why did you lie? Because you didn't want me to know what you were up to today?"

"Because you'd send someone to follow us, wouldn't you? Even though we are perfectly safe from an abduction. I don't appreciate being tended to like a child."

"Or is that your guilty mind, Miss Dunaway? What sort of mischief are you planning now?"

"Mischief?"

"Another protest? Have you Women's Rights signs tucked up under your skirts?"

Elizabeth should have gasped in outrage, but the sound turned instantly into laughter. "You must be joking."

"Oh, no, madam. I can see your plan now: just as the Speaker opens the debate, your ladies launch into a chant."

Elizabeth caught her hand over her mouth to quiet her laughter, but Blakestone only drew her closer, his sultry whisper dashing against her temple.

"I warn you against this, madam. A single outburst from your ladies in the gallery and the sergeant-at-arms will haul you away to jail, and then you will have your precious press coverage in spades."

"Excellent news, sir." Delighted to find the man so disgruntled and so unable to freely chide her in such a public corridor, she turned her head and whispered against the slight bristle of his very male cheek. "Any suggestions as to what we should shout to make the biggest impression?"

He scowled fiercely down at her, taking her chin between his thumb and forefinger. "Mocking Parliament is no way to win them over to your cause."

"We had planned to shout 'Give us the vote or give us death!' but that might not quite do the trick. However, it'll have to do for now since we're late and fresh out of ideas." She gave the startled man a huge smile, then started into the nearly empty Commons lobby, darting toward the gallery stairs.

"Oh, no you don't, madam!" He caught her arm as she reached the base of the stairs. "If it weren't for the Lord Mayor's inquiry, I'd be sorely tempted to let you go make a fool of yourself."

"Then what do you mean to do with me instead? Tie me here to the banister? Or put me in stocks out in the old courtyard? Think of the press coverage then!"

"A pity we've outlawed that sort of punishment."

"An even greater pity that you have no idea when I'm pulling your leg."

"What do you mean?"

"The ladies of the Abigail Adams have not come here to protest."

"Then what?" He narrowed his eyes at her, focusing their dark intensity on her own. "You're surely not here for anything but mischief."

"There's a great pity too, my lord. That men cannot fathom the fact that women might possibly be interested in the everyday workings of government. But we are."

"Why?"

"The same reason that men are interested: its laws affect every aspect of our lives. In these modern times, with so much at stake, we'd be fools not to keep abreast of Parliament. And to that end, from now on, the Abigail Adams will field a reporter to the Commons, every day of every session. That reporter will then relay to us what she has learned and we will be wiser for it."

"She?" He laughed. "A female reporter, turning up in the Press Gallery every day?"

"Why not?"

"Seems a waste of time. Why not just subscribe to the Hansard record?"

"Because Hansard only employs men, and the ladies of the Abigail Adams require a woman's point of view."

He went utterly silent, his frown deeply lining his forehead.

"So, my lord, if you have no further objection, I'll just go join the rest of my party in the Public Gallery. As is my right. I think."

Pleased with the squared-off confusion locked in the man's jaw, and still reeling from the fiery thrill of his touch along the inside of her elbow, Elizabeth started up the stairs, certain that the man would follow.

Hoping he would, because he did smell particularly fine today. Of laurel and musk.

Infuriating woman! Ross grabbed back the bellow that would have stopped her in her tracks and doubtless brought the noise from the floor of the Commons to a halt as well.

Instead, he followed her up the stairs, unable to turn

his eyes from the lithe trim of her ankles teasing him from beneath the crisply white flounce of her skirts.

Bloody hell, he felt like a besotted swain as he climbed into the warm air of the gallery.

There they were, Miss Dunaway and her gang of women, perched like an eager jury, six above six, on the tufted leather benches that overlooked the great brawling machine that was the British government.

The ladies were chattering to each other, craning over the railing, pointing down onto the main floor where the morning's proceedings were about to get under way.

"*Psst*, Blakestone!"

Miss Dunaway was beckoning to him with a subtle, utterly compelling crooking of her gloved finger, her green eyes flashing up at him. He might have actually had the strength to resist, but she splayed her fingers across the space on the seat beside her and patted lightly there.

Or was that a caress?

Lord help him find the strength to walk away.

But, of course, he sat down beside her anyway, his nerves tattered, already on edge.

"How can I help you, madam?" he asked, quite smoothly for a man who had just become thickly aroused in the gallery of the House of Commons.

And tempted to disaster by a woman who was fast becoming an element of his blood.

"Actually, my lord, the ladies have a few questions."

" 'Morning, my lord—"

"Good to see you, sir—"

"Will you be attending the charity ball, Lord Blakestone? It's for a very good cause. And I've heard you're up for auction . . ."

Damnation, he was going to have to clear up that particular error right away. "Well, I don't—"

But the women reached out for him from all sides, extending their gloved hands, shaking his vigorously. Doubtless they would have backslapped him if they could have.

None of that demure, sweet-miss stuff here. Damned if he didn't like that in a woman.

"Yes, and good morning to you all, ladies." He returned their enthusiastic smiles. "Miss Dunaway was just telling me that you had a few questions."

"About Parliament," the bewitching woman sitting so palpably beside him said. She was turned halfway around toward the group, her shapely backside making sound contact with the length of his thigh, taking his breath away. "Mrs. Niles, I think you had the first question."

Mrs. Niles stood, her hands clasped together. "My husband is a Conservative. He's always said that you can tell a Liberal devil in Parliament by the red tail that sticks out the back vent of his coat. Well, my lord, I don't see tails on any of the gentlemen down there. So, my question is . . ."

"Yes?" he prodded, when the woman's fiery glare into the pit below became fixed there.

"My question is this, my lord: am I to assume there aren't any Liberals in the Commons today? Or has my husband been playing loose with the truth?"

Though Miss Dunaway's head was turned mostly away from him, Ross could see well enough from around the narrow brim of her small bonnet that her jaw was working as hard as his to hold back a smile.

"Well, Mrs. Niles . . ." A perfectly good question, but without a good answer that wouldn't cause Mr. Niles to come find him with a swift punch in the nose. "Let's just say that one man's devil is another man's leader. Politics is a matter of personal opinion."

Mrs. Niles snorted and crossed her arms over her bosom. "Well, then, my personal opinion is that my husband's devil is no longer my own." She sat down with a plunk.

Miss Dunaway cleared her throat, hiding her unsubtle amusement beneath a delicate handkerchief that suddenly softened the warm dust-moted air with the barest hint of summer roses.

"I have a question, my lord!" A younger woman in the second row was waving her hand at him. "How does all this Parliament stuff work?"

Bloody hell, now there was a question for the ages.

"What I believe Mrs. Morriston wants to know, my lord," Miss Dunaway said, turning back to him with an unreadable glint in her eyes, "is how would a proposed measure which would, for example, grant women their God-given right to vote, become a law?"

Well, he'd walked right into that one.

The vixen was smiling at him in triumph.

"That's an excellent question, Miss Morriston," he said to the eagerly grinning young woman. "And an excellent example, Miss Dunaway."

Because the Government that seriously proposed "votes for women" to this august body would be laughed out of Westminster. The Government would crumble on a no-confidence vote and a new prime minister would be sitting on the Treasury Bench the very next morning.

But he could hardly burst the bubble of the ladies' success with an explanation as cold as that. Though Miss Dunaway was eyeing him as if she believed that was his intention.

Instead, he turned away from her silent defiance to the room below. "To begin with, ladies, the rows of benches on the left of the Secretary's bench are occupied by members of the current government in power. And you probably recognize Lord Aberdeen, the prime minister, there on the front bench."

"My my, his lordship's gone gray since last I saw him."

"Thinner too."

It was no wonder. These were trying times for the man and his cabinet.

"Now, ladies, can any of you tell me what party Lord Aberdeen belongs to?"

Mrs. Niles snorted in derision. "I don't see a devil's tail sticking out of the man's coat, so he can't be a Liberal, can he?"

The women laughed their approval.

"Lord Aberdeen is a Tory," Miss Dunaway said. "But he has actually formed a coalition government. One party working in concert with another, for the single purpose of running the government."

Leave it to Miss Dunaway to already know the details of her own personal opposition.

"Exactly right, madam. Last year, Lord Aberdeen, a

follower of John Peel, joined his majority party with a smaller faction of Whigs—"

"Excuse me, Lord Blakestone, but whatever is that man doing?"

He'd suddenly lost the attention of the women. They were staring at something in the back benches behind Aberdeen.

"That's no man, Mrs. Deverel, that's my husband." The woman sniffed toward the man at the very back of the benches who was waving both arms directly at her, glaring up into the gallery, his face blotched with red fury.

"I didn't know your husband was a member of Parliament, Mrs. Sayers."

"He is indeed, Mrs. Niles. My husband is the Conservative member from Nesbit Grange."

Now the man was gesturing toward the entrance to the Commons.

"I think he's trying to tell you something, Mrs. Sayers."

"Seems so, Mrs. Barnes."

Miss Dunaway's brow was a wing of troubles. "Didn't you tell him you'd be here today?"

"Why should I?" She snubbed her chin at her husband. "I decided that if Mr. Wilton Sayers wanted to make a fool of himself by telling me that I shouldn't be here, he was going to have to do it in front of all his friends."

The ladies actually applauded.

The very quiet Miss Dunaway merely arched a bemused brow up at Ross, unapologetic about the poor clod's reaction.

All the while Mrs. Sayers was the image of calm, ignoring her husband entirely, though he'd begun to make enough noise that the other members were now staring at him as though he had gone mad.

"You heard me, Vita Marie!" Sayers's strangled voice ricocheted off the benches and rattled around in the vast, vaulted ceiling.

But stubborn Vita only tilted her chin higher.

With another shout, Vita's husband dashed out of sight beneath the gallery for a moment then reappeared at his bench, shaking his fist at them.

"Well, now, ladies"—Miss Dunaway turned back to her distracted group— "would anyone like to ask Lord Blakestone another question?"

"I was wondering, my lord—"

The rest of the woman's question was cut off by the sound of heavy footsteps pounding up the gallery stairs, followed an instant later by two men in police uniforms who burst into the Public Gallery. They drew their nightsticks with great drama, then began striding toward them.

Bloody hell! What the devil was going on here?

"I'll take care of this, madam," Ross said quietly to Miss Dunaway.

Feeling suddenly protective of his horde and in a fighting mood himself, Ross blocked the way of the policemen in the aisle, aware that Miss Dunaway was also on her feet now, arms spread to protect her charges.

"That's enough, fellows," Ross said, meeting the men two steps up. "There's nothing here. Leave them alone."

"Sorry, your lordship, but the ladies are gonna have to leave." The older sergeant-at-arms wagged the stick toward the horrified women. "They're disturbing the proceedings."

"You're bloody wrong, sir. Now get on with you." Ross balled his fists at his sides, a natural reaction to an unjust claim, ready to take on both men, ready to let them retreat from this outrage.

"Your pardon, Sergeant," Miss Dunaway said from behind him, remarkably evenly, slipping her hand into the crook of Ross's elbow, "but we have every right to be here."

The man ignored Miss Dunaway completely and leaned in to Ross as though they were fellow conspirators. "It's for the best they leave, sir," he whispered with a debasing nod toward the women.

Ross wanted to plant his fist in the middle of the man's nose. But now the sounds from below had grown immensely, a chorus of bellowing voices, the Secretary shouting, banging the gavel against the podium.

"Let it be, Sergeant." Ross gestured to the wide-eyed women. "Sit down, ladies. You're staying here."

But then a shrill voice came barreling up the gallery stairs.

"Vita Sayers, what are you doing here with those"—and then Sayers himself appeared above them at the top of the stairs, standing spread-legged, jabbing a finger toward the beleaguered group—"those, those, those . . . women?"

Ross had never seen a man's face as molten red, or

such hatred throbbing in a man's neck. Fearing what Sayers would do next, Ross tapped aside the two security officers and put himself in front of the man.

"Come on, now, Sayers," he said, approaching carefully, "let's you and I go on down to the—"

"You're a woman, Vita! You don't belong here. Go home, do you hear me?"

"You don't scare me, Wilton."

Ashamed for his entire gender, Ross caught the man as he tried to plow past him to his wife, who was now frowning stubbornly at her husband, the other women filling in around her.

Sayers leaned hard against Ross, still trying to get past him, hissing his words through his teeth. "Are you deliberately trying to humiliate me, Vita?"

"Only you can do that, Wilton, dear."

"Vita!"

Again the Secretary banged the gavel from below, this time shouting, "Quiet up there! Do you hear me? Quiet in the house, everyone, or I'll have the hall cleared!"

But Sayers was nearly apoplectic at this point.

The women were calling down curses on the man.

And the gentlemen of the Commons had joined him in a clamorous protest over whatever trouble those damned women up in the Public Gallery were causing the honorable member of Parliament.

Furious at the lot of them, Ross himself was about to tackle Sayers and throw him over the railing, when he heard Miss Dunaway from beside him, her voice clear and in complete control.

"Please, everyone!" she said, raising her hand to the

gallery, and then to the rioting below. "Stop this foolishness immediately."

The roar of outrage flared, then moments later the entire House of Commons and all its galleries fell to a breathless silence, every eye trained on Miss Dunaway.

"Come, ladies," she said, with confident dignity, taking up her wrap from the bench in front of her. "We know when it's time to leave."

Her ladies objected en masse.

"But, Miss Elizabeth—"

"I don't think we should go—"

Vita pointed at Sayers. "Shut up, Wilton."

"Ladies, please." Miss Dunaway held up a gentle hand to her rowdy confederates. "I'm afraid we've reached the point of resentment and of diminishing returns. There's nothing more for us here."

She turned her quiet dignity to the enormous well of silent, upturned male faces below, ministers and peers, country squires and captains of industry, all of them staring up at her in what Ross could only interpret as awe.

Then, in perhaps the greatest show of statesmanship that he'd ever been witness to, the remarkable Miss Dunaway squared her slender shoulders and spoke an unerring challenge in a resolute voice that she surely meant to echo across the centuries from the diligent pages of the Hansard record.

"Make no mistake, gentlemen," she said, scanning the Commons with that utterly bewitching smile, "we'll be back. And one day we will stay."

Brava, madam.

"Good day to you, Blakestone."

Then she turned up her chin again and walked past him. She started up the aisle to the sound of a befuddled Commons, leading her proud band of women past the sagging jaws of the two sergeants-at-arms and then the stunned Sayers himself.

Bloody hell, what an exit! The woman was magnificent, from her gilded auburn hair to those lovely ankles. Doubtless right down to the succulent tips of her toes and all the luscious parts in between.

He let her go, though he desperately wanted to chase after her with his congratulations. But that would surely take away from her triumph. Besides which he didn't want to seem too approving of her impossible campaign. Didn't want her to hear the pride in his voice. Or to learn that her group would be followed by his operatives.

And most certainly didn't need her to catch on to how firmly she aroused him.

He would wait and see her tonight. All through the night. In her private sitting room.

With her private smile.

And that particular pleasure would have to carry him through a busy day of diplomatic jousting.

Feeling as though he'd just battled a bully in the street, he waited until the chaos in the main chamber below had settled and Sayers had slinked off. Then he dusted off his clothes and left the gallery himself, nearly late for a meeting with Lord Clarendon.

Only to be met at the bottom of the stairs by a familiar face and a familiar smile.

"There you are, Blakestone, old man!" Lord Scarborough clapped him on the back. "I thought that was you up there in the gallery, tussling with those disorderly women."

Ross felt himself bristle, his jaw tightened for another fight. "A lot you know about it, Scarborough. They were treated deplorably, from all sides."

"Damn, I guess I missed that part. Only just came in on the end of the fracas."

"They were merely a group of women from the Abigail Adams, interested in—"

"Ah, yes, that new ladies' club." The man was grinning broadly, a cat with cream on his whiskers. "My wife joined up a few months ago. Takes classes and goes to meetings of some sort."

"And, of course, you object to it." Taken aback by his own defensiveness, Ross waited for the usual diatribe against the very concept of a club for and by women.

But Scarborough only chuckled fondly. "Good God, no, Blakestone. I encourage the woman."

"That's very modern of you."

"To hell with modern." The man sent a glance around the lobby as though ready to whisper a state secret. "Best thing that ever happened to our marriage."

"How's that?"

"Let's just say that I don't know what they do over there at the Abigail Adams, but ever since Arlene joined them, well, the nightly activities in our bedchamber have become more . . . well, exotic."

"More exotic?" Ross drew a complete blank. Though the image of a silvery warm beach in the South Seas shimmered before his eyes.

Naked love . . .

"You know . . ." Scarborough twitched his brows, then clicked his tongue twice. ". . . more *romantic*."

Ross was feeling thoroughly dense, because exotic and romantic couldn't possibly mean what it sounded like the man meant.

Not about the Abigail Adams.

Not about Miss Dunaway.

"I'm sorry, Scarborough, but I don't—"

"Good Lord, do I have to spell it out? Arlene and I have been married ten years and suddenly my wife can't get enough of me. You know, old man. In bed."

"In bed?"

"God, yes! Bless the Abigail Adams and all who dwell within. I've become an object of my own wife's lust, and I don't mind it one damn bit."

"Well, I guess you wouldn't." All this just because his wife joined the Abigail Adams?

What the devil was the innocent Miss Dunaway teaching in her classroom, anyway?

Scarborough brushed at the lapels of his waistcoat. "Yup, just like a pair of lovebirds, are my Arlene and I."

"The more power to you, Scarborough."

"Hell, I was just going to recommend that you have your own lovely wife join up with the ladies, Blake-stone, but you haven't married yet, have you?"

"No, I haven't." He'd been about to spout the usual "Haven't found the right woman yet," but the comment hung up on the scent of roses still clinging to his coat sleeve.

Hung up on a pair of flashing green eyes.

On a voice that had just laid bare the entire House of Commons.

"Well, enough about this old married man, then, Blakestone. Clarendon's expecting us in Aberdeen's office. It seems that the Russians are kicking up another fuss about the sultan's treatment of Prince Menshikov."

"That was three months ago. Great." Ross followed the man's jaunty step, doing his best to keep track of Scarborough's prattling about the tsar's newest diplomatic insult against the Sultan of Turkey.

But there was only one stream of thought running through his head, boiling his brain, lodging its heat in his loins.

And her name was Elizabeth Dunaway.

Chapter 10

If the first woman God ever made was strong enough to turn the world upside down all alone, these women together ought to be able to turn it back, and get it right side up again.

Sojourner Truth, abolitionist and orator, 1851

"**H**ave you any family in America, Lydia? Any good friends there?"

The weary woman looked up at Elizabeth across the small library table, her eyes wet and red-rimmed and steeped in unwarranted guilt. "No, I haven't. I'm sorry."

"No need to be sorry about anything." Elizabeth took hold of Lydia's trembling hands and held tightly. "You *do* have friends in America. You just haven't met them yet. But you'll find them all along the way. Waiting to help you, from the moment you disembark in New York until you've become comfortable in your new life."

"Friends." Lydia's smile sagged at one corner. "I'm so very glad to hear that. I'd be utterly lost otherwise."

"That's why you came to us."

"I thank God that I did." Her simple face filled with gratitude. "That Helen convinced me to come. Because though I'm terrified of the future, it can't possibly be worse than what's come before."

Elizabeth had learned only a portion of Lydia's current situation. As it should be, as it always was. The husband's wrathful nature. The beatings. An unsympathetic family. Nowhere to turn. Just enough information to help determine the best plan of escape.

And who might come looking for her.

"It's perfectly natural to be frightened. Leaving your homeland, your family and friends, a whole new life in front of you."

"A whole new name to learn." Lydia smiled bravely. A spark of hope flickered in her haunted eyes for the first time since she'd arrived.

"Speaking of that, you still have a day or two to decide on your new name. The only rule is that you can't use any name that would connect you to your old life."

"My husband's life, you mean. We never had children, and my own family's gone now. So I have no reason to hold on to my past."

"Then look to your future for your new name. Start with women you admire the most."

"That would make me Elizabeth Dunaway." Lydia actually laughed.

"I'm thoroughly honored, Lydia. But it wouldn't be wise to have two of us running around. Though I could use the extra pair of hands."

"Then put me to work. Please." Lydia opened her hands in a gesture of hope. "Any way you need me."

"Ah, then, perhaps you can help me decide on the best location for your abduction." The moment she spoke the words, a chill raced across her shoulders. A feeling that Blakestone could hear her every word.

"My abduction! How exciting! Rather like attending one's own funeral. What kind of location are you looking for?"

Elizabeth found herself leaning toward the woman, nearly whispering. "It has to be a very public place, large and thronging with people. Lots of movement, passersby, wagons, carts, vendors. And in broad day light."

"Good heavens! So public? Won't people see everything we do?"

"That's the most important part, Lydia. I want them to see. Or think they see. The brighter the sun, the larger the mob, the blinder they are. An old Indian snake charmer's trick that works every time."

"But won't they hear something? A scream or a scuffle in the street?"

"No, because you won't scream, and we never scuffle. That's the beauty of the operation. It's an abduction that never really happens."

Lydia considered the scenario for a moment and then grinned from ear to ear. "Oh, I see! How amazing! Ascot and the Derby would have been perfect, but they've already been run. Now there's a blind mob for you."

"Exactly." A pity that Lady Maxton's Charity Ball was so soon. And the end of the Season was fast approaching.

"How did you . . ." Lydia looked around for the word. ". . . *emancipate* the other abductees?"

Emancipate was the perfect word.

"Well, take the first one, for example. We picked high noon on the busiest day in the mummy room of the British Museum. In the crush, Lady Hayden-Cole merely dropped a chloroformed handkerchief on the floor, then slipped secretly out a service door into the stairwell, where she dropped her bonnet and a man's leather glove. By the time she reached the ground floor she had aged thirty years and looked to everyone on the street just like a ragged old flower seller who then hobbled off into an alleyway. Never to be seen again!"

"Oh, my! How brave!" Lydia's eyes had widened to saucers. "Lady Hayden-Cole did all that by herself?"

"It took a crew of four, including me."

"Four?"

"Like a well-oiled machine, Lydia. We'll be there for you too. Everything will be worked out to the finest detail. We'll rehearse until you know exactly what to do when the time comes."

Because each woman needed to be an intimate part of her own liberation or it wouldn't count, not deep down in her heart. Taking possession of her destiny with her own two hands would set her free.

"Gracious!"

"In the meantime, we'll decide where, and that will determine how and when. I'll need to buy the steamship tickets, design the initial escape route, and make sure you reach Southampton in time for your voyage to New York."

"New York." Lydia shook her head in wonder. "It sounds like so much to do."

"That, my dear Lydia, is only the beginning of a—"

A brisk, familiar knock, low on the library door, made Lydia jump behind a chair. "Oh, dear, God!"

Elizabeth had seen that reaction too many times before; that helpless fear of being stalked and found and dragged back to her abusive homelife would haunt the poor woman long after she'd put the blue Atlantic between her and her nightmare.

"It's all right, Lydia." Elizabeth opened the door to her three-member crew of kidnappers.

"Cocoa!" Jessica carried in a tray of steaming hot chocolate.

Skye followed with a two-handled basket of hats and folded costume pieces. "Fresh from the seamstress."

"And orange cakes from the tea shop." Cassie winked at Lydia as she set the platter down on the table in front of the skittish woman.

"These three young ladies, Lydia, are your . . . shall we say, travel assistants?"

Elizabeth couldn't have asked for three more enthusiastic and committed young women. A shopgirl, an actress, and a retired pickpocket—the perfect background for their work at the Abigail Adams. Footloose and undirected, they each took to their well-paid jobs with relish and cunning.

"Have we a plan yet, Miss E?" Skye was already picking through the basket of clothes, holding pieces up to Lydia's chest.

"Not quite yet. We have a fortnight. That's when Mrs. Bailey's husband, who is currently at home in Derbyshire, expects Mrs. Bailey home from visiting an old friend in Hampstead."

"My dear friend Helen, who told me about you courageous ladies at the Adams."

"You know you'll never be able to go back home again, Mrs. Bailey." Jessica handed a cup of cocoa to Lydia, her pretty face awash in earnest sympathy. "From this moment on. Not ever. Not your home or your friends. You must leave your old life behind."

Lydia caught her upper lip between her fingers and nodded. "Yes, I know."

Cassie offered the woman a plate with a cake. "As my dear Irish papa so often said before he died, 'Stick with me lass, and you'll be fartin' through silk.' "

Silence fell against the bookcases and settled into the overstuffed chairs.

"How's that?" Lydia's brows had drawn tightly together, her gaze fixed and wide at the very prim-looking Cassie's very streetwise advice.

Needing to do something quickly to smooth the situation, Elizabeth put her arm around the woman's shoulder. "What Cassie means is—"

"Through silk? Oh! Oh, my!" Then Lydia started laughing. And kept laughing. And laughing.

Absolutely roaring, until they were all convulsed in tears, holding their stomachs.

"Cassie, really!" But Elizabeth hadn't laughed so much in months and months. Laughed until her stomach ached and her eyes were flooding, until suddenly she felt a breeze at her back.

Lydia and the three young women had stopped laughing and were now looking over her shoulder at the door.

Blakestone! She'd know that devilish scent any-where. That steamy presence.

She turned to him, carefully steeling herself for the sight of all that smoldering maleness.

It didn't work this time either; he was just too overwhelming.

And there was Lydia, standing beside Skye, as big as you please. All the evidence the man needed in his investigation of London's fiendish kidnapper.

"Can we help you, my lord?" she finally asked against the rise of her pulse.

"I didn't mean to interrupt, Miss Dunaway," he said with that dark, quirking eyebrow, those intelligent eyes that swept the room and caught up every nuance.

"Actually, you didn't. We were just finishing up."

In a flash her three keen-witted assistants had cleared the library of the cocoa and cakes, the costume basket and Lydia, the changed woman.

"Are you sure I didn't interrupt something, madam?" He reached back and closed the door behind him, clearly curious, amused. "I could hear your laughter all the way from the back stairs."

"Just a bit of humor between us women."

"With us men as your bull's-eye, of course."

"Of course. Turnabout is fair play."

"Turnabout is it?" He was looking quite smug at the moment. As though he'd just learned something highly personal about her, but was going to savor the secret power for a while, before using it. "Are you implying that men are in the habit of making jokes about women?"

"Come now. You must admit that men rarely take the opinions of women seriously."

"That might be true of some men, however—"

"Excess baggage. An anchor around the husband's adventuring spirit. A brood mare. A cash cow. Livestock. Chattel. It's all very funny, isn't it?"

"Hardly, madam." He furrowed a dark brow at her, a forged injury.

"You saw for yourself this afternoon, my lord. That little entertainment in Parliament. By the time our contingent left the chamber, the members' protests of outrage had turned from derisive laughter to a thundering celebration of the male intellect triumphing absolutely over an uppity, feather-headed female prank."

The sharp planes of his jaw hardened as he came toward her. "Do you really believe what you're saying?"

"I believe in what I have observed my whole life long, sir. Just as surely as I believe in the course of the sun and the stars."

He narrowed his eyes. "If that's true, then you purposely went with your ladies to Parliament, with your trap baited and set, fully expecting to snare your quarry?"

Had she really?

"Possibly. But I was truly hoping against hope that the members of your sex would prove me wrong this time around. We would have loved to have been left to our harmless mission in the gallery; to observe for ourselves the workings of government. To be defended by our men folk instead of publically reviled by them."

He had made his way to her end of the worktable. "Not all men are as intolerant as that idiot Sayers."

"But there are enough of them for the rest of you to hide behind."

"Me? You're calling me a coward?" He leaned back against the edge of the table, arms crossed over his broad chest. "Including me in your blanket condemnation."

The poor man looked more stricken than angry. And he was, in truth, generally undeserving.

"To be honest, sir, I was surprised and quite impressed when you came so quickly to our defense in the Commons."

"Sayers is a madman."

"Yes, but you forcibly held him back from reaching his wife. And that took courage."

"Nonsense. Sayers is a scrawny bastard, for all his blustering, and I—"

"Yes, and you could have pounded him into the ground with a single blow. But that's not the kind of courage I am talking about."

He seemed suddenly pleased with himself. "What other kind is there?"

"The most important kind. Moral courage. You stood up for us in front of your peers. That says a great deal about the strength of your character."

"Madam, I merely stood up to a bully." He shrugged those massive shoulders as though to dismiss her compliment, which had so obviously pleased him, then left her for one of the walls of bookshelves. "Any man would have done the same thing, in the same situation."

"Pardon me, my lord, if I don't count on it next time. You did the courageous thing, and the ladies of the Abigail Adams agreed that your behavior was exceptional."

"Did they?" He turned back from his browsing and arched a brow at her, then went back to scanning the shelves.

"They talked about you all the way home. And told me to thank you the next time I saw you." She'd been giddily hoping he would come tonight. "And here you are, so . . . thank you. From me, as well."

"You're all very welcome, though I'm not nearly as deserving of praise as you are."

"Me?"

He stopped in front of the neat rack of newspapers and turned back to her. "For your grand exit from Parliament this morning."

"Are you mocking me?" His comment stung. Though she'd only known the man for a week, she'd come to expect so much more from him.

"I would never." He leaned against the bookcase strut, appraised her for a long sweep of his dazzling gaze. "I thought you were . . . spectacular."

Spectacular? Me?

She tried to calm her heart, tried not to read anything into his admiring eyes, because there was danger here, of untold dimensions. "In what way, sir?"

He was smiling again, nodding as though he approved of her stance. "You stood up to the most powerful governmental body in the world, with great composure and dignity, and rightly chided them for their rude behavior."

She shrugged lightly, hoping to stave off the flush

that his unexpected praise was beginning to cause. "I only spoke my mind."

"You challenged their petty universe to a duel of wills."

"A duel? I didn't mean—"

"And, make no mistake, Miss Dunaway, you rattled more than one conscience."

"Oh, I doubt that."

"And had you stayed to listen instead of sweeping down the stairs with your entourage, you would have heard one of those rare moments that sometimes overtakes the House of Commons in times of national distress."

"Rare, how?"

"Silence, my dear. Utter silence."

"Oh." At the time, she couldn't actually hear anything for the anger and embarrassment ringing in her ears. And her heart had been pounding as wildly as it was now.

"Of course, all hell broke loose a moment later, madam, but you did substantially affect the morning's proceedings. They will remember you."

But will you remember me when you're gone, my lord, as I'll remember you?

He stared at her a moment longer, then turned back to the bookshelves, taking a sudden interest in reading each of the titles.

The titles! Oh, dear, this wasn't an ordinary library, for ordinary readers.

"Well, my lord, I will certainly remember my promise to *them*." Sensing his prowling interest in the contents of the shelves, Elizabeth gathered up the newspapers strewn across the surface of the table.

"And, though I don't know what the reporter from the *Times* will write about the your battle for the Public Gallery, you'll have some press again tomorrow morning."

"Then we're sure to be the object of ridicule at every breakfast table in London and in every dining room of every gentleman's club in St. James."

Looking much like a stalking bear, Blakestone pulled a burgundy leather-bound book off the shelf, then frowned at the cover.

Surely at the controversial title: *Rebel Wives and Household Revolutions*.

He glanced back at her with that weighty, unreadable glint in his eyes, tilting the book at her. "Was your childhood home a household of revolutions?"

She'd never considered it before, but, "Yes, I suppose it was. That is to say, my great-aunts were both wildly revolutionary for their time."

"Somehow that doesn't surprise me."

"What I mean is that they didn't bend their values to suit public opinion."

"So that's where you get your . . ."

She knew exactly the word he was searching for: "Pigheadedness?"

"Confidence, madam. An essential ingredient in all revolutionaries."

"I'd hardly call myself revolutionary." But she liked that he thought of her that way. Liked too much that he thought of her at all.

That he looked at her with such heat in his eyes, in the curve of his mouth.

"Neither of your aunts ever married, did they? The Hasleton sisters."

Blast it all, the man seemed to know everything about her and her past.

"The choice was theirs, Blakestone. They were both legendary beauties in their day, as well as wealthy heiresses, from an old family. They could have married anyone. However, to their dying days, they both preached loudly against marriage."

He gave a quick grunt. "I do hope you didn't listen."

Lord, what could he mean by that remark? And by the wry tilt of his frown, as though he were disappointed? Or cared.

"What does it matter to you, my lord, what I think about marriage?"

"I . . . well, I just think you ought to keep your options open."

"To paraphrase my Auntie Clarice: after marriage, the husband and the wife are one person, but that person is always the husband."

"Ah, and your Aunt Tiberia's words of wisdom?" Of course the lout would know her other aunt's name as well.

"Aunt Tibbs firmly believed that the law should not force the woman to surrender her independence or her fortune to her husband. And that men are only good for one thi—"

She stopped her words abruptly enough, but could

do nothing about the flush of crimson spreading like a wildfire out of her bodice.

She probably could have stopped the flush by sheer dint of will. If only Blakestone hadn't suddenly shifted the heat of his gaze from her bosom to her face.

If he hadn't slowly smiled at her, like an artful, unsated pirate.

"Good for one thing, madam? And what would that one thing be?"

"Ummm . . ." There was just a humming occupying her head at the moment, the burring drone of a little bee, then a whole hive of them.

"Escorting a woman to the opera? Or as an object in a charity auction?"

"No, certainly, my lord, but . . . you see, my Aunt Tiberia was a . . ." With every beat of her heart, he came closer and closer, until he was peering down at her.

"Your aunt was a . . . ?"

Great heavens, what a ninny she'd become. Cowering like an innocent in the face of Blakestone's rather simple question. A test of her mettle, which she knew she could easily pass.

Elizabeth squared her shoulders. "Aunt Tibbs was very broad-minded. Both of my aunts were."

"And this 'one good thing' about men?"

She looked him straight in the eye. "Intercourse, of the sexual type."

He had been peering at her, one eyebrow raised. Now it drooped. "What did you say?"

There! That had gotten him!

"Sexual intercourse," she said, landing hard and deliberately on every syllable, as though he might not understand, when she knew perfectly well that the man never missed a nuance.

Certainly not a sexual one.

And this moment was getting very sexual. Very hot.

"I see."

She could see too; she could see the bronze muscle playing in his jaw, the smile lurking in the corners of his mouth.

"You're a man of the world, my lord. You must realize that just because a woman like my Aunt Tiberia isn't married doesn't mean she can't enjoy the pleasures of the flesh with the man of her choosing."

"I've heard as much."

"Once in a while."

"Once in a while?"

"Absolutely."

"Ah."

"And safe enough, if precautions are taken against conception. *Interruptus*, for one. *French letters*, for another."

"English papers, in France."

"I didn't know that."

He blinked at her, then took a huge breath and cleared his throat. "So, I can assume that you agree with your aunts' philosophies, Miss Dunaway."

"I'm a modern woman, Blakestone, with modern ideas. In charge of my own destiny. My own body."

Oh, but not in charge of that charming, runaway blush, my dear Miss Dunaway, Ross thought, but didn't dare say for fear of spooking her. He was enjoying this banter far too much to risk her ejecting him from her sultry presence.

He'd never known a woman whose emotions played so plainly, so perfectly, on her flawless features as they did on Miss Dunaway's.

Spots of velvety pink blooming on her cheeks, peeking out of her bodice, making him want to explore his way to the source, with his mouth, his tongue.

"Ah, then," he said, turning away from all that boldly inviting beauty and going back to the wall of bookcases with its provocative selection of titles, "that would explain it, my dear."

"Explain what?"

He said nothing for a moment as he combed carefully along the amazingly eclectic titles.

Ancient Queens of Britain, Exotic Indulgences, Atlas of the World, Home Repairs Made Simple . . .

Ah, and now there was at least part of the answer. Scarborough's wife must have been borrowing books from the Adams library. *Mistress of the House, Mistress of the Bedchamber.*

"What is it that needed explaining, Blakestone?" She was standing at his elbow, her voice impatient at his silence.

"Just an interesting comment made to me today by a colleague."

"About me?"

"About secret goings-on here at the Abigail Adams."

Her dazzling smile flickered out for a moment, then returned with her laughter. "Secret goings-on? How exciting!" She was smiling as though playing along with his game. "Did your colleague say what kind of goings-on?"

"Apparently his wife is a member here."

"Who is it?"

"Now that would be telling."

She shrugged, plainly more comfortable now with his inquiry. "Well, then what did he say? What secret?"

"This colleague of mine hinted that his wife of nine years has suddenly found him . . . attractive."

"Perhaps he's gotten a haircut. Had his suits better tailored? A good tailoring can do wonders for a man's general physique."

"Perhaps I didn't make myself clear, Miss Dunaway. The man's wife's demeanor in their bedchamber has changed dramatically."

"How so?"

"Apparently she's become the . . . uh . . ." Now how to say this correctly? ". . . the seducer in the marriage bed."

"And?" So nonchalant. Making him wonder if she was as virginal under all that steamy bluster as he'd first assumed.

"And according to him, the only thing that's changed in their nine years together is that a few months back his wife became a member of the Abigail Adams."

She quirked her head, a tinge of confusion on her pouting mouth. "Is your friend complaining about his wife being a member of the ladies' club?"

"Hardly. In fact, he says he encourages his wife to attend as many meetings and classes at the Adams as she pleases."

She leaned forward, raised a teasing finger. "Don't you mean secret goings-on?"

"Bloody hell, woman! What the devil kind of classes are you teaching here?" He had no idea where his sudden irritation had come from. But it doubtless had a great deal to do with the fact that the woman danced around the truth like a moth around a flame.

"Just ordinary classes . . ."

"Balderdash! An ordinary thirty-year-old wife of an ordinary husband doesn't just change into a vixen in the bedroom overnight. Not without . . . hell, I don't know, Miss Dunaway." He really had no ready ideas for an explanation. "What have you done with the woman? And how many other women of London have you turned into sirens?"

"Sirens, my lord?" She gave a scoffing laugh. "Your friend was surely exaggerating his good fortune."

"Don't play your word games with me. You're flirting with fire here."

"How can adding a joyful dimension to a marriage cause any trouble at all?"

"Because, my dear, not every husband would be as pleased as my friend is to find a frisky wife in his bed. Especially his own."

"Frankly, that's not the husband's decision to make; it's the wife's. The pleasure isn't all for him, you know."

Oh, God, he'd plunged head first into that one. "So I've heard. But what you fail to understand is that you can't teach . . ." Bloody hell, had he suddenly become a prude? "You can't teach sex."

"We don't, my lord. We teach responsibility." Now

she looked like a chiding governess. "I don't see how anyone can object to that!"

"Responsibility, Miss Dunaway? For what?" Scarborough's wife had been an upright, responsible woman long before joining the Adams.

"Good heavens, do I have to explain everything in detail?"

"Please do, madam. You've lost me." In any case, he had long ago ceded control of his visit to the woman who was now shaking her head at him.

"In the simplest terms: if a woman desires more romance from her husband in the bedroom, then she must take responsibility for her own share of the seduction."

"Her share?" Bloody hell! "How do you mean?"

Now she huffed her impatience, as though he was a blockheaded man without a clue as to a woman's needs, then took off toward the sideboard at the far end of the room.

"There are certain techniques a woman can employ to help her husband understand how to please her in bed. Which, in turn, will please him as well." She had plucked a small booklet off a stack on the sideboard and proudly held it up for him. "*Unbridled Embraces; or Proven Techniques for an Intimate Marriage.*"

"Techniques?" In bed. *Proven?* By whom? Good Lord, she couldn't possibly mean—

"I compiled the book for our classes because learning how to be an adventurous wife in bed, and a flirt in the bedroom, is every bit as important for a woman's happiness as learning to read or write."

"Adventurous?"

"Here." She handed the booklet to him, and he

nearly flinched for the fire he feared must be hiding between the pages. He felt her eyes on him as he opened to the center pages, as he squinted at what might be there.

An explicit drawing, detailed instructions . . . but no, thank God.

Just words, dancing around in his uneasy hands, leaping off the page and into his groin.

"After all, Blakestone, today's bride goes to her marriage bed terrified because she's been left completely in the dark as to what's to happen to her. Her trepidation is well-founded, as she is then quickly and summarily deflowered by an equally ignorant bridegroom, in a ritual of pain and degradation."

Not my *bride*, he nearly said, but the remarkable woman was talking blithely to him just now, about an unspeakably taboo subject, as though she was at the head of a classroom and he was her ignorant student.

"Our mothers tell us nothing about the pleasures available in the marriage bed, because they know nothing about it themselves. Because *their* mothers knew nothing about it, or their mothers, and so it has gone for countless generations. And though a marriage may last fifty years, the supreme act of intimacy between husband and wife remains a bumbling assault on the marriage itself."

Still too shell-shocked to be thinking clearly, Ross found himself nodding at her, with her.

Wanting her.

"And so, in order to help combat such ignorance, we women of the Abigail Adams are merely claiming our right to our marital bliss."

"*Your* rights in particular, Miss Dunaway? I thought you were never going to marry."

She raked her fingers through the hair at her temple. "As I said before, a woman doesn't have to marry to find intimacy."

Dear Lord, he didn't dare follow that trail any closer. "Are you telling me, madam, that the Abigail Adams is running a school for unfulfilled wives?" He held up her scandalous, possibly illegal, booklet. "And that this is the primer?"

"Not a primer. Suggestions for a more satisfying married life. For example . . ." She took up another of the same booklet, tossed through the pages, then read aloud from one. " 'Be bold with your seduction; be playful in your intentions and you will soon feel the flush of passion rising in your own blood.' "

Good Lord!

She looked up at him with the clear, unflinching green eyes of a zealous evangelist. "Your turn, my lord. Try one for yourself."

"Try one?" He jabbed his finger against a page. "Of these?"

"Read one aloud and see what you think."

I think I'm going mad.

And bloody hell, he was terrified. Could barely breathe, let alone read. His mouth dried out, his thoughts stuck to his tongue, as he tried to focus on the first passage that caught his eye.

" 'Run your fingers . . . slowly through his hair—' " He cleared his throat, fearing the worst of it was just ahead. " ' . . . as you tell him how proud you are of his accomplishments.' "

Well. That wasn't so bad. Suggestive perhaps, but surely not explicit.

"Now what man wouldn't appreciate that, my lord? Fingers running through his hair."

"Well, I suppose that—"

"Shall I demonstrate on you?"

Had he heard right? "Demonstrate? On me?" Like a lunatic, he glanced around the empty library.

She smiled and shook her head at him. "Since you're the only man in sight . . ."

"Madam, please . . ." But he couldn't possibly say no. Couldn't breathe. Couldn't think past the rigid arousal he had been unable to restrain.

"Are you ready, my lord?"

I doubt it. "If you must." He tried to disconnect, to act bored with it all.

It was just an act.

"Just stand right there by the table." Then the astonishing woman placed herself a half-dozen paces from him, straightened her skirts, cocked her shoulder and her hip, and smiled the very smile that Eve must have offered to Adam in that long ago garden. Lush and beckoning, loaded with promises. "I'll show you exactly what I mean about a wife running her fingers slowly through her husband's hair. . . ."

He'd like that, like that a lot.

And so he stood there patiently, braced hard against the end of the huge library table.

Watched.

And waited.

Thoroughly unbridled.

Chapter 11

A man of sense only trifles with women, plays with them, humours and flatters them, as he does with a sprightly and forward child; but he neither consults them about, nor trusts them with, serious matters.

Earl of Chesterfield
Letters to His Son, 1748

She took long, lavish years in her approach, hips innocently tarty, shoulders swaying slightly, her eyes glinting at him with crystal fire in their depths.

And he was throbbing for her, a thick ache in his groin that only grew more unyielding with every step she took toward him.

"And do you teach this class yourself, Miss Dunaway?" he asked, just to keep his brain from exploding. And because he was suddenly beginning to wonder where she'd come by her "techniques."

"I teach sometimes."

"Sometimes, madam? I . . . Christ, woman!" He

nearly bucked backward as she brazenly stepped between his legs. Pushed right up against his erection.

"But the class was created by an experienced woman who knows about such things."

"Experienced? How, by God?" Not that he wanted to know.

"Let's just say that she was a professional woman in her day—"

"A prostitute?" Teaching a classroom full of aristocratic wives of aristocratic men? Good God!

"More than twenty years ago, before she married a member of the House of Lords who calls himself the most satisfied man in all of England."

He cast around in his head for a name, a peer. A man still in love with his wife.

But the rest of his thoughts went spinning out of control as the sublime Miss Dunaway then reached up with one hand and slipped her lithe fingers through the hair at his nape.

"Your hair is surprisingly soft here, my lord. If I were a wife, I would adore running my fingers through your hair like this."

She was actually killing him, slowly, scorching his skin, raking her short nails softly up the back of his head, the heat of her belly mixing with his at the apex of his legs, shocking him with its power.

"And, according to *Unbridled Embraces*, if you were my husband I would lean closely and gaze deeply into your eyes. Like this . . ."

She was doing more than that. She was dallying with his ear, teasing the ridges as her gaze feathered its way up his cheeks to his eyes, where he noticed for the first time an amazing pattern of gold embedded subtly in the aquiline.

"Goldenrod," he whispered, touching her cheek.

"What's that?"

"Your eyes. I see goldenrod."

"Then it's working." She smiled, her breath breaking against his chin.

"God, yes."

"In that case, my lord, next I would tell you how proud I am to be your wife."

His heart took a jump into his throat, cutting off his words. A stunning leap of elation, because it sounded so right.

"Then I'd thank you for my latest bonnet, and tell you that I bought it because I knew how much you'd like to see me in it. Do you?" She ruched her hand against her hair, tilted the imaginary hat, then turned her head from side to side, revealing the perfection of her profile.

"You're beautiful, wife." Wife? Good Lord! Did he just call her that? "I mean, Miss Dunaway."

"And how very brave you are, husband, the wife would say. And how intelligent—meaning every word, of course, because truth is the watchword of every successful marriage." She caught up her fingers in his neckcloth, still gazing, still a red-hot, pulsing heat between his legs, firing his brain to a brick.

"Truth, is it?" Because he was truthfully ready to toss that damned book across the room and put its lessons into practice.

"At this point, the wife would possibly run her palm over his chest or kiss him on the chin." She was breathing deeply, her eyes pools of brookwater, eddies of green and blue and gold, her cheeks flushed with the unintended passion of her own successful seduction.

Bloody hell! The woman was glorious. With a wanton heart and a spirit that thrilled him. He could take such delicious advantage of her innocence, of her eagerness to prove her revolutionary independence. But as she slipped her palm down the front of his chest, he pinned it flat with his own. Regretting it even as he warned her.

"Enough, madam."

"So you understand now, my lord?" Her eyes were half lidded as she gazed up at him, her knees sagging, her belly pressed fully against the bulge of his groin, nearly driving him mad with a roaring desire.

"I understand completely." Deeply, like a river of molten stone.

She straightened herself somewhat. "We teach nothing more scandalous here than that of paying attention to the one you love. At very close range."

"I noticed that too."

"It's only logical, my lord. After all, if I look into your eyes and search out all the colors there, all the meaning, then you must look into my eyes for just as long." She cupped his chin, frowned in concentration. "Right?"

"That's true."

"If I smile at you . . ." She did so, a lopsided, bewitching half grin. ". . . then you can't help but smile back at me."

Couldn't help it at all. Found himself falling toward a giddy smile of his own.

"If I kiss your mouth right here . . ." She leaned forward and touched just the corner of his mouth. ". . . you automatically kiss me right back."

God knows he shouldn't, dared only enough to catch the arc of her cheek, but remained there, resisting his deepest urges, reveling in her scent, his hands gripping her upper arms.

"And if I take your next breath, you must take mine."

Vanilla and chocolate, heated and sweet.

"My lord?" She suddenly leaned back from him, her hips still pressed against his, her eyes wide in amazement. "What is that here?"

The vixen shifted her hips against his rock-hardness just enough for him to understand her question.

To understand that his brazen instructor was indeed virginal to the marrow.

And killing him slowly, sweetly.

"You're the teacher, Miss Dunaway. Surely you are acquainted with the shape of the male anatomy when it is . . . fully engaged."

"When it's . . . ? Oh!" She gasped, then her eyes flew even wider, the jolt of discovery plain on her flushed face. "Oh, my! How amazing!"

"That, my dear, is the uncivilized reaction your eager sirens are finding in their unsuspecting husbands when they put your instructions into practice."

"As big as this? I had no idea!" She wriggled her belly against him again, more of a grinding movement, pulling an involuntary groan out of him. Then frowned and caught her lower lip between her teeth. "Ohhhh . . ."

"Yes, oh."

Any other man might have expected a fainthearted swoon from this unblushing innocent standing in the fork of his thighs, but Ross knew the woman better than that.

Wanted to know her even better.

Her beautiful eyes filled to the brim with a perilous gleam of adventure and then slyly dipped to the distended front of his trousers, her smile now a challenge to his tattered self-control.

"And this is a pleasant sensation for you?" More wriggling, more grinding. "This swelling?"

"Oh, yes, my dear. More than pleasant." The muscles in his arms had turned to quaking stone. His gut was on fire.

And her eyes were glinting mischief at him. "You've got me wondering, my lord, about what it looks like." Now she was flat out staring at his crotch. A starving woman eyeing a chocolate eclair.

"Sorry, Miss Dunaway, but you'll just have to keep wondering." A woman with fearless hands and that unquenchable sense of adventure. Not a chance in hell that he could keep control over that situation. At least not tonight.

Not with her grinning slyly up at him. "So, how did I do?"

"Do?"

"I've never practiced on an actual man before. Did I do all right with my seduction?"

Bloody hell, she'd done fine. So fine that his urge to finish what she'd started was shoving at his gut, pumping the breath from his lungs.

And so, with great regret, he set her a safe arm's length from him while he still had the moral courage.

"Madam," he said, standing away from the table, adjusting his clothes from her unexpected fondling, "if you'd done any better, I'm not sure I'd have lived through it."

She touched his arm, deep concern lining her brow. "Did I hurt you?"

Lord, she had a lot to learn, this guileless woman of seduction. And he suddenly couldn't imagine letting any other man teach her.

Or hold her.

Or kiss her for the first time.

"No, madam, you didn't hurt me in the least. I doubt you'd know how to."

"I certainly wouldn't want to!"

"Now, Miss Dunaway, if you'll please excuse me. I have some work to do before I come back here for the night."

Elizabeth watched the man leave the library. Specifically, watched his legs as he took his great strides through the doorway as though he couldn't wait to be away from her.

She stared blatantly at the power of his thighs, his calf muscles working hard against his trouser legs.

And those strong, broad shoulders that could carry her up and away. That could shelter her from the storms.

That could come between her and the rest of the world, which sometimes pressed too hard against her.

And his arms, so rippling thick with muscles, so visibly strong.

So inviting. As inviting as his eyes, his mouth.

And that marvelous phallus of his. Unbelievably thick and hard. Throbbing. With a life of its own.

Just a peek would have lasted her a lifetime without him.

But he seemed reluctant. And rightly so. He was a stranger. And one shouldn't fondle the private parts of a stranger, no matter how intriguing.

Just as one shouldn't kiss a stranger—

"Dear God, I kissed him." Just hauled off and planted her lips against his.

Nearly set her bodice on fire, shimmered against her skin, crackling ends of her hair.

Nearly let the man get away with her heart!

"Ah, there you are, Miss E!" Skye breezed into the library with a handful of papers. "And I see his lordship's gone."

"He is." Though she could still feel the heat of him in her belly, waves of him simmering up into her chest.

"A fine piece of work he is, don't you think?" The girl spread out a set of papers across the tabletop.

"He might be." Might be perfect. Too perfect to let herself be speculating about him any further. To be imagining him at breakfast, with the newspaper and his toast, and that sated, husbandly look in his eyes.

"Take my word for it." Skye grinned at her. "He's the kind of man that a girl wants to take home and keep."

"Is he?" Elizabeth laughed at the absurdity of the idea, and sighed out her regrets. A man to take home and kiss perhaps, but she couldn't keep him. There was too much at stake to risk on a permanent pleasure like the Earl of Blakestone. "You know as well as I that his lordship wouldn't fit very well in my home."

Skye frowned at her, clicking her tongue. "Perhaps not, but a girl can dream, can't she?"

"Only if that girl can get some sleep first." Feeling suddenly weary, Elizabeth bent over the papers. "What have you got here?"

"We sat around in the kitchen with Mrs. Bailey, plied her with more cocoa and orange cakes, talked a bit, you know, woman-to-woman. She even picked out the perfect hat. And we managed to tease out a few more facts that might help her find the best possible situation once she gets to New York."

"Amazing work, Skye, as usual. Thank you." Elizabeth spent the next half hour plotting Lydia's future with Skye, a big-hearted, beautiful young woman with the mind of a master criminal, plotting and scheming until finally the plan was clear and the arrangements were ready to be made.

And if she was going to make the convoluted travel arrangements in such a short amount of time, tonight would be the best window of opportunity for the next full week.

"All right, Skye, I'll leave you to make up an official schedule. Tomorrow will be fine. And I'll go see to the telegraphing."

Skye scowled fiercely. "You be careful down there, Miss Elizabeth. I don't know what sort of place it is, but if they ever find out . . ."

Whoever *they* are. "If they do, you know where I keep the bail money, don't you, Skye?"

But Skye didn't seem to appreciate that particular bit of humor. "You'll need this, Miss Elizabeth."

"Thanks." Elizabeth offered a pale apology and took Lydia's itinerary, feeling roundly chastised for being flip about such a real possibility.

She made a circuit of the Adams, checking on the few overnight guests, the kitchen, and the whereabouts of Blakestone's three unnecessary guards. It was well after midnight by the time she stepped into the back stairs and made her way down into the basement workrooms.

With any luck, her prescient earl wouldn't go looking for her once he returned from his own late night excursions, because she couldn't let him find her in the midst of her errand. Not where she was going.

She hung her oil lamp on a sconce hook in the corridor where it would cast just enough light to be a beacon when she returned, and then stepped into the long storage room. She worked her way through the dimly lit alleyways of crates and barrels to the large cabinet against the back wall.

The tallboy was empty inside, where she'd conveniently cleared it of its shelves. Which made it much easier for her to climb inside, slide the back off the cabinet, then push open the inmost and then the heavy, rusted iron outermost door that led through the cabinet into her secret passage.

She closed up the doors behind her and started forward into the long, dark passage that stretched out for an entire block under the street. It jogged and twisted and turned its way beneath what must have been some ancient medieval system of croft arches, until the passage finally ended at the backside of still another wooden door.

She put her ear to the panel, listened for a long time, but heard nothing of the footsteps or voices that she'd heard the first time she found her way through the odd passage.

Since then she'd learned that the vast complex of rooms beyond the panel were generally deserted after midnight, and her panel opened up into a tailor's shop behind convenient rows of clothes hanging against the back wall.

Still, she cracked open the door enough to make sure that the shop was dark, before pushing through and heading for the telegraph room.

Gaslights were burning low along the paneled passageways, as they usually did this time of night, softly lighting the various rooms in the elaborate underground installation.

A nameless headquarters of some sort. Probably a secret government building that she shouldn't be skulking around in. But she was hardly a risk to the security of the Empire. Besides, she was just borrowing a few services.

Because there was so much here to borrow.

What with a tailor's shop and a huge printing office, three different laboratories, and who knew what else locked behind heavy metal doors . . .

Still, she was grateful to have discovered the bank of telegraph machines. She could send private messages to her underground contacts without having to worry about the local telegraph operator remembering her or the subjects of her messages.

Secrecy was imperative in her activities. So was obscuring the trail of paper and plans and all the other clues that followed after her runaway heroines. Because their already miserable lives depended solely on her ability to camouflage and misdirect every step along the way.

Failure meant an angry husband or father or fiancé following the hapless woman to the ends of the earth. And then dragging her back to her own private hell.

She slipped into the telegraph room, vowing once again that she simply could never let that happen.

She'd learned telegraphy from the station master in her little village of Waverlock. He'd been a sweet-natured, childless old fellow who was everyone's grandfather. She'd often taken his place at the key when he was feeling under the weather, and had manned the station for a full month after he died.

But tonight she sent three messages, to three different contacts: one to Southampton, one to be sent via steamship to New York, and the third to the owner of an elegant but very private boardinghouse in Winston Quay. Each would reply to her in code, to any one of a dozen telegraph offices across London.

So far, so good.

But just as the thought slipped through her brain, she heard a door open somewhere above her.

Then a pair of male voices, then three of them, their words unclear.

But the sound of one of them made her pause and

listen dangerously long to the rumble of something oddly familiar.

And in the next moment she was too terrified to stick around and find out why. So she slipped silently out of sight through the wall of the tailor shop. But not without grabbing a boy's cap on her way out.

After all, she could always use another disguise.

"Wait, did you hear that?" Ross came to a halt at the bottom of the stairs, the hair at his nape lifting on end as he listened.

Jared stood stock-still beside him, and Drew on the step behind, both listening without comment until Ross broke the silence himself.

"Damnation, I could have sworn . . . no, wait!" He moved forward into the oddly moving air, sniffed at it, at the out-of-place scent. "There. Do you feel that?"

"Feel what exactly?" Drew raised his palm.

"That breeze. Where the devil is it coming from?"

Jared snorted lightly, then clapped him on the back and started toward the library. "Phantoms, Ross."

"Oh, phantoms is it, now?" Ross would have teased Jared further, but he recognized the sudden melancholy that had set into his jaw.

A phantom named Thomas. A past they would share until the end of their days.

"You know, he would have been thirty at the end of the month," Jared said, wrenching out of his jacket and hanging it on the coat tree. "Thirty, by God! That's makes me old."

"See here, Thomas!" Drew dropped his attaché case onto the table with a thunk and looked up at the chandelier. "If you are the one who's been bumping around here at night, we'd appreciate you raising a fright under that bastard Nicholas in St. Petersburg."

"Along with his bloody ambassador here in London," Ross said from the map wall, yanking at the cords of two different maps before finally rolling down the map of Europe and the Ottoman Empire.

Jared laughed. "Frankly, I'd settle for old Thomas shutting down the *Times* for a few days. Delane has everyone on the street taking sides in a conflict they know nothing about."

"And suddenly all things Turkish have become the height of fashion."

"What the hell is Stratford up to, Ross?" Jared stuck his fists into his pockets as he stared at the map. "Is he truly whispering into the sultan's ear to reject anything Russia throws his way?"

"Bloody hell, Jared, if he isn't, he should be. Why would anyone advise the leader of a country to hand over his empire to his enemies?"

"Because the war is, after all, inevitable, Ross. Because the Russian tsar has equipped hundreds of thousands of soldiers with the most modern weaponry and they are perched on the sultan's backside?"

"Modern weaponry, Jared?" Ross dug around in his attaché for the folio with his report. "Are you sure? Where do you suppose they bought these cannons? I haven't found a source, and I've looked in all the usual places."

"Like Jared said, Ross, the war is going to happen, sooner or later. At least according to Caro, who knows all the players."

"Because she's related to all of them," Jared said.

"Now there's a brain you should pick, Ross," Drew said. "We'll be at the charity ball."

"I might just do that. Maybe your wife can give me a hint about those bloody Austrians. They're as slippery as a box of newts."

Drew laughed and leaned against the edge of the table. "Say, Ross, how's your beautiful little revolutionary?"

Jared turned back from staring at the map. "What's this, Ross? A revolutionary what?"

"Nothing." At least he'd thought it was nothing. That she was nothing. An impossibility.

Drew wiggled his eyebrows like the utter devil he was. "Ross has been seeing a woman."

"Really? Which woman? Not Captain Tyson's daughter from last season? I couldn't bear that laugh. Please don't make me live through Twelfth Night and Easter and every last holiday of my life with that laugh."

"This one's much better than the hyena, Jared." Drew, the lout, knuckled Ross in the upper arm. "He met her in a jail cell at Scotland Yard."

"A jail cell?"

Ross sighed, knowing he'd been trapped again. "It's a long story."

Jared narrowed his eyes at him. "Sounds serious, Ross."

Drew answered for him. "I think it is."

"It's not."

"Sit." Jared pulled up a chair and shoved Ross into it. "Tell me all about it. Everything. Because Kate will have my head if I don't wrench every last detail out of you."

Somehow he thought Jared would say that.

Kate was that kind of woman.

Caro too.

Sublimely perfect in every way.

And until recently, he believed there were only two such women in the world.

Now it seemed there might be three.

Chapter 12

A king is always a king—and a woman always a woman; his authority and her sex ever stand between them and rational converse.

Mary Wollstonecraft,
A Vindication of the Rights of Woman

"**A**nd I'll have another copy of that perfectly shocking Mary Wollstonecraft, please," the elegantly dressed woman was saying to Skye as Elizabeth entered the bookshop from the street. "I want to take this one to my sister."

"Good afternoon, Mrs. Farnham." Elizabeth sat the box of books on the counter beside the woman, then exchanged a quick embrace with her.

"Oh, indeed it is, my dear," Mrs. Farnham said from under the massive brim of her lavish hat. "*A Vindication of the Rights of Woman*. Ha! That ought to send my blockheaded brother-in-law right into a fit of apoplexy. Doesn't like his wife getting above herself, you know. If my sister doesn't stand up for herself, then I'll just have to do it for her."

189

Dear Mrs. Farnham, the crusading widow, with all the force of a cyclone and all the money in the world to spread her newfound cry of freedom.

"Knowledge is power, Mrs. Farnham."

"From your lips to Parliament's ear, my dear Elizabeth! See you at the charity ball!" The woman took her paper-wrapped package by its silk ribbon handle, then dashed out of the shop, nearly colliding with Jessica and Cassie as they entered, each with their own boxes.

"Thank God, you two made it safely across that bloody street." The traffic was a gauntlet of London's most lunatic drivers. Crossing at any time of the day or night, especially with an armload of boxes, was a risk to life and limb. "I really need to move the book-shop into the Adams. Maybe connect it to the tea shop, or at least have it on the same side of the street. I can't have you dodging death every time you take a simple trip to the bookshop."

"Now, where'd be the fun in that, Miss E?" Skye was already two steps up the ladder, unloading the new books onto the shelves.

"You three already risk enough for me and the Adams." Prison time the least of it.

"All in a good day's work, right, ladies?"

As usual, Cassie's cheery disposition drew a rasp-berry from Jessica.

"Oh, Miss Elizabeth, before I forget—this came for you just moments after you left your office." Jessica handed her a telegram, then set to work dusting the display in the front window. "Good news, I hope."

"It very well could be, Jess. It's from Mrs. Frederick, in Winston Quay." Elizabeth unfolded the telegram and quickly read through the elaborate hand-writing. " 'Eagerly awaiting special package. Send anytime. Will forward per instructions.' Excellent. At least Lydia will have a safe place to stay before she—"

"Oh! Why, look, Miss Elizabeth! We have a customer!" Skye spoke overly loud, then jerked an eyebrow subtly toward the sunlight glaring in through the doorway.

But it wasn't a real customer.

It was him. Blakestone. The amazing man she had tried to seduce three nights before, bits of sunlight lighting his broad shoulders, making a halo of his hair.

"Good afternoon, Miss Dunaway." Such a rumbling, compelling voice, reaching out for her from across the bookstore.

She'd missed the sound of him, the encompassing sense of him. Three nights, three days, with only the briefest contact, had been too long to be without his teasing banter, his taunting smile.

"Good afternoon, my lord." Elizabeth tucked the telegram into her apron pocket, her fingers afire with the sudden need to hide it from him. "Welcome to the Bookbox."

But he was turning away from her, gesturing behind him. "Come in, my ladies, if you want to meet the remarkable Miss Dunaway . . ."

Remarkable? With that odd introduction, two of the most enchanting women Elizabeth had ever seen swept into the bookstore, locked eager eyes with her, grinned at each other, then made a beeline toward her.

"Miss Elizabeth Dunaway," Blakestone said, standing directly behind them, a most charmingly fond smile tucked into the corners of his eyes, "it's my great pleasure to introduce Princess Caroline—"

"Lady *Wexford!*" the young woman at his left said sweetly, from between her perfect white teeth. "It's Lady Wexford, Ross. How many times do I have to remind you?"

"Sorry, Princess." He didn't seem at all sorry; as though he was as perfectly used to teasing the woman as she was to teasing him right back. "Miss Elizabeth Dunaway, this is Lady Wexford, the ex-Princess of Boratania."

Oh, *that* princess! The one who had given up her whole kingdom for the love of her life. At least that had been the gossip at the time. A full two years ago, and she still looked radiant.

Elizabeth began to sweep into her best curtsy, but the princess had already taken her hand, as though to terminate the gesture.

"I'm very pleased to meet you, Miss Dunaway. So very pleased. We both are. This is Lady Hawkesly." She handed off Elizabeth to the other grinning woman.

"Truly delighted, Miss Dunaway." Lady Hawkesly drew her close as she shot a glance up over her shoulder at the imposing man behind them. "Ross claims that he's told us everything he knows about you and the Abigail Adams. But he's a man; and you know how men are."

She was beginning to know how this particular man was. His smile, the deep, deep brown of his eyes.

"He didn't tell us you also owned a bookstore, did you now, Ross?"

"A woman of initiative." Lady Hawkesly winked at

Elizabeth, her smile dazzling. "And utterly beautiful as well! How did you manage, Ross?"

Manage? Elizabeth rarely found herself speechless, but she was completely without words at the moment. With a wad of evidence in the abduction cases stashed in her pocket, a supply of *French letters* hidden in the storage room, a princess and company treating her like a long-lost sister standing in her bookstore. Her three steadfast companions cowering together behind the counter.

And Blakestone, looking quite pleased with himself through all the teasing, following her every move, the heat of his glance slipping into the thrum of her pulse.

"I'm very glad to meet both of you," Elizabeth finally managed, beginning to feel her old spiky self again. "Lord Blakestone told me he had friends, but frankly, I didn't actually believe him until now."

The women laughed and Lady Wexford nudged the stoic Blakestone in the ribs. "Take care, Ross. She's miles ahead of you."

"Leagues and leagues, Princess." There was that smile again, cocky and wry and clinging too tightly to her heart.

Lady Hawkesly was scanning the shelves now. "Caro, just look at these titles. All the Brontës, both the Brownings, Shakespeare, children's books."

"Shelves of Dickens and Trollope and every magazine imaginable. Even writing cases and a lovely collection of tortoiseshell pens."

And while the two amazing women converged at the counter and swiftly put her three assistants to work with their requests to see this book and that teapot, Elizabeth could feel Blakestone's presence at her back, warm and rousing, reaching out to her.

"I knew you managed a bookstore, madam," he whispered above her head. His breath steamed against her hair, his broad hand shaped intimately against her waist. "But you told me nothing of being the proprietor as well."

"I didn't think I needed to, Blakestone." She turned slightly, whispering up at him. "After all, you knew about my aunts, and my financial status. The color of my favorite stockings. My slipper size. I assumed you knew everything about me."

"The more I learn about you, Miss Dunaway, the more I realize that I don't know a thing. But that's not the point. I told you I don't want you traveling anywhere without a bodyguard."

"Don't be ridiculous."

He spun her easily to face his frowning anger. "Good God, woman, how many times a day do you cross that very busy street to come here to the store?"

"Two or three." More, but she didn't want to alarm him further.

"Don't you see the danger? A kidnapper who is bent on eliminating the Abigail Adams by eliminating you has merely to study your methodical movements, wait for the perfect moment, and then snatch you into his black carriage on your way across the street and you're never seen again."

For the first time she could see the genuine fear in his eyes. Intimate, caring.

Oh, what a shameful spot to put him in. Allowing

him to do battle against a phantom that she had conjured herself.

"It won't happen, my lord."

"It already has. Three times."

Not exactly. She was in complete control of the kidnapping situation.

Though she was quickly losing control of her heart, her sense of guilt. The remarkable earl had taken on the case with an uncompromising ferocity. Leaving no stone unturned.

No clue undiscovered, no question unasked.

Her heart tangled up in the tailings, while she planned still another kidnapping.

She could only hope and pray that he would never catch the perpetrator. Because he didn't seem inclined to compassion for those who deceived him.

And she was doing just that. Openly. Freely.

He probably despised such people to the depths of his soul, and that would be impossibly difficult to bear.

Because under all that bluster, beneath that fierce scowl, was a good man with an unyielding sense of honor.

"What I do know, madam, is that every lead I've followed in these three kidnapping cases, every speck of evidence, has come to an absolute dead end."

What a great relief. But for reasons so different than she ever could have imagined.

"As though these women never existed after the moment they were abducted."

Even better. Because he'd never have to discover the extent of her falsehoods. As long as she remained clearheaded in her decisions and meticulous in her methods.

"What do you think that means, my lord? Professional kidnappers?"

"It means that once you've been taken, madam, you'd be gone for good, just like the others." He held tightly to her upper arms, nearly growling at her, his voice low and coming from deep inside him. "And by God, I wouldn't like that one damn bit."

She was about to ask him why, when she heard Skye come beside her, whispering,

"Miss Elizabeth, may we give the two ladies samples of the creamy chocolates from Coraleigh's Confections? Nothing like word-of-mouth advertising to help Miss Cora find steady customers."

Elizabeth turned and nodded, a bit dizzied by the earl's intensity. "A fine idea, Skye, please do."

"Delicious!" The candy disappeared in a flurry of female whimpering that left her haunting exchange with Blakestone unfinished, her heart wanting more of him.

"And now, Miss Dunaway," the princess said, her eyes twinkling as she handed her brown-wrapped paper bundle to Ross, "about this ladies' club of yours. . . ."

"Yes, yes, how do we join?" Lady Hawkesly stuffed her package under Ross's free arm.

"Join? You?" Why would either of these highly accomplished, so obviously independent women need to belong to a scandalous ladies' club?

"I don't think that's wise, my ladies." Blakestone frowned down upon the room.

"Why?" Lady Hawkesly shot back, her chin thrust at him.

"Because . . . well . . ." He looked suddenly wordless, sheepish as they stared hard at him. "Shouldn't you consult with your . . . never mind."

"Oh, pish-tosh, Ross." The princess waved him off in a playfully regal way and hooked Elizabeth's arm with her own. "Now, Miss Dunaway, if you don't mind, we'd love to see the Abigail Adams for ourselves."

They were out the door a moment later and plowing across the street like the prow of a great galleon, the traffic miraculously coming to a complete stop in the wake of the ex-Princess Royal of Boratania and her entourage, including the tall, brooding earl and his leagues-long stride, pulling up the rear.

The royal tour of the Abigail Adams included nearly every inch of the club, except the cellar and the guest room floor, finally ending in the foyer, where they had left Blakestone behind in the visitors' parlor, where he'd taken up residence like a palace guard.

"You've done a perfectly wonderful job, Miss Dunaway," the princess said, "with everything. A true home away from home."

"A den of revolutionaries." Ross hadn't meant to speak aloud, but now every female head had turned to him in the doorway of his cave, as though he had just tossed his boot into their punch bowl.

"What I mean, ladies, is . . . a place where you can kick off your shoes and exchange . . . never mind." He'd been about to say recipes, but decided he would rather live.

More silent scrutiny. Kate had begun to slowly shake her head at him.

Miss Dunaway raised a tolerant brow at him. "Thank you, Lord Blakestone."

Then they all went back to their animated discussion, as though he hadn't spoken at all.

Which was just fine. He had plenty of things to do before his meeting with the Lord High Admiral.

He had just decided to leave his two charges to the princess's burly driver and the carriage that was parked in the drive up when Hawkins burst from his little side room and threw open the front door to block the way of two men.

"Sorry, sirs, but this is a ladies' club—"

"You were right, Jared, they're still here!" Drew and Jared both stalked past the befuddled Hawkins and into the foyer, then went straight to their wives.

Jared lifted Kate's hand to his lips. "Have you forced the women's vote on Parliament, my love?"

"Tomorrow, sweet. Afternoon session."

"Don't tell me you're checking up on us, Drew," Caro said as her husband collected her into his arms for a quick waltz around the floor.

"Never more, my dear. I had enough of watching your every move two years ago to last me a lifetime."

Bloody ballocks, Ross thought. The man was, and always would be, a hawk when it came to his princess and their new little son.

And damned if he wasn't beginning to understand why. Even now he found himself intently watching Elizabeth, who was herself closely watching the two effusive couples in their own *Unbridled Embraces*. A smile of wonder in her brilliant eyes, a softness to her brow.

Happiness in marriage, my dear rebel. It's possible.
He'd seen it. Felt it in his dreams.

And as though she had heard his thoughts, she
turned her head and met his gaze, a worried smile now
caught between her teeth, her eyes glinting like emer-
alds. His heart stuttered at the sudden intimacy, dancing sideways before it righted itself.

"Hey, Ross! This came for you at the Huntsman."
Drew left Caro with the others long enough to hand
him a message, a serious cant to his brow. "From the
Foreign Office."

"A declaration of war, do you suppose?" Ross
asked wryly as Jared joined them, weary of the tangle
of personalities as he thumbed open the envelope and
gave the message a quick scan. "Ah, not quite yet.
Merely a few tempers to soothe."

"The Austrians?" Jared asked. "Or the French?"

"The Russians this time." Ross tried to read
Clarendon's dashed-off message, but the man's hand
was nearly inscrutable. "Apparently one of their
diplomatic couriers was knocked down this morning
in Euston Station by someone who wanted his attaché
case badly enough to try to grab it in broad daylight as
he stepped off the train."

"Please tell me the Russian courier is alive."

"Apparently alive and kicking, Drew," Ross answered to the group now gathered around them.
"Now, if you'll excuse us, ladies, Drew and I have to
pay an official visit to the Russian Embassy."

But Caro persisted, the most doggedly curious

woman in the world. "Did they get the attaché case, Ross?"

"Apparently not, madam." Ross folded up the note and stuck it into his pocket before the woman could decide to join the hunt. "Come, Drew. And no, Princess, you can't come along."

"But I can help. I know Brunnov's weaknesses. He's terrified of spiders—"

"That's why Ross said no, my love. Jared and Kate will see you get home safely."

Drew gave his wife the smacking good kiss that Ross suddenly wished he could give to Elizabeth, and a very few minutes later he and Drew were on their way in a hackney to the Russian Embassy to forestall a political scandal.

"So, Ross, why exactly are we racing over to the embassy? No harm's been done. Making more of the confrontation than it actually is will only aggravate the situation."

"A diplomatic mission. Clarendon's request."

"Ah, we're to soothe Brunnov's temper. Maybe we should have brought Caro."

"The ambassador's blaming Aberdeen's government."

"For a simple robbery attempt?"

"He's making noises about an intentional act of sabotage by the British Foreign Office."

"That's absurd."

"But it's got everyone dancing to his music. He's demanding that Scotland Yard and the Foreign Office investigate the assault. And insists upon an apology not only from the prime minister, but Victoria herself."

"That's not going to happen any time soon." Drew leaned back against the coach seat, his longtime distinction as the queen's favorite diplomat granting him an invaluable insight into the woman's personality. "At least not an apology from the queen."

"Which is why Clarendon wants us to defuse the situation immediately—"

"Express Her Majesty's concern for the Russian mission in London—"

"Without actually issuing a formal apology." Ross rubbed at his suddenly aching shoulder. "Bloody hell, Drew, I hate this. I'm a soldier, not a nanny. How do you stand it?"

"Diplomacy," Drew said with a grunt, "is not for the faint of heart."

A quarter hour later they were met at the door of the Russian Embassy by a liveried page, then ushered into the elaborate receiving room.

They waited the obligatory ten minutes until the deputy ambassador finally strode in with his effusive apologies for keeping them waiting, though he knew as well as they did that he had purposely lingered upstairs the prescribed length of time, and that they had been expecting him to do just that.

"Diplomacy," Drew had whispered again.

The other formalities rang just as dry and hollow to Ross, and their questions about the assault on the courier were expertly deflected. As though the targeted attaché case had held something of a highly delicate nature.

Troop movements, weapon strength, fleet conditions, the royal pearls.

"If we might speak with the courier himself—"

The deputy ambassador shook his nattily coiffed head firmly. "I'm afraid that's not possible, Lord Blakestone. He is indisposed."

Ross heard Drew's muffled grunt beside him on the settee, but tried again. "We wish merely to ask him a few questions about the incident—"

"You may ask me, my lord. He has told me everything."

"Then shall we start from the beginning, Mr. Deputy Ambassador? Were you—I mean, was your courier—able to get a description of the man who attempted to grab the attaché case?"

"Well, now as I understand it, Lord Blakestone . . ."

By the time they left the Russian Embassy, Ross's notepad was a snarled web of the deputy ambassador's wild-ass suspicions, pointing the blame at nearly everyone the man could imagine, including Prince Albert, and the President of the United States.

He dropped Drew off at his town house, where Caro yanked open the door with young Andrew in her arms and pulled him inside with a quick wave to Ross in the carriage.

They made it look so simple.

When he knew very well that their road had been long and difficult, a road he would gladly take should the right woman ever come into his life.

A woman with a warm, deliciously rebellious spirit.

The sort who couldn't be flattered.

Or cajoled.

Who wouldn't turn from a challenge.

Or walk away from an injustice.

Bloody hell! What was it Drew had said about diplomacy? That it wasn't for the faint of heart.

But then neither was protecting Elizabeth Dunaway.

"Oh, I hate jam pots!" Elizabeth held her breath, gripped the lid of the jar with all her might, then put all her weight into a grunting twist.

"Blast it all!" She let up on the pressure. The lid was glued down by its own sweetness. And she dearly wanted to top off her late night crumpet with the last of the cook's brandied cherry preserves.

It was after eleven; all the staff was in bed. However, Blakestone's guards weren't. They never slept.

But they were always hungry, always courteous and ready to help.

She quickly set up a tray for the night man in the drive up, including the stubborn pot of preserves, and slipped from the kitchen through the darkened tea room and into the foyer. But as she approached the front door, she noticed a light flickering around the door frame of Blakestone's makeshift office and couldn't help looking inside.

Now, here was a man who could open a jam pot! Among other feats of strength and daring.

She set the tray on the entry table, took the pot with her to the door, then peered through the cracked opening.

He was bent over the desk, his fingers raked through his dark hair, his arm propping up his forehead. He was shuffling papers across the surface.

"Lord Blakestone?"

He whirled around and shot to his feet, looking so vulnerable in his shirtsleeves and waistcoat.

"Can I help you, Miss Dunaway?"

She felt utterly ridiculous now, with the pot of preserves and her petty request. But she held out the pot anyway.

"Can you open this please, my lord?"

"With the greatest pleasure." He smiled like a rogue, then drew himself up, even flexed an arm muscle for her, before he got a grip on the lid and opened the pot with ease.

"Thank you." She felt even more ridiculous as he handed it back to her. "Sorry. I had a craving for brandied cherry preserves."

"Please, I appreciate the friendly face." He leaned back against the desk and winced slightly as he began to absently knead a muscle in his shoulder.

"Working late I see."

"There's never enough time during the day." He yawned and rolled his shoulder. "If it isn't a diplomatic uproar, it's the Lord Mayor wanting to know how far I've come in the investigation of the abductions."

"No luck?"

"It's the most frustrating case I've ever worked on. Utterly useless evidence."

She felt like a traitor asking the question. "Useless?"

"Our serial kidnapper has used the same manufactured glove in each of his three crimes. Made by a factory in Manchester. As undistinctive as a copper penny." He dropped into the desk chair, looking weary and pained by his shoulder.

Which made her feel even more guilty. "Did you hurt yourself?"

He snorted a laugh. "A little over a year ago. Took a bayonet across my shoulder, and it sometimes stiffens up."

"A bayonet?" Dear Lord, she'd forgotten he was a soldier. In constant danger. "How did it happen?"

"Carelessness on my part. I put myself in a sticky situation and I lost. Well, nearly so."

Feeling like she ought to do something for the man's obvious pain, she put down the pot of brandied cherries and went to his side. "Can I try something?"

He cast her a doubting look. "Be my guest."

"It might hurt at first." She stood behind him, fit her hands around his shoulder, and the first squeeze of his muscles bucked him backward with a groan of obvious relief.

"Oh, God, thank you!"

"My pleasure." Distinctly so. She smiled as she worked at the muscle, amazed at the power contained beneath her hands. Ashamed of prodding him about the abductions, but unable to stop herself.

"I'm sorry the culprit has given you such trouble."

"Trouble is putting it mildly, my dear. The blackguard uses a standard mixture of chloroform, obtainable in large quantities from any one of a thousand chemists in London alone."

She kneaded slightly deeper, lower on his arm, and her patient let out a long, low groan, went lank and loose, then slumped and stuck his legs out in front of him.

"A pity, my lord." But all for the best. "Is the other evidence as troublesome?"

"As for the Wallace hat—oh, God, that feels good." He sighed and rolled his head. "There's not a shop within a fifty mile radius of the city that will lay claim to its apparently unfashionable design. The same goes for the hats from the other crimes."

Because Jessica makes all the distinctively ugly hats in the workroom of the Abigail Adams, not three dozen steps from where they were.

"We do, however, know that—oh, yes, right there, Miss Dunaway." He groaned and sighed and made her want to kiss the back of his neck and his temple. But she had to keep her senses about her as she quizzed her opponent.

"What is it you know, my lord?"

He roused some, tried to sit up, but slumped again. "We know that the feathers of the Wallace hat were pheasant."

"Well, that's something, my lord."

This time he groaned in exasperation. "But only if our kidnapper happens to be a pheasant."

"We'll just have to hope for the best then, won't we?"

Though she hadn't the faintest idea what the best could possibly be.

In the course of the next three days, Ross made dozens of trips between the Russian Embassy, the Austrian Embassy, the French Embassy, and the Foreign Office, and the world was still on the brink.

His own world had come to a halt. He'd seen Elizabeth all of four times in passing. Each time leaving his thoughts more battered and bruised than the time before.

She'd begun to fill his dreams and the quiet part of his days. He craved her touch and her scent. Looked for her around every corner.

And prayed that she wouldn't do anything foolish while this madman was still on the loose.

Now he was sitting in the map room of the Huntsman, preparing still another report for the late night session of Parliament. Where he would spend hours in a stifling room, just off the Commons, on call with nonsecret facts for the Foreign Secretary and the Lord Admiral about French and Russian ship movements in the Mediterranean. The ministers would then use these facts as they were needed in the open debate over the possibility of war in the Crimea.

A war that seemed ever more probable as the tsar played his games so near the brink.

And the Austrians dithered.

And Napoleon watched with glee.

By eight o'clock he was finished and gathering up his reports when Pembridge appeared at the door, his collar and cuffs as crisp as morning.

"Excuse me, sir, but there's a young lady here to see you."

Elizabeth! He steadied his rocketing pulse and tried to sound cool-headed. "Green eyes, Pembridge? Hair a reddish-blond, unruly?"

"Bluish eyes, sir. Hair tending toward the golden from what I could tell from beneath her bonnet."

Not Elizabeth? "Did she give her name?" Ross stuffed his portfolio with the ship reports.

"She did, after I calmed her down and put her into the receiving room."

"Calmed her down?"

"A Miss Jessica Fallon, from the Abigail Adams, sir. In quite a panic. Said something about a Miss Dunaway needing your help."

"Bloody hell!"

Ross arrived at the receiving room at a dead run, terrified to find the normally unflappable Miss Fallon, wringing her hands inside her apron.

"There you are, sir!"

Ross grabbed her by the upper arms. "Where's Elizabeth? Is she all right? Please tell me she hasn't been abducted."

"That's it exactly, my lord!" Tears welled, then streamed out of her eyes, spiking her lashes. "Stolen right out of the tea room at the Adams!"

Christ! Resisting the urge to bolt after the woman— which would do no good without more information— Ross plunked the startled Miss Fallon into a chair. "Sit. Now, tell me exactly what happened."

She snuffled back her fear and spoke clearly. "We were closing up the shop about an hour ago when three officers from Scotland Yard came bursting through the front door, demanding to see Miss Elizabeth."

From Scotland Yard? Or were they kidnappers in disguise. "Are you sure the men were actually policemen?"

She narrowed her eyes as he'd so often seen Elizabeth do. "Oh, yes, sir, they were definitely policemen. We demanded to see their identification before they went a step farther. Then one of them asked for Miss Elizabeth again, and when she came out of the kitchen, he stuck a piece of paper into her hand and told her she was under arrest."

"Arrested?" Not abducted. "Arrested for what?"

Surely not for marching in the street.

"She didn't say, my lord; it all happened so quickly. But she went white as a ghost when she read the warrant. And then they just took her away. In handcuffs! Though she didn't resist at all."

Damnation! "Please, Miss Fallon, are you absolutely certain these men were from Scotland Yard?"

"Believe me, my lord, I know what a policeman's uniform looks like close up. Besides, Skye and I followed the cart all the way into Whitehall. And that's where they took her."

Thank God for resourceful young women.

And for the strong cell doors in Scotland Yard, because, for the first time in the few weeks that he'd known her, Elizabeth Dunaway was safe from herself.

And doubtless she was spitting mad.

Which made him ask, "Did she tell you to find me, Miss Fallon?"

"Not likely, my lord. She wouldn't then, would she? Not you. But the three of us thought you'd know just what to do for her. Whether she likes it or not."

Indeed. "Thank you for coming to me, Miss Fallon." He picked up his nearly forgotten report case and headed toward the door. "Come along with me."

She followed on his heels. "Are we going to go break Miss Elizabeth out of jail?"

He had no doubt the charming young woman

would jump at the chance to try. "I'm going to drop you at the Adams, my dear, and then I'm going to pay a call on Miss Dunaway."

"You'll make them release her, won't you? Please, sir!" The girl grabbed two bold fistsful of his lapels and held him in place with a strength he couldn't have imagined. "She's done nothing wrong!"

Nothing, except to taunt authority with a march down Whitehall in front of hundreds of witnesses. As well as that dust-up in Parliament.

Someone in power might just be trying to teach uppity women a lesson in humility. And he damn well wasn't going to let that happen.

"Miss Elizabeth will be home tonight, Miss Fallon, if I have to saw through the bars myself."

"Oh, thank you, sir!"

Though the real question was: where would home be?

Should he let her stew in jail while he was attending the debate in Parliament, or rescue her immediately, permanently, as he yearned to do.

In any case, just to be safe he made a quick visit across the Thames to the Archbishop of Canterbury. And by the time he left Lambeth Palace for the debates at Westminster, he was armed to the teeth with all the tools he would need to deliver his bewitchingly troublesome rebel from the evil clutches of Scotland Yard.

Right into the hands of her worst enemy.

Chapter 13

Do not put such unlimited power into the hands of husbands. Remember, all men would be tyrants if they could.

Abigail Adams, to her husband, John
March 31, 1776

"Excuse me, please! I'd like a blanket." Elizabeth clutched at the familiar bars in the cell door, her fingers as bloodless and cold as the iron rods. "Anyone there?"

But her voice carried down the empty, dimly lighted hall like a reedy echo, spending itself long before it could reach the front desk.

Not that rousting one of the officers would help. It was well after ten and there was a small but watchful contingent of men on guard against her escape. No one had offered a single shred of compassion or concern when she was brought in. Why would they care now if she was a little cold? A little scared. For all they knew, she was just another woman picked up off the street for selling herself to keep food in her children's bellies.

At least that would be a simpler crime to explain than the litany of legal trouble she'd stuck into her pocket. A warrant so long that she might never again see the light of day.

Worst of all, she would never see Blakestone again.

Except possibly if he ever felt charitable enough or curious enough to come visit her in prison after her multiple convictions.

Disturbing the peace!

Bank fraud!

Distributing salacious materials!

Charges that were complete exaggerations. Merely her petty efforts to enlighten the ignorant and emancipate the imprisoned.

And yet here she was, imprisoned herself, her teeth chattering with the cold. In sore need of one last chiding by her unforgiving earl, one last chance to look into those coal dark eyes.

But one thing was certain: she'd never survive if she allowed herself to succumb to this sudden weepy feeling. She banished it and climbed up on the narrow plank bench for a glimpse out the window.

The glass was cracked beyond the bars and filthy. But she could still make out a single star through a wedge of open sky, could smell the velvety moonlight pouring in on the chilly air.

Freedom. It seemed so terribly remote just now. So very precious.

"Disturbing the peace, madam?"

"Blakestone!" she whispered. Her heart took a soaring leap as she whirled around on the bench.

He was standing at the door, in the same place he'd

been the very first time she'd seen him. Every inch as large, now a profound presence in her life, a warmth in her belly.

And more thunderously angry than she'd ever seen him.

"Bank fraud?" The charge blustered from him, rattling the iron fittings and the stone flags that stretched out between them.

"Good evening, my lord." Her voice had gone as creaky as her joints.

"Distributing salacious materials? By God, woman!" He was bellowing now like a bull elephant in full rut as he dragged a cowering policeman into view from behind him. "Dammit, officer, open this bloody door immediately!"

"What are you thinking, Blakestone?" She ran to the door. "No, officer, don't listen to him!"

She didn't know what she wanted just now, but it wasn't to be rescued by this bear of a man with dark fire spitting from his eyes.

"Sorry, ma'am." The timid young man was reaching for the lock with the huge ring of keys in his quaking hands. "Orders from the Lord Mayor. I'm to release you to your husband here."

"The Lord Mayor? My *what*?"

Husband?

The door clanked open and she backed away as Blakestone came through it like a war wagon. "When I get you home, wife, I'm going to paddle you good."

Wife?

"Paddle me? Like hell you are, Blakestone! Don't you come a step closer!" Elizabeth dodged out of his long reach, leaping back onto the bench and pressing herself against the cold stone wall.

Which only gave him better access to her to break her out of jail!

"There's a lesson in all this, lad," the blackguard earl said to the officer, ignoring her protests and her battering hands as he wrapped his arms around her hips and flung her over his shoulder like a sack. "If you want a happy home, keep your woman barefoot in the kitchen, and large with child."

"Oh, yessir!"

"How dare you! I'm not your wife, Blakestone!" She kicked out at him and squirmed. But he had clamped one arm over her backside, and was holding her legs flat against his chest with the other, leaving her to look backward into the face of the policeman. "He's not my husband!"

"There you go sassing at me again, woman!" Blackstone swatted her bottom with the gentlest hand, then held it there, his fingers spread possessively, intimately. "Give your wife a sniff of freedom, lad, and she's likely to start disowning you in public."

"Cor, I'll remember that, sir!" The officer was trailing eagerly after them, staring up at Elizabeth perched on Blakestone's shoulder, his eyes wide with admiring awe at the domineering treatment she was receiving from her conquering warlord.

"And I'll remember this outrage, Blakestone!" she said, whipping back to him.

"I should hope so, wife."

Wife, again!

"Damn you, I'm not your wife! Don't believe him, officer! Now let me go!"

But the lout was already stomping down the stairs into the courtyard, leaving the young officer waving at them from the stoop, defying the law!

"Keep still, madam, or I'll leave you right here in jail where you belong!" He stood her for an instant on the carriage step then pressed her backward into the darkness and onto the upholstered seat.

"Then please leave me here, Blakestone! I have to stay!"

"No, you don't." He slammed the door shut.

"You just broke me out of jail!"

"You're welcome, madam." He knocked on the side of the carriage and it plunged forward.

"Don't you understand, Blakestone? Thanks to you, I'm now a fugitive from Scotland Yard!" Hoping for a chance to right this horrible gaff, she waited until he turned to take the bench opposite before she reached across to grab the door latch. But he was there first, his hand a vise around hers.

"You're staying here with me, madam." He removed her hand and drew her back onto the bench beside him, then wrapped his arms around her, holding her fast, hip-to-hip, her back fit against his chest. "Now, sit still and behave yourself."

"*Me* behave myself? What about you? You just told that gullible young officer a bold-faced lie and then snatched me from the custody of the Metropolitan Police under false pretenses."

"Actually, I didn't." He was staring out the window in the carriage door, watching for something, his chin raised and squared off in his resolve.

"Are you mad, Blakestone?" She twisted in his arms and glared up at him, still stunned that the law-abiding earl would have actually broken her out of jail. "I've been charged with three serious felonies."

"Yes, I know, love."

"When Captain Robins learns that I skipped out in the middle of the night with an accomplice who claimed that I was his wife, and that the Lord Mayor had ordered my release into your care, they'll come looking for me. And when they find me, they're going to throw away the key."

He dropped his gaze to hers, his mouth wolfish as he turned her chin toward him with the end of his finger. "No one will come looking for you, Elizabeth, because the charges have been dropped."

Her heart went racing like the wind, riding a miracle. "What do you mean? How do you know that?"

"I know because I arranged your release with the Lord Mayor."

"You did . . . oh, you blackguard!" She ought to be throwing herself around his neck and kissing him for the relief that flooded her. Instead she wanted to throttle him! "You think you can just walk into my life and sweep up after me!"

"Believe me, it badly needed sweeping!"

"Then I will do it."

"Actually, madam, the deed has been done. Or will be done before the night is over. Come hell, high water, or an ill-tempered suffragist."

"What do you mean by that?" The man had tangled his fingers in the ends of her hair, was looking at her with a good deal of heat and hunger. "Do you and the Lord Mayor plan to hang me in secret before dawn?"

"We considered it."

"But you'd rather humiliate me instead." Then something in the unusual rocking of the carriage made her struggle out of his arms and put her face to the window. "Wait a minute! This isn't the way to the Adams."

"No, it's not."

"And that was St. Paul's Cathedral." She whirled back to him. "Where are you taking me?"

He smiled. "To a wedding."

"A what? A wedding?" She pressed her nose against the window, just to prove the darkness to herself. "But it's after midnight!"

She turned back to find him smiling at her with a lift of that rascal brow. "Rather last minute, I admit. But it's a special wedding."

But that was impossible. "But I can't attend a wedding, Blakestone. I'm not dressed for it." She held up the skirt of her kitchen apron, with its huge pockets and blotches of blackberry stains. "Just look at me!"

"Oh, I am." He was leaning casually against the carriage wall, studying her.

"I'm sure the bride won't appreciate me showing up dressed like a rag doll."

That made him laugh heartily and sit forward as the carriage slowed and turned a final corner before it came to a stop in front of a huge building. "Believe me, the bride won't even notice."

The carriage door popped open and, before she could get a good look at the attendant's livery, Blake-stone leaped down the steps.

"Then she's not much of a bride." Elizabeth stepped forward into the carriage doorway as he reached up to encircle her waist with his huge, hot hands. "After all, who gets married in the middle of the night?"

He stopped. Held her there suspended in time, his eyes glinting as they searched her face until he said finally, softly, "Indeed, madam, who?"

But there seemed to be so much more to his evasive answer, an inference in his dark eyes. Something he seemed to have decided in that instant to hold back from her. That set her heart knocking around between her ears.

"Come, love, the Lord Mayor's waiting." He lifted her out of the carriage and set her on her feet, then caught her hand inside his elbow and started toward a set of stairs at the side entrance to this imposing building.

"The Lord Mayor!" Dear God, that's where they were! At Mansion House, the Lord Mayor's residence.

For a wedding?

An impossible image wobbled through her head: the Lord Mayor getting married in the middle of the night. A clandestine, candlelit ceremony, a mysterious bride, and a sea of attending policemen.

And a man who had just called her *love*.

Possibly a symptom of a sudden madness.

Perhaps the madness was hers. Her pulse was feathcry and fast, and she'd begun to imagine even more impossible things.

Another wedding.

Hers.

To him.

But before she could sort through that terrifying absurdity, her inscrutable earl was leading her up the steps, past two liveried guards and right on into the Court of Justice.

"Blast it all, Blakestone! You and the Lord Mayor have proven your point. I am thoroughly rebuked. I don't need to see the man in person."

"It's the only way, my dear."

"The only way to what?" He wasn't making any sense, but she followed him on her unstrung legs, over the marble floor and down a dimly lighted corridor toward some unknown fate that had something to do with a wedding. "Please take me home."

"You're not going home, Elizabeth. It's too late for that."

"Then it's certainly too late for a wedding."

"Unfortunately for both of us, a wedding is the only way to keep you out of prison for the next twelve years of your life."

How could her attending a wedding keep her out of prison? She planted her heels against the slick marble floor, but Blakestone's momentum merely skated her along behind him. "Are you mad, Blakestone?"

"Probably. But for some bloody reason that I can't fathom, I've decided to save you from yourself. At great cost to myself."

To himself? "You needn't bother, my lord, I don't need saving."

"Bloody hell!" He stopped abruptly in the middle of the corridor and turned her around to face the brunt of his fury. A roiling heat that had filled his eyes with a dark alarm, that rattled in his throat as he spoke. "Don't you understand?"

"I do." At least she thought she did. "And I'm very grateful that you—"

"Listen to me, Elizabeth. The Bank of England—the most formidable financial institution the world has ever known—has charged you with fraudulently opening an account with them. Do you know what that means?"

Possibly. If she only knew which account they were questioning. Her very large, very legitimate portfolio that she kept in her own name in the Bank of England? Or all those little accounts she'd helped women like Lady Ellis open against their husbands' wishes?

Dear God, was that what this was all about? The warrant hadn't been specific. And if they knew that, then what else did the authorities know?

"I'm sorry, Blakestone." She tried to look past his outrage, tried to shrug off his disturbing alarm. "I don't know what the bank is talking about."

He pulled her closer, glaring into her eyes. "Who is Adelaide Chiswick?"

Adelaide? "Oh, Adelaide!" She gulped back a deep sigh of relief. Maybe she could talk them out of that charge after all. The Bank and Scotland Yard and Ross Carrington, the powerful Earl of Blakestone whose breath was dancing warmly, deliciously, against her mouth.

"Who is she?"

"Well, my lord, she's . . . *me*. Sort of. It's my account."

He grunted and wheeled her backward onto a wooden bench and then stared at her from just inches away. "You opened a bank account in the name of Adelaide Chiswick?"

She tried to wet her lips, but her mouth had dried up on the blatant lie she was about to tell to the man who was only trying to protect her from her own risky affairs. "It was last Christmas."

"Why?" The word came out like a growl.

"I was . . ." It had seemed like a fine idea at the time. A test of her skill at deception. A way to see if she could pass herself off as an elderly widow and open a little account in the completely false name of Adelaide Chiswick.

Because if she could do it, then she could help other apparent elderly widows do the same thing.

Like Lady Ellis and her alter ego, the widowed Althea Moore.

But she couldn't confess that little ruse to Blakestone. There were too many of her innocent followers to protect. And besides, the Bank only seemed interested in Adelaide.

Still, she would have to think fast to come up with a suitable explanation for the man who was still glaring at her.

"It all began, my lord, when a young woman came to work for me when I was getting the Adams ready to open. A very sad case, very poor. She lived with her old mum and eight siblings somewhere in the Seven Dials." This was going well for an instant story. Though she couldn't let it take on too much of the penny dreadful.

"Tragic, Elizabeth, but what has this to do with the Bank of England?"

"Her name was Addie Chiswick. And I felt sorry for her and her family. I tried to help her out with some extra money, but she said she wouldn't take charity. So I opened the account for her, in her name, thinking that I would send a solicitor to her home a few months later to tell her that she had inherited a few pounds. And to give her the bank book. But, sadly, Addie quit working for me after a few weeks, and when I sent off the solicitor, he couldn't find the house or any sign of Addie or her family."

The lout blinked at her, skepticism dripping from his reply, "Oh, really?"

"Yes, my lord, and to this day the account sits unused, waiting for the solicitor to find Addie." She offered him her most saintly smile, pleased with her little fabrication. But not sure that he believed her.

He chewed on his cheek for a while, assessing her from every angle, then shook his head. "You're either lying, Miss Dunaway, or a damned fool. And I've known you long enough to know that you are no fool."

"And I'm not a criminal. I didn't defraud anyone. It's my money. I'm not trying to steal anything. Who cares what name I use on my account?"

"That's not the point, madam." He knelt in front of her and wrapped his huge hands around hers, frightening her with the clarity of his concern. "You can't confound the Bank of England like that and expect not to be punished for your insolence."

"Because I'm a woman?"

No, my dear Elizabeth, because you terrify them.

Because the woman couldn't help herself. Because her heart was filled up with a restlessness he knew only too well. That he'd had to learn to manage in his own life.

"Because you're an upstart, my dear. You're not playing by their rules and that makes them spiteful." Willing to put this bright, uncompromising woman in jail.

She harrumped and leaned back against the bench. "Which is the very reason I've also been charged with disturbing the queen's peace."

"Indeed."

"Because I'm a woman. And I've dared to inform the emperor that he has no clothes. That his laws have no place in the natural order of life." She stood and paced away from him to the opposite wall, bringing him to his feet, making him want to follow after her. "That charge against me is completely unfair. Our march down Whitehall was peaceful. And that bally-hoo in Parliament the other day wasn't our fault."

"I'm aware of that, Elizabeth." And newly aware of the injustice she was battling against, of his own growing sense of outrage on her behalf. "However, the worst of the charges against you are undeniable."

"By that you mean my printing and distributing salacious material."

"That's how the warrant reads."

"It's wrong." She crossed her arms beneath her

breasts, plumping them above her bodice, causing havoc in his groin and blowing up a fire in his chest. "*Unbridled Embraces* is not salacious, nor is it meant to be, as you well know!"

"In fact, my dear, should I ever be asked the question in a court of law, I would have to state that I highly approved of Miss Dunaway's unbridled embraces."

"There, you see!"

But she obviously didn't. Couldn't see the effect she was having on him, on her freedom.

"However, Elizabeth, according to the solicitor I consulted on your behalf, the law deems that the publication of your little booklet constitutes a threat to public safety."

"Suggesting that a wife make herself attractive to her husband is a threat to public safety? That's absurd."

Bloody shortsighted. "But it's the letter of the law. And that's all the courts know."

"But you know differently, Blakestone. You know my intentions. You can testify in my defense. They'll believe you; you're a man."

To the marrow. He could feel the pulse of her spirit thrumming through his veins. A new brightness in his soul.

"And I've learned to play by their rules when it suits me to do so."

"Like breaking me out of jail."

He was finished listening to her debate, more sure than ever that he had made the right decision. For the both of them.

"I told you, my dear, I've had the charges against you dropped."

"Then why are we here?"

Braced for the mother of all battles, Ross put himself between Elizabeth and the door. "Because, madam, there is one condition to your release."

She narrowed her brow up at him. "That we attend a midnight wedding?"

Indeed. "A simple accord that I reached with the Lord Mayor."

"What kind of accord?" She fisted her hands against her hips and scowled up at him. A scowl that he was sure would turn to horror in the next instant. But he was ready for that.

He hoped.

"I intimated to him, madam, that since you and I were planning to be married anyway—"

"Married!" Her eyes had grown to saucers. But for the moment he had her full attention.

"That I would advance that date, my dear, marry you tonight by special license in exchange for dropping the charges, thereby taking you off the streets and out of the court docket for good."

"Now you've lied to the Lord Mayor." She was shaking her head at him in horror. "I'll be swinging from Tyburn for the noonday rush."

"I didn't lie to the Lord Mayor, Elizabeth. We are getting married tonight."

He didn't like the stark stillness of her silence. Didn't like that her fine mouth was set firmly in a frown. Or that she was blinking at him from under a thunderous scowl.

"Is that why you brought me here to the Lord Mayor's? So that you could take charge of me like a wayward lunatic?"

She looked that way at the moment, with her gold-tipped hair gone slightly wild, her cheeks pinkening to crimson, her kitchen maid apron stained every which way. But at least she wasn't pitching a tantrum.

"The choice is yours, my dear," he said, trying to keep his own breathing steady, his temper in check, because this was not the way he would have chosen a wife and a wedding day. "Marriage to me, or a lengthy trial by a jury of men. A lifetime as my wife, or twelve years in prison."

She raised a very wry brow and focused her glare into the deepest part of him. "The rock or the hard place? The fire or the frying pan? Is that the choice you're offering, my lord?"

A slap in the face that he felt all the way to his heart. "Have I been such a rogue?"

"No, damn you." She paced to the wall and back to him, scrubbing her fingers through her hair. "But you're still a man. And the law is on your side. My fortune becomes yours. My every decision. My children. My bookstore. My friends. The Abigail Adams."

And here he was, as good as forcing her to marrying him. No wonder she couldn't trust him.

"If I tell you that I'm not like that—"

"What's that old saying, my lord? That absolute power corrupts absolutely."

"That's unfair, Elizabeth."

"But it's the truth: that as my husband, you'd wield absolute power over me. You could so easily shut down the Adams, forbid my friends, grow tired of me. . . ."

He couldn't imagine ever growing tired of her enterprising spirit, or the challenge in her eyes, or the goodness of her heart.

But how to convince her that he would do his best by her to the end of their days?

"Elizabeth, I can't force you to sign the registrar's book. The choice to marry me has to be yours alone."

"How can you do this to me?" Her face fell to a flood of tears. "Offer me my freedom as long as I surrender my independence to you?"

"That's not my intention, love." But he was beginning to understand her terror, could see it in the trembling of her chin. "But you've finally pushed them too hard. And they've got the power to remove you from the sunlight. And I wouldn't like that a bit."

"But I—" Her chin wobbled. Her hands were quaking, her knees knocking against his. Panic welled in her eyes as she shoved herself away from him with a cry. "No, no, no, no, no! I can't do this."

Then she turned and sprinted toward the door they'd come through.

Fortunately, he was faster, scooping her into his arms, the force of her flight sending him into a spin. He stopped in place, then held on tightly as he carried her back down the corridor.

"Running won't take you where you want to go, love."

"But I want to go home!" She clutched her arms around his neck, holding on for dear life, as though he might drop her. "Back to the country."

"That's no longer an option for you. They'll find you there too. Home is with me from now on, Elizabeth. You've left yourself no choice but to marry me. Tonight."

"But I can't—"

"Ah, there you are, Blakestone!" The Lord Mayor himself came strolling down the hall on a bouncing heel, grinning madly at them. "And you, Miss Dunaway. Good evening."

"Has the registrar arrived, Callis?"

"Just before you did, my lord. Everything's in place for your wedding to Miss Dunaway."

The man was looking at Elizabeth with a ready smile, obviously expecting a delighted bride.

But her eyes swamped with tears again and she turned her face into Ross's collar, wetting his neck, steaming against his nape. Then a huge sob rolled out of her, roaring through his chest.

But she didn't say no.

Didn't try again to bolt from him.

Ross nodded back at Callis to ease the moment, feeling only somewhat like a cad. "Overcome with emotion."

"My wife cried on our wedding day," Callis said, starting off ahead of them. "Come to think on it, she cries most days, for one reason or another."

That set the woman in Ross's arms into a howling sob.

A lamb to the slaughter.

His lamb.

Chapter 14

His designs were strictly honorable, as the phrase
is; that is, to rob a lady of her fortune by way of
marriage.

Henry Fielding, *Tom Jones*

Ross carried his reluctant bride-to-be all the way
into the Lord Mayor's office, surprised that she
was still clinging so fiercely to his neck when they arrived. As though he was threatening to throw her over
the side.

"You'll be all right, Elizabeth," he said as he stood
her on her feet, halfway expecting her to bolt again.

But she merely clung to his sleeve with her warm
fingers as he and the registrar exchanged formalities
with the Lord Mayor about the matter of the special license that the archbishop had so kindly issued to him
earlier that evening.

Her only moment of resistance came after the quick
ceremony, when she paused with the pen poised above
the document that would officially make her his wife.

He'd never seen such melancholy on such a beautiful brow, had never felt so personally responsible for a crushed spirit as he watched her worry her lower lip between her teeth.

Though he yearned to assure her of his honorable intentions, he also knew that she wasn't ready to listen. He would have to prove himself worthy of such a prize.

After the longest minute of his life, and two false starts, she finally bent her hand to the registrar's book and signed her name. When she finished, she righted her shoulders and sighed as though she were bidding farewell to a loved one being put into the ground.

It wasn't until he had lifted her into the carriage that Ross realized that he hadn't thought through where they would spend their first night together. The choice between her rooms at the Adams and his substantial suite at the Huntsman seemed suddenly no choice at all.

Hardly the stuff of hearts and honeymoons.

But since he was sure that the staff at the Huntsman would be available to serve his bride's every need, even at this late hour, he chose the devil that he knew.

"The Huntsman, driver. My private entrance."

His new bride said nothing all the way to the club, only watched in silence out the window as the gaslights flicked by on the darkened streets.

He carried her from the carriage over the threshold and in through his private entrance at the back of the Huntsman. And since she still wasn't objecting, he carried her up the two flights of stairs and into the sitting room of his suite.

The troubled frown remained on her captivating

mouth even as he set her on her feet in front of the cold hearth. Her thoughts seemed distracted, wandering with her gaze, racing ahead of her, lagging behind. But withheld from him.

He slipped a lap blanket over her shoulders where she stood then left his rooms to speak with the night attendant about bringing up a tray of tea and firing up a hot bath in the next room.

But when Ross returned, his bride was standing by the window, looking out onto the rooftops, her shoulders sagging.

"I thought you'd like a bath and a meal. And I've sent word to the Adams not to worry. That you're fine and safely out of jail."

"And married to you."

"I thought I'd leave that news for you to deliver."

"Thank you, my lord." When she turned back to him, he realized exactly where he'd seen that haunted look before. On the battlefield. The walking wounded wandering aimlessly amidst the carnage, unaware of the bullets and cannonballs whistling past them.

She'd lost something dear to her tonight.

Until this moment, he hadn't realized just how dear her independence had been to her. And didn't quite know what he could do to ease her road.

But one thing was sure: he much preferred her spitting anger to this silent despair. Preferred the sparkle in her eyes rather than this abject surrender.

"Are you warm enough there, Elizabeth?"

"Fine." Even her nod was halfhearted, her eyes stricken.

He went to her anyway, just to be close, to be resourceful, honorable. Not knowing what else to do, he bunched the blanket up around her shoulders and then gave in to the need to fill up his arms with her, blanket and all.

Amazingly, she let him stay.

"A room in my gentlemen's club," he said against the silky softness of her coppery hair. "Hardly a proper setting for a wedding night."

She shook her head slowly, back and forth beneath his chin, leaning her weight against him, rocking, swaying with the beat of his heart. "I couldn't very well expect a beach in the South Seas."

Where lovers met on the warm sands? Was that part of her silent fears? That he would insist on making love to her tonight?

"You've nothing to fear on that count, Elizabeth. I've no intention of seeking my husbandly rights tonight."

She leaned away and quirked a brow at him. "I'm not afraid of your husbandly attentions, my lord."

"Well, good. You've no reason to be." Indeed, she didn't look afraid, not with the steadiness of her gaze, that sizzling flash of green. "I'm not a complete cad, you know. Despite what you might have thought about the methods I used to rescue you tonight."

More frowning, a stiffening of her shoulders. "I don't consider you a cad at all, my lord. Believe me, I've known my share of cads, and you are not among them."

"Indeed?" A good thing to know. Amazing, considering. Although he could only wonder where she'd come by knowing a brace of cads in her sheltered life.

"In fact, my lord, I believe that had you turned your

husbandly attentions on me tonight, I would have welcomed them."

That was not the praise he was looking for now. Not with him standing so close to his newlywed wife, in all her magnificence. With his unfettered, husbandly attentions meeting her fiery, wifely initiative.

Not with an enormous bed waiting for them in the next room, piled high with pillows and dense with bedclothes.

And a rock-hard erection throbbing in his groin, which wanted relief, wanted to be buried inside her.

And yet he couldn't help but ask. "Excuse me, what did you just say, wife?"

"I'm sure you would have been a most gracious and attentive lover." She looked up at him, her mouth a deep shade of rose. "You are the quintessence of the very *Unbridled Embraces* which, ironically enough, led to my imprisonment, your kidnapping me, and forcing me to marry you."

He filled his lungs with a long, unsteadying breath of her meadowy scent. "For your own good, wife."

"We'll have to see, won't we?" She shook her head, then pulled her warmth away from him, hugging the blanket close around her shoulders as she stalked away from him.

"Well, then, I appreciate your . . . candor, Elizabeth." He might not survive it, but he managed to speak through a throat grown tight with a fortitude he hadn't known he possessed. "As well as your confidence in me and my unorthodox remedy against your legal woes."

However ill-conceived.

"It may have been your remedy, my lord. But it's my responsibility." She slid her hand along the back of his desk chair as she walked idly behind it, her mood grown dark again. "I brought my legal troubles upon myself."

"With cause, madam."

"Nevertheless, you were right. I jumped right into each of those perilous projects with my eyes wide open, knowing full well who I was baiting. As well as the consequences. And I lost. Everything."

Everything. Now he felt like a true cad. Male and monstrous, because he'd always taken for granted that the power he wielded against her was a natural process. That it had been bestowed upon him and his fellow men by glorious, unalterable tradition.

Everything. As though he had beaten her at a game she hadn't known he was playing against her.

And the extraordinary woman had felt every blow, struck against her heart.

Christ! How could he convince her of the possible, when he wasn't certain of it himself?

"Surely you haven't lost everything."

She studied him from the end of the desk, a wariness in her voice, as though she were regrouping. "I think I understand exactly how Princess Caroline felt when she lost her kingdom. Though I know she did it for the love of her life. For Lord Wexford."

Oh, my dear, for a love much larger than the world would ever know. "I can assure you that Caro and Drew are living happily forever after."

"That was plain. A love to be admired, my lord."

My husband, he wanted her to say. But now was not the time to press the issue.

Now was for courting her. Because, for good or ill, they were married.

"And Drew and Caro nearly missed it completely. Would have, if the princess hadn't taken matters into her own capable hands. Nearly caused an international incident in the bargain."

"But she was a royal. They couldn't very well put her in prison, could they?"

"Nearly put her in the grave."

"Good heavens!" She put her fingers to her lips. "They tried to kill Princess Caro? When? Who? I never read anything about it in the newspapers."

"And you won't ever." His wife was far too easy to talk to, to share with. A dangerous temptation when he had so many great secrets to protect from so many enemies. "Pretend I didn't say that, wife."

She raised a brow, then went back to touching her way through his room, as though trying to steady herself. "Somehow I'm not comforted in knowing that they—whoever *they* are—treat royal princesses worse than they treat common women. That's hardly playing fair with the weaker sex."

"No, it's not fair. Not in the least." He caught up with her capricious pacing as she reached the pair of upholstered chairs in front of the bay window. She stopped and looked up at him, leaving him to marvel at the brightness of her eyes. "I understand the subtleties of fairness more than you can imagine I do."

"I doubt that, sir. A wealthy man of rank and privilege. A life of carriages and foxhunts and a fat goose at Christmas. Let me guess: you're an Oxford man."

Now there was a topic they hadn't covered in their oh so brief courtship. He laughed and touched her cheek, just to convince himself that she was real.

His *wife*.

"Not Oxford." He threaded his fingers through the strands of hair at her temples, which had come loose in all their wrestling.

"Cambridge, then?" She gentled against his fingers, though reluctant, wary of meeting his strokes. "I see you as a helmsman at the Henley Regatta."

"You'd have been more likely to find me dockside on the Thames, larking for goods that I could then sell on the streets. Or scouting the railyards for an unlocked freight car."

"Oh? When was that?" She narrowed her eyes at him, silently accusing him of spinning a tale for her benefit.

"I was eleven and a bit when we started out."

"Eleven! Did you run away from home?"

"As fast as our little legs could take us, the first chance we got."

"Your parents must have been frantic."

"We hadn't any parents to worry about us." He sat down in the high-backed upholstered chair, the memory always taking the wind out of his sails for a moment. "Home was a brutal workhouse run by Squire and Mrs. Craddock. And if they missed us, my dear wife, it was only because we'd stolen the gold buttons off the old bastard's coat and run off with them."

She stared down at him, her eyes dark with disbelief. "A workhouse? You must be joking."

He shook his head. "Not a bit. We were halfway to Newcastle by the time they found that rat-faced squire, naked as a plucked chicken and tied to the village market cross."

"You said *we*." She knelt at his knee, catching up his wrist with her warm fingers. "Have you brothers or sisters?"

Brothers to the marrow, no matter that they shared not a drop of blood between them.

"Friends."

"Who?"

But his answer was cut off by a knock at the door to his private entrance, followed by Pembridge's voice. "Tea tray, sir."

"Blast it all, Pembridge! You should be in bed."

Ross flung the door open a moment later, and found the elderly man holding the tray of tea and cakes, his clothes in perfect order, as though at this hour, well after one, he hadn't been fast asleep, hadn't just scrabbled out of his nightclothes to wait on Ross's every whim.

Or to verify the staff's gossip about the beautiful woman that Ross had stolen up the back stairs and hidden away in his suite.

"I was just taking care of some last minute details, sir." Pembridge plowed his way into the room and headed for the table between the two upholstered chairs, only to come to a full stop a few feet shy of Elizabeth. "Good evening, miss."

"Not *miss*, Pembridge." Ross came to stand behind

him. "I'd like you to meet Elizabeth Dunaway Carrington, the Countess Blakestone. My wife."

"Your what, sir?"

Ross plucked the tray out of the old man's hands. "The countess and I were married this evening."

Pembridge nodded to Elizabeth, not hiding his fond smile at all well. "It's a great pleasure, my dear countess." Then he turned that glinty old accusation on Ross. "Your lordship, if you had just informed me earlier, I would have appointed your rooms appropriate to a wedding night. A tea tray and a douse in a tub will hardly serve the lady."

"That was my fault, I'm afraid, Mr. Pembridge." Elizabeth took the old man's hand and smiled at him with those inviting eyes, then raised her gaze to Ross himself, as though she were laying claim to her actions in order to protect her pride. "I was in such a hurry. You can imagine that I was an anxious bride. The tea tray looks delicious, and a quick wash-up in warm water before bed sounds heavenly."

Pembridge blinked at her. "If you're sure then, your ladyship . . ."

"Absolutely sure."

Then he blinked at Ross. "Shall I keep the news to myself, my lord?"

"For the time being. Thank you."

"Excellent." Pembridge poured two steaming cups of tea, then muttered his way to the washroom door. He opened the panel with a nod to Elizabeth, then muttered his way back across the room, where he finally made his most elegant exit.

Leaving his bride to stare at him, a dozen questions in her eyes.

"An old family retainer?" she asked, looking thoroughly vulnerable as she reached behind her head and loosened the pins from her hair, as though she meant to stay.

"A savior, actually. Showed the three of us how to dress, how to eat, where to live."

"Your workhouse friends?"

"Jared and Drew. You met them at the Adams."

"You mean Hawkesly and Wexford?" She dropped her hand and her hair fell in a soft, auburn curtain around her shoulders. "Aren't they both earls?"

"With a few more titles amongst us."

"How?"

"Let's just say that we've all come a long way in this world."

"As I thought I had." That realization seemed to take her down, shook her from the easy banter they had been exchanging. "So what happens tomorrow, Blakestone? And the day after." She huddled her fingers around a sip of tea, casting her gaze over the top of the cup. "And the day after that. I have responsibilities."

Here it came. Sooner than he'd hoped. Like a storm off the sea. Ready to blow up onto the shores and flatten everything in its path.

"And so do I, Elizabeth." He would have to stand firm on the matter, make her understand from the outset. Else they would both end up in jail. "From this day forward, my dear wife, your responsibility must be to me. Because the law holds me responsible for everything you do."

She took her time lifting her cup to her lips again, savored the taste overlong. "Ah, yes, wasn't there a saying? 'He that keeps a woman is like he that keeps a monkey; he is responsible for their mischief.' "

Ross refused to take the bait. Let her vent her anger, let her storm.

"Believe me, my lord, I'm painfully aware of your legal rights and responsibilities." The cup clattered as she set it on the tray. "They are the very reasons I never wanted to be married. But when you took on this monkey, you took on my responsibilities as well."

"Yes, I know. The Adams, the bookstore—"

"I can't afford to neglect them for a moment. But since they belong to you now, what do you plan to do about them? Along with my income of ten thousand pounds per annum, which also now belongs to you. You're going to be a very busy man, my lord. What with your duties to the Foreign Office and the Admiralty and who knows what else."

The room had became tinder dry, the air prickly with her spent anger. Her blanket had long ago fallen from her shoulders, and now she was clutching her hands around her arms, trembling all over.

"Indeed, wife. But I'm exhausted. As you are. It's too late to decide such matters tonight. If you want a bath, you'd best go take it while you can still stand."

She glared at him for a very long time and finally huffed at him. "Where do I sleep?"

He nodded into the bedchamber. "In there beside me."

Inches from him. Tormenting him through the night with her heat, with her scent. It would serve him right.

"And what will I wear to sleep in, sir? I completely forgot to pack my wedding trousseau before my little trip to jail."

He turned away and tried not to smile as he pulled a nightshirt out of the bureau and tossed it to her. "Take your time, Countess."

She snatched the nightshirt out of the air, then glared at him for a moment as though digesting her new title. Then she spun on her heel, tromped into the washroom, and closed the door with an overloud clunk.

He stood there in the silence for a long moment, feeling roundly chastised for merely being a man.

A bridegroom without a wedding ring for the bride. Let alone a blasted home.

He listened for her beyond the door until he was satisfied that she hadn't climbed out the window to escape him. He went to the table and was about to pour himself a cup of tea when he heard a sighing sound, like an autumn wind blowing through dry branches.

A murmur so low, so restrained, he'd nearly missed it. He went back to the washroom door and listened again. And heard exactly what he didn't want to hear.

His fearless bride who had declared war on him, on injustice, on the entire male population of the world, was quietly weeping, alone, trying not to let him hear.

Bloody hell.

Elizabeth had barely shut the washroom door before she collapsed against the paneled wall, bending over to force her sobs into her balled-up apron.

But they just kept coming and coming and coming. Rolling out of her chest.

In a single stroke of a pen she'd lost everything she had worked so hard for.

Her ladies' club.

Her bookstore.

Her friends.

Her freedom.

I'm so sorry Aunt Tibbs! Oh, Aunt Clarice! I've lost it all.

But that's what came of reckless impatience. Of taking foolish chances with the lives of others.

Now they would all be forced to rely on the conceits of the Earl of Blakestone. Her husband. Her jailer. What would he do about dear Jessica and Skye and Cassie? She'd promised them a home for as long as they needed.

Blakestone would doubtless close down the Adams and the bookstore and then watch her like a hawk for the rest of her days.

And what about Lydia? How would she get the poor woman safely away from that despicable husband of hers? Or the next woman who knocked on her door?

There must be more than one way to divert Blakestone's attention from her most clandestine activities. She might have to go deeper underground. Apply more cunning and guile. Take fewer but more significant risks.

Perhaps things wouldn't change so much after all.

What had Aunt Clarice always added to all that talk of independence and determination? Something about there being many roads to a single goal, about taking time to reconnoiter the bumps and ruts along the way.

Well, there could hardly be anything in the world more bumpy than Ross Carrington, the Earl of Blakestone.

As for the man being rutty—well, wasn't that just another word for lusty?

And wasn't her husband simply shimmering hot with lust? Steaming with heat. Smoldering with something else that seemed to spark from his eyes when he looked at her. That arched from his fingertips when he touched her, and played in the corners of his deeply sculpted mouth.

In his voice.

In the sultry way he said her name.

"Elizabeth?" A soft rap hit the door just inches from her.

She leaped to her feet and landed in the center of the room. "What?"

There was a pause on the other side of the panel, and a gentleness that gripped her stomach. "Are you all right?"

No, Ross. I'm terrified. I'm angry. I'm lost.

"I'm fine, my lord. Thank you."

Or she would be fine as soon as she could reconnoiter the man's bumps and ruts.

"How's the water? Warm enough?"

"Thank you. Yes."

"If you need to warm it further, just turn the tap with the red cap. Oh, and pull the plug when you're finished." She heard the firmness of his footsteps as he walked away toward the bedchamber.

Toward the beginning of a marriage that she had feared might happen all her life.

A shadowy cliffside with a precipitous drop-off and a crumbling footing.

Was there such a thing as an independent wife? If not, she would just have to make up her own rules as she went along.

Teach her husband to follow them, without him noticing.

Mr. Pembridge's bathwater was perfect; warm as an exotic ocean current, the enamel tub itself huge enough for her to float in. Right-sized for a tall man with shoulders as broad as her husband's.

Which brought forth a sudden image of Blakestone standing naked in front of her. At least the way she envisioned him to be.

Bronze and dark and well-endowed with masculine vigor. In full rut. That fabulous rod of flesh doing whatever it did when it rutted.

Not frightening in the least.

Exciting.

A dangerous venture. But something she could definitely do to distract her husband whenever he came too close to her intrigues.

Her skin was tingling as she dried off; her nose sensitive to the faint scent of him caught up in the nightshirt he'd tossed to her.

Which made her wonder what he was wearing, or wasn't wearing, just beyond the door.

"Ready . . . or not, my lord," she whispered. Exactly the tumbled state of her mind. Ready. Not ready.

But she certainly wasn't ready for the sudden shiver

of nerves when she found the sitting room empty and dark, with nothing but the soft light from the window powdering the paisley of the carpet. The only other light gleamed from the bedchamber beyond.

The lair of a wolf. Her wolf, whether she liked it or not.

Her husband was just dousing a globe lamp on the bedside table when she found him, his hair mussed and overlong. He was larger than she had ever realized, wearing a dark, silken robe that flowed to his ankles and was belted too casually at the waist, revealing a striking slice of his bare chest.

He was surely naked under there.

The very thought made her smile and blush to her bones as she draped her clothes over the back of a chair.

"What are you smiling at, my dear?"

Caught. "You, my lord. You look very . . . domestic." Very rutty.

He canted an eyebrow, the picture of a pillaging pirate. "And you, madam, look far too tempting for a man to get a good night's sleep on his wedding night."

"What do you mean?" Surely he wasn't going to leave her alone tonight. That suddenly didn't feel at all right.

"Only that it's going to be a long night."

"Why, because I'll be in your bed? I don't think I snore."

"Because you'll be in *our* bed, wife." He started past her toward the door to the sitting room. "And I've promised not to touch you."

"Ever?"

"Tonight."

"Does that mean you're leaving me alone here?" She took hold of his silky sleeve, catching a hint of his warmth beneath.

He looked down his aquiline nose at her, a quizzical slant to his brow. "Do you want me to leave?"

What a trap of a question that was! "After all, this is your room."

"And yours."

"But you shouldn't have to give up your bed just because you . . ."

"Because I stole myself a wife tonight."

"You didn't steal me."

"I carried you bodily to the registrar."

"You swept me off my feet."

He laughed and cupped her chin in the palm of his hand. "Now, there's a good one to tell our children."

Children. Dear Lord, she'd never allowed herself to imagine herself a mother. A family of her own. A real one.

"Then you will tell them that I went with you, because I agreed to it." And his hand was so warm against her throat, her nape. "Because, my lord, I won't have anyone feel sorry for me. Especially not you. I wouldn't have said yes or signed the papers if I hadn't wanted to."

"Very well, then." He gestured toward the huge bed with its inviting pile of bedclothes. "Now, if you know what's good for you, for us, wife, you'll get yourself to sleep before I come back."

"From where?"

She wondered if he knew just how devilishly seductive his smile was. "The bath."

Then her husband was gone, disappearing into the darkness of the next room, taking his warmth with him.

Another glance at the bed took her up the step stool and under the sheet and the silky counterpane. She plumped herself up against the cushiony wall of pillows and settled back to wait for his lordship.

Blakestone.

Ross.

Her husband.

Which made her, irrevocably, a wife.

A lover.

Responsible for making a success of a marriage she hadn't wanted.

Now, if she could only remember what she'd so innocently written in *Unbridled Embraces*. Something about practice and desire . . .

"Ah, yes! 'Put into practice what makes him cry out with desire for you and he will come back for more.' For more."

She could easily see a man like Blakestone coming back for more. And more.

" 'Be creative.' " Now that was still a puzzle. Since she hadn't really seen him close up, hadn't had the nerve to part his robe for a good look.

" 'Explore his body . . . ' " she whispered to herself, yawning as she snuggled more deeply into the silken covers.

" 'Praise him . . . ' " She closed her eyes, but couldn't get them to open again.

Feed him grapes.
Laugh with him.
Let him know.
Love him.

Elizabeth dreamed of a shimmering, silver-sanded beach. Of nuzzling sunlight. And murmured embraces.

Dreamed of her handsome husband, her excellently attentive lover wrapping her in his arms, keeping her safe.

But she woke in a cold, empty bed, in a masculine room she'd never seen in the daylight.

She sat up and looked over the top of the pile of covers. "Blakestone?"

Silence.

"Husband? Are you here?" She climbed down the bed steps and padded into the sitting room. "Ross?"

Nothing. No one.

Deserted before her wedding breakfast!

"Excuse me, madam!" Pembridge was calling to her from the corridor, knocking politely.

Not knowing what to expect, Elizabeth ran to the door and opened it a modest crack. "Have you seen his lordship this morning?"

"Left early for a place called the Adams."

"The Adams?" Dear God, the man was possessive! Gone to claim his new property already.

"He said to tell you that there's a carriage waiting at the rear entrance and that you're to come to him as soon as you are ready. Would you like a breakfast tray?"

"No. No, thank you, Pembridge. I'll get dressed and be downstairs in five minutes."

Five minutes of sheer terror!

Because her files and shelves were brimming over with evidence that would give away the names and locations of her escapees. And Lydia was there. What if he searched the upper floors?

And why wouldn't he? They belonged to him!

"*I* belong to him!"

And she had lulled herself into some giggling romantic stupor. Dreaming of the man's touch, when all along the blackguard had been plotting to seize her assets and overthrow her empire while she wasn't looking.

She was about to make sure that it would never happen again.

She needed to remember to add a suggestion to *Unbridled Embraces*:

Keep your husband busy in your marriage bed and he'll never wander off and get himself into trouble.

Chapter 15

How you talk, husband. Don't you see that I am too busy. I have a committee tomorrow morning, and I have my speech on the great crochet question to prepare for the evening.

"The Parliamentary Female," *Punch* cartoon
Mistress of the House and Member of Parliament, 1853

"Here's this morning's *Manchester Guardian*, Lord Blakestone," Skye said, dropping still another newspaper onto the library table.

His wife's three young assistants seemed to have been laying in wait for him the moment he left the visitors' parlor and started across the foyer. They had summarily shuffled him into the library, plunked him down into this very chair, and strewn the table with heaps of newspapers.

That had been ten minutes ago, and they were still feeding him tea and pots of coffee, and one delicious pastry after another.

Hell and damnation, he'd come to the Adams to

pack up the visitors' parlor, but he'd barely gotten the chance to breathe.

And just as he was about to bellow in protest, he heard a voice in the library doorway that brought him to his feet.

"Good morning, Lord Blakestone."

Bloody hell, she'd grown even more beautiful in the few hours since he'd left her peacefully sleeping in his bed. Though her face was flushed now, her eyes wide and bright, and her hair swept up into a loose knot instead of fanned out across his pillow.

"Good morning . . . Miss Dunaway." He'd almost called her *wife,* but her assistants didn't yet know what had passed between them last night. He would leave it to their mistress to break the news.

"Look who's here, Miss Elizabeth!" Jessica said, as though the woman had trouble with her hearing.

"I see that, Jessica." His wife smiled at him, a businesslike show of trust.

Or a flat-out lie.

Because as he took another look around him at the chirpy behavior of his wife's efficient assistants, he saw the sudden flash of a pantomime.

Three amusing clowns.

Three agile dancers.

Three sleight-of-hand jugglers.

And their beautifully inscrutable ringmaster.

Of course, Elizabeth hadn't had time to tell them that he knew about the bank fraud charges and the other activities that pointed back here to the Adams. They might have been protecting her. Working in concert to keep him from getting too close to Elizabeth's secrets.

"Thank you for taking such good care of his lordship, ladies." Elizabeth gave them all a pointed smile. "I'll handle him for now."

"Is that a promise, wife?" he asked after the young women were well out of earshot. "You'll handle me?"

But it must not have struck her as witty. She was frowning at him.

"Why are you here, Blakestone?" The subject was obviously as tender now as it had been the night before. Pursed lips, clipped words, brows drawn together.

"To clear my things from my makeshift office in the parlor."

"Why?"

"Because I won't be using it anymore."

"Why?"

"Because you'll be sleeping at the Huntsman with me until I can . . . we can temporarily hire a town house."

"Why didn't you just wait for me?"

"I did wait, love." He couldn't help his smile as he left his place at the table to be closer to her. "I watched you sleep for nearly an hour."

"Why?" She blinked at him, feathering those thick lashes that he'd marveled at that morning, watching her flawless cheeks begin to flame.

"I couldn't help myself." Could barely contain his lust for her at the time.

Or now.

"So you finally grew bored and made a beeline for the Adams. *My* Adams!"

Hers, his, theirs. Such a prickly obstacle. But how to

state his position clearly enough so that she would trust his promise not to get in her way.

At least not much.

"I was far from bored, wife." He could have watched her all day.

"Then just get it over with. Tell me that you've decided to close down the Abigail Adams, sell the building, and send everyone home to their husbands."

Damnation, he'd always wanted a wife with mettle enough not to back down from her opinions. And it seemed he got one.

"I don't recall saying anything about closing the Adams."

"No, but it's what you mean to do. As soon as you can manage it."

"At my own peril, my dear Elizabeth." He caught her around her slender waist, feeling thoroughly possessive of her parts. His wife. The fit of her shapes against his palm. "With you and Kate and the princess ganged up against me? Not to mention those three mountebanks who just left here. I'd stand a better chance as a snowball in hell."

For a moment he thought she was carefully weighing his words as she gazed up at him, holding fast to his arms as though to study him better. But her breathing had deepened, her pupils had darkened, the sea green of her eyes had brightened with a new kind of intimacy.

"Then I can go on with the Adams just as I have been?" She held his gaze. "You're not going to insist that I change anything?"

"Nothing at all. My word of honor."

She studied him for the longest time, doubtless weighing his word against that of every other man in her life.

She finally sighed. "I shouldn't have to thank you for allowing me my God-given rights, my lord. But I will."

She smiled and was rising up on her toes, a rosy, moist kiss on its way to his hungry mouth when his bloody conscience made him add: "Of course, my dear wife, you'll have to pass everything you do by me first."

She stopped abruptly, her eyes even wider, greener, her lips a scant inch from his. "I knew it. You don't trust me!"

She dropped back down off her toes with a huff, rescinding her kiss before she had bestowed it, a juicy plum stolen right out of his grasp.

"Madam, it's not a matter of trust."

"Ballocks!" She pulled out of his reach, her body fiercely tense, her voice a wall of calm. "You would never dare treat a man this way, would you? Insist that he clear his plans with you before he acts. Checking up on him in case he does something foolish. Is that what you think of me? That I'm incapable of making a rational decision?"

He opened his mouth to deny her accusation, but he knew she was right—he wouldn't have questioned a man's logic. Not on the surface.

What a bloody mess.

And what a lot of dancing he was going to have to do around this subject.

"In truth, Elizabeth, you're one of the most rational people I've ever met."

"So *I'm* your model of rationality? How frightening for you. To be surrounded by lunatics." She folded her arms against her chest, daring him to continue, when he'd so much rather take her up into his embrace.

And then the answer came to him. A truth.

"Think about it, Elizabeth. The greatest leaders in the world seek counsel from others. Good Lord, the prime minister has a cabinet to advise him. The queen has her privy council. In fact, I'm the current chairman of the board of the Huntsman; I never act alone."

She narrowed those lashy eyes at him. "So you're offering to be my privy council?"

Now there was an enchanting proposal. "As privy as you'll allow me, my dear wife."

She studied him to the whispered beat of her dainty foot tapping beneath her skirts, her hands balled into fists and jammed against her hips. And the blush that looked so fine on her cheeks.

"Let's just say, for example, husband, that I want to offer a new class to our schedule at the Adams. Let's call the class 'How to Be a Scantily Clad Music Hall Dancer.' According to your rules, I would then convene a meeting with you, my privy counselor, and we would discuss it between us. Say you advise against it. But I think it's a marvelous idea. What then? Who wins? You or I?"

The minx. "Neither, madam. We obviously don't have enough information."

"And so?"

"We would then consult a solicitor, perhaps the Lord Mayor, the prime minister, the *Times*."

"And receive a resounding no! That's not fair." She flicked him a dismissive frown.

He caught her hand and turned her, hungry for her. Overwhelmed by this new realization that she was his wife. His unkissed bride.

"It might not be fair, my dear . . ." He slipped his hands around her waist, shaped them over the gentle rise of her bottom, trying to refocus her thoughts toward him, toward them, on this morning after their wedding night. ". . . But in this case, we would both agree that London is not yet ready for their ladies to learn how to be scantily clad music hall dancers. Am I right?"

"Possibly." She frowned down at his shirtfront, then fussed with a vest button, tapping it, tapping away her reluctance. "In that particular case."

"And so the Abigail Adams avoids a scandal and your den of subversion survives to protest another day." He lifted her chin, lifting her gaze to his, exposing the soft ivory length of her throat to his fingers. And then to his mouth.

She tasted of roses. A garden. Bent her petals for him to kiss more lushly.

"Oh, my!" She grabbed fistfuls of his jacket, his arms, and used that to pull herself closer to him. To his mouth. To moan against his cheek. "That's . . . so . . . nice. Oh, Ross."

"So you see my point, wife." Now this was much better. With his bride trembling in his arms, offering herself to him, belly to groin, his mouth trailing over her skin wherever he could uncover it. "We work together. You and me. A team. Elizabeth and Ross."

"Don't you mean Ross, with Elizabeth in the back room?" She drew a long, sighing breath that ended in her bright, whispering laughter breaking just under his ear. "Or in the cellar?"

Christ, she was magnificent! "In the bedroom, wife. In my bed."

"That would keep both of us occupied and out of trouble." She was trailing the cool tips of her fingers along the back of his neck, riffling through his hair, ringing his collar, blowing little bursts of air against his temple.

"With any luck, we'd never get anything done." Her touch had stolen his will, and his remaining air, else he would have done more than growl out his pleasure. He leaned back hard against the bookcase and drew her with him, sinking into her glorious exploration.

"You smell of cinnamon, Ross." Her nostrils flared as she nibbled at the underside of his chin.

"Your . . . assistant . . . Ah, hell!" He'd endured the pussyfooting, gut-knotting restraint long enough. Tossing away all sense of decorum, he filled his aching arms with his bride, caught her hips between his bent legs, then pulled her belly tightly against his groin.

"Ahhh, there it is again, Ross." She was looking up at him from beneath her fawn-colored brows, the sultry vixen, fragrant with honey and steamy vanilla. "That hard place of yours I've suggested wives must become well acquainted with."

"You seem well acquainted." Downright possessive, with the pressure she was wielding against him. A rolling motion. A music hall dancer.

She shook her head gravely, wetting her lips with her tongue. "Not well enough at all, husband."

Dear Lord, would he live through this long day? Would he survive the restraint? Would he make it to their bed without taking her here on the floor of the library, or there on the table? Right here against the wall of bookcases?

"May I take that as an invitation?" May I take *you*, wife? Swallow you whole, drink at your lips, drown in your bosom?

"We have to start somewhere, Ross. Someplace." She pulled away from him just slightly, but only to stagger him breathless as she reached up to put her fingers flat against his mouth, as though trying to memorize their shape.

"That's a good place, wife. Very good." His muscles had long ago seized up in his arms, in his thighs as they gripped her around her lithe hips, aching with the dizzying need to mount his own exploration of her mounds and valley. But this was a busy, bustling library.

And he wanted to strip her to her bare skin. Rip off his own clothes. Naked love.

"Now, husband, for that kiss." Then his thoroughly bewitching wife smiled like a wily cat, rose up the rest of the way on her toes.

He was beyond waiting, beyond starving for a taste of her. As she wrapped her fingers indelicately in his hair and pulled him closer, Ross cradled the back of her head with his hands, covered her full mouth with his own, then dove deeply into her kiss.

Plunging into her softness, then nibbling, tugging, dancing with tongues and teeth.

"Oh . . . Ross!" Her little moan came immediately, burst into his chest like sunlight. She broke off a moment and looked at him with startled eyes.

Then she smiled and met his mouth again, her kiss wet and torrid, as hungry as his.

Lord, and there was all that smooth, unexplored skin beneath her chemise, lean legs beneath her petticoats, silky thighs, the humid heat of her.

But he repeated to himself inside the steaming muddle of his brain: *we're in a library just now.* A library. As public as the Reading Room at the British Museum.

"Enough for now, Elizabeth," he whispered against her delving kiss, whispered over and over, "Enough, enough." And then caught his lips against her ear. "Tonight."

But he suddenly sensed something out of place in the room. Something crowding them. And when he finally glanced up from the heat of her searing kiss, over her head, he realized they were no longer alone.

"Ah. 'Morning ladies," he said to the three pairs of bright eyes staring at them from the doorway.

"Will you look at that, Skye!"

"Am I seeing right, Jessica?"

"It's the earl!"

Already light-headed and breathless from Ross's intoxicating kiss, Elizabeth felt the room spin as she turned quickly inside the circle of her husband's embrace. She tried to focus on the figures in the library door but all she could feel was Ross's thick erection, throbbing against her bottom.

"Ah, there you are, ladies." Her skin still on fire, she drew his jacket together from behind, then popped out of Ross's arms and strode toward her three gape-mouthed assistants. "Can I help you? His lordship and I were just . . . discussing something."

And her knees weren't working.

Cassie nodded, obviously unconvinced. "We just came in to let you know that your . . . uhm . . . your *gown* for the charity ball tonight has arrived."

"Ah! Good. Thank you." She'd forgotten all about Lady Maxton's Charity Ball. Had good reasons to have forgotten so many things in the course of the last day.

Tonight was the scheduled night of their Turkish trousers fashion rebellion. Not enough time to send out messages to her members to change their plans now.

Certainly no time to consult her handsome privy counselor. He would just have to be surprised along with the others.

Jessica pointed weakly toward the upper floors. "The seamstress is upstairs in your sitting room, Miss Elizabeth, ready for your final fitting."

"Very good." Since she was still wearing the same clothes she'd worn to jail yesterday. With a too short visit inside her husband's nightshirt.

"Shall I tell her that you're coming right up?" Skye was still staring between Elizabeth and her husband.

A man who seemed a giant presence just a dozen feet at her back.

"Yes, please." She glanced back at Ross, and found herself marveling at his easy composure when only moments ago his large hands had been everywhere, inside every tuck and fold of her dress, his mouth breaking boundaries with his pleasures, and unstringing her knees. "His lordship was just leaving. Weren't you?"

He smiled slyly as he pushed away from the bookcase. "Ah, yes, Miss Elizabeth. Though I'll be back at, say, eight, to pick you up for the ball."

She hadn't thought about tonight, let alone tomorrow. Where they would live, their social calendar, their acquaintances. Lydia. And of course, Ross was due to appear on Lady Maxton's auction block.

Her husband! Hers! Slave to another woman's desires. *I think not*, came the sudden thought. As shockingly possessive and jealous as a fishwife.

"Yes, of course, your lordship," she managed, as the man who was now bound to her by every means possible took her hand and put it to his lips, dizzying her with the pleasure of it all. The significance of it all.

"Good day, ladies," Ross said from the doorway, nearly knocking them all into swoons with the casual elegance of his nodded exit.

Elizabeth stared after him, as immobilized with awe as were her three faithful assistants.

Until they finally broke into a tangle of questions and surrounded her with speculation.

Skye waggled a chiding finger at her. "That man was kissing you."

"He was." He was fondling her.

Cassie looked utterly scandalized. "And you were kissing him back."

"Yes, I was." And fondling *him*. Wanting him so fiercely she could still feel the pressure of his hard places, his ridges and heat.

Jessica frowned. "Where were you last night, Miss Elizabeth?"

"With him?" Cassie jerked her head toward the door. "The earl?"

"That very earl. My husband."

They gasped together like a great, sucking furnace bellows.

"I married the Earl of Blakestone last night."

Another gasp of disbelief.

"That's amazing, my lady!"

"And wonderful!"

"But what about Mrs. Bailey?" Jessica asked. "And all others who need our help?"

As bright a star as her husband might turn out to be among the constellation of men, there were surely some details that even a queen must keep from her privy council for as long as possible.

And damn the consequences.

More than the simple fact that a pair of Turkish trousers were waiting upstairs for her to try on for tonight.

"Come then, ladies, the seamstress is waiting. I'll tell you all about everything on the way upstairs."

The seamstress did the last of her tucking and stitching under the watchful eyes of Elizabeth's entourage. She was gone within the hour, leaving careful instructions for putting it back together for the ball.

That was hours ago. Now it was after seven and the minutes were flying past. Ross would be here any time now, and she didn't want to give anything away before the last possible moment.

"Oh, it fits perfectly, my lady! Turn! Turn!" Skye laughed as she clapped her hands, setting off Jessica and Cassie with their ooos and ahhhs.

"You'll be the talk of the ball," Jessica said as she tried to catch up with the unruly curls let loose against Elizabeth's nape.

"Let's hope there'll be more women than just me to set tongues wagging tonight."

Please let her husband approve. At least a little.

Whatever the outcome, the Turkish trousers made Elizabeth feel utterly exotic. The blouse was richly cut in the sleeves, the bodice set off by a short vest with a tasseled hem.

The folds of silk sluiced against her bare skin when she moved, like cool, cascading water. The fabric draped freely around her limbs like a heated caress from an unblushing lover. The colors were a celebration of autumn, with sunny yellows and deep violets, oranges and browns, all of it shot through with leafy designs in the finest gold thread.

"And now the skirt that will hide my shocking little act of rebellion until the most proper—or dare I say *improper*—moment."

Her three assistants giggled and gossiped as they hooked and tied and tucked the elegant skirt to its waistband, then put the rest of her costume together, just as the seamstress had shown them earlier. A dashing cap of lush velvets adorned the crown of her hair, exotically hued, yet subtle enough not to draw attention to her.

Although when eight o'clock and her husband arrived at the same time, and she appeared at the top of the stairs, she thought at first that he'd caught on to her ruse.

He stood unmoving in the foyer below, magnificent in his evening clothes, his gaze locked on hers, following her every step as she descended.

He met her at the bottom of the stairs, his gloved hand extended toward her. He slipped it into the warmth of hers, then tucked it into the crook of his arm.

His eyes were hot with something that she had come to learn was desire for her.

"You will dazzle them tonight, my love," he said with a prideful smile.

Oh, I intend to, my lord husband. The rebellion had been set in motion long ago. Like an avalanche on the brink, she couldn't send it backward now.

She could only hope that she didn't dazzle her husband beyond his capacity to forgive her.

Chapter 16

The time draws nigh, and is at hand,
When females will with courage stand!
Each heart united will decree,
We'll have our rights, we will be free!
We'll sever ne'er, but steadfast be!
We'll die to have our liberty!

Mrs. Collie, "Chartist Song"
Scotland, 1840

"We leave the ball at the stroke of midnight, wife," Ross whispered in the wake of his beautiful bride, who had once again been swept away from him and onto the dance floor by another lumbering oaf.

His skin had always felt too tight whenever he was forced into the midst of London society, the balls and soirees and other such dry-boned galas. But this particular charity affair was proving to be of an even more diabolical nature, conspiring to remind him that he had by the dumbest of all good luck married the most bewitching woman in the kingdom.

She hadn't merely dazzled them tonight, she had laid them flat.

And yet finding an empty slot on her damnable dance card had been nearly impossible. Worse than that, not a soul yet knew that she belonged to him, lock, stock, barrel, and bookstore, as Elizabeth would doubtless accuse.

Because this truce of theirs was untested. As untested as their marriage.

So far, three eligible bachelors had fallen to Lady Maxton's charitable endeavors. With any luck, he'd be long gone, in bed with his wife, by the time his own name came up. He would have pulled it from the auction already, but then he'd have had to admit that he was no longer an eligible bachelor.

Gossip that would have spread like wildfire. And he owed it to Jared and Drew to tell them in person about his hasty marriage to Elizabeth.

And, bloody hell, he dreaded the moment that Kate and Caro found out they hadn't been invited to the wedding.

Fortunately, the two couples hadn't yet arrived. At least he hadn't heard their names announced. And these charity ball matrons always made a great deal of noise over the attendees, hoping one donor would choose to outdo the next one who ventured down the stairs into the pit.

He'd been willing to pledge his left arm to the orphans, but Elizabeth had insisted that he pledge his right leg as well, and so he had.

Indeed, Lady Maxton was the consummate professional. The manor house looked like a pasha's palace, from the filigreed arch at the front door, to the staircase, to here in the ballroom. There were delicate lanterns and potted palms, huge brass platters and bejeweled jugs, tendrils of incense and pantalooned footmen. Every spare inch had been richly draped, dripping in deeply hued silks, colors much the same as his wife was wearing.

Indeed she wasn't the only woman who had come dressed with the hint of the Ottoman. He could count more than a dozen others.

But all that was beside the point. At the moment he would offer up his life just for a moment in bed with his pink-cheeked bride.

"Why aren't you out there dancing with her, Ross?" Caro appeared suddenly at his elbow, her eyes flashing up at him. "She's liable to slip away from you forever into the arms of some other swain."

Kate joined up at his other elbow. "Or has she already danced you silly?"

He saw Jared and Drew then, striding toward them along the edge of the dancing, each with a huge grin and a pair of champagne flutes.

"Left at the wall without a partner, Ross?" Jared cuffed his shoulder and handed him one of the glasses. "You need this more than I do."

Ross handed it back. "No thanks. I want my wits about me tonight."

Which was exactly the wrong thing to say to his overly vigilant friends.

"An odd turn of phrase, Ross."

"He's hiding something, Caro."

"Or is he planning something big?"

Planning to announce the news of his marriage to these barbarians, in private. But with Elizabeth at his side. If she could only break free of the dancing.

Caro tugged on his sleeve. "Are you hoping she'll bid for you, Ross?"

"What?" he asked absently, scanning the dancers. Damn, he'd lost her again in the crowd.

"Miss Dunaway. Surely she'll bid for you until she wins you." Caro tugged again, and he glanced down into her smiling eyes. "During the auction."

Kate nudged Caro. "I suspect the bidding will be fierce for our Ross. After all, he's the most eligible bachelor in the kingdom."

Not anymore. He wanted to laugh out loud. But that would only bring on more questions.

And the waltz had ended. His wife was finally being escorted back to him on the arm of an eager young man, who tripped over his own feet on the way, oblivious, because he was grinning, unblinking, at Elizabeth.

Ross reached for her just as another lummox started toward her, but he stepped directly in the man's way.

"Sorry, Bollensburg, but the lady is engaged."

Married, actually. To me.

"Thanks, Ross," she whispered, blowing out a weary breath as she lifted a loose strand of hair behind her ear.

Wishing he'd done that himself, Ross took his smiling wife by the hand and strode past his friends, nodding for them to follow him out onto the terrace. Arriving first, he tucked Elizabeth slightly behind him and faced down the four people he loved most in the world.

That was until Elizabeth had come marching into his life, protesting all the way.

Jared and Kate stared at them with baffled smiles.

Caro clung to Drew's elbow, her eyes wide and watching until she finally said, "Well? What is it, Ross?"

"Look, I'll just say it right out." He reached back to find Elizabeth's hand, relaxed a bit to feel the fierceness of her grip. "We should have said something earlier, but the situation changed too quickly."

"Oh!" Kate gasped and clapped her hands together then pointed at them. "You two are getting married!"

"Are you?" Caro grabbed Kate's hand. "Is that what you're trying to say, Ross? If so, you're not doing a very good job of it."

Bloody hell, he should have sent them a note. From Paris.

"Please, ladies." He felt his wife's hand at the small of his back, so wonderfully familiar. "No, actually. Elizabeth and I are not *getting* married."

"Ooohhhhhhhh, no!" The two women wound down like a pair of case clocks, visibly sagging against their spouses.

Blast it all, this wasn't going at all well. Jared and Drew weren't helping either, looked confused while their wives fluttered around the truth.

"That is to say . . ." *Just blurt it out.* "Elizabeth and I were married last night."

They went utterly silent. No sound on the terrace but the strains of the orchestra trailing through French doors.

"What?" Jared said a second before Drew's own befuddled, "When?"

"Married?" Tears welled in Kate's eyes—just as he'd feared they would.

"Married!" Caro reached out for Elizabeth, who'd been standing safely out of the fray, and pulled her forward into an unsparing embrace. "Elizabeth, how wonderful!"

"Well, thank you, Lady Wexford!" His wife looked surprised, then pleased, giving back an equal embrace.

"Please call me Caro."

"Welcome, dear Elizabeth!" Kate was next, with a smiling hug and then a kiss on his wife's flushed cheeks. "And please call me Kate."

"Well done, Ross!" Jared and Drew had finally come smiling out of their stupor and were now boxing him around like a couple of bears and a beehive.

"You're an old fox, man."

"Now then, Ross Carrington." Kate was standing in front of the men, frowning, looking perfectly scandalized. "You'll tell us why you didn't bother to invite us to your wedding. Your own family."

Another complication that he wasn't yet ready to explain in a crowd. Not without Elizabeth's consent.

"Sorry, Kate," Ross said, taking her hand, "but there was no time for invitations."

"We would have come at the run. We were even here in London. A moment's notice and we'd have been there."

Now it was Caro's turn. "You said last night, Ross. What time?"

"In truth . . ." Elizabeth cleared her throat. "It was actually this morning just before one. The very middle of the night."

"At the very last minute," Ross said, taking Elizabeth's hand.

The four of them went silent again and just stared until Caro spoke. "Why?"

Elizabeth gave his arm a shy squeeze. "Because Ross was good enough to save my life."

"Now that sounds like our Ross!" Jared clapped him on the shoulder.

"Saved you from what, Elizabeth?" Kate quirked her brow.

"Myself, really."

"That's not enough of an answer." Caro shook her head.

Ruthless woman. Ross tucked Elizabeth behind him again. "That's all you're getting tonight, Princess."

"What's more, if you got married last night, you surely haven't had a proper send-off."

"Don't worry about it, Caro." This wasn't going at all well. He smelled danger. The Kate and Caro kind of danger. "And now, if you don't mind, Elizabeth and I are going to join the dancing."

He grabbed his wife's hand and led her toward the dance floor.

They didn't quite make it.

Lady Maxton hove into view as they reached the glittering ballroom. She bore down on them at full steam, resplendent in her own silk extravaganza and wearing a bright orange Turkish-style turban.

"Dear Elizabeth, you look simply glorious tonight. Don't you think so, Lord Blakestone?"

"Indeed." *But I'd rather have her home with me in our bed.*

"And you, Lady Maxton." Elizabeth grinned at Ross, then turned to the hostess, and the two exchanged a burst of whispering and giggling into each other's ears.

"So you're ready, my dear?" Was the only thing he heard, besides his wife's, "Oh, yes!"

And for no reason that he could imagine, as Lady Maxton glided away, Elizabeth's words struck fear into his heart.

"What was that all about, wife?"

She swung into his arms and looked up at him, her eyes wide and bright. "Just a little woman talk, Ross."

"Well, that's . . . uhm . . . just fine." He lost track of the rest of the world, felt only her fingers playing at his nape. "Another move from your *Unbridled Embraces*."

"Number seventeen, husband." She closed her eyes for a moment as though trying to recall something. "'Touch him fondly in private moments, a knowing squeeze at his waist during a dance'"—she slipped her hand beneath his jacket, then her fingers into his waistband— "'a flirting promise of intimacies after the ball.' Effective, husband?"

"Very, wife. If you mean to have me sweep you out of here right now, long before midnight."

They danced then, caught up in the music. He ignored the trail of men who tapped him on his shoulder. One after another, wanting to partner with his wife.

Ignored Drew.

And Jared.

The Lord Mayor.

Jonathan Effington, the very eligible Marquess of Helmsley.

Even the fretting little Austrian deputy ambassador tried his best to steal her away.

But Ross cheerfully monopolized his bride's every moment, making her laugh in delight when he actually stopped in the middle of the floor, struck out the other names on her dance card then added his own all the way down the list.

And Elizabeth adored him for it.

For being such a powerfully accomplished dancer. Probably the reason for the looks of envy she'd received from all those sad-eyed spinsters who waltzed past them.

For being so enchanting and attentive, so different from the raging beast he'd been when he stormed Scotland Yard to rescue her from the evil clutches of the law.

For stealing her breath away with the brush of his lips against her temple as they danced.

But for all his magnificence, he was still an impossible threat to her plans and programs. Because he seemed to have the terrifying power to addle her wits.

"You look delicious tonight, Elizabeth."

To make her weak in the knees.

"Will the backs of your knees taste of roses, I wonder?"

And fill her head with illusions.

"Will your nape smell of cinnabar?"

Would she wake up from this lovely dream and find that he had stolen her will along with her independence?

"Eleven o'clock, my dear," he said like the chime of

a hall clock, ticking off every five minutes with his wolfish smile.

As they danced to the edge of the crowd, Elizabeth glanced out to the deserted side terrace and caught a glimpse of a tall, well-dressed man shaking his fist at a young woman.

Another turn around Ross and Elizabeth could see that the man was furiously scolding the woman. He grabbed her chin and shook it.

"How dare he!" Elizabeth whipped her head around to follow the scene.

"What are you looking at, sweet?" Ross slowed and followed her gaze, but the brute was already stalking back into the ballroom, and the young woman had faded into the shadows.

"Who is he, Ross? That blond fellow grabbing that glass from the waiter's tray." She was finding it very difficult to focus on the man, waltzing as they were.

"Lord Stopes. Why?" Ross obviously hadn't seen the man's shamefully abusive behavior.

"Is he married?"

"You already have a husband, madam." The blighter pulled her closer than proper and turned her madly in his dance.

"Is he married, Ross?"

"I don't think so."

"Engaged?"

"Wouldn't know." Her husband only shrugged and kept dancing.

Whoever she was to the vicious Stopes, the terrified young woman stepped gingerly down the stairs from the terrace, visibly shaking, hiding her flushed face with a lace fan as she tried to fade into the mirrored wall.

Elizabeth wanted desperately to run to her and take her into her arms, to soothe her fears and give her strength. But that would call attention to the poor girl, at the expense of her beastly assailant. And he didn't seem to be the sort of man to suffer embarrassment without doling out punishment to the nearest innocent.

Fleeing the country was the very last resort in a case like this. But the beleaguered young woman could doubtless use a friend and a bit of subversive counseling. If only to fortify her spirits.

Elizabeth had been about to excuse herself to her husband when the music faded and Lady Maxton appeared in all her glory on the dais, waving her tutti-hued fan in the air.

"Time to sacrifice another bachelor, madam?"

"Not yet, Ross."

Her one-woman diplomatic mission would have to wait for the moment. It was time to shock a few people out of their donations.

"Ladies and gentlemen!" Lady Maxton called into the quieting room. "Yes, thank you all for being so generous tonight. We'll have another bachelor to auction off in just a few minutes. And you can be sure that every last ha'penny will go to the Relief Fund for Abandoned Children."

The applause rose nicely and rolled through the crowd, then settled back as Lady Maxton signaled for silence.

"I would also like to thank the members of the Abigail Adams ladies' club, for offering their time and their generosity to the affair." A dubious rumble followed the light applause, as though even the slightest mention of her club was scandalous.

"Pay them no mind, Elizabeth." Her husband's unexpected whisper of support caught her right in the heart, right where she was the most vulnerable to him.

"I would especially like to thank Miss Elizabeth Dunaway, the owner of the Adams, for her inventive ideas for making this charity event one that will be remembered for years and years to come."

"We'll have to tell them we're married, sooner or later, wife," he whispered against her temple in the wake of the applause.

"I guess later, Ross."

"Miss Dunaway, if you could come up."

Well, here goes!

But before she could step safely away from her husband, he slipped his hand through her elbow and pulled her back against his chest. "What's this about, Elizabeth?"

Fearful of his wife's inventive ideas, Ross made sure he was looking directly into her eyes when she answered.

But she tilted her head up to him with one of her devastating smiles and whispered back, "You'll see, husband."

"That's what I'm afraid of." But he let her go anyway, trusting in her sense of fair play, in her common sense, and watched her wade through the admiring crowd.

"Don't be shy, Miss Dunaway!" Lady Maxton was beckoning with a finger. "Come on up, dear. Please, let her through. That's it."

His wife mounted the three short steps onto the dais, drawing a murmur of admiration from the crowd. Only making him more impatient for her. He pulled out his pocket watch for the umpteenth time.

Eleven-fifteen. And counting.

"Now, ladies and gentlemen," Lady Maxton continued, "as each of you can see for yourselves, the members of the Abigail Adams chose as our theme tonight 'A Thousand and One Arabian Nights,' in honor of our beleaguered Turkish brethren."

A highly political cheer rose up in the room, followed by a few huzzahs tossed in for good measure.

From all but the Russian contingent, which stood in a sullen knot at the rear of the room.

All things Turkish might be a popular theme in the press these days, but pro-Turkish sentiment was quickly becoming a flash point among the diplomatic corp.

Yet, he doubted that Lady Maxton or the ladies of the Abigail Adams had an international political motive for their mischief.

But mischief it was bound to be. He could tell by the twinkle in his wife's eyes and the looks she was exchanging with Lady Maxton as she turned her back to the crowd to work at something at the front of her waist.

"And what, ladies and gentlemen," Lady Maxton called out like a festival barker, "could be more Turkish than . . . a harem full of lovely ladies. As Miss Dunaway will demonstrate . . ."

Good Lord, no! She wasn't—

But his suspicions lagged way behind reality. He watched helplessly as Elizabeth turned back around to face the crowd, at the same time dropping the skirt from her waist and smiling that jaunty, self-assured smile.

The crowd gasped.

Ross gulped. Christ, look at those legs! Long and lithe and shapely beneath the erotic draping of satiny silk.

And now everyone else in London knew it too.

"Ladies and gentlemen!" Lady Maxton shouted over the growing tumult. "Turkish trousers!"

And there went Lady Maxton herself. A few years his wife's senior, but showing a pair of legs that would do any husband proud.

Other women among the crowd on the dance floor began discarding their skirts with a flourish and revealing silk-trousered legs by the dozens.

The spectators parted with a collective gasp, leaving the happily scandalous women standing in the center of the uproar, preening.

And his magnificent wife standing at the dais, stripping him of his will, taking his breath away.

Elizabeth hadn't known what to expect of her opinionated bridegroom. She'd kept her eyes on him through it all, had easily found his gaze when she revealed her trousers, hoping he wouldn't be too scandalized, too angry.

She still couldn't read him as he stood stock-still, staring at her across the heads of the crowd.

It's all for a good cause, husband. Lost children, unloved children, frightened children.

You were one of them once.

And still he stared, and then frowned more deeply when Lady Maxton waved her arms and slowly quieted the crowd.

At least they hadn't rioted. Perhaps they were spellbound.

Or paralyzed.

Now it was Elizabeth's turn to speak, and she seemed to have every eye. She swallowed hard.

"We've auctioned bachelors tonight. And sold tickets to a lottery. Lady Maxton has resorted to outright blackmail in some cases."

They laughed, their wallets nearly empty.

"But now, gentlemen, it's your turn." The men in the crowd took a few steps closer as though they were indeed interested; Ross took a dozen steps toward her, still frowning.

She hurried on while she still had their attention.

"For the rest of the night, whenever you partner with a member of our delightful harem in a dance, you'll be asked to make a generous donation for the opportunity."

They began to grumble and bluster; Ross looked ready to spring.

"And, to make your giving as simple as possible, my lords, the footmen will come around as you're dancing to accept your contributions."

And instead of letting the momentum die on the vine, or turn into a complete imbroglio, Elizabeth clapped her hands together twice then motioned to the band to begin.

Then complete pandemonium erupted below the dais.

"That went quite well, Miss Elizabeth!" Lady Maxton gave her a hug as Elizabeth watched the dance floor churn with confusion below. "Just as I knew it would."

"Unless they take us off to jail."

"Not to worry, my dear. It's all for such a good cause, it can't fail."

"And speaking of good causes, do you know whether Lord Stopes is married or engaged?"

A quick frown quirked the lady's mouth. "Recently engaged to a very wealthy young heiress. Why?"

Elizabeth stepped closer. "He's a monster, isn't he?"

"A profligate of the first order. I was forced to invite him; her uncle is my husband's first cousin. If he's been bothering you, I'll—"

"He hasn't." Wouldn't stand a chance with her husband. She'd never felt quite so well protected as she did with Ross in her life. "It's just that I saw him berating a young woman—"

"Doubtless his fiancée, a Miss Preston. Damn the man."

"Perhaps Miss Preston needs to join us at the Abigail Adams?"

And Lady Maxton was just the sort of revolutionary to join up with her in her most underground operations.

"An excellent idea, my dear, I'll sponsor her myself."

"Thank you." *And woe betide any fool who tried to get in their way.*

Lady Maxton planted a kiss on her forehead. "Now you'd best go claim a dance from that handsome Earl of Blakestone, else he's liable to start a brawl over you."

Or lock her up and toss the key into the Thames if he ever discovers the growing depths of her conspiracies. "A very good idea." She could see him waiting at the base of the dais, blocking the stairs.

"Better yet, my dear," the woman whispered, with a lift of her brow, "marry the man."

Elizabeth smiled and whispered back, "I already did."

Lady Maxton's approving laughter followed her to the top of the stairs. To the sight of her husband's stubborn face.

He tapped the crystal of his watch with the teasing scowl of an impassioned lover. "It's nearly midnight, madam."

And he still wanted her, wasn't shocked beyond speech. "But, sir, I'm wanted here in the seraglio."

"You're wanted in my bed, wife," he said from between his teeth.

Heavens, he was a joy to tantalize. And she might as well play out her fantasies with him for as long as she could.

For there were so many dangers ahead of them.

"But, husband, just think of the money I can make for the children."

He sighed with great drama and whipped out his wallet for the third time tonight. "How much?"

"For what?"

"If I danced with just you the rest of the night, how many dances would that be?"

"From midnight until the wee hours . . . I'd say eight, maybe ten dances. In fact, make it twelve, my lord, just to be on the safe side."

"Then I've just bought out your dance card."

"Excellent, sir. At a shilling a dance, that's twelve shillings. But perhaps you ought to just make it twenty; an even pound. Per dance. A crisp twenty-pound note ought to do nicely."

"Blackmail, madam, pure and simple." Her delightfully impatient husband handed her down off the dais, a smile lurking inside him somewhere.

"As they say, Ross, charity begins at home."

"Then consider me a man in dire need of your charity." He pulled a twenty pound note out of his wallet, caught a passing footman then tossed the note into the man's brass pot. "Come, wife, before I haul you over my shoulder and carry you home. You've caused enough scandal for one night."

"If you think so, Lord Blakestone!" Elizabeth held fast to her husband's hand as he steamed with her out of the ballroom and into the gravel drive up.

What a grand difference twenty-four hours could make. Last night she had fought the arrogant man every step of the way, from her jail cell, into a forced wedding, right into a loathsome marriage.

But tonight she was snuggled against him in the circle of his arms, wrapped in his coat, eagerly waiting for their enchanted carriage to speed her off to their marriage bed.

However fleeting that peaceful happiness might be.

Fortunately, their carriage pulled up a moment

later, but as Ross handed her up the steps, she could see something moving in the darkness of the cab.

"Is there someone there?" She stopped at the top step and peered into the shifting shadows, wondering if she was getting into the wrong vehicle. "Excuse me, please, but—"

"Shhhhhhh!" came the hissing noise from inside.

Then someone grabbed her by the wrist and pulled her forward into the carriage. The door slammed behind her, plunging her into darkness as the carriage jerked forward.

She flew to the rear window in time to see Ross ambushed by two men. "Ross!"

"It's all right, Elizabeth! It's us!"

She made a grab for the door latch, ready to fling herself out of the carriage, but stopped short when she recognized the laughing voices.

"Kate?" Her pulse was pounding against her eardrums, her limbs as loose as a rag doll's.

"And me! Caro!" The princess was peering at her from the opposite seat, obviously pleased with herself and her confederate.

"Dear Lord!" Elizabeth collapsed back against the seat. "You nearly frightened me to death!"

"Oh, dear, we didn't mean to." A match flared in Kate's hand, lighting her impish, unrepentant smile. "But we decided that the bride and groom should have a proper send-off after all."

"Good heavens! What did you do with Ross?" The man was going to be seething.

"We left him to Jared and Drew." Caro lifted the

glass for Kate to light the candle in the carriage lamp. "He'll be fine."

"He'll be furious."

They giggled like a couple of schoolgirls. "Perfect!"

"That's what he gets for not telling us you were going to be married." Kate scooted forward on the seat and tucked a few curls behind Elizabeth's ear. "The man's always been a bit preemptive."

Elizabeth couldn't let them keep thinking that Ross was to blame. The fault had been hers entirely.

"But the timing wasn't his doing at all," she said. "He had no idea that I would actually marry him until five minutes before it happened."

"Kept him guessing, did you?" Caro scooted in beside her. "Excellent. Very romantic."

"And just like a man," Kate said, suddenly fanning herself and leaning back against the seat. "Couldn't plan their way out of a pasteboard box."

"It wasn't exactly that way." Confession was good for the soul. The basis of a growing friendship. "You see, I either had to marry Ross or spend the next twelve years in jail."

The two women froze, mouths open, but absolutely silent. Giving her the horrid feeling that she had disappointed them beyond repair.

"Oh, Elizabeth," Caro finally said, gathering up her hands between her own, "you are simply one of us."

"I am?" That seemed a very good thing.

"We can spot them a mile away." Kate handed down three lap blankets. "Now just settle back and tell us all about your romance with Ross. Every gory detail."

Caro snugged herself back into the corner of the seat. "We've got plenty of time."

Her head swimming with confusion, she peered out the window into a softening landscape of trees and fields. "You mean you're not taking me back to the Huntsman?"

Kate laughed. "That fusty old gentleman's club? Not a chance!"

"We're delivering you to your perfect honeymoon lodge."

No, this was some fairy tale. And she'd managed to hook up with a pair of mischievous wood sprites. "Where would that be, Caro?"

But Caro only smiled slyly and tucked the blanket around her knees. "Not far. You'll see."

Not far was good. She really needed to see Ross. To prove to herself that he was real.

"We've sent ahead to make the place perfect for you and Ross. Food and a fire and privacy. You won't be wanting for anything."

"But when did you arrange this? You couldn't have been planning beforehand. You found out less than two hours ago that we were married."

"True." Kate smiled at Caro. "But a princess works in mysterious ways."

Caro winked back at Kate. "So does a mother of twenty."

"Twenty children?" Not possible! The woman couldn't be more than twenty-five. "You and Jared have twenty children? How?"

"No, no, you first, Elizabeth," Kate said, pulling a wad of knitting out of her bag. "Tell us everything."

She told them *nearly* everything.

About the protest march and Scotland Yard.

The set-to in Parliament.

The arrest warrant and Ross's overwhelming gallantry.

The wedding and the nonexistent wedding night.

But she didn't have to tell them how much she had come to love him.

They seemed to have known that before she did.

Chapter 17

For God's sake hold your tongue,
and let me love.

John Donne, 1572–1631
The Canonization

"Damn it all! First we made circles around London and now we're in Hampstead. On the way to God knows where." Ross glared at the two men sitting across from him in the carriage as it jounced and jolted along the rutted country road. "I'm going to kill you both."

"I'll risk it. What about you, Jared?" The blighter was doubtless grinning like a chimp.

"I'm in with you for the whole pound, Drew. Besides, if I remember rightly, Ross was instrumental in tricking my Kate into stepping into my lair at the lodge."

"At your own request, Jared."

"Still, turnabout's fair play." Drew laughed. "Because we all knew it was for her own good."

"Kate and I both benefited." Jared whistled. "Damn, if we didn't have the finest wedding night in the history of the world. No matter that it was two years late."

"Pardon me if I'm a bit more driven, but I'd prefer that my wedding night occur sometime within a month of the wedding. Now let me out of this carriage at the next—"

"I agree with you, Ross." Drew sprawled back against the carriage seat. "Caro and I had our wedding night first and then got married the next morning."

The carriage rounded a sharp curve to the right as the road left the village, then started down a hill.

"Where the hell are you taking me?"

"Oooo, the boy is eager, isn't he, Drew?"

"Can hardly blame him, though. We all did marry beauties."

Ross ignored them and glared out the tiny window.

A quarter mile outside the village the carriage slowed as it rolled through a hedge gate then came to rest.

Without waiting for an invitation, let alone an explanation, Ross leaped out of the carriage, and stopped dead on the gravel walk.

"See, Ross," Jared said, following him down a step. "Grousemeade Cottage."

"Good Lord." Ross laughed. Hard-won ages and ages ago by Jared. In a day-long dice game. With their pooled funds from the first of Craddock's gold buttons. Their erstwhile home for nearly two years. He'd almost forgotten it.

"Your bride is inside."

Ah.

"The family moved out a month ago," Drew added from the coach. "It's yours for as long as you'd like it."

"There's a gig out in the carriage house and a horse in the paddock, should you ever wish to leave your paradise."

"Now, are we forgiven, old man?"

Ross laughed again and, without a backward glance, started toward the front door and the softly amber glow from the mullioned windows. "Good night, gentlemen."

The carriage sped out into the darkness, stirring the cool, rose-scented air into billowing clouds that drew him closer to the arbored entry.

With a quaking hand, Ross merely touched the door latch and the oak panel drifted open like an invitation.

The main room was just as he'd remembered it, though neater and more substantially furnished. The hearth blazed from the center of the room, flanked by wide, timbered arches on either side of the large-stoned structure. Its flames danced shadows across the carpet, up the walls, and into the parlor behind the chimney, where the hearth was open between the two rooms.

"Elizabeth?" He stood in the entry, his nerves jangling as he scanned the room for his wife's lovely face in every curve and darkened corner, but without any luck.

Grousemeade Cottage wasn't large at all. Three rooms up, three down, and a snug kitchen attached in the rear. Difficult to get lost in.

Unless, of course, his pals had dumped him here without a bride. For which they would pay the rest of their stinking lives. If they lived.

"Your friends are quite wonderful."

"Elizabeth?" His heart leapt toward the sound of

her, somewhere in the weaving shadows of the candlelight beyond the arch to the right of the fireplace. A silky voice without substance.

He could feel her, could sense her heat, taste her savory fragrance on the air.

"They're devious too. Caro and Kate, especially." And then she appeared like a spirit just inside the arch. A shape, a shadow. His willful harem dancer.

She had been dazzling in the ballroom tonight; here in the cottage she was sumptuous, glittering. Her hair cascading freely across her shoulders, her cleavage deep and lush.

"You call *them* devious, wife? What of you and your trousers?" He shrugged out of his coat and dropped it across a chair back, savoring her smile, the glint of her eyes. "Shocking London to its marrow. Exposing your legs to the world, when I, your ravenous husband, haven't yet had the pleasure."

"All for a good cause."

"Ha! You'd wear those trousers every day for your own convenience if you could get away with it."

"I don't see why I shouldn't. Skirts can get in the way of doing all sorts of chores. What would you do without your trousers? Oh, I . . . ah-ha!" She paused in her realization, then sent him a teasing smile so beguiling that he would follow it to the ends of the earth.

"Are you threatening my trousers?"

"Come see for yourself." She cocked an eyebrow, dipped her shoulder at him, then disappeared into the flickering shadows beneath the arch.

And he followed like a wake follows a ship. Followed her exotic scent of sandalwood, the soft shoosh of silk that stirred against her legs. Followed her through the arch and into the parlor.

But the back parlor had never looked quite like this when he'd lived here with Jared and Drew. Opulent drapes against the rear windows, a scattering of thick carpets littered with piles of huge satiny pillows. A steaming tub, a low table laden with cheese and bread and succulent fruits. The whole scene shimmering with a forest of candles.

And standing in the midst of this breathtaking landscape was his exotic wife, in her exotic trousers and . . . Lord help him, the only garment between him and her pouting, perfect breasts was that short vest, precariously fastened in the front.

Those tiny silken tassels dancing where his hands ought to be exploring.

The full-sleeved, blowsy shirtwaist she'd been wearing beneath the vest had disappeared somewhere along the way. And now all he could do was stammer and stand there aching for her.

"I understand your journey here has been long and difficult, sirrah." She came toward him with a delicious glint in her eye, her arm extended as she approached, her fingers beckoning.

"Grueling, madam. Across arid deserts and raging seas." Oh, yes, he could play her game, would play it gladly. He could stand here and watch the gentle, purposeful swing of her lithe hips, the shifting, clinging silk against her thighs.

And the hypnotic bobbing of her breasts beneath

that singular vest with all its shadows and snickle-ways, waiting for one of them to show itself to him.

"Then settle your thoughts. I'm here to serve you." She stopped just shy of him to entwine her fingers in the front of his waistcoat. "After all, I'm told that you purchased a night full of scented delights with me."

"Indeed. A bought-and-paid-for night in the seraglio, madam." A night he might never survive, though he would die the happiest man on earth.

"A night in *my* seraglio, sir. Designed with you in mind." She tugged down on his waistcoat, bending his mouth to hers like a willow in the wind. "Hungry?"

"Starving."

"Good." She produced a succulent blackberry be-tween her fingers, then popped it into his mouth and kissed him lightly, slowly, on his mouth, nibbled along his jaw until she reached his ear, and whispered, "If you'll follow me, my lord."

"Anywhere, anytime." He was dazzled as she pulled on his cuff, dumbstruck by her scent as she led him toward the low table. "I have since the moment I saw you marching down Whitehall with your outra-geous sign."

She turned back to him and smiled, quirking her head as though she thought he might be teasing. "You saw me in the street that day?"

"Watched you from the moment you left Trafalgar Square." He slipped his hands around her slender waist, finding warm, bare skin beneath his fingers, and suffering a jolt of lust that pulled her forward against his erection and made her eyes flash.

"You said you hadn't."

"Every blessed step you took, my love."

"Why?"

"Hoping like a fool that you would glance up at me." He lifted her into his arms, holding her fast against him, length upon length, unable to get enough of her.

"Where were you, Ross?" She hugged her arms around his neck, clinging to him, scrubbing her fingers through the hair at his nape.

"In the Admiralty." He kissed her eyelids, the side of her nose. "At a meeting that held no importance after the moment I saw you."

She caught him by the ears and peered into his eyes. "Is that what brought you into Scotland Yard that day? My protest sign?"

"You did, Elizabeth." He laughed, slowly lowered her to her feet in front of the table and lifted her hair back off her shoulders. "While you marched past me with such determined pride."

"I was terrified," she whispered, catching her lower lip with her teeth.

"And I was besotted with the beautiful woman scowling out at the world from the back of that paddy wagon."

"That's not like you, Ross." She offered another blackberry between her fingers, and he took it eagerly, her fingertips and all, nibbling and licking them until he was holding her hand, kissing her palm.

"It isn't at all." To think, he might have walked away, might never have met her. And he suddenly couldn't imagine the loss. "But believe me, my love, you're worth every penny of blackmail you wrung out of me tonight."

"So far." She was now tugging on his sleeve, lifting

herself up onto her toes, the tips of her breasts a teasing, white-hot pressure seeping through his waistcoat, the linen of his shirt.

He steadied himself, restrained his urges and took hold of her elbows. But a shudder ripped suddenly through him, a lightning blue thirst for the woman he'd married but had hardly kissed.

He took her mouth with his, possessed her lips completely, tasting her and teasing. Sending him into an ecstasy when her tongue found his and played and flickered, until he was groaning like a bear and clutching her hips and lifting her into his arms again.

Mindlessly hungry for her, he carried her to the carpet, as he had imagined so many times, and drove her deeply into the mounds of pillows, deeper and deeper with his kiss against her hair and her eyes, then back to the lushness of her berry-flavored lips.

She sifted her fingers through his hair and looked up at him, her mouth rosy and moist. "My lord, I'm supposed to be pleasuring you."

"Believe me, love, you are."

But his little vixen gave a quick twist to her hips and he was suddenly, amazingly, trapped beneath her. Trapped by her devilish grin, by the simmering thrall of sandalwood caught up his nostrils.

"Now isn't that better?"

"God, yes!" She was straddling his hips with her knees, and his shoulders with her arms, settling another kiss on his lips, a long, leisurely kiss, a mad exploration of his mouth, a waltz with his tongue.

And then she was dangling a deep red cherry above

his mouth, dragging it across his lips until he caught it and chewed.

She crossed her arms over his chest and rested her chin on the back of her hands. "According to Kate, the cherries are from a tree here at the cottage."

"I remember." He sat up slightly and tossed the pit into the fire.

"So the three of you lived here in the cottage?" She slowly poked a cherry into her own mouth, making him want to follow after it.

But he'd vowed to pace himself through the night, to restrain himself for the sake of his eager, unbridled wife.

"Our headquarters for nearly three years, until Jared was twenty and we all went off to sea."

"My amazing husband." She cut off his words with another juicy blackberry then another kiss nuzzled against his mouth, another endless, honey-warm kiss. "And then, Ross?"

"Canada—" He was breathless for her. "—where we foiled a royal embezzlement plot and gained the queen's everlasting gratitude."

"The queen's champion, as well as my own." She was silk and sleekness from head to toe. He could barely think for the need to pull off her clothes, roll her onto her back and plunge inside of her. But that was for later, if he could last.

And still she nuzzled and squirmed against him until she finally stood up and over him. Her silk trousers shimmering like a warm river, the undersides of her breasts like shadowy crescents beneath her skimpy vest.

A sultry haven he intended to visit as soon as he could manage to regain his senses.

"I've more for you, my lord." She held out her hand to him.

Transfixed, not sure he could take much more, he gathered her soft hand into his and rose up onto one knee. She planted a kiss on his mouth and lifted him the rest of the way to his feet.

Then she stood back and raked him with her gaze while he waited as silently as he could, breathing like a bull.

"Your bath awaits, sir." When he reached for the buttons of his waistcoat, her fingers followed, tangled with his. "Let me do that. You're to relax here in my harem."

He laughed and took her chin between his fingers. "If I let you undress me, I can guarantee I'll not be relaxed in any way."

"I can see that already. Felt you as well." She grinned up at him as she started up the front of his waistcoat, button by button. The backs of her warm fingers sifted heat through the linen of his shirt, taking his breath away.

"These buttons, Ross." She peered closely at one of them. "I noticed this very crest carved into the hearth in your rooms at the Huntsman. And tonight on Jared's and Drew's buttons. Is it the Huntsman's official crest?"

So much more than that. "A symbol of freedom, success, and loyalty."

"Ah, the three of you." She went to work on the rest of the buttons, admiring them.

"Indeed." A reminder of how precious life could be.

"Perhaps the Adams should have a crest of its

own." She opened his waistcoat and toyed with the buttons on his shirt. "Our own symbols."

"A book, madam, a protest sign, and—"

"And Turkish trousers?" She slipped her hands inside his open shirt and slid them across his bare chest. "Oh, my, you're warm here."

He caught her face between his palms and kissed her upturned mouth. "Actually, wife, I had been thinking of a heart."

She put her ear to his chest. "Yours is beating just fine."

And Lord, his pulse was thundering through his veins, churning against his sinew, battering his resolve.

"But your shirt has to go, my lord." A moment later she had shucked him of his waistcoat and shirt, and his braces were hanging at his sides.

And she was appraising him again, the tip of her finger tucked beneath her chin, as though she were considering the purchase of a new vase.

"Heavens, Ross, Aunt Tibbs and Aunt Clarice would think you a marvel of manhood."

Now there were two women who had left their mark on his wife. "They'd approve of me?" That seemed important.

"In her younger days Aunt Tibbs would have thrown herself at you headlong."

"A woman who knew her mind."

"And her manflesh."

A surge of molten heat shot through him. Sweet-hot anticipation. "Indeed."

"You're also recklessly handsome, husband, and Tibbs admired that in a man."

"And in a husband?"

Aunt Tibbs would have thought I was a damned fool for marrying you, Ross.

But with any luck and a lot of work, her remarkable husband would prove that jail hadn't been the better alternative to marriage.

He was certainly the most amazing man to look at. His shoulders wide, his arms powerfully muscled as he ran his fingers through his hair, his chest bare and bronze and corded like a Greek god's. With a dark swath of hair plunging to well below his narrow waist, like a fine, sleek arrow.

And below all that dizzying maleness, his wonderfully bulging trousers.

"Time for those," she said, pointing to the bulge, still amazed at the size of him, everywhere she looked, everywhere she touched.

But when she reached for the top of his trousers, he grabbed her hands and put them around his neck, then pulled her against him, which only made his rock hard penis more prominent.

More thrilling.

"You'd best let me do that, wife."

"Why? Yours aren't the first set of men's trouser buttons I've encountered."

"Is that so?"

"Well, there wasn't a man in the trousers at the time, but I figured it out on my own." And so she went to work on the topmost button, hampered somewhat by the fact that she couldn't see what she was doing because the man was kissing her fiercely.

"Have you figured out that I'm bursting for you?"

"Definitely." He groaned against her mouth as she brushed up against his arousal, nibbled at her lips as she slipped the top button through its hole.

Then, curious beyond measure, Elizabeth dropped to her knees in front of him and reached for the next button. But Ross caught her hand and drew her to her feet.

"No, Elizabeth."

"Then how am I going to get your trousers off?"

"You're not."

"You simply can't take a bath in your clothes, sir. And your paid-for night in my harem includes a personal bath."

"Personal bath?" He raised his brows, smiled broadly, then, without losing a beat, hauled off his trousers and his drawers, his shoes and socks, all at the same time.

And when he was finished, he stood naked in front of her. Gloriously naked.

"Much better, husband." Though her cheeks were afire and her pulse was thumping against her ears. "Much bigger." Thicker.

Grand!

And waiting for her.

Chapter 18

And on her lover's arm she leant,
And round her waist she felt it fold,
And far across the hills they went
In that new world which is the old.

Alfred, Lord Tennyson
The Day-Dream, 1842

And she really ought to encourage him to get into the tub, but she hadn't any words at the moment. They were stuck in her belly, like a whirlwind of embers.

But he was already making his way there, the muscles of his backside flexing as he moved, as he stepped into the water like a beast out of legend.

And groaning all the way down, until he ducked under the water, stayed overlong, then came up scrubbing at his hair, shaking his head like a water dog.

His skin gleamed gold in the light of the candles, inviting her touch, but sending her heart into a plummeting spin when she noticed a thick, uneven scar running at a downward angle across his left shoulder, from the ridge line well into the muscle of his upper arm.

Graphic proof of her husband's vulnerability in his work, as well as his courage.

She went to his side and pulled a candle closer for a better look. "No wonder your shoulder gets sore now and then."

"If it's sore at the moment, wife, I can't feel it." His smile was wolfish as he leaned back against the tub. But as she began massaging the thick muscles, his head fell back and his mouth dropped open with a moan. "That's just . . . oh, you're so fine."

She worked on his shoulder, kissing his ear and his neck, cupping his jaw for a better purchase for her kiss against his mouth.

"I like this, wife. Being here in your harem." He held her face with his wet hands, held her mouth against his, romped there. "Pampered and massaged."

Fondled, my lord. But that was to be a surprise for later.

"A wife's responsibility," she said, her hands soaped now and scented with lemon.

"To create a harem for her husband in their bedchamber?" He sighed even more deeply as she worked the slickness of the soap into his shoulders and along his arm.

"A one-woman harem, sir, though she would, of course, soon come to expect the same intimate treatment from her husband."

"Wise woman."

That's when the soap slipped out of her hands, landed on his chest, then slid downward into the soapy darkness between his widely spread legs, where it hit the bottom of the metal tub with a clunk.

"Oops," was all she could manage.

He looked up into her eyes as though challenging her courage to go after it.

She not only had the courage, but a burning, deeply abiding curiosity.

"I'll get that, Ross." Hoping for the best, yet not quite knowing what that would be, she judged his position under the water then stuck her bare arm between his legs.

"Careful." He was gripping the edge of the tub as though he feared she would pull him under.

She found the soap immediately, but, like the shameless hussy she was, pretended she hadn't while she gathered her courage and kept her hand down there, having to lean her breasts against his knee.

He focused a narrowed, suspicious eye on her. "What are you doing, wife?"

"I'm trying to remember the suggestions from my booklet."

"Which suggestions would that—oh, God! What are you—oh, Elizabeth!" He bucked.

"Oh, Ross!" Oh, my, his erection was splendid! Hot and thick and stiff beyond her imagination. And his scrotum was a marvelous wonder, along with all the other shapes of him.

"Careful where you—ahhhhh!" He was sitting bolt upright, breathing hard and fast, like a tethered beast, holding onto the rim of the tub with a white-knuckled grip.

"Now I remember! 'Tend to his every part in the

bath, fondle his manly shapes, linger where he seems to most enjoy your touch.' "

"And that's enough fondling, for now, sweet!"

"So soon?" Disappointment deflated her. But only until Ross grabbed her upper arms and rose out of the tub, drawing her upward with him.

"Barely soon enough!" He stepped out of the water and snagged the nearest towel.

"I should be the one to dry you off, my lord. After all—"

"Not this time. Can't risk it."

"Then you owe me."

"And I always pay my debts." Elizabeth loved to see him in such a tempest of passion, striding toward her in full rut, the towel tossed aside, his nostrils flaring.

"But, good sir, I haven't given you anywhere near your donations's worth tonight."

"You will, my love, you will."

A thrilling threat, a breathtaking promise from a man who was huge and stark naked and looking too pleased with himself as he engulfed her with his embrace.

The steaming heat of him seeped through the silk of her trousers, his penis a rod of fire, rolling against her belly, making her want to reach down for him, to touch him again.

But when she tried, he growled and dipped her backward over his arm, exposing her neck to his mouth, to his trailing kisses, her name whispered again and again.

"Oh, Ross . . . that's, oh!" Her skin was alive and on fire for him, his hands skimming everywhere along her silky trousers, shaping her bottom and against her belly, cupping her between her legs, a touch that drove the air from her lungs and dizzied her.

Just when she was about to beg him to . . . to do something more intimate, faster or slower, he hooked his deft fingers through the loop holding her vest together between her breasts and popped the button right off.

The sides of her vest fell away to each side, and when she looked up he was the wolf again, staring hungrily at her breasts.

"There they are," he whispered, "the sweet things."

She was ready for anything, but when his mouth closed over her nipple, she nearly fainted with the force of the pleasure. It shot through every part of her. The more he nuzzled and squeezed and tugged, the tighter he was winding her. Like a watchwork spring in her belly, winding and winding, growing hotter and hotter.

He held her suspended backward, exposed to the sweet torture of his mouth and his tongue as she writhed her hips into his steamy hot erection, clutched at his shoulders and called out his name in a most shameless way.

"Is this among your *Unbridled Embraces,* my dear wife?"

"No, but it should be. Will be!"

Ross wondered how he'd gotten so damned lucky in his brashness. Dutifully rescuing a rebellious woman from a prison sentence and finding a brazen, wanton wife instead.

She was nearly singing his name, taking tiny little

gasps of air with his every tug, grabbing his bare buttocks and urging his hips and his hardness against her belly.

The vest was long gone, but the woman was still wearing those Turkish trousers, still hiding her scented mysteries beneath the silk.

He straightened with her, pulled her against him, belly-to-belly, roused by the growing urgency of her wriggling.

"Did you know, wife, that there are techniques a husband can use in order to please his wife in their marriage bed? An 'Unbridled Embraces for Men.'"

Her mouth was rosy and thoroughly kissed. "Making love to his wife as though she were his mistress?"

"Exactly." He found the two buttons at the back of her trousers and freed them a moment later. "It's time for these to come off."

She lifted her arms over her head, and swayed her hips in a little dance as he spread his fingers over her hips and slipped the trousers slowly down. He knelt as he went, his efforts tantalizing him with the softness of the silk, the sight of her bare belly, then her fleece and the sleekness of her legs as the silk gathered in a pool around her bare feet.

"You're beautiful, Elizabeth."

She gazed down at him, still swaying, though completely naked now. "You make me feel that way."

The woman did that all on her own. And here he was, on his knees in front of her, with a tantalizing view of her womanhood, and a driving hunger to taste her.

"Hold on, wife."

"Are we going somewhere?"

"Indeed we are." He reached his hands around her hips to her bottom and splayed his fingers across the coolness of her cheeks. He planted kisses on her flat belly and then moved his mouth downward.

"Oh! Ross! Oh!" She gasped with every inch of his descent toward her curls at the cleft of her legs, her fingers winding tighter and tighter into his hair.

He kept her close with one hand on her bottom and began to toy at her mound with the fingers of the other. Playing among her curls and the slickness he found there, gently sliding a finger inside her where he wanted to be thrusting his throbbing erection.

"Ross, what are you—oh!" She grabbed his shoulders, then his hair again, her hands unsettled and pulling him closer as he stroked and plunged with his fingers.

But when he plunged with his tongue, delving deeply with his strokes, her knees buckled against his arms and she let out a keening moan that would have thrown her backward in a free-fall if he hadn't carried her safely to the ground onto the pile of pillows.

"Oh, Ross! Shall I add this one to my *Unbridled Embraces*?" Her knees were bent, her hips thrusting upward and writhing into his kiss, pulling at him as though she couldn't get enough of him.

But bringing her too close to her climax. Too soon for the first time.

"We'd best keep this marital suggestion between us." He kissed his way from her belly all the way to her mouth, until they were face-to-face, and he could see the dizzying passion in her eyes. "Or we'll both be locked up for distributing salacious materials."

"They'd never believe me anyway." She was crooning against his cheek, rolling his hotly distended, much beleaguered erection against her belly, inching him ever closer to her sheath with her determined squirming. "Take me there now, please."

He felt suddenly like he was falling. "Where?"

"Wherever it is you were taking me. Because I don't think I can wait any longer."

And there would always be other times with this remarkable wife of his. Tomorrow. An hour from now. Other nights in their own special harem.

And she was so eager. Wouldn't want to frustrate her the first time around.

So he rose up on his elbows and let her find him with her fingers, with her impatient grasp, which nearly cost him dearly.

"Here?" she asked, fitting the tip of him unerringly against her cleft, then sliding it back and forth along the slick heat of her until he caught her hand.

"Let me."

"Oh, yes!" She lay back like a cat lounging in the sun and wrapped her legs around his hips.

"I see you're ready."

"Mmmmm . . . ready for you." She closed her eyes and brought her heels against his backside.

Slick and open and, dear Lord, this might just kill him.

He lifted her hips and fit her better against the tip of him. He thrust slightly and met a firmness that widened her eyes, then made her smile and catch her hands around his waist.

He thrust again a little deeper, encouraged again by her smile and the brightness of it, until she finally buckled forward and propelled him mindlessly all the way inside her.

Until he was buried to the hilt and quaking, and she was kissing him as though she were starving.

"You're very large, Ross, and very warm and, oh, how I want you here."

Elizabeth loved the way her husband was hovering above her, gazing down at her so possessively, his eyes as hot as his breath. His growl of pleasure rumbling through his chest and into hers. Into every part of her.

Oh, my, what all those unfulfilled husbands and wives of London were missing.

And then, as though they had formed a silent pact between them, she began to move with him in a spell-binding rhythm, meeting each of his strokes measure for bewitching measure. An earthy pleasure that built like a summer storm, bristling with bolts of blue light-ning.

An urgent heat that leadened her limbs and lit up her fingertips. That centered on that splendid place where they were joined. Her husband kissing her madly, as though he couldn't get enough of her.

The rhythm increasing, surging like a wildfire, fo-cusing its tension, coming faster and faster, lifting her up toward the clouds.

Until she finally felt herself splintering into bits of giddy light in an unimaginable bliss. Heard herself calling out his name against his mouth, catching his every breath, his every pulsing moan.

Until he caught her fiercely around the waist and lifted her against him and began to quake and shudder above her. His muscles turned to stone, his bellowing breath turned to grunting groans as he pulsed and drove into her, spilling his seed deeply, completely, inside her.

A blissful sharing so profoundly moving that she began to weep quietly and stroke his hair out of his handsome face.

"Well, my lord, did you find pleasure enough in my harem?"

His coal dark eyes took on a brilliant glint. "Not nearly enough, my lady. I'll be wanting more of this."

"Really?" She hadn't thought of that, but the very idea made her skin tingle. "You mean we can do it all again tonight?"

He lowered himself to her side, his breathing still coming in long drafts. "Technically, we're well into tomorrow. But since I'm all paid up for my night of pleasure . . ."

She sighed and slipped her arms around him. "Delighted to oblige, sir. Simply delighted."

Elizabeth had never in her life been treated so like a pampered fairy queen. Complete with a quaint, enchanted cottage. With a heaping sideboard of heavenly dishes delivered twice the following day, as if by magic. With an attentive husband who seemed to adore her.

Just as she adored him.

They took a walk on the grounds and ended up playing naked in the stream. They toasted chunks of bread in the fire and ended up drizzling warm honey and butter over each other's skin, snacking off the excess, and snacking and snacking. They arm-wrestled for erotic wagers, and he always lost to her questing fingers.

Always, the lout.

And in the last rays of daylight, after feeding each other a delicious meal of thick beef stew and steamed asparagus, cucumber salad and fleshy fruit, all the while wrapped in a tangle of bed linens and pillows, Elizabeth found herself unable to stay awake any longer. She finally began to drift asleep, her dreams and her heart caught up in Ross's powerful arms.

And those splendid dreams spun out as she slept, tendrils of joy twining around every part of their lives. Happy children and meadowlands, acts of Parliament and games of whist.

Each new strand amazed her, because Ross was a husband right out of legend. The converse of each of her closely held prejudices against men and their arrogance.

Votes for Women, the signs still read.

And husbands still wielded their absolute authority over their wives.

Boys grew to men, girls to women, and still the cycle repeated.

And repeated.

And she felt the cliff begin to crumble out from beneath her shoes.

Felt herself falling, heard herself crying out into the darkness—

"Ross!"

She woke with a shock, sitting bolt upright in the darkness. And alone. Chilled.

"Ross?"

No sound at all.

She slipped out of bed and into a nightgown, then wrapped herself in the silky counterpane and padded out into the main room.

She wasn't alone after all, but the reedy figure bending to the hearth wasn't Ross.

"Ah, Willie!" The young son of the caretaker who lived in the village and had faithfully delivered the meals from his mother's kitchen. "Don't tell me you've brought more food? As you can see, we're full up. And it's after ten at night."

And where was Ross?

"No, my lady. I brought a note to his lordship. Straight from London, it was. And urgent, said my ma."

"Where is he?"

"Left here on my horse 'bout a half hour ago, right after reading the note I brung him."

"And he didn't tell me?"

"Didn't want to wake you," he whispered, as though recreating Ross's exit. "Told me to stay here and keep guard over you."

Good grief. Was she never to move again without a pair of dutiful, male eyes watching over her, by command of her beloved, still overbearing husband?

"That's it, Will? I'm to guess why he's gone?"

"Oh!" Will jumped to the hob, plucked a folded

note off the mantel then jabbed it at her. "Also told me to give this to you in the morning when you wake up. But I guess you're awake now, aren't you?"

"Quite." And disappointed beyond imagining. "Thanks, Will, you can go home now."

"No, my lady. I'm to stay here and keep—"

"Guard over me, yes, yes, I remember," she said, unfolding the note and turning up the lamp at the side table. "Then relax. Have something to eat. Take a nap, lad. I'm sure I'll be awake for a while."

You have a lovely hand, husband. His script was plain and clear and firmly struck.

But, oh, there was a world of trouble in the contents.

My dear Elizabeth,

Forgive me for not waking you with a farewell kiss, but I hadn't time to risk that a taste of your honey would keep me from my sudden call to action.

As I feared, and warned you, wife, the monstrous kidnapper struck again late last night.

"Again? But that's impossible." Lydia wasn't due to make her escape until the end of next week. Surely her assistants hadn't advanced the schedule without telling her.

This time he has not only abducted the wife of the Russian deputy ambassador, but he has taken her from her own chamber in the Russian Embassy.

"Dear God, no!" Not Lydia at all. But a stranger! A completely innocent woman.

As you may know, an embassy and its grounds are considered sovereign soil, its fences as sacred to the home country as its own borders. The mere act of breaking into an embassy can be considered an invasion. Abducting one of its citizens at the same time can precipitate a declaration of war.

I've been called back to Whitehall to help smooth over the situation with the Russians before it becomes an international incident which might force us into an unwanted, unwinnable war. I'm also to use all my resources from the investigations into the previous abductions.

Oh, but Ross, you have it all wrong! Whoever kidnapped the hapless deputy ambassador's wife was using her own methods for his evil deeds!

To misdirect everyone! Ross and Scotland Yard and the Foreign Office! The press and the public!

"Dear Lord, what have I done?" Thanks to her, they were investigating the wrong crime.

"Anything the matter, my lady?" Willie must have been watching her the whole time, listening to her babbling. His eyes were wide as the moon and worried for her.

"Uhm, well, Willie, it's nothing I can't handle."

As long as I can get to London in time to save that poor, helpless woman from my own bloody foolishness.

"Good, my lady, because his lordship wanted me to be sure not to let you leave before he comes back for you."

She'd been afraid of that. Her overprotective husband and his ever-present henchmen. Though a nicer henchman she had never met.

I'll send my carriage to pick you up at noon. In the meantime, love, stay abed in our honeymoon cottage and think of me.

Your adoring husband,
Ross

Well, she'd be thinking about him, all right, but while speeding into London, not while lying abed.

Chapter 19

All tragedies are finished by a death,
All comedies are ended by a marriage.

Lord Byron, *Don Juan*, 1819

"I understand the need for haste, Clarendon," Ross said as patiently as he could manage, "but I can't make a definitive pronouncement to the ambassador about our investigation until I know something more."

"Can't you go back there now and do a little diplomatic lying?" the man asked, scraping his bent knuckle across his unshaven cheek. "Just stir the facts a bit, muddy them if you must. You saw Brunnov. He looked positively apoplectic."

"My lord, the only thing I can tell the Russian ambassador at the moment is that we haven't a clue as to who abducted the three women before he got the princess. Only that the criminal is getting bolder with every attack."

"He might listen to—"

"Bloody hell, sir! If I do anything to lead him to be-

319

lieve that we're incapable of finding Princess Lenka, we'll be at war come morning. Look, I've surrounded the place with my operatives. I've covered every railway station, every dock in every harbor. I've set the world in motion. That will have to do until we've got more solid evidence. Besides, it's nearly three in the morning."

"Damn, damn, damn." Clarendon yanked off his spectacles and rubbed his eyes. "I'm going home to bed. Though I doubt I'll sleep a wink. Just find the bloody princess, Blakestone. Alive, if you please."

"I'll send word the moment I have anything for you, sir."

Clarendon gave a final scowl, then clapped his hat down on his head just a bit too far, wrinkling folds into his brow. "Good night."

A better night would have been another one in Grousemeade Cottage with his unbridled wife. And with a miracle or two, he would be back there tomorrow night.

But in the meantime, he had a long night of research to do down in the Factory archives.

"Good God, Ross, you're supposed to be dallying with your wife in your wedding cottage." Drew was standing at the club room door, bleary-eyed and yawning, scratching the top of his head.

"Don't bloody remind me." Ross lifted the box of evidence he'd collected at the embassy and started toward the back stairs. "Let's see what we can do about getting us both back to our brides."

The guard held open the door that led into the security vestibule of the Factory, leaving Drew to stalk down the stairs after Ross.

He led the way into the evidence lab and put the box on one of the examination tables, feeling older than dirt and completely at a loss. Blind where he normally could see through stone.

"What the hell is going on here, Drew?" Ross dropped onto a tall stool and tossed his nearly useless pad of notes into the middle of the table. "I've never seen anything like it. Four abducted women, four identical crimes."

"What's all this?" Drew peered into the box.

"Besides a folded white handkerchief doused in chloroform and a man's leather glove, nothing."

"No bonnets this time around?"

"The princess was sleeping. Hardly the time for bonnets. The rest of this is all for the benefit of the embassy officials. I had to do something. The whole delegation was in an uproar. Brunnov was bellowing for satisfaction. Dueling pistols at dawn. And he didn't care if his opposite was Aberdeen or Prince Albert, or the queen herself."

"So you collected a clock?" Drew lifted it partially out of the box.

"Someone heard it ticking in Princess Lenka's room sometime in the night."

"Lenka? Oh, hell." Drew hitched his hip onto the table. "The moment Caro hears about this one, she'll be beating down the Factory door."

"A second cousin?"

"First."

"Well, what could it hurt if Caro joined the fray? She's damned good and certainly no stranger to the secret operations down here."

"Not to mention all those state secrets that need to be kept from—" Drew frowned, lifted his eyes to Ross. "Did you hear that?"

But Ross was already out the lab door and heading silently down the passage toward the tailor shop and the noises in the dimness.

Toward the soft footfalls, moving toward him.

The whisper of fabric.

A familiar scent.

And then someone crashed into him, squarely against his chest. The person flew backward, out of his reach with a bellowing shout as Drew went dashing past them, deeper into the passage.

"I'll go see if there are others."

"Come here, you!" Ross made a lucky grab in the dark for the burglar who was scrabbling away from him, and must have caught a sleeve.

Then a hand.

A very soft hand.

Dismissing the distracting sensation, he hauled the little sneak thief behind him along the corridor toward the light from the lab, wondering how the devil the Factory's defenses had been so badly breached. How many of these ruffians were prowling through the rooms? And what could be done to keep them quiet?

"In here, you bloody bastard!" He pulled the rumpled clump into the room at the same time he realized that he was looking at the back of a rounded woman, righting herself.

At her skirts. An apron. Slender arms and long hair. Burnished red hair, golden tipped, tumbling out of its loosened bonds as she turned.

Silky, shining hair.

Elizabeth's hair.

Bloody hell!

"Elizabeth?" A stupid question. He was looking right into her beautiful sea-green eyes.

At her stunned, crimson-cheeked, open-mouthed face.

"Ross?" She squinted right back at him, tilting her head. "What are you doing here?"

"Me? What the devil are you doing here? I left you in Hampstead." Left her sleeping and naked, but now . . .

"I'm very aware of where you left me."

"How the hell did you get back to town, madam?" He reached out and lifted her hair back over her shoulder, if only to convince himself that she wasn't simply an illusion. "And where's that blighter Will? I ordered him to stay with you."

"Good heavens, Ross, he's a boy. He hadn't a chance. I tricked him. But you'll not take it out on him. Really, that's all beside the most important point. What I want to know is, what are you doing in here?" She pointed at the floor, her eyes still puzzled, flashing with exasperation. "In this place?"

"What are you talking about, wife?" They were utterly at cross purposes, speaking riddles to each other. "And how did you get in here?"

"How did *you*?" She seemed increasingly incensed, as though he had followed her here instead of the other way around.

"I came down the stairs, madam. And you?"

"The *stairs*?" She quirked her brow. Pursed her lips and looked to the ceiling.

"How did you get past the guard?" Hell, he'd just seen the man upstairs. The two other entrances were manned by multiple sentries.

"The guard? Oh."

He didn't like the sound of that. "What do you mean, 'Oh'? How did you get in here?"

She opened her mouth to speak, but pulled back her words and moved away from him as Drew came bowling through the door with a lighted candlestick.

He raised a brow when he caught sight of Elizabeth. "Well, good evening, Lady Blakestone."

"Wexford?" She canted her head as though she was looking at a ghost.

"I thought you left your wife at Grousemeade Cottage, Ross." Drew set the burning candle on the table next to the evidence box.

"So did I." He pointed at the candle but kept his eyes on his nervous wife. "Where did you find that?"

"In the tailor shop. And I doubt Mr. Puckett left it burning."

Ross took hold of his wife's arms and turned her around to face him full on, better to catch the nuances so alive in her eyes. "Well, madam, explain yourself. How did you get in here?"

But her mouth took on an even more stubborn slant as she glared back at him. "Here's a better question, Ross: where *are* we? What kind of place is this? And what have you and Drew to do with it?"

Bloody hell, did she really not know that she was in the basement of the Huntsman? "Let's just say that Drew and I have a right to belong here. We work here. You don't. Now what are you doing in our cellar?"

She glanced at Drew, then back at Ross. "All right, then, my lords, since I am obviously the one who found my way into this so-called cellar by way of the . . . unofficial route—"

"Which is from where?" Drew asked in an overly diabolical voice, his arms crossed over his chest.

"In . . . uhm, through the paneled wall of the tailor shop."

"The what?" Ross asked, with a glance at Drew. "How? From where?"

She wrinkled her brow and rubbed the end of her nose with a crooked finger, as though wishing to muffle the truth. "From . . . from the Abigail Adams."

Impossible! The place was three blocks away. "You must be joking."

Drew snorted. "I'll go check it out. If she's right— and I'm assuming your lovely bride wouldn't be spinning a tale for us—then I should end up at the Adams."

"You might as well go home from there, Drew. I'll see you back here this afternoon."

Drew sent a gracious, encouraging wink toward Elizabeth, and then arched a brow at Ross. "Welcome to the *husbands' club*, old man."

Drew stuck his hands in his trouser pockets, turned on his heel and left the lab, trailing that damned contented tune behind him.

"Now, listen, Elizabeth—" Ross whirled back on his wife, ready to get to the bottom of all her dodging and deceptions, then realized that she was three sizes larger than she'd been when he left her. Her bosom matronly, her waist larger around, her dress oddly old-fashioned . . .

He opened his mouth to ask what the devil she was up to, but the woman reached out to him, caught her fingertips in his coat sleeve as though to soothe him.

"Look, Ross, I promise to show you everything later. But just now we don't have much time."

"No time for what?" It never ended, this riddle of his wife. One puzzle after another. One surprise before the next one, an even larger one.

She was flicking an impatient frown at him. "I thought you were trying to find Princess Lenka. Isn't that why you left me to pine away in our wedding cottage in Hampstead, while you came flying back here to London?"

"Yes, but the case of the abducted princess isn't your affair."

She took a stout breath and set her brow. "Actually, Ross, I think can help."

"Thank you, but I've got plenty of help. My own operatives, the Home Guard, the Metropolitan Police, the Foot Guard, the bloody cavalry—"

"Isn't that going to be a little crowded for a quiet investigation?"

God, it was late. And she was more beautiful than ever with her adventurous spirit. But he was tired enough to sleep a week, had hoped for just a few hours.

"Please, Elizabeth, I appreciate your concern for the princess. It's not your problem."

But it's completely my problem! Elizabeth had never dreaded anything quite so much as she was dreading this. Telling Ross that she'd been responsible for the three previous abductions. That they weren't abductions at all.

But that the princess's kidnapping was terrifyingly real.

She had to tell him everything, if only to make him believe her.

Even this new little bit of treachery. That not only had she and her operatives already been at work on the case, but that they might have broken the first clue.

A very large clue.

Best to just say it right out.

"Look, Ross, I know you're not going to like anything I'm about to tell you, but . . ."

He took his time pinching out the candle flame then casting her a weary glance. "But what?"

"I know where the princess is being held."

He rubbed at his temples, sighed. "Please, Elizabeth—"

"You have to listen to me, Ross. When I got back to London, I didn't know where you were, but I had to do something."

"You had to do something about the kidnapped princess? Why?"

The full truth would surely mean a battle between them, and would slow them down, so she didn't answer completely. "So when I couldn't find you, my assistants and I . . . well, we went over to the Russian Embassy to see if we could do anything."

He came fully alert and plunked her down in the chair behind her. "Bloody hell! You did what?"

"Good heavens, Ross, we didn't knock on the door.

We posted ourselves across the street, around the perimeter."

He towered over her, his arms crossed against his chest, as though daring her to continue. "But why?"

She was leading up to the reason. "A short time after we arrived—one o'clock maybe—I saw a shadowy figure on the roof, skirting the eaves, in the rear of the building. Apparently he was looking for a way to get inside, maybe to drop onto a balcony or something."

"Well! Did he get inside?" He scowled his question at her, plainly interested, plainly not wanting to be.

"Something must have spooked him because he listened for a moment, then scuttled down a drainpipe. He ducked through the garden shadows and then disappeared down an alley."

"No one else saw him, wife, none of the guards?" He stood there looking down at her, the muscles in his arms flexed.

"I doubt it. Nobody moved, Ross."

"And then what?"

Her overprotective husband wasn't going to like this part at all. "Well, I couldn't just let him go. So . . . I followed him into the alley."

"Bloody hell! You could have been killed!" He dropped down on his knees in front of her, his eyes flashing with dark horror. "How the hell far did you follow him?"

"All the way to an import shop on Huggett Lane." She swallowed hard, just now realizing that she might have been in a bit of danger after all.

"And then what did you do? And please don't tell me that you went inside."

At least the stubborn man was finally fully engaged in what she was trying to tell him. Furious, but he obviously believed her.

And she had so many more secrets to tell him.

But his eyes were so bright she had to look down at her fingers for a moment before she could bear the intensity. "I waited, to see what he'd do next. It was still dark, and a light flared up in the attic almost immediately. That's when I tried the shop door and it opened. I didn't hear a bell, Ross, so I went inside."

"Christ!" He dropped his head into both hands.

"A few steps only." She raked her fingers through his hair, just for contact, to make sure he didn't hate her completely. "But I'm sure I heard something upstairs of the shop. Harsh voices, whispering. Angry words, though I couldn't understand them. As though something had gone wrong."

When he raised his head, he was still looking at her from under a thunderous brow. "And then what?"

"I heard someone coming down the stairs. So I ducked outside and hid in the doorway of the next shop. Then I followed him another ten minutes until he disappeared into a large building somewhere in Kensington. So we can't wait another minute. You know how quickly things change in a kidnapping."

After all, her three assistants were already waiting for her in Huggett Lane, ready to put their plan into gear as soon as it got light enough.

Though that might be a bit difficult just now, given her husband's stare of disbelief.

"Where do you come by this whole mad idea?" He captured her chin between his fingers and bent to her, palpably frightened for her. "Besides the danger involved in skulking outside the Russian Embassy, you haven't any understanding of what it takes to foil a kidnapping."

Oh, but I do, husband. I just don't know how to tell you where I came by that understanding.

"Please, Ross. At least let me show you where I think she is. That's all I'm asking. Please."

Ross heard himself growling. His mind a muddle. His heart rattling against his throat, terrified for his wife. Getting involved when the danger was so real.

But bloody hell, she sounded so sure of herself, her story so plausible, he had to look into it. And if she came along with him, at least he would know exactly where she was at all times.

"Very well, madam, we'll take a drive past the import shop." If there was anything to it, he'd take it from there.

"Wonderful!" She grabbed his arms, lifted up onto her toes and kissed him. Then she picked up the large fabric satchel she'd dragged in behind her, grasped it in front of her in both hands and waited for him.

Not a patient bone in her body. And if she was right, if the Russian princess was locked in an attic in Huggett Lane, then she'd just possibly saved the day.

"This way, madam." He closed the lab door and led her up the stairs through a series of locked doors, a vestibule, past two guards, and finally into the back hallway.

"The Huntsman, Ross?" She stopped and touched his shoulder. "Is that where we are?"

"You're very good at secrets, Elizabeth." Too good,

it seemed. "Please keep this one. Because a whole lot of people are depending on it."

She snorted as if he'd just accused her of treason. "I'll carry it to my death, Ross. As if you didn't know."

The sun was up and the morning beginning to bustle as they left in a carriage from the rear of the Huntsman.

"To the Russian Embassy, Henry."

Ten nearly silent minutes later, with his lunatic wife tucked under his shoulder and his heart rammed up against his throat, the carriage came to a halt in a narrow street a block short of the Russian Embassy.

"There, Ross." Elizabeth slipped to the seat across from him and tapped on the window glass. "I was posted in the doorway of that flower shop, just opposite the northwest corner. It was dark at the time, but that's how I was able to see the man on the roof."

He followed the point of her finger, hoping she'd been wrong about the whole thing, or delirious. Yet knowing in his gut that she was rarely wrong about anything.

Russian guards were everywhere. His own operatives posted quietly out of sight. But her story was becoming all too credible. And that could only mean trouble.

"Which direction did he go when he left the grounds?"

"Through that alleyway. There, next to the bakery on the corner."

"Then use this to tell Henry which way to go." Feeling as though he was putting his wife directly in the

line of fire, Ross handed her the speaking tube, then
sat back against the seat, to watch out of sight of the
window.

"Thank you, Ross." She smiled at him, suddenly,
suspiciously, looking every bit the commander in the
field as she spoke into the bell. "Are you there,
Henry? . . . Oh, good."

The route led from the embassy along the most narrow of snickleways, perfect for a conspirator.
Through two squares, then finally into Huggett Lane,
a street lined with small, well-cared-for shops.

"He went in there." His too clever wife had in-
structed Henry to pass the shop before she stopped
him, and pointed farther down the street. "With the
green awning. An import shop, as I said. Foodstuff
and fabric and porcelain from the continent."

A tidy, bayed display window. A floor above and an
attic.

Nondescript.

It could be anything. Or everything. Making him
wonder who the devil he'd married.

"Show me where the man went next, Elizabeth."
He wanted to get this over with quickly. Wanted it to
end without involving his wife in the danger that he
felt prickling the back of his neck.

She picked up the speaking tube again. And Henry
followed her directions.

But in the midst of her instructions he was struck by
a thought. The perfectly logical reason that Elizabeth
had felt compelled to rescue the princess!

My God! Why hadn't he thought of it? His heart
gave a wild thump.

"Elizabeth . . . ?"

"Two more blocks, Henry, then to the left." She looked from the window back to Ross, the bell of the tube stuck against her ear. "Yes?"

"Princess Lenka." He leaned forward, elbows on his knees, his heart slowing with relief. "Is she, by chance, a member of the Abigail Adams? I didn't think to ask because—"

"No, no, she isn't, Ross. I've never met the woman." Yet her face went white, her eyes filled with dread again. She caught her lower lip between her teeth, her voice growing quiet as the carriage rattled on along over the cobbles. "But if you think about it, that's . . . uhm . . . that's a problem with this case, isn't it? The common factor among the other abductions that's missing this time."

"The Adams." Or Elizabeth herself.

She looked stricken. "It's more than that, Ross, much more."

"But if we're not dealing with a—oh, bloody, bleeding hell."

"What is it, Ross?"

He hadn't been paying attention to the route or their surroundings, but now he pressed his face closer against the window, praying he was wrong.

"Elizabeth, is that the building you saw the man go into?"

She peered through the window on the other side of the door as their carriage approached from the south. "The large limestone, with the grounds taking up the whole block. Yes."

Bloody hell! He grabbed the speaking tube, called

out for Henry to stop, and the carriage swung up against the curb.

"You're absolutely sure, Elizabeth? It was dark when you were here. You might have missed him entering. It's very important that this is it."

"Definitely. Someone greeted him as he entered from the porte cochere. Why? What is it?"

His heart and his hopes fell. "The Austrian Embassy." Christ Almighty.

The Austrians had invaded the Russian Embassy and kidnapped a princess of the blood.

And, bloody hell, he would never have known about it if his confounding wife hadn't pointed the way.

"That's the Austrian Embassy?" She peered more closely, then looked back at him, her forehead deeply fretted. "How do you know? There's no sign."

He couldn't help staring at the building out the window, a catastrophe in the making. "I had dinner there two weeks ago."

"What does it mean, Ross?"

He leaned back against the seat, exhausted by what was to come.

"War."

Chapter 20

Man with the head and woman with the heart:
Man to command and woman to obey;
All else confusion.

Alfred, Lord Tennyson, *Song*

"**D**ear God! Then what happens next, Ross?" His usually unflappable wife's voice cracked on his name. She was sitting across the carriage from him, upright against the seat back.

"The inevitable, my dear, when this whole thing blows up." He crossed his boot over his knee, assumed an air of aplomb he didn't feel. "Russia will declare war on Austria, followed by the British declaring war on the Russians and possibly the Americans, piling on the French, then the Turks, resulting in a massive war—"

"Then would you like to hear my idea, Ross?" Panic darkened the emerald green of her eyes.

"Go right ahead, love. You've cracked part of this case wide open all by yourself." And he could use the help. Every idea he'd entertained in the last few moments had ended in a global disaster.

"All right, then, from what I know about the current mood between all the parties, Russia will use any excuse to invade Austria and take over the Danube Territories completely."

"True."

"The fact that the Austrian Embassy is involved in any way in the kidnapping of a Russian princess is excuse enough for the tsar to overrun Vienna this very afternoon."

"Also true." His remarkable wife even knew her current affairs.

"If, at any point during the rescue of the princess, the Russians discover that the Austrians are involved, it means war."

"Indeed." A lit match flicked into a mountainous stack of powder kegs.

"So the sticky part of the operation, Ross, is going to be rescuing the princess and returning her to the Russians without them guessing that the Austrians were involved."

"That's it in a nutshell." A direct hit on a complex political truth that few in the government even understood. "A secret rescue without involving a horde of police or the army or the press, or, God knows, the idiots in the Foreign Office. Not possible."

"Are you sure?"

"Diplomatic secrets are like so much smoke."

"So, really, Ross, the operation is left to us, then." She shot a sober smile at him, one that only confused him. "You and me and my three stalwarts."

"You, wife?" His neck tightened suddenly at her inference, that he would even consider sending her out on a dangerous mission. Whatever her plan. "I have seasoned operatives who know how to keep secrets."

"So do I, Ross. But the difference is that I have a plan." She scooted forward into the seat well, wedging her knees between his. "You see, the trick to a successful abduction is to do it in broad daylight, in public."

"In case you haven't noticed, love, the princess has already been abducted."

"And we're going to abduct her back. From right under the noses of her abductors."

"An interesting fantasy. You mean we just walk into the import shop and take her?"

Her smile brightened. "Exactly. Except that we create a whole fiction and play it out in front of whoever is holding her in the shop. Dodge and distract. And then we have her."

"Just like that." Ross sat back and studied her, suddenly deeply suspicious of the strength of her certainty. As though her strategies were well-practiced, timed right down to the minute. As though she'd done this sort of thing before.

As though she had already donned a costume and would have set her preposterous plan into motion if he hadn't caught her in the catacombs of the Factory.

"What the devil are you wearing?" Those weren't the breasts he'd spent the last two days making love to.

"Well, it's my . . ." She caught her lower lip between her teeth as she lifted a bulging satchel into her lap. "That's what I have to tell you."

They were already eye-to-eye across the carriage, her breath breaking against his chin. "Go on."

"You're not going to like it, Ross, but here it is."

She took a huge, worried breath then sighed through it. "The first three women weren't kidnapped. Lady Wallace and the other two."

His heart went still. "What do you mean 'not kidnapped.' Has someone contacted you? Are they dead?"

"Of course not. They're very much alive. All three of them."

A bloody odd thing to say. "How could you possibly know this?"

She straightened her shoulders, growing taller in the seat. "I know they weren't abducted because . . . well, because . . ."

"Because . . . ?"

"Because I . . . because I helped each of them plan and execute an escape from her husband."

Her words had become a wall he couldn't see past. Dizzied him with its height. Or maybe he was just tired to death.

"You did what, love?"

"I had to make it look like the women had been taken against their will and never found, otherwise they might look like a runaway wife." When he could only nod, the impossible woman pushed on. "That's how I knew that the princess wasn't kidnapped by the same person who had kidnapped the other women. Because I had."

"You can't be serious." His ears were still ringing with the impossibility of what he was hearing, with the morning traffic rattling past them in the street.

"That's why I'm suggesting that we mount a similar

fiction to rescue the princess. Because I've done it three times already, Ross. More, really."

"I still don't understand, wife." His brain felt mushy and slow. "You kidnapped Lady Wallace? How? Then who left all those clues behind?"

"Me. I merely arranged for temporary lodging and a steamship ticket to New York for her, then executed a broad-daylight abduction, on Regent Street in front of as many reliable witnesses as we could manage. And then we slipped her safely out of town in a disguise."

Elizabeth had expected Ross to be angry or shocked or stunned or raving when she finished confessing her role in the so-called abductions. Outright bellowing would have been good.

But she hadn't expected him to be so completely silent.

Dumbstruck.

Though his dark eyes with their fathoms-deep fires were shifting across her face, watching her every breath, her every blink.

"Don't you see, Ross? You can't use any of the evidence from the first three abductions in your investigation of the abducted princess. The hat, the glove, the handkerchief with the chloroform. Because there were no abductions. And none of your information applies."

The only muscle that moved was his jaw; it squared and flexed and squared again.

"That's why I had to come to tell you the truth in person after I read your note at the cottage. The princess must be frightened to death. And I'm frightened for her. She's truly been abducted by some fiend who has copied my clues from reading about the details in the newspaper. Her life is probably in danger! We have to rescue her as soon as possible."

"Christ, Elizabeth, what the hell have you done?"

Too much to explain right now.

"Please, Ross, I know how to do this. How do you think I managed to make three women disappear without a trace?"

"Because you're mad?"

"Did you or Scotland Yard ever find a single piece of evidence against me?"

He bucked backward as though he'd caught her dead to rights. "Their membership in the Adams."

"Which led you absolutely nowhere. You know I'm right, Ross. If I hadn't just now confessed that I'm responsible for the abductions, you would never have discovered it on your own."

"That's beside the point."

"The point is that we're running out of time for the princess. Maybe for the entire world."

He had stopped his ranting and now looked at her through one eye. "I know the princess. She knows me. I've danced with her. How exactly do I explain to her the reason that I've come to her rescue without the Russian delegation demanding a full investigation?"

"You've danced with her?" Well, good. He was willing to listen. Thank God.

She softened her voice, hoping to sound more reasonable to him. Less the lunatic.

"Whoever took the princess must have actually used the chloroform in the handkerchief to get her quietly out of the embassy. Which would render her unconscious for a time, and disoriented for a number of hours."

Ross was leaning forward, nodding, frowning. "She might not have seen the kidnappers. Wouldn't know they were from the Austrian Embassy."

"Exactly. With a blindfold and absolute silence the moment we lay our hands on her, she won't know who rescued her or even how she got back to the embassy."

"The Austrians certainly won't be able to cry foul for fear of bringing down the wrath of the tsar on their heads. It's a damned near perfect stalemate, Elizabeth." And he looked appalled by the very idea.

"But only if we can make the princess disappear, in a public shop, in broad daylight, then deliver her back to the Russian Embassy. No questions asked."

He studied her for the longest time, his breathing deep and controlled. Scrubbing at his jaw, weighing the gains and losses in his head.

Until he finally said so softly that she barely heard him over the traffic, "Hell and damnation."

Ross had begun to believe that he was dreaming. Or writhing in purgatory for the brief happiness he'd discovered with Elizabeth. The world had gone topsy turvy.

But here he was, wide awake, crammed into a carriage with his wife, actually considering her antic strategies as the only rational risk.

Because time was a critical commodity. As critical as secrecy. The last thing he needed at the moment was to have the little shop surrounded by the police, or the Home Guard, or the entire Russian Army.

The tsar screaming bloody murder at the affront of it all.

Bloody hell!

"What kind of fiction, madam?" he asked carefully, knowing that he would be setting off an operation that would put the woman he adored into harm's way.

"It's already in progress, Ross. The girls are in place on Huggett Lane. Shopping, chatting, having tea—"

"In place? Do you mean right now? At this very minute?"

"We've no time to waste. Everything is set. They're just waiting for me to—"

"For you to show up in your disguise and rescue the princess single-handedly. That's why you're dressed that way."

"Not just me. There are to be four of us."

"You're wrong, wife." He couldn't believe he was about to say it. "There will be five."

"Five! Oh, Ross! Thank you!" There wasn't a lick of triumph in her eyes, only urgency and terror. "It's an easy plot. All you have to do is follow my lead."

"No, madam, you'll do as I say, when I say it." He needed to be able to put himself between his wife and a bullet meant for her. "That goes for your confederates. Now, how were you going to deliver the princess back to the embassy?"

"I've hired a private hack to meet us at the Adams."

"No. I'll take care of that at the Factory." If this madness worked, he'd have a huge mess to clean up afterward.

"The Factory?" Her eyes widened at his admission. "Oh, I see."

Then she nodded soberly and went back to wrestling things out of her ponderous satchel.

A substantial bonnet. A wig box.

"What the devil have you got there?"

"A few things for our pantomime. Remember, you're the father, Ross." She opened the lid of a small wooden box, pulled out a black hairy thing the size of two caterpillars and started fiddling with the back of it. "I'm the mother. And we have three teenaged daughters."

"Three teenaged . . . bloody hell!"

He'd married a quick change artist with the tracking skills of a Seminole warrior.

Twenty minutes later Ross was stepping out of the coach onto the limestone curb a block down Huggett Lane from the import shop. As well-rehearsed in his wife's bloody fiction as he was ever going to get.

The pair of them dressed to the teeth in costumes that would fool the most discriminating audience.

Elizabeth wore a slightly old-fashioned dark wig, shot with strands of gray, a fashionable hat, a heavier bosom, a thicker waist, a beige, flawlessly tailored skirt and bodice, and a gold pince nez on her nose, secured to a brooch with a black silk ribbon.

Ross felt like a bloody orator, his frock coat enhanced by an unfolded walking stick, a silk hat, kid gloves, grayed temples, spectacles. And a rather virile moustache, the ends of which he could see when he glanced down.

All of which his wife had conjured out of her satchel like a magician.

"Mama!" Down the street came their three stylishly

dressed teenaged daughters, waving exuberantly. Decked out with parasols and shopping baskets, bundles of brown wrapped packages.

"Good morning, Papa!" Jessica and Cassie each grabbed an elbow, unfazed by his addition to their theatricals.

But while he had them gathered around him, he needed to be sure they understood the gravity of the situation. This was no longer a freelance operation.

"One thing to keep in mind, ladies," he said, including his wife in his hushed tones and the sweep of his gaze. "You're now acting as official agents of the crown. Everything you do or say reflects directly back upon Queen Victoria. And since I am Her Majesty's champion and she is a longtime friend to me, you will do everything in your power to behave in her best interest."

Their mouths opened to perfect O's. Hopefully awed. Hopefully aware of the stakes. The threat to each and every one of them.

"Now, don't dawdle, girls," Elizabeth said, breaking out of the group with a noisy trill. Instantly transforming herself into a sophisticated matron on a shopping spree with her family.

She preened at a windowpane, then waved to someone across the street, and even added a little waddle to her stride.

The girls fell into step behind her, like a mama duck and her ducklings.

The Carter P. Norris family on parade. And he was their proud father.

Their protector, should anything go wrong. And it

damned well better not. Because his wife had a lot of explaining to do when he got her back to their rooms in the Huntsman.

Elizabeth and the girls trolled the various shop windows ahead of him, exclaiming over hats and lamps and china displays until they finally reached the import shop.

It was an odd thing to be looking into that window. Not at the tins of herring and the bolts of cloth as Elizabeth and the girls were doing. But *through* the window into the small store itself; at the layout, the single clerk and the woman customer, the play of light and the stairway that he could see through a break in the curtain in the rear.

A long counter on the right, a wall of shelved goods on the left. The perfect setup for their ruse.

"After this customer, wife," he whispered as she slipped her hand through his crooked elbow and smiled primly up at him, "and then we'll go."

He had the strangest urge to kiss her.

For show.

For luck. For love. Because this was a bloody dangerous business and he'd grown quite used to her being in his life. In his heart.

He bent his head and caught her smile on his mouth, the deep impression of petals and roses. The exotic sensation of having a thick moustache between his upper lip and hers.

She kissed him right back, her eyes wide open and serious. Then she pulled away in mock ire. "Why, Mr. Norris, you dear cad, you!"

"And here we go," he whispered against her ear as

the woman inside the shop completed her purchase and pranced out the door.

Perfectly on cue, the girls laughed, then flounced into the store, a dangerous cloud of crinoline, exclaiming over everything in sight.

"Ah, good afternoon, ladies, sir," the clerk said with a chortle, thickly laced with an Austrian accent. A medium-sized man that Ross knew he could easily take down with the back of his hand should it be necessary.

Hopefully, it wouldn't come to that.

But Elizabeth had hung back just outside the doorway, raising a terrified sweat on the back of his neck, though her actions were exactly as they had planned.

"Mr. Norris, have you seen our Patrick? Oh, my stars! Where did that boy go?" Then she cupped her hand to her mouth and shouted down the street like a fishmonger's wife. "Paaaaaaaaatrick!"

His heart had never felt so exposed, so vulnerable. These were dangerous men with dangerous intentions.

"Oh, look, Papa! Humbugs!" Jessica had stopped near the front door, just as they'd planned, drawing the clerk's attention.

"May I help you, miss?"

"Papa, please!" She poked her finger against the big jar of candy. "Humbugs are my favorite! And sherbet lemons and licorice and bonbons!"

"Helen, you know your mother doesn't like you eating candy." Ross moved into place on Jessica's left as he carefully blocked the clerk's view of the back of the shop.

"It's bad for your complexion, dear."

"Oh, Mama, please!"

"Mama, come smell this rosewater! It's lovely!" Skye and Cassie had positioned themselves at the end of the counter, taking up the entire aisle with their skirts and bonnets, not more than six feet from the curtain into the next room that led to the stairs beyond.

Again they looked too vulnerable. No match for someone who wanted to hurt them.

"Oh, I do love a good rosewater, sweet." Ross felt Elizabeth brush past him, her skirts as wide as fashion would allow. But she waddled those matronly hips down the middle of the aisle with all the confidence of a professional operative, making him wonder if she wasn't.

She took the open bottle from Cassie and gave a long sniff. "Isn't that delightful! Mr. Norris, dear, I'm going to be wanting a bottle of this. Maybe two. Heavenly days, any sign of Patrick?"

Ross cleared his throat and put his mind to the task before he lost the sense of the moment, and his yearning to protect them became the danger to the mission.

"He's somewhere, dear," Ross said to the clerk in his most beleaguered, husbandly derision. "He always is."

"Oh, Helen, look at this pretty gingham! It's you!" Cassie and Skye were unrolling a bolt of yellow cloth between them.

And damned if it wasn't becoming a perfect screen across the back of the shop.

"Oh, Josey! It is!" Jessica left Ross with the clerk and added her flouncing ruffles to the end of the counter.

The aisle now looked like a decorated wagon in a

mummer's parade. Four skirts and four bonnets all
swinging and bobbing. Four female voices raising a
clamor against a wall of yellow gingham stretched
here and there.

All because of his amazing wife. Hell, this might
work out after all.

"You have quite a lovely family, sir!" The clerk
lifted a sympathetic brow.

"Don't mean to be such a handful for you today, sir.
With just one of you here and all."

The man gave a telling but nearly imperceptible
flick of his eyes to the ceiling, then shook his head.
"As usual, sir, a bit shorthanded this time of the day."

Pray God that he was right.

"Mr. Norris, dear, has our Patrick come past you
there? Or is the lad still outside somewhere?" Her
eyes locked with his, alert to the play of the shop, as
aware of everyone and everything as he was. "He'll be
wanting a look at the toy trains there on the shelves
behind you."

"Yes, my dear." Ross smiled wanly at the clerk and
pointed wearily to the jar of humbugs. "A half pound,
if you please. And make sure none of them are broken.
Our Helen is a very . . . particular child."

Ross glanced at the chattering chaos at the back of
the store, and noticed with a jolt of terror that Skye
was missing from the mob. The core of their plan had
been set in motion.

Elizabeth could feel the concern in her husband,
could see it in his dark eyes, his mouth drawn and
deadly serious under that expansive moustache.

A man wound tightly, ready to spring should anything go amiss. And if anything was going to go amiss, it would be right now.

"Here, Helen, dear," she said, holding up the length of gingham to cover Skye, who was on her knees, slipping through the curtain at the back of the shop.

Seconds stretched out to minutes as she pictured Skye approaching the princess. Hopefully blindfolded, hopefully alone and unharmed. Dressing the hostage in a jacket and a pair of britches, cramming her hair into a cap.

"Yellow is just perfect for my hair, Mama!" Jessica stood in front of the mirror, nearly dancing with the long length of fabric.

While Elizabeth listened closely to the sounds from above, the soft brush of a footfall, a small voice, a creak. She was ready to rescue Skye or any of them, if it came to that. Armed as she was with a short cudgel and the will to use it.

Just as she knew that Ross was prepared to do the same; she could see it in the broad set of his shoulders, in the powerful flex of his arms.

But the amazing man kept the clerk busy with the rosewater and a box of cigars and a promise that he would purchase the entire length of yellow gingham.

She held her breath and tried to steady her heart. Still, it was a full five grueling minutes before she finally heard two quiet sets of footsteps on the stairs.

Quiet because it was Skye and the princess and not a brawling end to the mission.

"Oh, good heavens, look at the time, girls!" she

said, giving the signal that the princess was in hand and to prepare to leave the shop. "Your grandmother will start to fret if we're a minute late."

"Can I have the gingham, please, Mama?" Jessica held out the bolt as Skye and the other figure slipped through the curtain and into the middle of their cluster.

"Yes, child, your father's already bought it for you, haven't you, dear?"

"Yes, dear."

They started forward from the rear of the shop as a group, then Elizabeth let out a loud snort. "Why, there you are, boy!"

"Did you see the trains, Patrick?"

"No trains for *him*, Josey; he missed his chance! Where have you been, boy?" Flooded with relief, Elizabeth clamped her arm around the small rounded shoulders of the princess and yanked the cap farther down over the blindfold. "Out gallivanting in the street, I'll wager. Come along now, or you'll not be getting your allowance this week."

While the three girls blocked the clerk's view from the counter, Elizabeth led the stumbling, confused hostage through the aisle toward the door.

They were just steps from freedom when a wiry man in a cap and a shop apron came striding through the door.

He stopped abruptly in his tracks, blocking the whole of their exit.

Elizabeth's heart dropped into her stomach. She'd know that walk anywhere, even in the dark. She'd followed him here to the shop and then to the Austrian Embassy only a few hours before.

She maneuvered herself and her skirts in front of the princess and gave the man an enormous smile.

"Well, good afternoon to you, sir," she said as brightly as she could manage.

Still the man studied her for a moment, then the rest of her brood. Then cast a look above and behind them, doubtless at Ross towering above them all.

The man then smiled and nodded. "Thank you for your patronage." He stepped aside with a bow.

"You're most welcome, sir." Her knees quaking, Elizabeth led her delegation through the doorway and out onto the sidewalk, with the princess disguised as her son and overwhelmed by the sea of crinolines and bonnets.

The Carter P. Norris family, larger by one, paraded back down the street and around the corner to the waiting carriage, with Ross silently bringing up the rear.

The rest happened quickly, silently.

Henry opened the door and Elizabeth climbed in behind her husband. The girls surrounded the blindfolded princess and helped her up into the carriage, then down into a ball in the well between the seats.

Then they hooked arms and kept walking down the street, chattering. Three young women on a market outing.

What would she do without them?

And what would she have done without Ross?

Elizabeth wanted to bubble and blather to him about the terrifying parts of the operation and the nimble ones, the things they might do better next time, and how perfect he'd been at the spur of the moment.

But her husband was pensive, unmoving; his gaze

fixed out the window, his face unreadable, his mouth still masked by that ridiculous moustache.

And with the princess at their feet, they couldn't speak anyway. Not without risking her recognizing their voices at some time in the future. Or Ross's immediately.

But the princess was safe now, the world as well.

And it was barely ten in the morning.

And so Elizabeth watched out the window, startled when, instead of stopping in front of the Russian Embassy, they pulled through a pair of gates that opened into an unfamiliar courtyard that she couldn't ask Ross about.

Even as he silently handed her out the carriage door.

A small group of equally silent men, doubtless more of her husband's operatives, swooped out of a doorway then set to work gently moving the princess out of the carriage into the back of a van painted with the words FINEST HOUSEHOLD GOODS in deep arcs on each side.

The poor woman was just as silent. Must still be terrified, though she must also have guessed at their good intentions because she had never struggled against her bonds or her blindfold, never cried out.

Thinking that she ought to ride in the back with the princess and lend her a bit of comfort, Elizabeth looked around the busy courtyard for Ross. But he was nowhere to be seen.

She was about to scour the place for him when she saw a bearded man with a slouching cap climbing into the driver's seat of the van.

Ross! She'd know those unforgettably dark eyes anywhere, that finely sculpted mouth. She went toward him, but he put up his hand to stop her and gave her a nodding salute, when surely she deserved a walloping kiss.

More than a kiss!

After all, they were still in the midst of their honeymoon!

"Blast it all, Ross!" she whispered under her breath as her arrogant husband pulled the van through the gates and out into the street, taking the princess and all the risks with him.

The blackguard! After all she'd done for him!

"My lady Blakestone, if you please . . ."

"Pembridge!"

"His lordship said he might be away for a few hours, maybe more." The man's face flushed crimson. "So he wanted me to see you to your rooms at the Huntsman."

"A few hours?" Just to deliver the princess? Or maybe he had to report back to one of his many agencies.

"He also said to tell you that you'd best be there when he returned, if you know what's good for you."

"He actually had the nerve to say that?" No wonder Pembridge's cheeks were red and growing redder.

"Well, my lady, I'd certainly not be making up threats like that to another man's wife."

Nor should the husband himself.

"Then come along, Pembridge. Whether his lordship likes it or not, I have an excellent idea of what's good for me."

And it wasn't being locked in her husband's sitting room for the rest of the day.

Chapter 21

It is the nature of a woman to cling to the man
for support and direction, to comply with his
humours and feel pleasure in doing so, simply
because they are his; to conquer him not by
force but by her weakness, to command him by
obeying him. . . .

Thomas Carlyle, to his fiancée, 1826

*What's good for me, husband, dear, may not al-
ways be what's good for you.* Elizabeth was
still steaming mad a few minutes later when she went
bolting into Ross's empty suite at the Huntsman, prepared to do battle with the man the moment he returned. She was going to have to set him straight
before their marriage grew another day older.

She had just begun scrubbing the greasepaint off
her face in the washroom when she thought she heard
a knock at the door.

It couldn't be Ross, he hadn't been gone long
enough. Thinking it was Pembridge with a heaping
tray of tea and biscuits, she opened the door to a

stoop-shouldered old man peering at her from the private corridor.

He was dressed well, his white hair neat and trimmed, his gray eyes drooping but surprised.

"Oh, dear, miss. I must have knocked on the wrong door." He glanced both directions down the hallway.

"You're looking for Lord Blakestone?"

"Yes, is he here?" The old man looked past her shoulder.

"I'm afraid he's not right now. But I'm his wife. Elizabeth . . . uhm, I'm Lady Blakestone. I'd be happy to give him a message from you."

"His wife?" The man quirked his brow and studied her face. "I didn't know the boy had married."

"It's only been a day or two." Worried about his balance, she caught his thin wrist. "Would you like to come in and leave a note?"

"No, no, my lady." But he came forward into the room with the gentlest tug. "The name is Tuckerton, Lord Tuckerton. I just came by to ask his lordship if he'd found my lass yet."

His lass? A lost, dreamy look had come into the man's sad gray eyes. A long-dead wife, or a grandchild? "Have you lost someone, then?"

"Oh, no, my dear. I wouldn't be so careless with someone I love. My lass was taken."

Elizabeth drew back. "Taken where?"

"I don't know where, Lady Blakestone. Don't know who took her either." Tears began to soak into his leathery cheeks. "But she's been missing a couple of weeks now. That's what young Blakestone is looking into for me."

"Missing." A chill slid over her skin. "What was your lass's name?"

"Eugenia." The man wobbled as he sank onto the ottoman. "She's my grandniece. She's married to that bastard Wallace. You might have heard of him."

Dear Lord, no! Her heart plunged into her stomach. Her throat closed up, filled with tears.

"My Genie's the only family I have now, and someone took her from me."

Eugenia Wallace! He was waiting for Ross to find a phantom! She knelt in front of the old man and wrapped her arms around his thin shoulders. Hot tears brimmed in her eyes and spilled down her cheeks. "I'm so sorry, Lord Tuckerton."

"I came by to find out if the lad's heard anything at all about my Eugenia. Do you know if he has?"

"No, my lord, I don't think so. But I'm sure he's working very hard on it." What a terrible lie to tell a heartbroken old man.

An innocent soul that she hadn't anticipated in all her conspiracies. But she couldn't very well confess to him that his Eugenia was fine and on her way to a happier life in America. A slip of his doddering tongue and the old man wouldn't stand a chance against Lord Wallace's interrogation.

But there must be some way she could make things right for the dear fellow.

"Good, then, my Lady Blakestone, Eugenia ought to be coming back to me any day now." Tuckerton patted Elizabeth's hand as he stood and started toward the door. "I'm glad I've got his lordship working on the case."

"I'm sure he'll do his best, my lord."

And I will too, she promised as he hobbled off down the corridor. One way or another.

Weighed down by more than a bit of guilt, Elizabeth finished cleaning up, then stuffed her costume into her satchel and was back at the Abigail Adams a few minutes later, the memory of old Tuckerton trailing after her like a ghost.

The true, untold cost of Lady Wallace's liberty.

She made her daily rounds at the Adams, the tea room, the bookstore, the library, then into the workroom with her three assistants, to celebrate their first and probably final international success.

"We were wonderful, my lady!" Jessica said, popping a humbug into her mouth.

"Skye, you were the bravest of all." Elizabeth gave the young woman a hug, her nerves still on edge for the danger they had all evaded.

"I was lucky, my lady. The princess was blindfolded when I found her and very cooperative after I whispered that we'd come to rescue her."

"His lordship was magnificent as well." Cassie dropped back into a chair. "Especially his moustache."

"I'll tell him that, Cassie." If she ever saw the man again.

Elizabeth would have stayed at the impromptu party, but she was called into the clubroom.

Lady Maxton was standing beside the besieged young woman from the charity ball.

A sight that filled her with relief for the girl, and a sudden trepidation for the future of her own married life. Because she couldn't give up on the lost and the aching, no matter her husband's objections.

"Lady Maxton," she said, sharing an embrace with the woman, "how delightful to see you again. Thank you again for giving the charity ball. Definitely the talk of the entire season."

"As we knew it would be, my dear. And just imagine! I've brought you a new member." Lady Maxton touched the young woman's shoulder. "Miss Preston, I'd like you meet Lady Blakestone. A woman of many miracles."

Would that were true! But Elizabeth smiled and offered her hand. "Welcome, Miss Preston."

To the rest of your life.

To the rest of her own life.

And this wayward marriage to the most confounding man she'd ever met.

Grousemeade Cottage had been a blissful paradise. Their own private South Seas island where their controversies couldn't find them. Where there weren't any fearful wives, or embattled embassies, or heartbroken old men.

Where Ross had been the ideal husband.

A paradise where she'd come to love her handsome privy counselor for his humor and the goodness of his heart.

And, blast it all, if they were ever going to put this marriage on the right course, they'd have to return to Grousemeade Cottage immediately.

Tonight.

And what better way to be sure that her husband

would come find her than to return to their paradise without him?

That is, if the lout knew what was good for him.

"Hell and damnation!" Ross cursed all the way from the Huntsman into the livery in Hampstead where he hired a mount and rode off toward Grouse-meade Cottage.

Cursing the darkness.

Cursing the Russian ambassador and the Austrians.

Cursing his wife's stubbornness.

Her bloody independence.

And this driving need to hold her in his arms at any cost.

He arrived at the cottage reeling in the saddle, exhausted from the lack of sleep. And certain that Elizabeth would be waiting for him on the doorstep, ready to do battle.

But the cottage was dark, save for a few low-burning lamps, the main floor quiet.

And his wife lying stark naked and fast asleep in their bed.

Her hair was spread across the bank of pillows in the moonlight, the counterpane dipped to her waist, revealing the soft perfection of her breasts.

His heart full, and pumping hot fluids to every corner of his body, he leaned over her gentle breathing and whispered softly against her ear, "Elizabeth?"

A dreamy smile flickered on her mouth, but she only drifted deeper into sleep.

Hardly a fit opponent for the hostilities sure to come. And Lord, he was sleepy. Compelling him to remove his clothes and slip in beside his wife, where he could hold her through the night and join in her dreams.

Knowing that the battle would come tomorrow.

But having no idea that it would come with the first rays of dawn and the smack of a pillow against his head.

"Ross Carrington, how could you!"

He sat upright, opened his bleary eyes and found himself face-to-face with his wife's lovely navel.

Dangerously close to her inviting triangle of curls, his groin already fully distended under the blanket.

"Well, my lord?" She was standing over him, spread-eagle and delicious, her eyes wide and filled with fury, the pillow hiked over her shoulder, ready to come across his head again.

"How could I what, wife?" Risking another swat for his insolence, he leaned back on his hands to enjoy the tempting view. All bobbing breasts and flashing eyes.

"First I worried that you were hurt. Then I worried you weren't coming at all. I waited up all night for you. I shouldn't have bothered."

"So eager for me, love, you fell asleep."

"When did you get here?"

"Last night. Just before ten." That brought the pillow down on his head again, but with half the force of the first blow and a good pouting afterward.

"After everything that happened yesterday, you didn't wake me up?"

"I tried, sweet. You were snoring."

"I don't snore." He got the pillow again.

"Then you drew me into your dreams, love." He

wrapped his arm around her knees and buckled her sideways across his lap, sending the pillow over the side of the bed.

"And you left me standing in the middle of a strange courtyard without a by-your-leave."

Just as he'd hoped, she swung around in his lap to face him with her fierceness, her bottom pressing against his thighs, her cleft just inches from his raging hot erection.

"I left you under the care of Pembridge." A lot of good that did.

"That's all the trust you have in me, Ross? After I helped you save mankind from a terrible war?"

"No . . . well, it's—" Habit perhaps. Though that might not be the most politic answer. "You said it yourself, Elizabeth, you didn't know where you were. I thought Pembridge could help you find your way back through the Factory."

She narrowed her eyes at him, setting her jaw in suspicion. "What happened to the princess?"

So that was the source of her ire, that he had finished up her secret operation on his own. He needed to step gingerly here.

"Just as you had planned, Elizabeth. We pulled up in front of the embassy. Drew opened the rear of the wagon—"

"I didn't see Drew get into the wagon!"

"Because he was already waiting there when we arrived." The benefit of a well-oiled system of messengers and private telegraph stations. "A moment after he set the princess on her feet on the sidewalk in front of the embassy, our wagon was disappearing around the corner, and the phalanx of Russian guards were just realizing that we'd dropped off someone."

"So Princess Lenka was all right?" Elizabeth seemed entranced with his story as she drew the end of the counterpane up over her shoulders like a tent.

And he was enjoying every moment of anticipation. The sight of her shapes, the sound of her wonder, the shifting of her hips, bringing her warmth closer and closer to him.

"Her Royal Highness seemed right as rain an hour and a half later when Drew and I were standing in the Russian Embassy with Lord Clarendon, offering our official sympathy that the princess had been kidnapped by a local mad man."

Her eyes few open. "She didn't recognize you, did she?"

"Not a flicker."

"They didn't wonder about who had rescued her?"

"Ambassador Brunnov speculated that it was a secret Russian agency that watches out for Russian royals."

"That's silly."

"Yet the very idea seemed to please not only the delegation, but Princess Lenka herself." He slipped his hands around her hips, wanting desperately to pull her forward and bury himself inside her. But the anticipation was too sweet and he was burning way too hot for her.

"What about the Austrians?"

"I paid a visit there and found the place eerily silent and nearly paralyzed with what seemed like a plan gone terribly wrong. I made sure that Prince Rupert understood how grateful Queen Victoria was that her cousin had been returned to the safety of the Russian Embassy."

"Do you think he was a part of the conspiracy?"

"Don't know. But when I lied and told him that Scotland Yard was on the case, his face went pale."

"He must know something. What were they hoping to accomplish?" She drew the covers more tightly around her shoulders.

"What matters is that they won't be trying it again. A ransom demand was never made, therefore no clues to trace, no pointing fingers. A clean slate. Thanks to you, Elizabeth."

"Thanks to me?" She drew back, her rosy mouth pursed in skeptical pout.

"I hate to admit it, my love, but without your help, Drew and I would still be in the Factory analyzing your clever red herrings. And Scotland Yard would be spinning in circles."

Elizabeth wondered if her husband would be so generous with his compliments when she confessed her many other sins to him.

Though she hoped he didn't pull away from her; the flex of his thighs beneath her bottom, and the ramrod sight of his penis, were just too thrilling to forfeit.

"Actually, Ross, I really couldn't have done my own work without a lot of help from the Factory." Without a lot of help from the man himself, though she hadn't realized it at the time. He looked the restive saytr just now, leaning back against the dense bank of pillows, bare-chested and ready to spring.

He raised that decisive, accusing brow. "Then yesterday wasn't the first time you were there?"

The scar across his shoulder looked darker this morning, more ragged, in need of her hands. She leaned forward and began to massage the thick muscle beneath, drawing a groan from him.

"You see, Ross, I've been borrowing your telegraph machines."

"Have you?" His growled question became a deeply rumbling moan. He leaned forward and dropped his head against her shoulder.

Might as well get it all over with, while she had the beast distracted, if not tamed. "And I've used the small handpress in the print shop. We needed a certain train ticket for Lady Hayden-Cole."

"Anything else I should know about?" His palms were hot against her hips, his fingers spread so wide that his thumbs nearly met across her belly, kneading slowly there.

Making it very difficult for her to think beyond the sizzling feel of his hands.

To remind herself that she still had a thriving underground to operate. That she had to tell him about it. As well as her determination to keep it moving.

"We've also borrowed a few pieces of clothing, now and then. And, my, but you have a marvelous archive of newspapers and the like."

"By 'we' you mean your three wily assistants?" He turned his head against her neck and and nibbled a slow path to her ear, took the lobe between his teeth and made love there and at her nape.

"Just them, Ross." Oh, my, he was making this difficult. "But while I'm confessing, and I really must confess all, before we continue a moment longer . . ." Before he drove her mad with his fingers toying with her nipples, stealing her breath away and all of her will.

"Keep talking, wife. I'm listening."

But *she* wasn't, not well. Not with him sliding her toward his thick erection, fitting her cleft hot against the full length of his penis, making her throb against him, when she wanted him to be inside her, thrusting.

"Ross! Oh, my!" Now she was writhing wantonly against him and he was chuckling while they both really ought to be paying attention. "You might as well know that the Bank of England has more than the fictional Adelaide Chiswick on their books."

"What?" He stopped rocking, stopped dallying and straightened, narrowed his eyes at her, dark fires suddenly flickering deeply beneath his long lashes. "You've opened other fraudulent accounts?"

"The devil was in the details. I set up the Adelaide Chiswick account as a test to see if I could do it as a wobbly old widow and not be recognized by the bank clerks."

"Why?"

"So that I could help other women open their own bank accounts, using false names."

"False names?"

"And disguises, so their husbands wouldn't find out."

"Elizabeth . . ." He closed his eyes as though she'd just punched him.

"Oh, and by the way, Ross, I carry an excellent collection of French letters in the back room of the bookstore."

"That's contraband, Elizabeth." He shook his head at her. "They have to go. No privy council discussion about it."

She'd just have to find another way to distribute them. Maybe in the Adams itself. Or as part of a workshop. But contraceptive devices were the least of her worries.

She could only hope that he would understand the strength of the convictions that drove her.

"Then there's Lydia Bailey."

"Who?" Though his hands were planted firmly on her backside, he was once more focused and listening, and all she could do was hope for the best of his understanding.

"I've made arrangements for Lydia's abduction to happen on London Bridge three days from now."

He pulled back and stared at her. "You must be joking."

"And I believe I'll be arranging a similar disappearance for another young woman very soon. Lord Stopes's fiancée."

"No, no, no, Elizabeth." He was shaking his head at her. "I won't allow it."

"That's between me and Miss Preston and the other women who help them along the way to freedom."

"You can't, Elizabeth, because Scotland Yard will learn about it immediately. From me."

"You'd actually tell them? Risk unleashing Lord

Stopes's brutality on his helpless fiancée? Risk him battering her face and breaking her bones because nobody will stop him?"

"Damn it, Elizabeth, I can't very well ignore you and still pretend I'm looking into the matter."

"Why not?"

"Because it's a waste of manpower."

"It'll just have to be that way, Ross, until the police start arresting husbands for assaulting their own wives. What if you had a sister who was being beaten by her husband?"

"I'd kill him."

"Then you'd go to jail, Ross. But if he killed your sister in a fit of anger, he would be excused because, after all, she was only his property. Don't you see the injustice? Sometimes we just have to take matters into our own hands and set things right as best we can."

Ross felt the familiar roar of outrage rising up in his chest, tried his best to blink away the stark image of Thomas lying dead on the steps of the doctor's surgery. The broken little body, bruised face, limbs at odd angles. He'd died in Jared's arms and they carried him to the surgeon's front stoop, a place where they knew he'd be found. Then they went in search of Squire Craddock, the savage bastard who had beaten him to death.

They'd come away with a handful of solid gold buttons, and a brighter, braver future.

The same future that Elizabeth was offering to Lady Wallace and the others.

No wonder he loved her so dearly, so deeply. She was his heart and his soul.

His past and his future.

But it couldn't be this way. "No more kidnappings, Elizabeth."

Her eyes flashed a rebellious emerald. "Ross, I—"

"But I can help." In his own way.

"How? Kill off all the husbands?" She scowled deeply, so ready to stand her ground for the defenseless. "Because that's what it'll take. When Lady Hayden-Cole sought a civilized separation from her husband, the man threatened to commit her to an asylum if she ever tried to leave him again."

"Madam, you're sitting on the lap of a man who has a vast network of power available to him."

She raised her eyebrows, only half amused. "Ross, your prowess as a lover is admirable—"

"Only admirable?"

"Staggering, then. Awesome, overwhelming. However—"

He cupped her chin and brought her closer, wanting her to understand his promise. "Bring them to me, Elizabeth, and I'll see them safely to their new lives without a single threat from their husbands."

Her face filled with doubting wonder. "You can do that?"

"In the blink of an eye." He winked, smiled because he couldn't help himself.

She sniffed at him. "You didn't know where the princess was until I told you."

"But you did tell me, Elizabeth." He touched his mouth to the arc of her lips. "I'm usually not as dense, but you unbalance me."

"Then you really will help me?"

He took her hand and flattened it against his heart,

hoping she heard it galloping there. "My word of honor, my love."

"Oh, Ross, you're my—"

He didn't let her finish, certain he'd just become her hero. He kissed her instead, covered her mouth completely and made love with her tongue. Caught her sigh inside his chest, and growled with the pleasure of her squirming, riding him without when he'd rather be buried inside her.

A lift of her hips and they would be connected there. Though he would surely spend himself immediately. And often.

A risk he planned to take—

But she pulled away, her eyes bright. "I have a brilliant idea, Ross!"

"And I have a great need for you." He cupped her bottom.

"We can take Lord Tuckerton to New York to live with his dear Eugenia."

"What?" Would the woman ever stop planning great escapes. And how the devil did she know Tuckerton?

"He's miserable, Ross. We have to tell him that his grandniece is well. But we can't let him stay here in London because Lord Wallace would surely find out where she was hiding." She cupped his chin, her eyes suddenly rimming with tears. "We can't let him just waste away in a club chair at the Huntsman. That would be cruel."

And he'd noticed himself that the old man had already begun to fade, in just these few weeks. His hair white, his eyes more dull, his back more bent.

"Oh, God."

"Next week, Ross? As soon as we can, please. I have excellent contacts at all the steamship companies! And what a grand honeymoon for us!"

"We're on our honeymoon, Elizabeth, in case you hadn't noticed that I'm ready to burst for wanting you."

Elizabeth had noticed, could feel herself ready to burst, ready to give her heart and her soul to this amazing man.

"I'm not exactly what you bargained for when you married me, am I, Ross?"

"Now, there's an understatement, wife. You are a wonder." He was looking at her in a very heady way, breathing like a bull, dropping hard, steaming kisses across her bosom. "And as it happens, Lord Clarendon agrees."

"The foreign minister?"

He looked up long enough to say, "He's arranging for a royal commendation for you."

"A royal commendation!" How amazing! "But what about Jess and Cassie and Skye? They were every bit as important to the mission as I was."

"I've already informed them of their commendations, when I was looking for you at the Adams. As I would have informed you, had you stayed put."

"I obviously don't know what's good for me." But she knew what was good for him.

And he must have thought so too as she closed her hands around the very hot shaft of his penis.

And then she leaned down and kissed him there,

suckled and teased and fondled this big howling husband of hers until the poor man just couldn't take it anymore.

He lifted her off his thighs and, with an unerring aim and a roar of triumph, he slipped his thickness inside of her and rocked her world with his wonder.

They made love until the noonday sun was piercing through the windows, until they were breathless and starving and her limbs no longer moved. Until her eyelids drooped and her dreams came nudging up against her.

She woke sometime later with Ross looking down at her. He was stretched out above her, looking every long inch the sated wolf, cleanly shaven and smelling of soap.

"Good afternoon, wife."

"A very good afternoon." She cuddled against him, amazed at the turn her life had taken.

"By the way, love, I made two stops after I left the Adams. Before I came here to look for my runaway wife." He lifted her fingers to his lips and kissed them, then gathered her right hand inside his.

"Two stops? For what?"

"Something I neglected to do the night we were married." His eyes sparkled as he lifted her hand to show her the wedding band he'd magically put on her finger sometime while she'd been sleeping. "Call me a little slow."

"Oh, Ross!" The band glinted gold and steadfast. "I'll call you wonderful to the end of our days!"

She kissed him long and hard, catching her name in

her heart as he whispered it against her mouth and her cheek and her temple until he was rolling her to the edge of the bed and climbing out.

"Where are you going?" She grabbed at his arm but missed as he left her for the wardrobe.

"Don't you want to know where else I stopped on my way here?"

"Not if it's going to keep you over there." Though he was a delicious feast for her eyes from this distance. Tall and bronze and still very nakedly aroused.

"Greedy." He returned with a smile and slipped back into bed beside her with a folded packet of what looked like legal papers.

"You went to a lawyer?"

"I had these started the morning after we were married." He handed her the packet, then laid back against the pillow with a catlike smile.

She unfolded the stiff pages. "What is it?"

"It's everything you owned before we married. I've deeded it all back to you."

"What do you mean, Ross?" She sat up and tried to make sense of the words swimming around on the pages, realizing that she couldn't read for the tears welling in her eyes.

"It's all yours again, Elizabeth. Lock, stock, and barrel." He crossed his arms over his chest, looking very pleased with himself.

"But, Ross . . . ! That's not what I want." It felt wrong. Separate from this man she loved with all her heart.

He frowned and sat up. "It's not?"

"I love you, husband!" She shook the pages at him, shocked at the turn of her own feelings. "You said we were partners."

"We are." He looked bewildered.

"Then I'm going to take these back to that lawyer as soon as we get to London and I'm going to make it right."

"Right?"

"My name and yours. That's what belongs on each of these deeds. Us, Ross. Together. Partners."

He scratched at his head as he looked at her in complete confusion for a long, unsettling moment. And then he started to laugh. And laugh. A roaring, belly-busting laugh that had him falling back against the pillows.

Leaving her completely clueless. "Just what's so funny?"

His laughter settled and he sat up, wiping at his eyes. "God, I love you, Elizabeth!"

"And that's funny?"

His smile changed from madness to the devil's own as he reached out and gathered her into his lap.

"Something Drew told me, love." He bent her backward over his arm.

"That wives are funny?"

"That diplomacy isn't for the faint of heart." He kissed his way upward from her navel to her mouth.

"And?"

"And that's what I get for not consulting all the parties in this treaty of ours."

"But, may I say that you do make an extraordinary ambassador to my kingdom, husband." She caught his handsome face between her hands. "Though I would definitely excuse you should you attempt an invasion."

"Point taken, my love." His laughter turned to a sultry growl as he carried her back against the pillows, his eyes alight with that glint she loved so well.

The man she trusted with her life, with the children they would someday have.

Because, in the end, when all was counted, it was his unconditional love that had set her heart free.

Summer nights are hotter than ever thanks to these July releases from Avon Romance . . .

The Marriage Bed by Laura Lee Guhrke

An Avon Romantic Treasure

Everyone in society knows that the marriage of Lord and Lady Hammond is an unhappy one. But all that is about to change, when John, Lord Hammond, begins to see what a beautiful woman he is married to. Now he prays it's not too late to win back the love of his very own wife.

The Hunter by Gennita Low

An Avon Contemporary Romance

In order for Hawk McMillan, SEAL commander, to succeed in his latest lone mission, he needs a tracker, and the best woman for that job is CIA contact agent Amber Hutchens. But when their mission requires Hawk and Amber to risk everything, they've got too much at stake to stay far away from danger . . . or from their passion.

More Than a Scandal by Sari Robins

An Avon Romance

Lovely Catherine Miller has always been timid—until the treachery of unscrupulous cousins threatens her childhood home. To save it, she steals the identity of the notorious "Thief of Robinson Square" who, years ago, preyed on pompous society to help the poor.

The Daring Twin by Donna Fletcher

An Avon Romance

When Fiona of the MacElder clan is told that she must wed Tarr of Hellewyk so the two clans can unite, she is furious. Fortunately, Fiona's identical twin sister Aliss is on her side. The two boldly concoct an outlandish scheme—to make it impossible to tell who is who—and it works. The only trouble is, one of the twins accidentally falls in love with the would-be groom!